By Samantha Young

On Dublin Street Series

On Dublin Street

Down London Road

Before Jamaica Lane

Fall from India Place

Echoes of Scotland Street

Moonlight on Nightingale Way

Castle Hill (novella)

Until Fountain Bridge (novella)

One King's Way (novella)

Hart's Boardwalk Series

The One Real Thing

Hero

The One Real Thing

Hart's Boardwalk

SAMANTHA YOUNG

PIATKUS

First published in the US in 2016 by Berkley,
a division of Penguin Random House LLC
First published in Great Britain in 2016 by Piatkus

All characters and events in this publication, other than those clearly in the public domain, are fictitious and any resemblance to real persons, living or dead, is purely coincidental.

A CIP catalogue record for this book is available from the British Library.

ISBN 978-0-349-41258-0

Printed and bound by CPI Group (UK) Ltd, Croydon, CR0 4YY

Papers used by Piatkus are from well-managed forests and other responsible sources.

MIX
Paper from
responsible sources
FSC® C104740

Piatkus
An imprint of
Little, Brown Book Group
Carmelite House
50 Victoria Embankment
London EC4Y 0DZ

An Hachette UK Company
www.hachette.co.uk

www.piatkus.co.uk

The One Real Thing

ONE

Jessica

One of my favorite feelings in the whole world is that moment I step inside a hot shower after having been caught outside in cold, lashing rain. The transformation from clothes-soaked-to-the-skin misery to soothing warmth is unlike any other. I love the resultant goose bumps and the way my whole body relaxes under the stream of warm water. In that pure, simple moment all accumulated worries just wash away with the rain.

The moment I met Cooper Lawson felt exactly like that hot shower after a very long, cold storm.

The day hadn't started out all sunshine and clear skies. It was a little gray outside and there were definite clouds, but I still hadn't been prepared for the sudden deluge of rain that flooded from the heavens as I was walking along the boardwalk in the seaside city of Hartwell.

My eyes darted for the closest available shelter and I dashed toward it—a closed bar that had an awning. Soaked within seconds, blinded by rain, and irritated by the icky feeling of my clothes sticking to my skin, I wasn't really paying much attention to anything else but getting to the awning. That was why I ran smack into a hard, masculine body.

If the man's arms hadn't reached out to catch me I would have bounced right onto my ass.

I pushed my soaked hair out of my eyes and looked up in apology at the person I had so rudely collided with.

Warm blue eyes met mine. Blue, blue eyes. Like the Aegean Sea that surrounded Santorini. I'd vacationed there a few years back and the water there was the bluest I'd ever seen.

Once I was able to drag my gaze from the startling color of those eyes, I took in the face they were set upon. Rugged, masculine.

My eyes drifted over his broad shoulders and my head tipped back to take in his face because the guy was well over six feet tall. The hands that were still on my biceps, steadying me, were big, long fingered, and callused against my bare skin.

Despite the cold, I felt my body flush with the heat of awareness and I stepped out of the stranger's hold.

"Sorry," I said, slicking my wet hair back, grinning apologetically. "That rain came out of nowhere."

He gave a brief nod as he pushed his wet dark hair back from his forehead. The blue flannel shirt he wore over a white T-shirt was soaked through, too, and I suddenly found myself staring at the way the T-shirt clung to his torso.

There wasn't an ounce of fat on him.

I thought I heard a chortle of laughter and my eyes flew to his face, startled—and horrified at the thought of being caught ogling. There was no smirk or smile on his lips, however, although there was definitely amusement in those magnificent eyes of his. Without saying a word he reached out for the door to the quaint building and pushed. The door swung open and he stepped inside what was an empty and decidedly closed bar.

Oh.

Okay for some, I thought, staring glumly out at the way the rain pounded the boardwalk, turning the boards slick and slippery. I wondered how long I'd be stuck there.

"You can wait out there if you want. Or not."

The deep voice brought my head back around. The blue-eyed, rugged, flannel guy was staring at me.

I peered past him at the empty bar, unsure if he was allowed to be in there. "Are you sure it's alright?"

He merely nodded, not giving me the explanation I sought for why it was alright.

I stared back at the rain and then back into the dry bar.

Stay out here shivering in the rain or step inside an empty bar with a strange man?

The stranger noted my indecision and somehow he managed to laugh at me without moving his mouth.

It was the laughter-filled eyes that decided me.

I nodded and strode past him. Water dripped onto the hardwood floors, but since there was already a puddle forming around the blue-eyed, rugged, flannel guy's feet I didn't let it bother me too much.

His boots squeaked and squished on the floor as he passed me; the momentary flare of heat from his body as he brushed by caused a delicious shiver to ripple down my spine.

"Tea? Coffee? Hot cocoa?" he called out without looking back.

He was about to disappear through a door that had *Staff Only* written on it, giving me little time to decide. "Hot cocoa," I blurted out.

I took a seat at a nearby table, grimacing at the squish of my clothes as I sat. I was definitely going to leave a butt-shaped puddle there when I stood up.

The door behind me banged open again and I turned around to see BRF (blue-eyed, rugged, flannel) Guy coming toward me with a white towel in his hand. He handed it to me without a word.

"Thanks," I said, bemused when he just nodded and headed back through the Staff Only door. "A man of few words," I murmured.

His monosyllabic nature was kind of refreshing, actually. I knew a lot of men who loved the sound of their own voice.

I wrapped the towel around the ends of my blond hair and squeezed the water out of it. Once I had rung as much of the water from my hair as I could, I swiped the towel over my cheeks, only to gasp in horror at the black stains left on it.

Fumbling through my purse for my compact, I flushed with

embarrassment when I saw my reflection. I had scary black-smeared eyes and mascara streaks down my cheeks.

No wonder BRF Guy had been laughing at me.

I used the towel to scrub off the mascara, then, completely mortified, I slammed my compact shut. I now had no makeup on, I was flushed red like a teenager, and my hair was flat and wet.

The bar guy wasn't exactly my type. Still, he was definitely attractive in his rough-around-the-edges way and, well, it was just never nice to feel like a sloppy mess in front of a man with eyes that piercing.

The door behind me banged open again and BRF Guy strode in with two steaming mugs in his hands.

As soon as he put one into mine, goose bumps rose up my arm at the delicious rush of heat against my chilled skin. "Thank you."

He nodded and slipped into the seat across from me. I studied him as he braced an ankle over his knee and sipped at his coffee. He was casual, completely relaxed, despite the fact that his clothes were wet. And like me he was wearing jeans. Wet denim felt nasty against bare skin—a man-made chafe monster.

"Do you work here?" I said after a really long few minutes of silence passed between us.

He didn't seem bothered by the silence. In fact, he seemed completely at ease in the company of a stranger.

He nodded.

"You're a bartender here?"

"I own the place."

I looked around at the bar. It was traditional décor with dark walnut everywhere—the long bar, the tables and chairs, even the floor. The lights of three large brass chandeliers broke up the darkness, while wall-mounted green library lamps along the back wall gave the booths there a cozy, almost romantic vibe. There was a small stage near the front door and just across from the booths were three stairs that led up onto a raised dais where two pool tables sat. Two huge flat-screen televisions, one above the bar and one above the pool tables, made me think it was part sports bar.

There was a large jukebox, beside the stage, that was currently silent.

"Nice place."

BRF Guy nodded.

"What's the bar called?"

"Cooper's."

"Are you Cooper?"

His eyes smiled. "Are you a detective?"

"A doctor, actually."

I was pretty sure I saw a flicker of interest. "Really?"

"Really."

"Smart lady."

"I'd hope so." I grinned.

Laughter danced in his eyes as he raised his mug for another sip.

Weirdly, I found myself settling into a comfortable silence with him. We sipped at our hot drinks as a lovely easiness fell between us. I couldn't remember the last time I'd felt that kind of calm contentedness with anyone, let alone a stranger.

A little slice of peace.

Finally, as I came to the end of my cocoa, BRF Guy / possibly Cooper spoke. "You're not from Hartwell."

"No, I'm not."

"What brings you to Hart's Boardwalk, Doc?"

I realized then how much I liked the sound of his voice. It was deep with a little huskiness in it.

I thought about his question before responding. What had brought me there was complicated.

"At the moment the rain brought me *here*," I said coyly. "I'm kind of glad it did."

He put his mug down on the table and stared at me for a long beat. I returned his perusal, my cheeks warming under the heat of his regard. Suddenly he reached across the table, offering me his hand. "Cooper Lawson."

I smiled and placed my small hand in his. "Jessica Huntington."

"Nice to meet you, Doc."

TWO

Jessica

Two Weeks Earlier
Women's Correctional and Rehabilitation Facility
Wilmington, Delaware

"You know, if you go running into any more doors I'm giving you a vision test," I said dryly as I applied antiseptic to Mary Jo's cut lip.

She glowered at me but didn't respond, which was unusual. If only she'd use that kind of restraint with the other inmates she might stop running into so many "doors."

I dropped my cotton swab and took off my latex gloves. "Nothing more I can do here. You can sit in the ward for a half hour with ice on your eye. It should take some of the swelling down." I strode over to the small freezer in my clinic and took out an ice pack.

When I turned back to Mary Jo she was squinting at me with her good eye.

"How come you don't talk to us like we're trash? That older bitch speaks to us like we're trash."

I ignored her reference to my colleague, Dr. Whitaker, who worked part-time at the prison infirmary. She didn't peer down her nose at just the inmates; she considered everyone beneath her. And despite the fact that I was the primary physician and worked the most hours, she still consistently tried to tell me how to do my job. "Maybe because I don't think you're trash," I said, slapping the ice pack into Mary Jo's hand. I guided her hand over her eye.

"How come?"

I heard the suspicion in her voice.

Working as a prison doctor for the last two years had taught me a few things. One of those things was that most of the female inmates were suspicious of absolutely everyone and their motives.

"How come I don't think you're trash?"

"Yeah."

I turned away to put the cotton swabs I'd used in the medical trash. The answer to that question was like the deepest root of a solid twenty-one-year-old tree—buried too far down to unearth it now without toppling the entire tree. "Mistakes don't make you trash." I pasted a bright smile on my face as I turned back to her. "You're good to go." I knocked on the glass pane of my door and the guard on duty, Pamela, nodded and strode over. She opened the door. "Doc?"

"Let Mary Jo sit in the ward for about a half hour with this ice on her eye, and then she's good to go."

"Sure thing. Come on, Mary Jo." Pamela ushered her out.

Once I was alone in my office again I sat down at my computer to update Mary Jo's record. I was just finishing up when there was a knock at my door.

Fatima marched in. Six foot one, proud, and physically fit, Fatima was like a warrior queen in a prison guard uniform. She was also a riot. I grinned. "What brings you here?"

She pulled a face and waved a dusty leather-bound book at me. "These girls have been watching too many movies." She sat down on my desk and flipped the book open.

Well, look at that.

The middle of the pages had been carved into, and sitting hidden in the hole was a makeshift shank. "That's a new way to hide a weapon."

"In Jane Austen," Fatima huffed. "They defiled Mr. Darcy for this shit. Don't they know that man is *fine*? No shank hole should be defiling such a gentleman."

I chuckled. "I don't think they care about how much of a gentleman Mr. Darcy is."

"See, that there is the problem. Instead of using library books to hide weapons, they should be educating themselves. No wonder they cut the freaking library budget."

"I heard they did that." I knew how much getting the women into the library, for reading groups and to teach them computer skills, meant to Fatima. "I'm sorry."

She sighed heavily. "Shit, I knew it was coming. I'll just make do with what I got. Anyhow, how was your date last night?"

"I told you it wasn't a date." Andrew and I didn't date.

She shook her head in disappointment. "You need your head checked. So does this idiot you're hooking up with. Nothing sweeter than coming home to your man after a long day at work."

I looked at the gold wedding band she was subconsciously touching. "That's not what you said last week when you were complaining about Derek forgetting to do the laundry, or the week before, when his idea of doing food shopping consisted of buying a year's supply of beer and Cheetos."

Fatima scowled at me. "Do you remember absolutely everything?"

"Pretty much."

"It's annoying."

"Noted." I laughed.

"Okay, so I want to kill Derek as much as I want to make sweet love to the man, but it's nice living with my best friend. You should get yourself one and kick that Dr. Commitment-Phobe to the curb."

"I told you, I like not being in a relationship."

She grunted at me like she didn't believe me, but the truth was I did like keeping things casual. I'd never had a serious relationship in my life. I came and went as I pleased. I made all the decisions in my life and got to live each day my way.

And on the days I got a little "fris-frisky" I had Andrew on speed dial.

"I'm setting you up." Fatima got up from the desk with determination. "How do you feel about chocolate?" She winked at me.

Laughing, I shook my head. "Chocolate is very nice, but right now I am happy with my casual dose of vanilla."

"That particular slice of vanilla is boring." She huffed and her pager beeped. She checked it and all amusement fled her features.

"Everything okay?"

"Fight in the yard. Gotta go."

"Be careful!" I called after her.

"Always am."

The door slammed closed behind her and I felt a wave of uneasiness in my stomach. The uneasiness wouldn't go away until she returned to let me know she was okay.

As I turned back to my computer my eye caught on the book Fatima had left on my desk. Curious, I took the old book in hand, feeling sad that the classic had been mutilated. I flicked open to the front pages and felt even sadder. The book was printed in 1940. A vintage copy of *Pride and Prejudice* would have some value. Not a lot, but some. Mostly its value was in its history.

And someone had destroyed it, completely oblivious to all that.

I flicked through the broken pages to the end and was just about to put the book down with a sigh when my thumb brushed over the back binding.

Hmm. It felt a little spongy—a little thicker than it should. With curious fingers I prodded at it. A faint line at the bottom near the spine drew my gaze. It looked like the paper that covered the leather there had been cut and opened and then resealed.

Why?

I pressed at the thickness.

There was something in there.

My heart rate started to speed up a little at the mystery of what the book might contain.

I looked up at the glass windows around my office. No one out there. No one watching.

The book and Mr. Darcy were already defiled so it wasn't like I could do much further harm—I picked and picked at the line until eventually I was able to rip the paper back.

"What the . . ." I stared down at what had been placed inside the binding of the book. Tipping them over onto my lap, I stared at four small envelopes.

There was a name and address scrawled on all four.

The same name and address.

Mr. George Beckwith
131 Providence Road
Hartwell, DE 19972

Had an inmate hidden these letters in the book?

And when?

My fingers itched to rip open one of the envelopes.

The phone on my desk blared to life, making me jump. "Dr. Huntington," I answered.

"An inmate on their way up. Yard fight. Nothing more serious than a deep cut."

"Thanks," I said and hung up. Without thinking about why, I stuffed the four little envelopes into my purse and hid it under my desk. I glued the paper back down on the binding of the book and put it aside for Fatima for when she came to collect it.

My door burst open as Fatima and Shayla, an inmate I was familiar with, came in. Shayla was hanging on to Fatima and clutching her stomach. "Fucking bitch!" she screeched. "I'm gonna fucking kill that motherfucking bitch!"

Fatima rolled her eyes at me as if to say, *Is this our life? Really?*

"Outstanding," Andrew grunted out as he came.

I had a little giggle to myself as he rolled off of me and collapsed on his back.

Every time Andrew climaxed he grunted out the word "outstanding." It was a nice compliment, but the longer our casual arrangement of sleeping together went on, the funnier I was beginning to find it. And comedy wasn't really high up on my list of dirty talk that worked for me. Although I did remind myself it was way better than the guy who kept referring to his dick as his rocket. Finally, while we were in the middle of sex, he told me that if I didn't do something quick his rocket was going to launch and detonate. I started laughing before I could stop myself and he had no choice but to pull out of me. I tried to apologize, because it really wasn't nice of me to laugh, but he stormed off in a huff. I never saw him again. I think that was for the best.

Andrew turned his head on the pillow and grinned at me.

I smiled back and he bounced up off the bed with the kind of energy a surgeon needed. Once he'd disappeared into the bathroom to dispose of the condom, I got up out of the bed. Inside my pants pocket I found my pager and checked it, even though I was pretty sure I hadn't heard it go off. Sure enough, it was quiet.

"You are so sexy."

I glanced up at Andrew. He was leaning against the bathroom door with his arms crossed over his chest, completely at ease with his nakedness. I felt the same way about being naked in front of him and grinned at him. "You're kind of sexy yourself." And it was true. The man worked out at the gym in his fancy-ass hospital between patients. He had a sleek, hard, athletic body that was a delight to explore in bed.

As for me, I normally wasn't this sexually confident woman who walked around naked with ease. It was just that Andrew and I had been at this whole fuck-buddy thing for about three years now on and off. About a year after we'd started sleeping together, he met a woman and started dating her seriously, so we stopped. They broke up after about nine months, and Andrew realized he was just too much like me and we started our casual relationship back up again. Once you'd been naked with a guy that many times and he kept coming back for more, you were pretty confident that he liked your body, so I didn't feel self-conscious around him.

"Just kind of?" He guffawed.

I didn't say any more. The man had enough of an ego to fill the entire state of Delaware. It was best to keep him on his toes so it didn't get even more out of hand than it already was.

"What are you doing?" he said as I began pulling my pants on.

"Going home."

He pushed off the door frame, frowning as he strode toward me. He picked up my shirt and held it out of my reach. "We just started. I put aside two hours for you."

I tried not to roll my eyes at him. Andrew liked to think everything should be done on his schedule since he was the big important cardiothoracic surgeon. And in the interest of saving lives it probably should, but that didn't mean I had to stick around when I didn't want to. "I can't stay. I'm sorry."

Pouting—yes, pouting—he continued to withhold my shirt.

I stared him down. When we weren't having sex it only reminded me of what a jackass he could be. Which was one of the reasons it would only ever be sex between us. His arrogance and self-involved sense of importance would drive me up the wall.

He thrust the shirt at me when he realized I wouldn't back down. "So what is so important that it's worth messing up my schedule?"

"I said I'd cover Dr. Whitaker's shift at the prison," I lied. In truth I was desperate to get home so I could finally open the letters I'd found. They had been on my mind my entire shift. For a moment I'd considered canceling my sex date with Andrew so I could read them, but I remembered he said he had a conference in Sweden coming up. Our sex dates were weekly and I'd gotten used to getting myself a little something-something on a regular basis so I figured I'd better get it while he was around to give it.

I watched his delicious ass as Andrew stomped across his bedroom to grab his neatly folded pants off a chair. "Why on earth do you insist on working in that shithole?"

My blood turned instantly hot at his condescending attitude toward my job. I swore to God, if the man didn't know what to do with those hands of his I'd have wiped my own clean of him long since. "Quit it," I bit out.

"No." He spun around, his hands on his hips. "Jessica, you're a fantastic, talented doctor. It's a crying shame that you're locked up in some dingy prison doctor's office when you should be a surgical resident." He donned his shirt, a look of disgust on his face. "I still can't believe you left your residency and gave up the chance of a fellowship at the hospital. No one can."

"Can we not do this again?" I snapped. We'd been having this argument for two years.

"Maybe if you'd tell me what the allure of the prison is, then yes. Why do you insist on staying there?"

Instead of answering I sighed, grabbed my bag, and walked over to him. I brushed my fingertips over the frown line between his brows and leaned in to press a soft kiss to his mouth. "Good night, Andrew."

I walked out of his apartment, knowing he'd gotten the reminder.

We were just fuck buddies.

He had no right to answers about anything in my life.

THREE

Jessica

Despite the fact that I spent little time away from work, I stretched myself financially to rent my two-bedroom apartment downtown. I'd wanted the extra space so that my best friend, Matthew, his wife, Helena, and my goddaughter, Perry, could visit whenever they wanted.

It was a spacious and airy apartment with an open-plan kitchen and living room. It was stylish and comfortable, and my whole body seemed to sigh with relief every time I stepped inside it. I didn't get much alone time here, but when I did, I savored it.

The first thing I did was shower, hurrying through the process and then speeding through blowing out my hair. It was still damp when I changed into my pajamas and wandered casually into the kitchen. The kitchen was the reason I chose the place. It was sleek, glossy, and white—white cabinets, white tile flooring, white sink, white stove: white, white, white. But the whiteness was broken up by the backsplash of leaf tiles—copper foil encased in glass. It was a glamorous touch of luxury, as was the huge picture window at the end of the kitchen that gave me a fantastic view of the city.

I grabbed a cold beer and stood at my kitchen counter, staring out the large window as if I hadn't a care in the world. But trying to relax was impossible when my eyes kept drifting to my purse. I'd left it sitting on my favorite armchair.

Screw it.

I couldn't wait anymore.

With cold beer in hand I curled up on the chair and pulled the envelopes out of my purse. Part of me wondered why whoever wrote them didn't mail them, and why they stuck them inside of a book. Did they want them to be found eventually? Or was it wrong of me to read them?

I let my conscience decide it was the former. Putting my beer down, I opened all the envelopes. Inside were letters with lovely feminine handwriting. I checked each for a date.

They were written in 1976, forty years ago.

Wow.

I got little goose bumps just from touching the decades-old paper.

Putting them into chronological order, I picked up the first one, along with my beer, and settled in to read.

Sarah Randall
Inmate No. 50678
Women's Correctional and Rehabilitation Facility
Wilmington, DE 19801

April 14, 1976

My darling George,

What you must think of me. I dread it. In fact, I can barely breathe under the weight of my secrets, secrets that have kept me from you. Secrets that have destroyed all the good you ever thought of me.

Perhaps it's too late to explain. It's definitely too late to change my circumstances. But not too late to change yours. Not too late to change how you think of me. I think I'd be okay if I knew you could forgive me.

You need to know that I love you. I have loved you from the moment we collided on the boardwalk and you picked up my books and asked me if you could carry them for me. It was such an old-fashioned gesture, when all the other boys were too busy trying to be cool. You were always just you. And you were the kindest, most thoughtful boy I'd ever met. And you made me laugh. I never knew I could laugh like that until I met you.

Do you remember the day Kitty Green put my clothes down the toilet after gym class? I had to wear my gym clothes all day and everyone knew and laughed and teased me. Not only did you stand up for me, you took me to the boardwalk after school and you did all these funny impressions of Kitty and the mean girls. You turned my tears into laughter.

You have always turned my tears into laughter.

It was real between us. You have to know that. From that first smile, to our first kiss, to the first time you made love to me.

I never wanted those moments with anyone else.

If you believe anything in this world, believe that.

Believe that I love you more than any other person and that that love will never die. You'll be the last image in my mind the day I leave this world, and I hope that image of your goodness, the love I feel for you, will be enough for God to recognize that I know of Heaven and I cherish its value. Perhaps in that knowledge He will forgive me and welcome me home.

Forever yours,
Sarah

It took me a moment to reach for the next letter. Already my chest ached. It was so desperately sad to read the woman's profession of love without knowing why this stranger had been separated from someone she cared so deeply for. A small part of me envied her, her love. The larger part of me knew I shouldn't. She had clearly suffered even though she had known love.

I picked up the next letter, desperate to know the reason for their separation and her incarceration.

Sarah Randall
Inmate No. 50678
Women's Correctional and Rehabilitation Facility
Wilmington, DE 19801

April 23, 1976

My darling George,

I am so sorry. I meant to explain everything in my first letter. I truly did. For a moment I lost courage. All that seemed important was telling you I loved you. But as important as that is, I realize it's just as important for you to hear that I didn't love Ron.

I pleaded guilty because it was the truth, George. I killed Ron. I killed my husband.

He didn't deserve the title. He was cruel. Beyond cruel. There is no excuse good enough for taking a man's life, I know that. But I was protecting myself. I'd taken so much for so long. He kept hurting me. From the night of our wedding until the day I shot him, Ron hurt me.

I didn't want to marry him. He forced my hand. On the night of our wedding he took . . . I never wanted him. Not once throughout our marriage did I want him.

I was becoming nothing. I lost myself and it was his fault. He took everything from me. He took you from me.

That night he came home angry about something. He was so angry. He'd threatened to kill me before, and the last time he'd been so angry that he'd almost succeeded. He beat me so bad I lost consciousness for hours. He had a doctor come in from out of town. He paid him a lot of money to keep quiet. Ron told everyone I'd gone to a spa for a few weeks. He almost killed me and yet he told people he'd paid for me to go to a spa.

So I knew. I knew that night when he came home that he was going to kill me. I felt it coming. I can't explain it. I just knew in my gut. He managed to get a few hits in before I got away from him and got to his gun. I knew where he hid it. I made sure I knew after that last time.

He sneered at me. Said I didn't have the backbone to do it.

I shot him in the heart. And I was surprised. Really surprised when it killed him. I just wanted him to stop.

I shot him.

Please forgive me, George.

I feel guilty. Ashamed. I do. But I also feel relief that I'm free of him. Maybe if you forgive me, I can forgive myself.

Forever yours,
Sarah

I was surprised at the splash of water that fell on the paper and I jerked it away from my tears. The ache in my chest had intensified as I read the second letter and for the first time in a long time I cried. I cried for this faceless woman. I cried for the powerlessness, the pain, and the truthful shame of that freedom that Sarah's words invoked.

My phone suddenly rang and I felt like I jumped a foot in fright. For a moment there, everything had disappeared, including the apartment.

Reaching into my purse for my cell, the irritation I felt at being interrupted melted away when I saw who was calling.

It was Matthew. Matthew and I had been friends for twenty-five years. He was the only remaining tie I had to my life back in Iowa.

"Hey, you." I smiled.

"Hey, sorry for calling so late."

"Don't be. Is anything wrong?"

He heaved a heavy sigh, causing the line to crackle. "Helena's mom has been admitted to the hospital with pneumonia."

I knew Helena was close to her mom. "Oh, God. What are the doctors saying?"

"Well, we're hoping she'll pull through, but even then she's looking at some recovery time. She's going to stay with us during recovery."

Suddenly I knew the other reason he was calling. Every year, during the anniversary of my sister's death, I went on vacation. This year I couldn't because my colleague, Dr. Whitaker, had already put in for her vacation for the weeks that I'd wanted. And she refused to even consider swapping vacation time. I hated the idea of working during what was always a hard time for me. The next best thing I could do was to plan a vacation with my best friend. In two weeks, I'd planned on meeting Matthew, Helena, and Perry in Key West for a shared vacation together. I never went home to Iowa, so these planned trips were the only chance we had to see each other.

Disappointed, but more concerned for Helena and her mom, I said, "Matt, it's okay. If you contact the owner of the house we were renting and explain, we should get our money back."

"I'm not worried about the money. I'm worried about you. It was our only chance this year to see each other."

"Don't worry about me. I'll figure something else out."

"You'll call me when you do?"

Smiling at his overprotectiveness, I said, "Yes. But more importantly, keep me posted about Helena's mom. And give my love to her and Perry."

"I will. We'll talk soon?"

I could still hear the anxiety in his voice and I wished I were a less complicated person so he could stop worrying about me. "I promise."

Once we hung up I stared at Sarah's last two letters.

An emptiness had struck me when I realized Matt was canceling, and it suddenly expanded and filled my chest. It was strange how such emptiness could cause an ache.

I didn't know what I was going to do. I had my three-week vacation time to use up and I knew I couldn't stick around Wilmington for it. I'd have to come up with a plan.

The thought exhausted me so instead I picked up the letters and started reading again.

Sarah Randall
Inmate No. 50678
Women's Correctional and Rehabilitation Facility
Wilmington, DE 19801

May 5, 1976

My darling George,

I will mail these letters to you. I will. It's just taking me time to find the strength. Now you'll get them all at the same time. At least you won't have to wait for the truth then. There will be no agonizing wait as I try to gather my courage to tell you what I need to tell you.

If I could save you from this truth I would. Perhaps it is selfish of me to tell you now, after all these years of protecting you, but it has taken me this long to realize that secrets are poison. You, of all people, are owed the truth.

I wish I had known then what I know now.

Everything would be so different.

Do you remember the weekend you went with your father to tour the Princeton campus? You were so excited. You'd never wanted anything more than to be a Princeton man. Except me, you said. You said you'd always want me more than anything.

Why didn't I remember that then?

I am so sorry.

You were gone that weekend and that's when Ron came to me. Remember he'd been bothering me for months, trying to get me to go out with him? He was becoming a problem. You two had that fight in Loretta's the night he touched me. Everyone on the boardwalk was there to see you best Ron. He never forgave you for that. I sometimes wonder if he came after me just to get his revenge for that night.

Ron came to me and he had proof that Anderson was involved in criminal activity. I know how much you love your father and how proud you feel of him. Back then you were secure in your place in life: son of a state senator and soon-to-be Princeton freshman. I couldn't bear the idea that you might find out, that all that would be taken away from you. But now here is the truth:

Ron discovered Anderson was making money illegally, mainly drugs and prostitution. He had photographs. Even I knew of Dot's place out near Route 1. Your father was pictured there. Incriminating photos. Money passing hands outside the brothel. And Ron suspected your father of buying votes. Finally, he showed me money transfers from Anderson to Ron. Ron was blackmailing him, which was all the proof I needed that what he said was true.

At the time.

I wish I could go back to that scared kid and tell her to trust you, to tell you, to let you take care of it. But I'd lost Mom and you knew how much that destroyed my world. I didn't want to destroy yours like that by taking away your father.

I realize now how wrong I was.

Please forgive me.

Ron told me he would go to the police and the newspapers with what he'd found and that not only would Anderson go to jail, but you would lose any chance you had of getting into Princeton. Your whole future was on the line. I was stupid. So stupid.

I agreed to marry Ron in exchange for his silence.

Everything fell apart anyway. You hated me. I still see your face when I told you what I'd done while you were gone. I will never get that look out of my head. And I understand.

About you and Annabelle.

I don't know if you slept with her to hurt me or if you genuinely cared for one another. When the baby came, when little Marie came, I was angry. I was hurt. I was . . . I lost my love and I lost my best friend. I lost my best friend when I needed her the most. But over time I've grown to understand. I hope you two found happiness in your marriage in spite of everything.

And I'm sorry that after everything I hid so you would have Princeton and the future you dreamed of, fate took it away from you anyway. But I hope that being a father has been a new kind of dream, better than the one that came before it. God, I hope that for you, George.

I'm sorry for keeping the truth from you for so long. I'm just so ashamed that something that could have been avoided grew so out of my control.

It's selfish of me now, I know, to tell you the truth. But there's so little time in life. I realize that now more than ever before. I needed to unburden myself. I just needed you to know that I love you.

Always have. Always will.

Forever yours,
Sarah

Heart thumping, I almost dropped my drink trying to get to the next letter in hand. I had to know what happened. Why hadn't these letters made it to George?

Sarah Randall
Inmate No. 50678
Women's Correctional and Rehabilitation Facility
Wilmington, DE 19801

May 8, 1976

My darling George,

I've made all the wrong choices up until now. I hope this isn't another.

I hope this is the right thing to do.

I have asked much of you in these letters, George, and now I ask one last thing: write me back, just once, telling me you got the letters, and letting me know whether you forgive me or not. Yes or no, I'd like to know. If you could do this as soon as possible I would be so grateful. So grateful.

I will never ask anything else of you. Not ever.

I love you.

Always have. Always will.

Forever yours,
Sarah

With tears on my cheeks, my nose running, and a sharp ache in my chest, I folded the letters up and slipped them back into the envelopes.

For some reason Sarah's letters had never made it to George.

My heart hurt for her beyond bearing.

A sob escaped me and I sat in my low-lit apartment with my heart breaking over a stranger's story.

Upon waking the next day the first thing I thought about was Sarah. I couldn't get her letters out of my head, and I realized that the ache in my chest wouldn't lessen until I found out what had happened to her.

"Any chance I can get into the old records room?" I said to Fatima during my lunch break. I always came down to the guards' room to eat my lunch with her and Shelley, Fatima's shift partner.

Fatima swallowed the bite of sandwich she was chewing and frowned. "Why? You can't check the computer's medical records?"

"I want to find out what happened to an inmate that was here in 1976." The computer held only the records for inmates of the past fifteen years.

Shelley pulled a face. "Who the hell did you know here in 1976? Suddenly the truth comes out about why this one is working here. Ghosts in her closet, huh?" Shelley winked at Fatima.

Fatima gave her a dry look. "You are the only person I will say this to in my life: stop reading so many damn books."

Shelley looked horrified. "And actually have to talk to Paulie? No, thanks."

Paulie was her husband.

Fatima chuckled and turned back to me. "Seriously, why do you want into the old records room?"

"It's for a friend. She knew of someone who served time here in 1976. My friend just wants to know what happened to her."

"You got a name? An inmate number?"

"Both, actually."

"Okay. I guess I can trust you. Remember, though, no stealing or photocopying those records," she teased.

I crossed my heart.

Man, it was dusty in the old records room. I slammed a drawer shut and sneezed for the fifth time as another cloud of dust floated up around me.

Thankfully, I was determined enough to get through the horror of the dustland.

Fourth drawer in, my heart leapt in my chest at the sight of Sarah's name and inmate number. I almost dropped the damn folder in my hurry to get it out of the drawer. Clutching it tightly in hand, I took it over to a table that was set up in the back of the room and clicked on the library lamp that sat on it. To my surprise the bulb in the lamp still worked.

I didn't completely understand my reaction to Sarah's story. All I knew was that she'd gotten under my skin in a way that surprised the heck out of me. I felt like I knew her. Like I understood her in some way. And more than anything I wished for a happy ending for her.

I flipped open her records. The first thing I saw was a picture of a frail-looking woman. There were hints of her once-upon-a-time beauty, but it appeared as if life had battered most of the prettiness out of her.

And as I read on, all my hopes and wishes for her died there on the spot.

Inside the folder was a copy of her medical records and her date of death.

May 8, 1976.

The day she wrote her last letter to George.

That was why he'd never gotten them.

I read through the medical notes with a heavy heart. Sarah had been diagnosed with non-Hodgkin's lymphoma in January 1976. All the time she'd been writing to George she'd been undergoing radiation therapy. The treatment had been aggressive because her cancer was aggressive, and she died of heart failure.

I closed her records feeling impossibly sad. Now I knew why Sarah had wanted George's forgiveness so quickly. She wanted it before she died, and he never got the chance to give it to her.

Wiping tears from my eyes, I quickly put her records back, wishing I could unsee them and frankly wishing I could unsee the letters. There were enough unhappy endings in this life. I didn't need to know about a stranger's.

However, as I worked that day, my mind kept drifting back to the man she had written to. I couldn't help wondering if George might still be alive. I knew from Sarah's records that she was twenty-six years old when she died. If she and George were the same age, then he would be only sixty-six years old.

How hard could it be to find a state senator's son who lived in Hartwell, a city so small I hadn't even heard of it until I Googled it? Turned out it had a pretty boardwalk and gorgeous beach so it was actually quite a popular vacation spot.

When I had another moment free I Googled "Anderson Beckwith." Sure enough it pulled up articles on the state senator, and before I knew it I found a photo of George Beckwith. It was taken in 1982 with his father at a political rally at Princeton University. The college of George's dreams. The college he never got to go to despite Sarah's efforts.

I stared at his handsome face and knew he and Sarah must have been a fine-looking couple. I wanted desperately to see a photograph of them together, when they were both young and happy.

"God," I muttered, clicking off the screen. Why was I so hung up on this? "You're going crazy."

"Why are you going crazy?"

I jumped, startled, as Fatima strode into my office with a cup of coffee for me. I took it gratefully but scowled at her. "Don't creep up on me like that."

"Why? So I don't catch you talking to yourself like a crazy person?"

I sighed. "I think I might be a crazy person."

Fatima frowned and sipped at her own coffee. "And why is that?"

"I did something." I pulled my purse out from under the desk and searched through it for the envelopes. "That book you confiscated. *Pride and Prejudice* . . . I found something inside the binding . . ." I told her everything, including my discovery of what had happened to the inmate who'd written the hidden letters.

"Why didn't you just say that was what you were looking for in the records room instead of lying?"

At her waspish tone I tried to appease her. "I didn't want you to think I'd gone nuts."

"I don't think you've gone nuts." Fatima looked over the letters and I saw my sadness reflected in her gaze. "This is heartbreaking shit." She glanced up from them. "And I know why they get to you more than they probably would anyone else."

For a moment I froze, wondering if she— Nah. She couldn't.

"You can kid yourself all you want that you're happy, but you and I both know there should be more to life than how you're living." Fatima handed the letters back to me, her eyes kind as she gave me some harsh truths. "You have no family, no boyfriend, and your oldest friend lives over a thousand miles away. Now, I'm glad you're here working in this prison, but I have to ask myself what the hell made you want to work here when you clearly had so many other opportunities open to you. Can you honestly say that at thirty-three years old this is where you always hoped your life would lead you?"

For hours I sat in my empty apartment later that evening, Fatima's words ringing in my ears. The woman had always known how to be blunt, but up until now I'd never felt the force of her words so much as I did today.

I didn't want to believe that she was right or that the reason I felt so much for the woman I'd met through her letters was because I, too, felt as if life had slipped away from me somehow.

That there was no hope of a happy ending for me.

And maybe there wasn't. Maybe I'd designed it that way.

I picked up my phone and called Matthew.

"How's Helena's mom?" I said as a hello.

"The same as she was yesterday. She hasn't gotten any worse so that's a good sign, I guess."

"Is there anything I can do?"

"You could tell me why you're really calling."

I rolled my eyes at the amusement in his voice. He knew me too well. "I really am concerned about your mother-in-law."

"I know that. But I also know when your voice gets all high and twitchy like that, you're worrying about something."

"Is my life empty?"

"Sweetheart," he replied.

And everything was in that one word.

Jesus Christ, Matthew thought my life was empty.

He would. In comparison to his it was. He was an architect and passionate about it; he had Helena, who he was in rapture over (still!); and he had his little girl, Perry, who he adored. And it wasn't hard to adore her since she was the coolest, most awesome thing that had existed since Jimmy Stewart! Of course my life would look empty next to Matthew's.

"You need that vacation, Jess. That's all I'm going to say. Get away from that prison, that apartment, and that idiot you're screwing around with."

"Get a little perspective?"

"Exactly," Matthew said. "Helena and I were in Hawaii last year and it was amazing. You'd love it there."

"Hawaii." I tried to picture myself lying on a beach, drinking cocktails for a few weeks.

"There are some nice treks in Honolulu. Water sports. Deep-sea diving. More to it than cocktails by the pool."

But even so, Hawaii didn't feel right. "I don't think so."

"Okay, so where do you feel like going?"

Honestly, the whole idea of taking a vacation to get perspective on my life scared me a little. What if I found perspective and realized I really did hate my entire life? That would suck, black-hole-style. And who needed to deal with a black hole, right?

"Jess?"

"Hartwell," I blurted out. "I'm going to Hartwell."

"Hartwhat now?"

"Hartwell. It's a boardwalk town here in Delaware."

"How adventurous of you."

"I'll have you know that it is an exciting place to be."

"It's Delaware, honey. The same state you live and work in. If it was an adventure it would be Hawaii or the jungles of South America."

"You're lucky I love you, you condescending ass."

"You're lucky I love you, you *pain* in the ass."

At the sound of his warm laughter, I felt better than I had since I'd found Sarah's letters.

FOUR

Cooper

Hartwell, Delaware

"It's your alternator, Ayd," Cooper said, staring down into the engine and pretending he couldn't feel his sister's best friend's breasts pressed up against his back.

"Really?" she said breathily. "And what about that squealing noise it was making before it died?"

"Drive belt needs to be replaced probably." He pulled back, taking a step away from her.

Aydan was a good-looking woman, but Cooper had a rule. He didn't fuck a woman who would care if he didn't call her again. He especially wasn't going to mess around with Cat's best friend. Not only because he didn't want to piss off his sister but also because Aydan was vulnerable. Her husband had run off a year before, leaving her alone with her teenage daughter, Angela. She was struggling to make ends meet, which was why he'd said he'd fix her car so she didn't have to pay the local garage to do it.

But Cooper knew from Cat that Aydan was also looking for a stable man in her life.

Cooper wasn't that guy.

For now, he was steering clear of relationships.

Despite the fact that they lived in a small town and everybody knew Cooper wasn't interested in settling down again, Aydan seemed to be testing his position.

When he'd turned up at her place to tow the car to the large shed he owned on the outskirts of Hartwell, he'd known something was up right away. It was the short jean skirt, tight tank top, and high red heels she was wearing.

Aydan usually dressed for comfort. He'd only ever seen her in a skirt and heels when she was on the prowl with Cat when they were younger.

Shit.

"I really appreciate you doing this, Coop," Aydan said, closing the distance between them again. She ran her fingertips down his bare arm. "Maybe I could have you over for dinner to say thanks."

Shit.

"Sure. You, me, Angela, Cat, and Joey." He said, deliberately mentioning her kid and his nephew. "A family dinner sounds good."

Her face fell. "Well, I was thinking—"

"It shouldn't take me too long to get the parts for your car. As soon as they arrive, I'll make time, get it fixed up for you. For now I've got to get the bar open. I'll give you a ride back into town."

He went to move past her, but she grabbed his wrist. "Coop . . . I'd really like to have you over for dinner. Just you. Angela is staying with friends next weekend."

Ah, hell.

She was staring up at him with those pretty blue eyes as if he could hand her the world with just one word, and it made him feel like the biggest asshole for not giving her what she wanted. She deserved a good guy in her life. Cooper just wasn't the guy. He reached out and brushed her soft cheek with his thumb. "If you were anyone else but my sister's best friend, I'd be over to your house for dinner in a heartbeat."

She blushed, her gaze dropping. "That's just your diplomatic way of saying you're not interested."

"Hey." He tipped her chin gently to raise her eyes back to his. "Ayd, you're gorgeous and you're sweet, but you know I'm not in the place to start anything up."

This time she gave him a sympathetic smile. "I get that. You know *I* get that."

"Good. So we're okay?" He grinned.

She rolled her eyes. "When you smile like that you know it's hard for any woman to be mad at you."

He winked at her and heard her laughing as she followed him to the truck.

Relief moved through him.

"How's Angela doing?" he asked as they rode back into town.

"Oh, she's doing great. She got a summer job at the fun park and she's helping out a lot. She's a good girl."

"She is that." Cooper smiled. "You're doing a great job there, Ayd."

She gave him a tired smile. "I do what I can."

"Which is a lot more than some." He pulled up to a stop at her small house. It was in the crappiest neighborhood in Hartwell. She'd moved Angela there nine months back. They used to live four houses down from Cooper, but when her asshole of an ex left them, he left them without the means to pay rent on the nicer house.

"Thanks for saying so, Coop." She opened the door. "And thanks again for the car."

"No problem. I'll call you when it's fixed."

She threw him a wave over her shoulder and Cooper pulled away from the house.

"Call Cat," he said to his truck's computer system.

His sister picked up on the third ring. "What's up?"

"Did you know Aydan was going to make a play for me?"

His sister groaned down the line. "Oh, please tell me she didn't."

"I wish I could."

"Well, don't feel special. She has a list of suitable guys and you're actually last on the list. She probably just went for it because the opportunity arose."

Cooper grinned. "You always know how to make me feel good about myself."

"Like you need me to inflate your ego."

He ignored that and asked after his nephew. "Joey okay?"

"At school. It's his last week, so you know he's more than okay. He's hyper."

"I'll swing by to see you tomorrow."

"Great. And I'll talk to Aydan if you want."

"It's okay. I already did."

"You weren't mean to her, were you?"

That didn't even deserve a response.

"Right," she said. "Stupid question."

"I'm pulling up to the house. Talk to you later."

"Later."

Ex-wives were hell.

Or at least in Cooper's experience they were hell.

For instance, he was supposed to be free and clear of his. That was what the divorce was all about, right? So why the fuck had he stepped out of his house, set for getting to his bar, to find Dana Kellerman—Dana Lawson until eighteen months before—leaning up against the passenger side of his truck?

Unfortunately for him, this wasn't his first encounter with his ex since they'd divorced. For a while he *had* been free and clear of the traitorous she-demon. Until a few weeks back, when, out of the blue, Dana was suddenly in his face again, wanting to talk and angling for reconciliation.

She was out of her fucking mind, that was all Cooper could say.

Sighing at the annoyance, he strode down his porch steps to his drive, completely ignoring her existence as he got in his truck. He could feel her eyes burning on his face. Once upon a time he'd thought those eyes of hers were stunning. Now he looked at her and he couldn't remember what the hell he'd seen in her.

Cooper guessed that was only natural since Dana had fucked his best friend behind his back.

He pulled out of the drive, ignoring her thumping her hand

against his truck and yelling his name. After getting angry at her calls, at her turning up at the house and his bar, he realized all he was doing was giving her a reaction. She was obviously taking that emotion to mean he still felt something for her.

Now he was out to get the message across that he couldn't give a shit about her. Maybe then she'd get out of his face and leave him in peace.

Irritation bubbled in his blood, but Cooper attempted to force the feeling out, to turn his mind away from his ex. The woman had monopolized too much of his life as it was.

By the time he got to his bar on the boardwalk he felt a little better. It was hard not to feel good as he walked the boards, knowing that he had a business there, in the one place in the world he wanted to be. The salt air, the clean light spray of the water, the mingling scents of sweet food, hot dogs, burgers, surf, and coffee—all of it was so familiar he hardly even thought about it, except to acknowledge that it smelled like home.

Cooper had barely let himself into the bar when there was a knock on the front door. The bar wasn't open yet. It didn't open until noon, when he served lunch five days a week. His cook, Crosby, wouldn't show for another hour to set up.

Even so, Cooper knew who was at his door.

He let Vaughn Tremaine inside and locked up behind him.

Without even asking what he wanted, he poured Vaughn his favorite scotch and slid it across the bar to him as he sat on a stool.

The businessman owned Paradise Sands Hotel next to Cooper's. The hotel was swankier than anything that had come before it on the boardwalk. Vaughn had bought the old hotel and completely renovated it, turning it into an upscale hotel and conference center. Some folks in town said the hotel was too swanky for Hart's Boardwalk; that the people who vacationed here didn't come for contemporary luxury but a little piece of tradition. Somehow, however, Vaughn had made it work. The conference center was always busy and the guy had made a success out of the hotel.

Cooper wasn't too surprised. The Manhattan-born businessman owned a number of hotels and was the son of a hugely wealthy CEO of an international real estate and construction company.

The boardwalk community hadn't exactly warmed to the New Yorker. No one could understand why a guy like him would choose Hartwell as his home. He wouldn't explain himself and people around there didn't like that much. Frankly, Vaughn didn't do much to make them like him. But he'd been coming into Cooper's every week for that shot of whiskey for the past year and Cooper had gotten to know him better. There was definitely more to Vaughn Tremaine than met the eye.

"Thanks," Vaughn muttered. "I need it this morning."

"Rough night?"

"Dentistry conference yesterday. Those assholes can party. One of them assaulted my night manager. It was a late night."

"Jesus. Your manager okay?"

"Fine. Just a swollen eye, thankfully."

"And the dentist?"

"Out on his ass. Fuck knows where he went."

Cooper grinned. "Did—"

A knock at the front door cut him off.

Dana?

"Coop, it's Bailey!"

Noting the way Vaughn tensed, Cooper smirked.

Idiot.

Ignoring Vaughn's reaction to the sound of Bailey Hartwell's voice, Cooper hurried over to let her into the bar.

"Coop, Dana is on the boardwalk," Bailey said a little breathlessly. Her hair was windswept, suggesting she'd been running. "I was walking to my place and I was just nearing the bandstand and I saw that bitch marching this way so I took off. I'm pretty sure she knows I was running to give you a heads-up that she's slithering around the boardwalk."

He laughed at her rambling, but he did it while he shut his blinds and locked his door.

When he turned back he nearly laughed again at Bailey's reaction to finding Vaughn in the bar. Her whole body had gone rigid.

"Miss Hartwell," Vaughn said with a mocking salute of his scotch glass.

He never called Bailey by her first name. Cooper knew it drove Bailey crazy and he more than suspected that Vaughn knew that, too, and that was exactly why he did it.

The two of them had clashed from the moment they met. There couldn't be two people more different from the other. If Vaughn Tremaine was the Prince of the Upper East Side, Bailey Hartwell was the Princess of Hart's Boardwalk. A descendant of the city's founders, Bailey had inherited Hart's Inn at the north end of their stretch of the mile-long boards. The inn was the last remaining piece of real estate owned by the once incredibly wealthy Hartwells. But the family Bailey was born into wasn't wealthy. They'd worked hard to run the inn, and when her brother and sister went off to live their lives elsewhere, Bailey's parents had left the running of the inn to her and took off for their retirement in Florida.

Nothing had come easy for this particular princess and she wasn't exactly gearing up to make friends with the arrogant, wealthy businessman she saw as her competition.

And, Bailey being the boardwalk's sweetheart, most people came down on her side of this particular war.

Cooper found the whole thing damn funny. The pair was a comedy act and didn't know it.

"Mr. Asshole," Bailey replied.

Vaughn just laughed and finished off his scotch.

Bailey whirled around to glower at Cooper. He assumed for having the audacity to serve Vaughn, especially while the bar was closed. "Don't tell me I'm stuck in here with this idiot, Lawson."

The door handle of the bar turned and rattled. A loud knock followed it. "Cooper! I know you're in there!" Dana yelled.

"Yes," he said quietly. "You're stuck."

"I have to get back to the inn. Can I sneak out the back?"

He nodded. "Go ahead. If you see her—"

"Oh, I'll take that bitch down before I let her in here," Bailey assured him and turned to go.

"I'm going with you." Vaughn slipped off the stool, slapping money down on the bar. "Cooper."

"Vaughn."

Bailey threw a horrified look over her shoulder at Vaughn. "Wonderful."

"You know, you really need to stop flirting with me, Miss Hartwell," Vaughn said as he strode toward her. "It's a little inappropriate."

She narrowed her eyes, ready to spit fire at him, but Cooper distracted her.

"Thanks for the heads-up, Bailey."

"Anytime. And remember, my bitch-slapping services are always available."

"How much do you charge?" Cooper heard Vaughn say as they walked through the staff door.

"Oh, I'll slap you for free."

"Kinky."

"You are such an asshole."

"I think you need to find a new word."

"Turd!"

"Careful, your maturity is showing."

Cooper laughed softly, but his amusement fled at the continued knocking on his door.

"Cooper!" Dana shrieked now.

He winced at the sound. Seriously, what had he seen in her?

"Cooper! Open up!"

"Well, that's enough of that," a familiar voice admonished.

Iris.

Cooper tensed.

Iris and Ira owned the Italian pizzeria next to Paradise Sands. They'd opened it twenty-five years back and named it Antonio's because they reckoned no one wanted Italian food from "Iris and Ira."

Iris and Ira were like family to him.

"Iris, this isn't your damn business," Dana snapped.

"Cooper is like a son to me so it is my business. You've done enough damage here. You are not going to harass that boy. Now go away. You are not wanted."

"I need to talk to him. Cooper!"

"He doesn't want to talk to you, by the looks of it, so get going. Get going before I call the cops."

"Stay out of it, you nosy bitch."

Enough was enough. His blood turned hot as he marched across the room. No way was he going to continue hiding in his own bar, and no way in hell would he stand by and let her talk to Iris like that.

He shoved open the door and Dana skittered back as it caught her elbow.

"Cooper."

"Don't you ever fucking talk to Iris like that again. You hear me?"

She licked her lips nervously, a gesture she thought got to him. "Coop, please. I just really need to talk to you."

"About what, Dana? About us getting back together? Are you out of your mind?"

"Cooper, if you just forgive me—"

"It's not about that anymore. I don't want you. I see you now. And I'm so grateful I'm free of you. You get that? I don't want you."

Tears spilled down cheeks he'd once found pretty and she let out a harsh sob before pushing past Iris. She half marched, half ran down the boardwalk in her four-inch high heels and Cooper was pissed off all over again because he could feel a twinge of guilt in his chest.

"Crocodile tears."

He looked back at Iris, who was staring at him sternly.

"Don't you feel guilty for anything, Cooper Lawson. Everything that woman does is a manipulation."

The reminder eased his guilt somewhat and he stepped forward to press a kiss on Iris's forehead. "Thank you."

Her eyes were bright when she smiled up at him. "Always here, you know that."

"Back at you. Say good morning to Ira for me." He pushed open the bar door.

"Will do. See you later."

Cooper walked through his empty pub, trying to will the tension out of his muscles. He took a beer out of one of the fridges and sat down at a table.

Thirty-six years old. Thirty-six goddamn years old. Just a little over ten years of those he'd spent with Dana. Ten years of his life gone. Thirty-six and divorced. A crazy ex-wife. No kids. No dad. No mom.

But he had his sister.

He had his nephew.

He looked around the pub.

He had his bar.

And he had friends on the boardwalk and they were like family.

If it felt like something was missing from his life, then Cooper guessed that just made him ungrateful.

Or maybe just human.

Finishing his beer, Cooper let all the crap of the morning disappear as Crosby came in to prep for the lunch service, and as he opened the bar it started filling up. The tourist season hadn't quite hit yet, but his place was never empty. He had his regulars, and as those people filled his bar, the emptiness left him for a while and the tension eased.

FIVE

Jessica

The two-hour drive to Hartwell had taken it out of me, but that wasn't surprising. I suspected my singular focus on my work had kept my body going for as long as it had. As soon as I'd decided on Hartwell for my vacation I'd felt myself growing more tired, as if just the thought of vacation had caused my mind and body to go, *Hey, thanks a lot; we've only been waiting forever for you to notice we're fucked.*

Two weeks I had to wait for vacation and it had felt like the longest two weeks of my life. Stress could be underlying. Sometimes you didn't even realize you were as stressed as you were. I should have known that. And as a doctor I should have been taking better care of myself mentally and physically.

Now was my chance.

I was at once kind of excited to take some time out, and also to see the town where Sarah had grown up, but also scared that all this vacation was going to do was prove that I didn't like the life I was living.

God, I hoped that wasn't true.

Those worries drifted away, however, when I began to smell the salt of the sea through the window I had rolled down. The closer my GPS took me to my destination, the stronger the ocean smell grew as I drove through the town of Hartwell. I seemed to be driving through the center—it was all shops, restaurants, and parking lots. The GPS turned me west and that took me into a residential area that was interspersed with a few restaurants. I drove slowly down the dark, tree-lined streets, my headlights catching on the white-clad homes with their brightly colored awnings and old-fashioned porches that reminded me a little of the neighborhood where I'd grown up. The smell of the sea got stronger and when my GPS announced I had reached my destination I swung into a nearby parking lot, my headlights catching on a sign that stated *For Hart's Inn Guests Only*, and relief moved through me that for once my GPS really had led me to my destination.

I got out of my car, glad for the streetlights that guided me (and my heavy suitcase) straight onto the boards of the boardwalk.

I stopped.

Lights lined the boardwalk and when I looked right I could see all along it. It was dark but not late enough for people to have gone inside for the night. Not quite tourist season, yet it didn't seem to matter. The boardwalk was apparently popular with locals. It wasn't heaving, but it was busy enough to feel alive with energy. Couples, groups of teenagers, and clusters of friends and family were laughing and talking as they strolled by the hodgepodge of architecturally different buildings. Bright Vegas-style lights glittered in the dark, announcing to the people, and to the ocean beyond, the names of the buildings housed on the boardwalk.

Waves crashed gently behind me and I turned to look out at the dark sea.

Was there anything more relaxing in this world than the sound of the surf? My body seemed to melt under its spell and just like that I felt exhaustion hit me.

It was only nine o'clock in the evening, but I was ready for bed.

On that thought, I turned left and looked up at Hart's Inn. It was a large version of the houses I'd passed—white-painted shingle siding, gorgeous wraparound porch, and blue-painted shutters on the windows. I knew from the photos I'd seen on the Internet that there was even a widow's walk on top of the building.

Rather than a bright neon sign, there was a beautiful hand-painted sign that rose up by the porch. A light had been attached to it so that it was lit up in the dark.

Lights glowed from behind the windows and I felt myself drawn to the warmth of them like a clichéd little moth. I was so damn tired.

I hauled my suitcase up the porch stairs and pushed open one of the beautiful double doors with its stained glass window inset. An old-fashioned bell tinkled above me, announcing my arrival.

A grand staircase rose ahead of me and a cute waiting area and reception desk lay to my left. To my right was a sitting area with a beautiful open fireplace. Bookshelves packed with reading material lined the walls on either side of the fireplace. Everywhere I looked there were signs the inn was all about quality and comfort, which was one of the reasons I'd decided to stay there rather than at the more contemporary Paradise Sands Hotel just down the boardwalk.

Beyond the reading nook area, a large archway led into a dining area, and from what I could see it looked pretty busy that night. I wondered how long it would take the manager to notice my arrival. At that thought, I immediately homed in on the waiting area and its comfortable-looking chesterfield sofa.

I'd just rest my legs and possibly my eyes.

"I thought I heard the bell!" a cheery voice called out, jolting me, and I turned from my journey to couch heaven and watched as an attractive redhead hurried toward me. She was smiling brightly and held out her hand as she reached me. "I'm Bailey Hartwell. You must be Jessica Huntington. Welcome to Hart's Inn."

I took her hand and managed a tired smile. "Thank you. Your inn is lovely."

She beamed at my sincerity and even in my tiredness it nearly knocked me over. Bailey Hartwell was pretty, with deep auburn curls that tumbled to the middle of her back. Her light green eyes were tip tilted, giving them an almost feline quality, and she had a cute button nose with a smattering of freckles over it. Pretty. Adorable even. But her smile was her best feature. It was so warm I had no choice but to smile in return. She was about my height, but in her skinny jeans and tight green thermal I could see she was more slender than me.

I curbed my envy at her elegant figure, blaming the flare of jealousy on my exhaustion. It had nothing to do with being a normal female with insecurities like everyone else. Nope. Not. At. All.

Bailey's smile wilted. "Oh, jeez, you're tuckered out, sweetie. Let's get you checked in and to your room."

I loved her.

"Thank you."

As she checked me in, Bailey informed me, "Breakfast runs from seven to ten a.m. We serve hot food and Continental and, best of all, great coffee."

I smiled at that. "Sounds like heaven."

Smiling back at me, she took my suitcase from my hands and I marveled at the way she hauled it up the stairs like it weighed nothing, considering it was probably heavier than she was.

"I'm so excited to have you here for three weeks," she said as she climbed, her breathing coming a little shorter, suggesting she was human after all. "I hardly ever get guests for that long. You'll feel like family by the end of your vacation, I have no doubt." She laughed and it sounded so musical I started to wonder if maybe Bailey Hartwell was part fairy.

I suddenly pictured her with little glittery wings on her back.

"I need sleep," I muttered.

"Sorry?" she said as she came to a stop at a door on the second floor.

"Nothing." I shook my head and followed her inside the room.

As she put my suitcase by the bed I stared in awe.

Decorated in a contemporary style with a nautical theme, the room was beautiful. But I barely took in the soft furnishings, the huge four-poster bed covered in inviting scatter cushions, or the living room area. I was too busy staring at the French doors that led out to a small balcony facing the sea.

"It's the best room in the inn," she said. "I thought you should have it since you're staying three weeks. I originally had you in another room, but we had a cancellation for this room for the week so I was able to bump you into here."

I turned to her and saw she was looking around at the room with pride and satisfaction. "Thank you. It's beautiful."

Bailey grinned and dropped the key in my hand. "Get some sleep. Tomorrow we'll get to know each other." She said it like it was a no-brainer, like all innkeepers set out to make their guests their best friends.

Honestly I didn't mind the thought of Bailey trying to get to know me.

At that point I was too exhausted to mind anything.

"Good night," she said as she closed the door.

"Good night," I called back.

That was when I really noticed the bed.

"Come to Mama." I gestured to it at the same time I stumbled toward it.

When I woke up the next morning, I was on top of the covers still fully clothed.

SIX

Jessica

The first thing I did after I showered was open the French doors in my room. I stepped out onto the balcony that overlooked the boardwalk and the ocean beyond and I didn't even care that it was a cloudy, gray day above me.

Instead I enjoyed the wind blowing up off the water because it carried with it the smell of sea and the sound of the surf. I closed my eyes, listening to that gentle rush, the lap of water against the beach, the cry of gulls in the air, and I felt a moment of complete peace.

I'd been so concerned about what this vacation meant because, like always, I was overanalyzing it. Maybe it didn't have to be this monumental trip that would somehow change my life. Maybe it would just be a vacation. Three weeks of peace and contentment.

I reluctantly walked back into my room, closing the doors and shutting out the sounds of the ocean. Digging through my purse I pulled out my cell and sent Matthew a text.

You were right. I needed this. x.

Once I was dressed, hair dried and styled, makeup on, I headed downstairs for breakfast. It was nine thirty, so I'd just make it.

The dining room was empty when I took a seat, other guests having gotten up way earlier than I had, or having slept in even later.

I was looking at the menu when a door at the back of the cozy room swung open, revealing a kitchen beyond it. The door slammed shut and I lifted my gaze to the person who was striding out of the kitchen toward me.

Bailey grinned at me. “Morning.”

“Good morning.” I smiled back at her.

“You slept well?”

“Yes, thank you. I feel so much better. I’m sorry if I was a little out of it last night.”

“Don’t even apologize. I could see you were dead on your feet. Will we start you off with some coffee?”

“Please.”

“Okeydokey. I’ll let you look over the menu.”

Bailey was back a few minutes later with my coffee. I wanted to snatch it desperately from her hands but somehow managed to refrain from doing so, waiting impatiently for her to take my order so I could descend on the coffee like the caffeine fiend I was.

“I’ll have the scrambled eggs, bacon, and pancakes, please.” My stomach practically growled just thinking about it.

“Great choice.” She cocked her head to the side. “I haven’t eaten yet. You mind if I join you? And please feel free to tell me ‘hell no’ if you want some peace.”

I laughed, surprised by her request but definitely not annoyed by it. “I’m happy for the company.”

“Great! I think I’ll have what you’re having.” She strode back to the kitchen, calling out as she pushed her way inside, “Hey, Mona, two scrambled eggs, bacon, and—” The door slammed shut behind her, completely silencing the room.

Not too long later, I’d had my first shot of heavenly caffeine and Bailey was back with both of our meals. She sat down in the chair opposite me to dig into hers.

I shoveled a forkful of pancakes and egg into my mouth as soon as the plate was put in front of me.

“So,” Bailey said once she’d swallowed, “I’m usually not this weird innkeeper who crashes her guests’ breakfast. My alarm didn’t go off this morning.”

I snorted, unable to laugh without spraying my breakfast everywhere. Once I'd swallowed, I said, "I really don't mind. It's nice, actually."

"Good." She grinned. "Tom would say this is so unprofessional."

"Tom?"

"My boyfriend. We've been together for nine years. He's the yin to my yang. Although yin is getting a little annoyed with the yang lately. I lost my deputy manager to New York last month and so I've been running around like a headless chicken while I try to find someone I trust to do the damn job, and Tom is all 'Slow down, Bailey, before you kill yourself.'"

I blinked at her rambling.

She laughed. "Sorry. He also says I talk too fast sometimes. He says it makes me sound twelve. I'm thirty-three."

I was surprised. She looked younger than me. "We're the same age."

"We are? What do you do? Say innkeeper and it'll freak me out."

Smiling, I shook my head. "No. I'm a doctor."

Bailey's eyes widened. "Really?"

"Yup."

"A doctor? In a hospital, or do you have your own practice?"

"I'm a physician at a prison, actually. A women's prison."

"No way!"

I laughed. "Yes way."

"Well, I was impressed by doctor, but I'm even more impressed by doctor in a women's prison. That is hard-core. You know, this town could do with a hard-core doctor. You lookin'?" She winked teasingly.

"Unfortunately, not at the moment. Hartwell," I said before she could ramble on again. "Your name. Does that make you a descendant of the founding family?"

"It does." She nodded, suddenly looking serious. "We used to own a lot of this town, but over the years the family lost most of it. My parents sold what was left with the exception of the inn. Boardwalk properties are prime real estate here. I offered to run the place because my brother and sister weren't interested. My parents are retired in Florida."

"Do you like running the inn?"

"I love it."

I could tell she meant it.

"Do you like being a doctor?"

"I do."

"How could you not? You're saving people's lives." She ate a piece of bacon. As soon as she swallowed it she said, "So what made you want to vacation here?"

I contemplated Bailey because as someone who had lived here her whole life, and whose family had lived here generations before, I could only assume she was pretty familiar with most of its inhabitants. "Would you happen to know George Beckwith?"

"Sure. How do you know George?"

"We have a mutual acquaintance," I said, evading the question. "Anyway, this place was recommended to me and I thought I'd stop in to see George while I'm here. He owns property on the boardwalk, right?"

Bailey wrinkled her nose. "Yeah, but George closed up shop a few weeks ago and took off for Nova Scotia. His daughter, Marie, lives in Canada with her family and George decided to spend the summer there."

For a moment all I heard were the names George and Marie. Sarah's story suddenly became even more real, hearing Bailey talk about the people mentioned in her letters.

That made the disappointment that flooded me even worse.

I hadn't even considered that I might not actually get to pass the letters on to George.

"So what's it like working in a women's prison?" Bailey interrupted my thoughts and I remembered why I was here.

To vacation.

I had to put Sarah's situation out of my mind and force the ache she'd caused out of my chest.

"It's like anywhere. You get used to your environment."

"Is it scary or am I being judgmental?"

I smiled at her wince. "We learn quickly if an inmate is going to be a problem, and there are always guards on hand. Mostly they're fine with me because I'm usually helping them out, but there is the minority . . . I've been spat on before." I wrinkled my nose, remembering the charming incident.

"Ugh, charming."

I laughed at her using the same word I'd been thinking.

"As I said, there are dangerous criminals in there and the not so dangerous. Many of those women are just people who have made mistakes and are now paying for them."

"I guess. Still, it must be stressful sometimes."

"I'm not sure running an inn isn't any less stressful."

"Running an inn *can* be stressful," she agreed. "But I love this place. I love Hart's Boardwalk."

"Hart's Boardwalk?"

"That's what the locals call this place because of the legend."

"What legend?" I leaned forward, intrigued.

"That if you're destined for true love, you'll find it on the boardwalk."

I grinned. "How romantic."

Bailey smiled softly, a hint of sadness in her eyes. "I know it sounds cheesy, but the legend grew from something kind of beautifully tragic, actually. Back in 1909 my great-grandmother's sister, Eliza, was the darling of Hartwell. Our family still had wealth and power and Eliza, being the eldest, was expected to marry well. Instead she somehow crossed paths and fell in love with a steelworker from the Straiton Railroad Company, which was based just outside of town. Jonas Kellerman was considered beneath Eliza and also a con artist. Her family tried to convince Eliza that he was only using her to gain her wealth.

"But Eliza didn't believe her family and she and Jonas made plans to marry in secret. Her father, my great-great-grandfather, found out their plans and he threatened harm against the Kellermans if Eliza didn't marry the man he had chosen for her. To protect Jonas she agreed to marry the son of a wealthy Pennsylvania businessman. But, devastated, on the eve of her wedding Eliza snuck out and went to the beach late at night. She walked right into the ocean. By chance Jonas was up on the boardwalk with some friends, drowning his sorrows, when he saw Eliza. He rushed down to save her and his friends say they saw him reach her. But the ocean carried them away together and they were never seen again."

Jesus Christ. This place was just brimming over with heartbreaking love stories. Now my heart broke for Eliza and Jonas as well as Sarah and George. "Wow."

Bailey gave me that sad smile again. "Over the years people have grown to believe in the legend that Jonas's sacrifice and the purity of their love created the magic. Also because townies who fall in love on the boardwalk stay in love their whole lives. There's a spot on the boardwalk near the bandstand with a brass plaque for tourists about the legend. It says if they walk the boardwalk together, and they're truly in love, it will last forever. Tom and I are of course evidence of its truth." She grinned.

"As for my great-great-grandfather," she continued, "he made a few bad investments and lost a lot of his wealth. People believed the Hartwells were being punished for what happened to Eliza."

"So you guys are big on fate here, huh?"

"Fate. Magic." She shrugged with a grin.

"It sounds to me like a lot of drama. I'm not too big on drama."

"That probably means you need some in your life." She winked at me playfully.

I decided to explore the boardwalk after my interesting breakfast with Bailey.

Despite the dark clouds above, the weather outside was mild with only a gentle breeze whispering up from the water. I strolled along the wooden planks. A mammoth sign above the porch door of the building next to the inn proclaimed in feminine script *Hart's Gift Shop.*

The gift shop was currently closed. I hoped it was on off-season hours and would be open sometime during my vacation. I wanted to buy something for Perry and there were beautiful dolls and jewelry in the windows.

After the gift shop were a candy store and arcade, and from there the boards ran along the main thoroughfare. A large bandstand sat at the top of Main Street. The street was wide enough for cars to park in the middle of it, and along either side were commercial buildings. Trees lined the street, where restaurants, gift shops, clothes stores, fast-food joints, spas, coffeehouses, pubs, and markets were neighbors in a well-groomed tourist environment.

I decided to explore Main Street later and kept heading along the boards. I passed a small ice cream shack, a surf shop, an Italian restaurant with a neon sign proclaiming *Antonio's*, and then the largest building on the boardwalk—it seemed to rise up among all the others like a giant of contemporary architecture. Whitewashed walls and lots of glass. There was no gaudy neon sign for this building. Huge gold metal letters three stories up spelled out *Paradise Sands Hotel* and smaller gold letters subtitled underneath it, *And Conference Center.*

I stared up at the mammoth place, wondering how it could contrast so sharply with everything else on the boardwalk and yet somehow add a quality to the place that I personally thought benefited it rather than detracted from it. I took a step back and turned toward the ocean. There were only a few people walking along the beach today because of the complete lack of sun. Even without the sun turning the sand what I assumed would be a spectacular gold, the beach was lovely. The sand was soft, rockless, and inviting. I couldn't wait for some sunshine so I could lie on a lounge chair out there.

But there was no sunshine and I could do with another coffee. On that thought, I continued my journey down the boardwalk, when the heavens suddenly opened.

My eyes darted for the closest available shelter and I dashed toward it—a closed bar that had an awning. Soaked within seconds, blinded by rain, and irritated by the icky feeling of my clothes sticking to my skin, I wasn't really paying much attention to anything else but getting to the awning. That was why I ran smack into a hard, masculine body.

If the man's arms hadn't reached out to catch me I would have bounced right onto my ass.

I pushed my soaked hair out of my eyes and looked up in apology at the person I had so rudely collided with.

Warm blue eyes met mine. Blue, blue eyes. Like the Aegean Sea that surrounded Santorini. I'd vacationed there a few years back and the water there was the bluest I'd ever seen.

Once I was able to drag my gaze from the startling color of those eyes, I took in the face they were set upon. Rugged, masculine.

My eyes drifted over his broad shoulders and my head tipped back to take in his face because the guy was well over six feet tall. The hands that were still on my biceps, steadying me, were big, long fingered, and callused against my bare skin.

Despite the cold, I felt my body flush with the heat of awareness and I stepped out of the stranger's hold.

"Sorry," I said, slicking my wet hair back, grinning apologetically. "That rain came out of nowhere."

Cooper

All Cooper could see at first were the stranger's gorgeous eyes. Big. Brown—*no*. Hazel. They were brown with flecks of light green and yellow in them. Thick lashes framed them.

Right now those gorgeous eyes held a mix of apology and amusement. The mascara streaks running down her cheeks didn't detract from how pretty those eyes were.

Warm eyes that moved from his face to travel over his body. His shirt was soaked through and clung to him, showing off the results of his early-morning workout and run along the beach. He gave a brief nod as he pushed his wet hair back from his forehead.

The stranger's eyes widened a little and Cooper didn't miss the feminine appreciation in them.

She wasn't short, standing at about five seven, but he was tall so she was tilting her head back to look up at him. That was when he realized how close they were standing.

Cooper felt what was almost like a warning tingle on the back of his neck. And it wasn't the cold.

He'd felt that tingle when he was walking home from school minutes before he got home to find out his dad had taken off. He'd felt the tingle the day his mom's brother died, leaving the bar to her, only for his mom to turn around and give the bar straight to him. He'd felt the tingle the first day he stepped into the bar as the owner. He'd felt the tingle the day his mom died of cancer. And he'd felt that tingle driving to the bar one day. That tingle made him drive home to check on Dana. He had found her fucking his best friend.

Standing in front of this bedraggled stranger with the prettiest goddamn eyes he'd ever seen, Cooper had to wonder whether the tingle was a good thing or a bad thing in this case.

Good or bad, it was worth listening to, he thought as he opened the door to the bar. He'd only stepped out for a few minutes to drop off mail that should have been delivered to Emery's next door. It was enough time to get soaked to the skin.

The woman now stood with her back to him, staring out at the rain. Her shoulders were hunched a little as if trying to protect herself from the dampness of her wet clothes. Cooper's eyes dragged down her body. She had a tiny back, narrow shoulders, and a narrow waist, but that waist swept out into a curvy ass Cooper appreciated greatly. Especially since that ass was attached to long, slim legs. She wore skinny jeans that showed off those fantastic legs of hers. The jeans were tucked into high-heeled boots.

Casual but sexy, he thought. It worked. At least it did for him.

He suddenly wasn't so cold.

And he was going to listen to that tingle. "You can wait out there if you want. Or not."

She swung around, staring at him with those big eyes. With her wet hair slicked back he got to see all of her.

All of it was good.

She wasn't a striking beauty like his ex, but there was coldness to Dana's beauty. There always had been. It used to intrigue him. Now he knew better.

Other than the wet clothes on her body, there wasn't a hint of coldness in this stranger.

She did, however, look uncertain. She peered past him at the empty bar. "Are you sure it's alright?"

He nodded.

The woman hesitated, obviously unsure about entering an empty bar with a strange man. She was definitely a tourist. And right now she looked like a teenager deciding whether or not to do the smart thing while oh so tempted by the stupid thing.

Amusement filled him.

As she nodded and strode past him, her perfume wafted over him. It was light, kind of flowery, nothing musky about it. She turned around, gazing at his bar in curiosity, and he took in the rest of her. Her black shirt clung to her, straining over full breasts. More than a handful. Fuck, but she had a body on her.

Then Cooper noticed that body was shivering.

Asshole. He needed to stop checking her out and get her warm.

"Tea? Coffee? Hot cocoa?" he called out, heading toward the kitchen.

"Hot cocoa," she called back.

He went to the linen closet in the hall first, where he kept dish towels and towels for the staff bathroom. He grabbed one and took it out to her.

"Thanks," she said, staring up at him, looking almost confused for some reason.

He nodded and got back into the kitchen to make them a warm drink as fast as possible.

When he returned to her with her mug of cocoa he noticed her hair was a little drier. There was a lot of it.

The mascara smears around her eyes were gone, too.

He glanced at the white towel he'd given her and grinned when he saw the black on it.

"Thank you," she said, taking the mug of hot cocoa and whipped cream from him.

She was soft-spoken and, for whatever reason, his lower belly reacted with a tugging sensation to the sound of her voice.

Cooper took the seat across from her and sipped at his coffee, enjoying the chance to study her as she studied him. There was an air of easy confidence around her that he appreciated. That kind of confidence usually belonged to women who knew and liked themselves.

"Do you work here?" she said after a few minutes of comfortable silence had passed between them.

Cooper nodded.

"You're a bartender here?"

"I own the place."

He watched her study his bar, and he had to wonder what she thought of it. She had little diamonds in her ears and was wearing a nice watch, plus those sexy boots weren't cheap, as far as he could tell, and he'd lived with Dana long enough to know a designer purse when he saw it. If he'd had to guess, he would have thought the tourist a cocktails-at-a-trendy-bar kind of woman. But just as he'd caught her appreciation of his body earlier, he saw a different kind in her eyes as she looked around at his place.

He felt a spike of pride. It used to be a dowdy little pub. Now it was a successful one. It was all him in that bar and it was nice that she liked what she saw.

"Nice place," she said, confirming her appreciation. "What's the bar called?"

"Cooper's."

She narrowed her big eyes on him. "Are you Cooper?"

"Are you a detective?" he teased.

"A doctor, actually."

Well, he hadn't been expecting that. "Smart lady."

"I'd hope so." She grinned at him.

Silence fell between them again and Cooper found that he liked that she could sit quietly with him without growing uncomfortable. He liked the quiet. He liked that she wasn't rushing to fill it with meaningless chitchat like most people did.

In the little time he'd spent with her he knew she was sexy, cute, smart, and nice to spend time with. All that meant Cooper wanted to know more. "You're not from Hartwell."

"No, I'm not." She sidestepped his unspoken question.

Cooper almost laughed at her taciturnity. "What brings you to Hart's Boardwalk, Doc?"

"At the moment the rain brought me *here*," she said. "I'm kind of glad it did."

Yeah, he was glad, too. He reached across the table, offering her his hand. "Cooper Lawson."

She smiled at him and took his hand, hers small and soft in his. "Jessica Huntington."

That tingle sprang to life down his neck again.

He tensed, his eyes sharp on Jessica Huntington. "Nice to meet you, Doc."

"You, too. Thanks again for the cocoa."

"You're welcome." He sat back, watching her sip the drink he'd made for her. A bit of cream stuck to the top lip of her pretty mouth. He eyed it, trying not to think about how much he wanted to lick the cream off her. Forcing his eyes from her mouth to her eyes, he said, "What brings you to Hartwell?"

"I'm on vacation."

"Why Hart's?"

"I didn't want to stray too far from work. I work in Wilmington."

Wilmington. It wasn't too far. A couple hours' drive at most. "At one of the hospitals?"

"No, actually; at a women's prison."

Again, not what he expected. Being a doctor wasn't exactly easy. Being a doctor in a prison was just adding challenge on top of challenge. Had to take a certain kind of person to want that kind of job. He just wasn't sure what kind of person that made Jessica. "That's different."

She gave a huff of laughter. "I suppose it is."

"So what makes someone want to work in a women's prison?"

"What makes someone want to own a bar?" the doc countered.

It was his. It was his vision. His hard work. And the locals were his family. Not many people got to have a business they loved like he did. "This place is home."

The doc tilted her head to the side, a lively humor in her hazel eyes. "Well, I can't say the same."

"So why a women's prison?" he persisted. It had been a long time since he'd been this curious about someone.

She considered his question for a moment and when she spoke her voice got even softer. "Even people who make mistakes need someone watching over them. When I became a doctor I took the Hippocratic oath. I said I would help people and do no harm. That means helping someone no matter who they are or what they've done. I take that oath seriously."

A flash of sadness, something deeply rooted . . . something personal . . . crossed her eyes and Cooper knew there was more to it than that. "There's taking that oath seriously and then there's working in a prison."

"I believe everyone deserves compassion," she said. "When I got offered the job I was concerned that if I didn't take it then some other doctor might take it out of necessity rather than interest. There's no guarantee such a doctor would have the right bedside manner for these women. I took the job because I can guarantee they feel safe coming to me for treatment."

Cooper stilled at her words.

Was she for real?

He knew kindness existed. After his dad left, he'd grown up in a house full of it. But unfortunately, he'd also seen a lot of selfishness lately. A complete and total lack of compassion, too.

There was something about that compassion on a woman like Jessica Huntington that more than intrigued him. She was tallying up a list of positives that were hard to ignore.

"Is that a bartending trick?" she said suddenly, her cute little nose all wrinkled up in annoyance. "Getting people to talk to you?"

Cooper grinned, liking the idea that the doc didn't usually share so much. Maybe she was feeling it, too . . . some kind of connection between them. "I'm just easy to talk to."

Jessica grinned back and he felt that hard tug of attraction deep in his gut. "Maybe so."

The door opened and Cooper's cook, Crosby, strolled in, distracting him from the ever-increasing tightness in his jeans.

Crosby saw Jessica but didn't acknowledge her. "Morning, boss."

"Morning," Cooper said as his cook disappeared into the kitchen. Crosby wasn't really the social type anymore. "My cook," he explained when he saw Jess staring after his employee with curiosity in her big, gorgeous eyes.

Those eyes swung back to his and she suddenly stood up. "Well, I better let you get on. Thanks again for the shelter and the hot drink."

He felt disappointment flood him and if it wasn't for the fact that he had a bar to open in an hour he would have convinced the doc to stick around.

"Do you know of any bookstores nearby?" she said as she grabbed up her purse.

"Emery's next door."

"Great. Thanks."

He stood up, too. He needed to know he was going to see her again. "You staying at the Paradise?"

She hesitated, as though she wasn't sure she should tell him. Cooper didn't like that so much. When she finally answered, "Hart's Inn," he smiled. Not only because he liked that she'd chosen Bailey's homey place over the luxury of Vaughn's hotel, but because he liked that she'd told him where she was staying.

Cooper hoped that meant she was single and looking to get to know him a bit better while she was visiting. "Nice choice. Bailey's a good woman."

"Yes, I'm getting that," Jess said and walked around the table to him to hold out her hand. "It was nice talking to you."

It was more than nice talking to her. His grip tightened on hers and he stepped in close, so she knew for sure he wanted to see her again. "You, too, Doc. You staying here long?"

"A few weeks."

That was plenty of time. "Then I'll be seeing you."

Her cheeks flushed a little and her eyes grew round with surprise at the obvious intention behind his words. She tugged on her hand, making him laugh.

So damn cute.

"I guess so," she said in that soft way of hers.

Cooper watched her leave, hoping that hint of vulnerability he saw behind her confidence didn't mean he'd have to track her down to spend more time with her.

He wanted her to come to him.

He'd done a lot of chasing around, especially after Dana, and look where that had gotten him. Just as he'd been trying to tell Aydan in as diplomatic a way as possible, there hadn't been anyone serious or special since Dana. The women he messed around with always came to him. Cooper liked it like that. He wasn't putting himself out there, chasing another woman around, only to get burned.

But as he stared at his now empty bar, he thought, *Fuck*, more than a little worried.

He knew that if Jessica didn't come to him he wasn't going to be able to sit on it. The doc was someone worth getting to know. He felt it in that damn tingle.

Jessica

It was difficult to concentrate on anything but the attraction I'd felt to Cooper Lawson. I'd paused a moment, wondering if it was a good idea to tell him where I was staying, but then I thought what the hell. I was here on vacation and there was no rule that said I couldn't flirt with a rugged bar owner while I was here.

Still, it was the kind of intense attraction that threw me a little, so I had to admit stepping into Emery's was a nice distraction.

To my left was a large counter and, behind it, coffee machines. To my right was the bookstore. Ahead and up a few steps was a seating area filled with cute little white tables and chairs. To the left of the table and chairs were comfortable armchairs and sofas situated near a lit open fireplace that crackled and snapped invitingly.

The place was empty, presumably because of the weather, but I couldn't see why anyone wouldn't want to hang out here.

A door behind the counter opened and a woman stepped out. She gave me a shy smile. "I thought I heard the bell over the door."

I smiled back and walked over to her. "It's miserable out there."

Her startling pale blue eyes took in my bedraggled state. "Would you like to get warm by the fire?" She asked it tentatively, almost as if she thought it was forward of her to offer me a kindness.

She was tall and willowy, with beautiful eyes and a heart-shaped face. She wore her long white-blond hair in an intricate plait that rested over her right shoulder. Wisps of hair framed her lovely face.

I glanced around at the bookstore with its white-painted bookshelves and hodgepodge of comfortable seating. A few Tiffany lamps were set here and there, adding warmth and color. All the woodwork in the store was painted white and it contrasted beautifully with the rich teal blue of the walls.

The place seemed to fit the woman and I couldn't even put my finger on why. I turned back to her. I'd had every intention of buying a book and heading back to the inn, but I suddenly liked the idea of getting warm here. "Yes, I think I will. Are you the owner?"

She nodded.

I held out my hand. "I'm Jessica Huntington."

She glanced at my hand a little unsurely and I was relieved when she lifted a long-fingered hand covered in silver rings and placed it in mine. The silver bracelets on her wrists tinkled together as we shook. "Emery Saunders."

"It's nice to meet you."

"You, too." She dropped my hand quickly, along with her gaze. "Would you like a hot drink?"

I frowned, wondering how someone so timid could like working with the public all the time. "I'll have a latte, please. I'm just going to peruse the books."

She nodded and turned away, busying herself with making my coffee.

I realized I was curious about her—and also wondered why this place had me so damn curious about everything and everyone.

Especially a certain bar owner.

A few minutes later I put down two books on the counter and pulled out my wallet to pay for them and the coffee.

"That's a good one," Emery offered quietly, touching the book on top.

It was a crime novel. I had a thing about crime novels.

"You read thrillers?" She didn't seem like the thriller type. She seemed like the magic and fairy-tale princes type.

"I read everything," she replied softly and put my books through the register.

I paid and grabbed my books and coffee, heading toward the fireplace.

"Happy reading," she said, just loud enough for me to hear.

I grinned back at her in thanks and got myself comfortable in an armchair with a footstool, right by the fire.

Heat suffused me and I soon lost myself in my book, my clothes drying without my even realizing it until much later.

Over the next couple of hours I was vaguely aware of a few people coming in and out of the store, but I was left to enjoy the fire alone. When a shadow fell on me I was surprised to find Emery standing over me.

She wore a pair of dark-wash skinny jeans and a white shirt with sleeves that were fitted from shoulder to elbow, where the fabric loosened out into long bells, like the style of a medieval maiden's dress. Short biker boots completed the look.

"Would you like something to eat?" she offered. "I have sandwiches."

It was only then I felt the growl of my empty stomach. "Sure, thank you."

"Another latte?"

"That, too." I grinned at her.

Not too long later she came back with both and laid them down on the reading table beside me.

"What else do you like to read?" I said, before she could escape me.

Emery seemed surprised by the question. "Oh . . . I like everything."

"Okay. Who is your favorite author?"

She wrinkled her nose and I saw a glimmer of a smile on her lips. "That's like asking which I prefer: oxygen or food."

I laughed. "Well, tell me *one* of your favorite authors."

Her lids lowered over her eyes, and I saw that her lashes, darkened with mascara, were enviously long.

For some reason I was charmed by this shy bookstore owner.

I was finding myself charmed by many people in Hartwell so far.

"J. D. Salinger," she offered suddenly.

I loved that answer. "*Catcher in the Rye* fan. Me, too."

She smiled at me and I felt triumphant that I'd won a grin from her.

There was something about her, something in the back of her eyes, that made me sad, and I liked that I'd made her smile.

I glanced down through the store to the front window to see the rain had started coming down in sheets again. "I doubt you're going to be busy anytime soon. Why don't you grab a book and sit by the fire?"

Emery followed my gaze to the windows and I watched her chew on her lip as she thought about it. "I probably shouldn't," she muttered.

"If someone comes in, you just put the book down and go help them."

It took her longer than it should have to consider it, almost like she was afraid to do the wrong thing. Finally, she gave me a small smile. "I guess it wouldn't do any harm."

"Not at all," I said encouragingly.

A few minutes later she was curled up on the sofa across from me and I watched with fascination as she seemed to get sucked into her book from the moment she opened it. In the time it would take me to snap my fingers Emery was immersed in the world of the story in her hands.

It took me at least a chapter before I became oblivious to everything around me.

But not Emery.

I had the fanciful thought that she was escaping, and that she'd escaped into pages and words so many times in her life that falling down the rabbit hole was like second nature to her. I wondered what she was escaping from.

This curiosity of mine was getting out of hand, I grumbled to myself as I bit into the ham and cheese sandwich Emery had brought me. In a way my curiosity had brought me to Hartwell. I didn't need to get wrapped up in the mystery behind the shy sadness of Emery Saunders. And maybe there was no mystery! Maybe Sarah's story had me imagining that everyone here had a tragedy hiding behind them.

Maybe even Cooper Lawson.

Don't think about him!

I had no time for his kind of temptation.

On that thought, I stared down at the pages of my book and willed myself to get caught up in fiction.

After dinner at the inn that night I sat by the fireplace in the front room with a glass of wine in my hand. I was hoping to catch Bailey before I went to bed and was waiting on the diners to clear out so I could talk to her.

Staring into the flames, sipping my wine, I realized that I'd spent the most relaxing, peaceful day I could remember having in a very, very long time.

Emery hadn't said much as we whiled the day away reading by her fireplace, but I didn't need her to. As much as there was something sad about her, there was also something incredibly soothing about her company. I thought it funny that I'd experienced the same comfortable silence with Cooper on the same day, when I'd never experienced that feeling with anyone before.

I left Emery late that afternoon, vowing to return before my vacation was over. That sadness I saw in the back of her eyes seemed to grow as she was saying good-bye to me.

And there it was. Despite myself, I was intrigued by Emery Saunders and I couldn't make myself not be.

And that intrigue only reminded me of Sarah's letters, which had brought me to Hartwell in the first place.

I'd decided to ask Bailey about her after all.

As the last customers were leaving the inn, Bailey trailed behind them wishing them a warm good night. The bell over the door rang as they left and a few seconds later Bailey flopped down on the sofa beside me.

She looked exhausted.

I handed her my glass of wine and she accepted it with a grateful but very tired smile. She took a sip and handed the glass back to me. "Thanks."

"You're welcome. Please tell me you don't work these ridiculously long hours every day. "

Bailey shook her head. "No. Like I said, I had a deputy manager and we worked around one another. I used to have a day or two off, if you can believe it."

"You need your own vacation."

"Yes, yes, I do." She grinned at me. "The rain didn't frighten you away today?"

I smirked. "No. Actually I got caught in it outside of Cooper's. The man himself let me into his bar to dry off until it calmed enough for me to venture back outside."

Sitting up straighter, Bailey eyed me with a mischievous smile. "What did you think of Cooper?"

I could spot a matchmaker a mile off and so I avoided her gaze. "He didn't say much." I sipped at my wine, pretending disinterest.

"That's because he's a good listener."

"You know him well?"

"I've known him my whole life. He's single, you know." She nudged me with another cheeky grin. "Divorced."

I laughed. "You are so not subtle."

"What's the point in subtlety?" Bailey studied me. "Are you single?"

I opened my mouth to say no and then sighed. "It's complicated."

"I'll take that as you're single."

"How so?"

"If you were really certain of this guy, whoever he is, your answer would have been a straightforward no."

I guessed that was true enough.

It was time for a subject change. "You know how I asked about George Beckwith this morning . . ."

"Yeah."

"There was a reason." I turned on the sofa to face her. "I actually don't know George. The reason I know *of* him is because I found letters in a book at the prison. They were addressed to George in 1976."

Bailey's mouth parted in surprise. "Sarah Randall," she said breathlessly.

At the sound of her name, that now familiar ache in my chest hitched. "You know the story?"

"Everyone knows the story." Bailey's green eyes darkened with sadness. "She and George were sweethearts. They fell in love on the boardwalk when they were sophomores in high school. Everyone thought they'd get married. But the summer they graduated from high school Sarah married—"

"A man named Ron."

Bailey raised an eyebrow. "Ron Peters. How . . . ?"

"It's in her letters to George."

I could see the blaze of curiosity in Bailey's eyes, but she continued recounting their history for me. "No one knew what made Sarah marry him. Most people suspected he had something on her, but she wouldn't say what. George was devastated. He started sleeping around and he knocked up Sarah's best friend, Annabelle. He married her. And then a few years later Sarah Randall shot Ron in the chest and she went to prison. And she died there."

My eyes stung with unshed tears.

Bailey reached for my hand. "You okay?"

I tried to smile reassuringly. "Sarah died of cancer. Before she could mail these letters to George. Letters that explained everything. She had a reason for what she did, Bailey."

She squeezed my hand. "That's so sad. Is that why you came here?"

I shrugged. "My vacation with my best friend got canceled . . . Sarah and George were on my mind so I decided to come here instead."

Bailey considered me. "You came to Hartwell to give George Sarah's letters?"

"Yes."

"I knew I freaking liked you."

I gave a huff of surprised laughter. "Thanks. I like you, too."

"Of course you do; I'm hilarious," she teased.

I laughed.

But Bailey sobered. "You know Sarah was Cooper's mom's cousin?"

I tensed. "Really?"

"His mom, Laura, passed almost ten years back, but she and Sarah were really close before Sarah went to prison. Coop was close to his mom and he knew how much what Sarah did broke Laura's heart. Maybe it would be nice for him to know the truth."

Uncertainty moved through me. "I don't know. Those letters were only meant for George's eyes."

"You don't have to give Coop the letters, but Sarah was his family. If there was a genuine reason for what she did, he deserves to know."

SEVEN

Cooper

Cooper had to admit to himself he'd been hoping the doc would come to his bar the night before. She'd made him impatient to see her again and he'd been counting on her feeling the same way.

Shit.

"Penny for your thoughts," Old Archie said as Cooper sighed.

He glanced down his bar. The place was filled with locals. In a week or two it would be packed with locals and tourists once the high season hit. Sitting in the same stool he sat in every night, Old Archie smirked at him over the rim of his beer glass.

"They're not that interesting."

"Right." Old Archie narrowed his eyes. "Hear your ex has been bothering you."

Cooper hadn't heard anything from Dana since he'd cut her down in front of Iris. Hopefully that meant she'd finally gotten the message.

Truth was he was too young when he married Dana. The sex had been fantastic. Looking back, the sad realization he came to was that there was more lust in their marriage than love. Cooper had thought it love at the time, but now he couldn't remember a moment when they ever talked about anything real. He didn't think much of it back then, but now he knew that wasn't right.

Sure, he'd made Dana laugh, and he'd gotten a kick out of making her laugh, but that wasn't enough.

She'd been so goddamn beautiful when they first met—the kind of beautiful that would have opened up doors for her if she'd been smart enough to look for the doors in the first place. But Dana liked being a big fish in a small pond. Cooper knew she was vain. He'd always known it, but he'd been so caught up in her beauty he'd decided to call it confidence and find it sexy.

He'd been an asshole kid.

And they'd both paid the price for their stupidity. With not much between them but lust, the marriage had fallen apart. Dana had betrayed him, and that betrayal burned so much Cooper wasn't sure he ever wanted to get involved in another serious relationship.

Yet . . . he wasn't that dumb-ass kid anymore.

He knew something special when he saw it.

And he knew not to ignore that tingle on the back of his neck.

Cooper couldn't put his finger on exactly what made Jessica Huntington different from any other woman he'd dated. She was sexy, true. She was incredibly smart—had to be if she was a doctor.

Maybe that was it, he thought.

Maybe it was the doctor thing. It said a lot about her. All good. Other than the obvious, it said she was probably an independent woman, and Cooper had never dated a woman like that before.

After his dad left, Cooper had become the man of the house. He was twelve years old. He'd looked after his mom and sister. Then when he met Dana she was looking for him to look after her, too. And Cooper hadn't minded that. At least, he hadn't thought he did. However, looking back on it, he saw Dana had been more like a kid than a wife. She didn't want the responsibility of making important decisions to do with their finances, their home, their cars, their bills. Nothing.

Unlike all the other couples they knew, he and Dana didn't have a partnership. He didn't have a wife to lean on when shit got hard. She had expected him to deal with it alone and shield her from anything bad, like she was a child.

For instance, when his mom died. *His* mom. She wasn't even close to his mother. But Dana couldn't cope with the sad reality of death. It made her question her own mortality and she didn't like that one bit. So she wouldn't talk about his mom's death. She wouldn't let him talk about it, and he'd needed to talk about it.

In the end it was Jack who had been there for him.

Huh. What a joke that was. He'd always considered himself a really good judge of character until Jack's betrayal.

Cooper sighed again and shook off the ugly memories.

Jessica struck him as a different sort of woman than Dana. Not only did she probably take care of herself, she took care of other people. The idea of dating an independent woman appealed to him now. Then again, he'd always thought Dana was sweet, until she'd showed him how bitter she could taste.

But that shouldn't be enough to put him off at least getting to know the doc. She was in Hartwell for three weeks. That was plenty of time to explore the chemistry between them if he was willing to give it a chance.

"Those look like some heavy thoughts," Old Archie said.

Cooper looked at him. "What do you know about heavy thoughts?"

Old Archie grinned and opened his mouth to say something, when his old lady, Anita, slid onto the stool next to him. Old Archie immediately frowned at her. "Woman, what are you doing here?"

She grinned and shrugged. "Thought I'd join you tonight." Anita turned that lopsided grin of hers on Cooper. "I'll have what he's having. He's paying."

Cooper grinned and started to pull her a draft while he watched Old Archie's reaction to Anita showing up.

It was fair to say that Old Archie was an alcoholic. He liked his drink and he made no apologies for it. He'd been married and she left him, taking their kids with her when she drove out of Hartwell for good. Things had gotten bad for Archie for a while, but then he'd met Anita. Anita didn't care that Archie liked his drink. All she cared about was that he was loyal to her and he loved her.

Cooper knew Old Archie loved Anita.

But there were days, like today, when Old Archie loved the drink more.

As Anita talked about some television show she'd been watching, Cooper saw Archie surreptitiously lean to his other side where Anita couldn't see, clearly counting the money in his pocket. He frowned and snapped up straight, shooting his old lady a glower. "Woman," he said, interrupting her, "what have you done to your hair?"

Anita frowned back at him, her hand hovering over her head. "I cut it. Last week," she snapped.

"Well, I don't like it."

"What do you mean you don't like it? You didn't even notice it until now."

"And I don't like it."

"What's wrong with it?" she practically yelled, and a few of Cooper's other regulars turned to watch the older couple.

Cooper crossed his arms over his chest, suspecting he knew exactly what Old Archie was up to.

"It's too short. You look like a boy."

"I do not look like a boy, Archibald Brown." She hopped up off the stool. "If you're in a bad mood, I'm going home. Sleep on the couch tonight." She stormed away.

"I like your hair, Anita!" Hug, a painter and decorator who had gone to school with Coop's mom, shouted out as she passed.

"Thank you, Hug." Anita preened, touching her hair. She threw a smug glower back at Old Archie, but he was too busy grinning into his beer to notice.

As soon as the bar door slammed shut behind Anita, Cooper shook his head at him.

Old Archie's grin got bigger. "What? If she'd stuck around I could only afford two more beers. Not I got four more to look forward to."

"And a cold couch." Cooper turned away, laughing at the way Old Archie's face fell boyishly at the realization.

"That was mean," Riley, his bar staff, said from the other end of the bar.

Lily, one of his waitstaff, dumped a tray with empties on the bar and glowered at Old Archie. "It was beyond mean. Anita looked real upset, Archie."

"Ah, she'll be fine." He waved them off, but Coop saw the flicker of guilt in his eyes before he lowered his gaze to his beer.

"Quiet tonight," Riley said, strolling up the bar to him and Lily. "Can't wait for the season to kick in."

Cooper had four bar staff working for him—Riley, Kit, Jace, and Ollie. Riley and Ollie worked nights, Kit and Jace worked days. There was Crosby, his cook, and four waitstaff—Lily, Isla, Bryn, and Ashley. During high season, everyone, including Cooper, worked more hours.

It was a lot of responsibility, but he didn't mind. He was good at that shit.

But it could get tiring.

Which made the thought of dating a woman who didn't need him to be responsible for anything more than making their time together enjoyable very appealing.

As if he'd conjured her, the door to Cooper's opened and in stepped Jessica Huntington. He drank in the sight of her.

Her long blond hair was now dry. There really was a lot of it. It spilled down her back in thick waves. Those big gorgeous eyes of hers moved around the bar, drinking in the sight of the locals, who stared at her curiously. She smiled at them and then looked over at the bar, and that pretty smile widened when she caught sight of Cooper.

He nodded at her.

His heart beat a little faster, a little harder.

"Hi, Cooper," she said.

Damn it, his name had never sounded so good. "Hey, Doc." He gave her a small smile back. "Nice to see you again."

She didn't smile. In fact, she looked a little nervous. He tensed as she leaned over his bar toward him. "Do you have a minute to talk?" Riley, Lily, and Old Archie all leaned in toward them in curiosity. Cooper ignored them, but Jess looked bemused by all the attention. "Perhaps in private?"

"Yeah, I'm thinking in private would be best." He gave Riley a look. "Watch the bar. I won't be long."

"Sure thing, boss." She grinned knowingly at him.

He ignored her, more concerned about what was up with the doc than about being subjected to his staff teasing him. He gestured to Jess to meet him at the end of the bar. She walked around, smiling at Old Archie, who grinned at her like a pubescent boy, and met Cooper at the end. He placed a hand on her lower back and guided her through the Staff Only door. "We can talk in my office."

Once they were inside the small, cramped space, and the door had closed behind them, Jess moved away from his touch. She turned to him and he couldn't help taking a moment to enjoy looking at her. She wore a fitted black leather jacket, a dark pink shirt underneath it, and black skinny jeans. She was also wearing those sexy-as-hell high-heeled boots again.

Her pretty features were taut with tension.

Cooper immediately stopped thinking about how good she looked as his earlier concern came back. "What's going on, Doc?"

"Uh . . ." She glanced around. "Can we sit?"

"Sure." He gestured to the chair behind her and he strode by her to sit on his desk. "Now, what's going on?"

Jess stared up at him and he tensed at the compassion he saw in her eyes. "I mostly came here for my vacation, but there was another reason I chose to come to Hartwell."

Curiosity definitely piqued, Cooper nodded at her to continue.

"As you know, I work at the Women's Correctional and Rehabilitation Facility in Wilmington." She paused to open her purse and pull out four little envelopes. "A few weeks ago I found these letters inside a book from the library. They were written by your mother's cousin, Sarah Randall."

Shock froze Cooper to the spot.

"I didn't know she was your mother's cousin until last night. Bailey told me of the connection."

Sarah Randall. Jesus Christ. He hadn't known her—she died before he was born—but his mom was only a few years younger than Sarah and they'd been close. She'd thought of her as a big sister. Coop knew from how choked up his mom got when talking about her cousin that the crime she'd committed, killing her husband, had had a huge impact on her. It changed his mom.

He didn't have the most positive feelings toward the woman because of that.

At his silence, Jess leaned forward in her chair. "These letters are for George Beckwith. You will of course know the story there."

Everyone in Hartwell did.

"I'm not sure it's right for you to read them. It wasn't right for me to see them, I guess, but I did. Now I feel it's only right that George gets them. But Bailey also convinced me you had the right to know the truth at least."

"And what truth is that?"

"That Sarah was blackmailed by Ron Peters into marrying him. He had evidence that George's father, the senator, was involved in criminal activity. He said that if he was exposed George would lose everything. Sarah was just a kid and naive and she stupidly gave in to Ron. He was very abusive. The night she shot him, it was because she knew he was going to kill her. It was self-defense. These letters . . . She wanted forgiveness, Cooper. From George and probably everyone she loved. She *needed* forgiveness and she died before she could mail them out and get what she needed."

Cooper narrowed his eyes on Jess. There was a lot of passion in her voice for someone she didn't know—it was almost like she was defending his mother's cousin. "No one knew why Sarah married Ron. Now we know. But my mother and Sarah's family knew something wasn't right in Sarah's marriage. They suspected he was abusing her and they tried to help her. My mom said Sarah was so changed by the marriage that she kept everyone at a distance. This . . ." He waved his hand at the letters. "Look, my mom was a good woman. She would have forgiven her because she'd already guessed that Ron was abusive. But she was hurt that Sarah cut them out, that she didn't go to them for help. It changed her. I didn't know Sarah, but I can't forget the way my mother got when she talked about her. I believe, no matter how hard things were, she had other choices available to her. My mom and our family were one of those choices. Sarah made the wrong choice."

More than that, Cooper knew what it was like to see a woman be beat down in every way by a man, and at no point in all his own mom went through would she have ever considered taking the road Sarah Randall did.

Jessica stared up at him with those big eyes and he saw something change in them. He didn't know what it was because he didn't know her well enough, but he got a feeling that it wasn't good.

That was made clear when she abruptly stood up, shoving the letters into her purse. "Okay," she said in that quiet voice of hers. "Bailey just . . ." She shrugged.

Sensing she might be feeling foolish for coming to him, Cooper cursed himself and reached out to touch her arm to halt her departure. "Thanks for telling me, though. I do appreciate it."

When she lifted her gaze to his, he frowned. Something was missing from her expression. Something warm that had been there before was now gone. She gave him a tight smile. "I should go."

Shit.

He'd fucked up. He must have sounded too harsh. "Doc, you obviously feel compassion for the woman."

"You disagree with me, though."

"Yeah, but compassion is not a turnoff." He grinned.

Flirting with her didn't work. She gave him another weak smile. "I really should go."

Annoyed by her retreat but determined to prove to her he wasn't some unforgiving asshole, Cooper touched her arm again. "I was hoping you'd be free Tuesday night to grab some dinner with me."

Jessica gave him a pinched smile as she moved away from his touch. As she pulled open his office door she said, "I can't. I have other plans."

Before he could say anything to change her mind, the doc was gone.

And Cooper was confused as hell.

If Jessica Huntington hadn't known Sarah Randall, why did she feel strongly enough to be pissed off at him for not . . . what exactly? He knew her crime wasn't completely black-and-white, but still . . .

Yesterday Jess was interested in him. He could tell. She'd felt the connection that pulled at him.

Now she was retreating over a few letters written by a woman she didn't even know.

What the hell was that all about?

EIGHT

Jessica

The sun spilled out over the water and the sand, transforming the boardwalk from a soothing gray to a vibrant scene. It also brought out dog walkers and sunbathers. High season hadn't quite hit, but tourists were starting to appear.

I sat on the balcony outside my room staring out over the ocean. The sea breeze moved through my hair and I reveled in the peace.

Seriously . . . I'd had no idea how much I was missing a sense of serenity in my life. I'd never have absolute peace, yet I was soothed by the knowledge that few people ever would. But back in Wilmington I never had anything like these quiet moments, these little ocean drops of contentment. I honestly hadn't even known it was a possibility for me. Maybe because I hadn't been actively seeking it for fear I'd find something more ominous in the quiet.

After Cooper's disappointing reaction to the revelations from Sarah's letters I found myself enjoying the peace more than ever. His lack of compassion had cast a pall over my attachment to the boardwalk town and I wanted to be like the sun and blast the grayness out.

It was difficult and I couldn't work out why. Why was I so disappointed and affected by his grim dismissal of Sarah's complicated situation? I barely knew the man!

My phone rang, pulling me from my frustration. It was Fatima.

"Hey. Aren't you supposed to be working?" I said in greeting as I wandered back into my room, closing the balcony doors behind me.

"Aren't you supposed to be on vacation? You sound depressed. What's up with that?"

I made a face. I even *sounded* depressed? Well, that was just wrong. "I'm fine," I chirped.

"That was so fake my teeth hurt."

"Your teeth hurt?"

"Yeah. Like too much sugar in fake frosting."

"Okay, strange lady, what can I do for you?"

"I was just checking in to see how the vacation was going, but I can tell it's going well. Not."

Sighing, I flopped down on the bed. "It *was* going well. I really like it here. It's peaceful. Pretty. The people are nice."

"So what happened?"

With another heavy sigh I found myself telling her about Cooper and his reaction to the letters.

Fatima huffed, "So her cousin's son who never knew her doesn't give a shit. Does that mean you let that ruin your whole vacation? Remember you're there for you, not Sarah. So quit moping around and enjoy the fact that you're not working in a place with too many bitches."

"You know I hate that word." I scowled.

"I know," she said, amusement in her voice. "That's why I said it."

"Despite using that derogatory term," I said, all uppity because I really did hate that word, "you're right. I'm on vacation. I'm going to enjoy it. And that means getting off the phone with you so I can get dressed for the day."

"Nice talking to you, too," she said with no small amount of snark.

I grinned. "Are you and Derek well?"

"Yeah, Jess, we're well. Now go va . . . cate? No, that isn't right."

I chuckled. "We'll talk later. 'Bye."

Once we'd ended the call, I threw my shoulders back with renewed determination. Fatima was right! I was on holiday. I needed to remember that, forget about Cooper, and enjoy the break away from the real world.

Bailey was nowhere to be seen at breakfast and a waitress named Natasha told me that it was the owner's day off. I'd smiled. Good. I was glad my new friend had decided to take a day off after all.

I was going to spend the day walking around Hartwell and getting to know it better. Strolling out of the inn, I slipped on my sunglasses and enjoyed the gentle heat on my skin as I walked down the porch stairs. Hitting the bottom step, I smiled in surprise when I saw Bailey striding through the front gate toward me.

"There you are," she said with a big grin. "I was worried I wouldn't catch you."

"Is something wrong?"

"Nope. Screw it, I said to myself this morning, I'm taking a day off. No one is checking in or out today, there are kitchen staff, waitstaff, and cleaning staff in and out all day if a guest needs something, and I have my phone on me if I'm needed."

"Good for you."

"So I thought we could hang out."

My day was looking up. "I'd love that."

"Great." Bailey started leading me out onto the boardwalk. "I cannot tell you how much I treasure my day off."

"You haven't found anyone to cover the management job yet?"

"I'm sort of picky." She shrugged. "I have to feel something from someone . . . you know, like, I can trust them."

"Sure." I spotted Hart's Gift Shop and noted it was still closed. "Damn. Will that shop open soon? I really like the stuff in the window display and there's a doll I want to get my goddaughter."

"Dahlia's?" Bailey smiled. "Sure. She's on vacation, but she'll be back soon."

"You know her well?"

"Of course. She's one of my best buds."

"Wow. That must be nice. Working so close to your friend."

"It is. Dahlia is a great person. She makes and sells her own jewelry. I'm sure you'll love it." She touched the silver necklace she wore. It had a long thin chain and the pendant was a beautiful silver cherry blossom tree. "She made this. My dad calls me Cherry," she explained with a smile and I read the love for her friend in that smile. If I were to go by the craftsmanship and detail put into that little tree I'd say Dahlia loved Bailey.

"It's beautiful." I felt a wistfulness come over me. I didn't have anything like a best girlfriend in my life. Matthew and I were close, but he lived so far away. Fatima was also a good friend but not the hang-out-on-the-weekends or share-deep-dark-secrets kind of friend.

"You okay?" Bailey frowned at me.

"I'm fine," I assured her with a grin. "Where are we off to?"

"Well, I was thinking we could walk around and then— Oof! Jesus Christ!" Bailey stumbled back when a guy came barreling out from an alley between buildings and straight into her. He caught her, steadying her, and I watched as recognition lit both their faces.

He immediately let go of her and she glared up at him. "Tremaine," she sneered.

He smirked. "Miss Hartwell."

For a moment they just stared at one another, animosity pouring off Bailey. It was so the opposite of the version of Bailey I'd been getting to know that I was immediately taken aback and then intrigued to discover who the man was. I studied him as he stared back at Bailey in amusement. I raised an eyebrow as I finally got a clearer picture of him.

Tall, with a swimmer's build, he wore an exquisitely tailored black suit and black shirt. His jet-black hair was thick and cut well, the dark color in contrast to his startling pale gray eyes. He swung those eyes to me and I found myself snared in them. They were rimmed with thick black lashes that only emphasized how pale they were.

Mr. Beautiful held out a hand to me. "I'm Vaughn Tremaine. I own Paradise Sands Hotel."

Ah. Bailey's competition. I shook his hand. "Nice to meet you. I'm Jessica. One of Bailey's guests."

"*Dr.* Jessica Huntington," Bailey put in smugly.

He just smiled at her pointed comment, albeit with a wolfish, predatory smile that dipped to her mouth and stayed there. "And here you said I would kill your business, Miss Hartwell. Yet a doctor chose your establishment over mine."

"Well, she has taste," Bailey said, grabbing my arm. "Now, we'll be leaving before you storm into me deliberately again."

"It was an accident," he said lazily as she started to pull me away from him. "It's not my fault you're always in my way. Enjoy your stay in Hartwell, Dr. Huntington."

"Pfft!" She tugged me forward and I had to quicken my steps to keep up with her.

"Well, there's a story there," I said, thinking about how the air had snapped and crackled around the two of them. "Ex-lover?"

"What?" she screeched, drawing to a complete halt on the boardwalk by the bandstand. There was horror in her pretty green eyes. "What would make you say that?"

"Sexual tension," I answered honestly.

The horror in her gaze multiplied. "Sexual . . . wha . . . pfft . . . huh!" she sputtered. "No! There is no sexual tension between us. Just pure dislike."

"Hmm."

"You don't believe me?" She pointed to Paradise Sands. "That monstrosity was a deliberate attempt to undermine my business."

"Wasn't it a hotel before Vaughn bought it?"

"Yeah, but a crappy one. Vaughn's place is affordable luxury."

"Has it affected your business?"

Bailey shrugged and turned toward the water. She leaned her elbows on the railing and stared out at the beach. "No. But that doesn't mean he cared whether it would or not. And what is he even doing here?" She glanced at me, frustration mingling with curiosity in her eyes. "He's this big fancy New Yorker, born and bred in Manhattan. Comes from big money, owns numerous hotels, and he decides to take up residence in the hotel in little Hartwell, Delaware? You don't find that suspect?"

I leaned on the railing beside her. "You don't think Hartwell has its charms?"

"Of course I do." She grew serious. "But not to someone like him. Vaughn Tremaine treats me like an uncultured country bumpkin, like I'm less of a person because I'm a townie who lacks ambition. I admire people like you, Jessica. You've worked for a long time and worked hard to become a doctor. But I never wanted a fancy education or to live anywhere but here. For me this is all I've ever wanted." She gestured to the sea. "I believe it's the simple things in life that make it great. My inn. My ocean. My family. My friends. I don't appreciate someone telling me that all the things I admire the most about my life are things to be sneered at as simple and folksy."

I nodded, understanding now. I'd be mad at Vaughn Tremaine, too, if he'd made me feel that way about my life. Gazing out at the water, I found myself envious of Bailey. All the things she thought made her life special were the things I didn't have.

"I just don't get why the smug bastard wants to be here. Why stay somewhere when he so obviously finds it provincial? He won't tell anyone. And I don't like it."

I grinned at her. "He didn't seem so bad."

"Oh, don't be fooled by his suave, cultured manners. That there is a wolf in Armani."

Funny, his expression had struck me as wolfish, too. "Maybe you're right," I murmured.

"He's worming his way in. I think he may even have Cooper softening up to him. Asshole."

I laughed.

"Speaking of Cooper, how did it go? With Sarah's letters?"

That pall from earlier threatened to return. "It didn't, really. He said the family had already guessed Sarah was being abused and they tried to help. He said she had choices and she made the wrong choice. I didn't find him very compassionate. At all." I shrugged sadly.

And that was just so crappy because even without realizing it I'd built him up in my head to be this . . . I don't know . . . someone I had really liked a lot from our one encounter. I hated that the second time around he wasn't who I'd hoped he'd be.

"You sound disappointed."

"I don't know the guy, so I wasn't expecting a reaction either way," I lied nonchalantly.

"But you didn't expect him to be so black-and-white about things."

No, I really hadn't.

Bailey contemplated me. "Let me buy you an ice cream cone and I'll explain a few things."

"An ice cream cone?" I grinned. I hadn't had an ice cream cone in years.

"From Antonio's." She pointed down the boardwalk to the Italian pizzeria that stood next to Paradise Sands Hotel. "But there's no Antonio—it's owned by a couple named Iris and Ira."

Antonio's décor was very 1950s diner, with black-and-white-check flooring, red leather booths, and high round black tables with red-leather-topped chrome stools. Every inch of the white walls was covered with black-and-white photographs of Hollywood stars and musicians. All the frames were red or black. It was sleek and it sparkled, it was so clean.

The restaurant itself wasn't so busy at that time of day, but the ice cream counter had a small line of people at it.

A man with a full head of dark gray hair, a beaming white smile, and a stocky build was manning the counter. He cheerily scooped up ice cream for his customers and as soon as Bailey and I stepped up to the counter that smile went full wattage.

"Sweetheart!" he boomed, lifting the countertop to come out and hug Bailey. "Iris!" he yelled in Bailey's ear, making her flinch and then giggle like a little girl. "Bailey girl is here!" He turned back to her. "How are you doing? Cooper says you're run off your feet at the inn. That you need some help. Remember Kevan? Iris's nephew's son? He's in Hartwell. He needs work."

"She's not hiring Kevan." A small, trim woman wearing jeans and a plaid shirt appeared. Her gray hair was cut into a perfect bob that swung as she moved in to hug Bailey. "He's a buffoon."

Bailey laughed. "Yeah, I need less buffoon in my life."

"Who else is a buffoon? Tom?" The woman frowned.

Bailey gave her a look. "No, Iris, not Tom."

Iris harrumphed at that before turning to me. I wondered what her problem with Bailey's boyfriend was. "Who's this?"

I held out my hand and opened my mouth to speak, but Bailey beat me to it. "Dr. Jessica Huntington. She's a guest at the inn and she's wonderful like me so of course we hit it off."

I laughed and shook Iris's hand. "It's nice to meet you."

"Ira." The man shook my hand as soon as I let go of Iris's. "Iris's husband."

"Pleasure."

"So what brought you to Hartwell?" Iris said with curiosity sharp in her eyes.

I decided to give the less complicated explanation. "I work in Wilmington. I wanted to go on vacation but not too far away from work."

"Hmm. Workaholic," she pronounced and then swung her hand to the wall behind the cash desk. "Our daughter, Ivy, is just the same."

I stepped closer to take a look at the photographs. One in particular caught my eye. A gorgeous brunette wearing a floor-length ivory evening gown stood on a red carpet. Standing next to her, his arm around her waist, was a handsome older man in a tux.

"Ivy is a Hollywood screenwriter," Ira said with pride. "Engaged to Oliver Frost, the director."

"Wow." Oliver Frost was a big-time director in Hollywood. He'd just wrapped up filming the last in a teen dystopian franchise that had shot its young stars into the celebrity stratosphere.

"Cool, huh?" Bailey grinned at me. "Ivy and I went to school together. We were best buds until she moved to Hollywood."

Iris threw her arm around Bailey's shoulders. "Bailey girl, you are still best buds. You know she loves you more than anyone." She sighed and stared almost forlornly at the photographs. "Kid just got busy."

Bailey gave her a squeeze. "I'm showing Jessica around and our first stop is ice cream at Antonio's. Nothing but the best."

The couple grinned. Ira moved to behind the counter. "Now, then, let's see. I recommend a two-scoop: double chocolate chip and mint chocolate chip."

"No, no." Iris followed him. "The strawberry delight with the white chocolate."

Ira made a face. "That's crazy talk, woman."

"Don't you call me 'woman' in front of customers."

"It's Bailey girl and her friend." Ira shrugged as if to say, *What's the big deal?*

"Move over and let me get them ice cream."

"The ice cream counter is my domain." Ira stood in front of it with his arms crossed over his chest.

"Are you seriously blocking my way?"

"Um, guys." Bailey cleared her throat. "Today would be nice."

"Fine." Iris nodded. "Two strawberry delight and white chocolate coming up."

"No, two double chocolate chip and mint chocolate chip coming up," Ira said equally firmly.

I stepped up to the counter, trying my best not to laugh and almost failing. "We'll have one strawberry delight and white chocolate and one double chocolate chip and mint chocolate chip."

Iris and Ira blinked at me.

Iris finally nodded and cleared her throat. "Well, alright, then."

A little while later we walked out of Antonio's with our cones.

I had the strawberry and white chocolate. And Bailey was right. The ice cream was creamy and smooth and delicious. I licked at it greedily, feeling like a kid again.

"They are always like that," Bailey said, laughing. "They argue about everything. But they really love each other. And Ivy."

I was curious about Ivy. "Is there a story there?"

"I'm not sure." Bailey tilted her head to the side in thought. "Ivy and I still talk, but it's not the same as it used to be. A year or so back she got really closed off and distant. With her mom and dad, too. They blame this Oliver guy, but I'm not sure what's really going on there."

I thought about how close-knit the community here appeared, with Bailey growing up with Ivy and being best friends with the business owner next door to her inn, plus her obvious affection for Cooper. It really was a small town.

It seemed so nice.

Like a big extended family.

I found myself envying Bailey again.

"So ice cream, check," Bailey said as we wandered past Paradise Sands. She stopped and my gaze followed hers to Cooper's. "Now the explanation I promised." She licked at her ice cream and turned to me with a smirk. "I'm not telling you it all, because it isn't my story, but I'll tell you something I think will help you understand Cooper's reaction better. Mainly what you need to know is that Cooper has had his share of betrayal. The latest was fairly recently, in fact."

She continued to walk and I practically twisted my neck craning back to look at the bar. I wasn't sure what I was looking for. Maybe a glimpse of the man himself?

"When you were looking for a place to stay here, did you come across the Hartwell Grand Hotel?"

"Yeah." It was a four-star hotel in the middle of town. "It looked nice, but I wanted to stay on the boardwalk."

"Most folks do. The Grand is owned by the Devlin family. Ian Devlin is the patriarch of that particular group of bandits. There are four sons and a daughter. They own a few stores on Main Street as well as the hotel and they own Ocean Blue Fun Park—the fairground a few blocks from here. They're wealthy . . . and they don't pretend to be nice on their way to accumulating more wealth. They're more than ambitious. They're ruthless."

Intrigued, I said, "How so?"

"We've all had our personal dealings with the Devlins and some of us are more than a little suspicious that they may have obtained buildings through underhanded means. There is a possibility they're paying off town officials to get what they want. Maybe even state officials . . . like health inspectors.

"I had a friend, Stella, who had owned a café on Main Street for a decade. Five years ago the café didn't meet the health inspection requirements even though there had never been problems before. Stella was meticulous about cleanliness. But they didn't pass her and every time she tried to get it sorted out there was a roadblock put in her way. She was already in debt and in trouble, so when Ian Devlin showed up and offered to buy the building she took the offer and moved out of Hartwell. Hers isn't the only story like that. Everyone knows Ian Devlin has been trying to get property on the boardwalk for years. When my parents were retiring and handed the inn over to me, Stu Devlin, the eldest devil, got pretty aggressive trying to get them to sell."

I was completely engrossed in her story. "Aggressive how?"

"At first it was just Stu constantly in their face about it. He sent them presents, which they sent back, and when they'd spurned about ten gifts, things got ugly. We started to receive threatening letters, stuff that pretty much said we should get the hell out of Hartwell or we'd lose everything, we'd get hurt, stupid stuff like that. We knew it was coming from them, but there wasn't enough evidence to prove it.

"Anyway, I get my stubbornness from my parents and they refused to be bullied. And that's all it was. As far as we know, the Devlin family is underhanded, but they've never resorted to physically hurting anyone. Anyway, my parents didn't want to leave me, but I told them that we would only be letting them win if they didn't go, so off they went. Sure enough, they backed off after that. It helped that the old Boardwalk Hotel went up for sale at that time.

"Until Vaughn Tremaine came on the scene. He just swept in with all his money and he so far outbid the Devlins there was nothing they could do. And oh, man, were they pissed. I dislike Vaughn, but the Devlins *hate* him."

"Wow," I said. "They sound like real-life villains."

"Oh, they are. Every town has 'em, right?"

And wasn't that the awful truth. "Right."

"Anyway, the point of the story is the third brother, Jack Devlin . . . he's gorgeous, charismatic, and down-to-earth. The rest of them, gorgeous, yes, but that's about it—well, his sister, Rebecca, was nice, which is probably why she left town as soon as she could, but the rest of them think they're so superior to everyone else. Jack wasn't like that. He was kind of the black sheep. He refused to go into the family business and . . . he was Cooper's best friend."

"Okay," I said, a little warily. If this was a tale about betrayal I didn't like where it was going.

"A few years back, out of nowhere, just after Vaughn outbid the Devlins on the hotel site, Jack quit his job as a construction foreman. As far as we were all aware he loved that job. But nope, just up and quit, and went to work for his father." She took a deep, shuddering breath, pain suddenly etched in her features. "And then one day, not too long later, Cooper walked in on Jack with Cooper's wife, Dana. Now his ex-wife."

The ice cream cone that I'd just eaten churned in my stomach at the thought of such a betrayal. I barely knew him, but I was overwhelmingly sad and angry for Cooper. "God," I whispered.

"Poor Coop stopped talking to Jack and Jack got even more immersed in his family's business. He's distant from all of us now. He doesn't seem to care about anything."

"And Cooper and Dana?"

"Well, Coop divorced her a while ago and went from a completely one-woman guy to a no-strings-attached lothario. All seemed okay, but a few months ago Dana started harassing him for reconciliation. He doesn't want her, but she's making his life hell right now." Bailey's green eyes darkened. "Not for long if I have anything to say about it."

I took in the hard light in her eyes and gave a guffaw of surprised laughter. "I really wouldn't want to get on your bad side."

She laughed. "In my case, the red hair . . . definitely a sign of a fiery temper." Bailey turned us around and we started walking back the way we had come. The boardwalk was a mile long and the southern end was occupied by a number of private residences so there wasn't anything touristy for me to see.

"The point of me telling you all this isn't just to beat the gossip queens of this town to it but also to let you understand where Cooper is emotionally. His ex is just a constant reminder right now of betrayal."

I understood and I felt my disappointment regarding him melt. But it didn't melt completely. Because the truth was I had fancied myself a little "in like" with the guy. I hadn't known what it meant or if it meant anything or if anything would come of it while I was on vacation, but now I knew for sure that nothing would come of it.

Plus Cooper was another no-strings-attached guy.

I had one of those already.

And Andrew and I had ultimately agreed to be each other's one-and-only hookup for the sake of health and safety. Cooper was definitely out of the question.

I had to remind myself of what I'd told Fatima: I was happy *not* being in a relationship with anyone.

"So does that change your mind about him?"

I blinked, jerked out of my thoughts. There was a spark of hopefulness in Bailey's expression and I recognized it as an ember from a matchmaking fire. I rolled my eyes. "I'm here for three weeks. I'm not here for a relationship."

"Yes, but clearly friendship is in the cards." She gestured between us. "So why can't you be friends with him, too?"

It was complicated. But Bailey didn't need to know about the complicated so I told her what she wanted to hear. "I guess I can."

Bailey seemed happy with that answer and from there she led me off the boardwalk through Main Street. She told me more about the town, its people, and her family as we shopped and explored. By the time evening was falling, she led me back to Antonio's for dinner. The place was packed, and Iris and Ira were too busy to stop and chat with us. I had their delicious pepperoni pizza and enjoyed the family atmosphere of the place.

"So all day I've been talking your ear off," Bailey said after swallowing a forkful of pasta. "And I haven't learned anything more about you other than you were a surgical resident—I repeat: I'm in awe—before you took the job at the prison. What about family? Friends? This not-really-a-relationship thing you have going with some guy?"

The pizza I was currently chewing became tough and hard to swallow. I felt cold all of a sudden, and a familiar tremble started in my hands. I was never very good at fielding personal questions. I wasn't exactly what you'd call an open book. Taking my time, keeping my expression neutral, I finally managed to swallow my food. I hid my hands under the table so she couldn't see them tremble. "I don't have any family left. Not blood, anyway. My best friend, Matthew, is my family. He lives in Iowa, where we grew up."

Bailey's eyes were bright with sympathy. "I'm sorry, Jess. You don't have to talk about them."

"Thanks. It was hard losing them, but Matthew has always been there for me and because of him I have Perry, my goddaughter, and she's just an adorable devilish angel."

She grinned at my description. "Do you get to see her a lot?"

"Not as much as I'd like." Partly my fault because of my work schedule and also because I didn't like going back to Iowa. "But we FaceTime a lot."

"And what about back in Wilmington? What about this guy?"

As we moved onto this safer topic, I felt the cold begin to leave me and my trembling eased. "Andrew. He's a cardiothoracic surgeon. We met at the hospital while I was a resident. The hours were so insane—even worse than my hours now—it was impossible to have any kind of relationship with someone who wasn't a doctor. And honestly I didn't want a relationship. I still don't. I like my autonomy and Andrew gets that. He gets all of it. We're friends with benefits." I thought about that term and snorted. "Except we're not really friends, either."

Bailey surveyed me. "And how long have you two been benefiting each other?"

I chuckled at the way she phrased the question. "We started a few years back and then he met someone so we stopped for the length of their relationship. That was about a year. He decided he didn't want a serious relationship after all and so we started up our thing again."

"And close friends in Wilmington?"

Until I arrived in Hartwell I hadn't realized how much I lacked a social life back in Wilmington. I had no time for the realization to dawn on me. "You know, it occurs to me that I don't have a whole lot going on in my social calendar. I have colleagues that I like, but we don't go out or spend our free time together. I work long hours."

This garnered me a worried look.

"It's fine," I said, but her expression didn't change. "What? Why are you looking at me like that?"

"I'm just glad you came here."

"Why?"

She shrugged and gave me this secretive, mischievous smile. "I just am."

NINE

Cooper

It was a fact that the coffee at Emery's was better than the coffee Cooper had at the bar. On days he wanted that coffee bad enough he would hit Emery's place first, before work, and he did this knowing he'd have to endure the painful shyness of the owner.

That day was no different from any other. As soon as he stepped into the bookstore-coffeehouse, Emery blushed from the base of her neck to her hairline at the sight of him and lowered her eyes.

It would have been cute if her discomfort didn't make him so uncomfortable.

"Morning, Emery," he said, approaching the counter. "I'll have the usual."

She nodded, her gaze aimed somewhere over his shoulder. In the entire time he'd known Emery Saunders he thought maybe she'd made eye contact with him once. Cooper would never understand it. She was a few years younger than him, probably about thirty or so, beautiful, and she'd managed to open her own business at a really young age. All of that should have given her plenty of confidence, maybe even a hint of arrogance, but as far as Cooper could see, Emery had none of that.

The first time he came into her coffeehouse, years back, he thought maybe she was attracted to him because of the way she blushed when he talked to her, but over time he came to realize she was shy with most folks, especially men. She blushed that pretty color of pink when Jack spoke to her, too.

He frowned. No need to think of that son of a bitch. But it was a hard habit to break, considering the man had been his best friend for the bigger part of his life.

"Anything else?" Emery said quietly, still not meeting his eyes.

"No, angel, that's it." He paid up, getting out of her place fast like always. It might make him a dick, but that woman was hard to be at ease around. He felt like his presence tortured her, considering the way she whispered or stammered around him. He felt he was being nicer getting the hell out of her way as quickly as possible so she could go back to breathing normally.

Cooper stepped outside her store and sipped at his coffee.

Pure heaven in a cup.

Made the awkwardness from the owner worth it.

Coffee in hand, he started walking toward his bar. His footsteps almost faltered, however, when he recognized the figure waiting under the bar awning.

Think of the devil and he shall appear.

Fucking Jack.

He felt a familiar cold hardness settle inside him and coil around his muscles, like it always did these days whenever he encountered his ex-friend around town.

"Here on business." Jack held up his hands defensively.

Cooper's anger toward Jack was so controlled he managed to keep his face blank. He stopped mere inches from him, sending a message by getting in his personal space. That message was, *You don't bother me, asshole; you're not even on my radar.* He sipped casually at his coffee as Jack stared back at him just as impassively. Ignoring the ugly regret in his gut, Cooper finally said, "And Ian thought it was a good idea to send you?"

Jack shrugged. "I gave up trying to figure out how my father's mind works a long time ago."

"And yet you work for the bastard?" Something Cooper never could understand.

Sidestepping his remark, Jack said, "He's upping his offer on the bar."

Jesus Christ, what was it with the people in his life that they couldn't take a hint? First Dana. Now Ian. It was good he had control over his anger because right now it wanted to simmer a little too close to the surface. He stepped even farther into his old friend's space to drive home his point. "You tell your father what I've told him every year since the bar became mine . . . I. Am. Not. Selling. And while I've got breath in my body I never will. You tell him if he ever comes back here with another offer, he and I will have a serious problem."

Jack nodded, face still blank, stepped back, and then walked away.

No fight. No argument. No cajoling.

This was the first year Ian Devlin had sent Jack to make his case. It was also the first year Cooper had gotten rid of a Devlin boy in under a minute. Usually they tried to irritate him into considering an offer for the bar.

He frowned, watching Jack walk away.

Nothing about his old friend's behavior made sense.

Unlocking the bar, Cooper took a moment after shutting the door behind him. His adrenaline was up. He wanted to throw his coffee at the wall or punch his fist through it. Anything to expel the horrible burn in his blood.

He took a sip of the coffee. Reminded himself that the coffee was too good to be wasted over Devlin.

But it wasn't Ian Devlin's persistence that had pissed him off.

As always, it was seeing Jack.

He just couldn't figure that shit out.

Thirty years he'd known Jack, ever since they were six years old and Jack defended him during recess when a bigger kid was picking on Cooper. Despite the fact that Jack was a Devlin and came from the moneyed south side of Hartwell, and Coop didn't have much and came from the north side, they'd become best friends. And then as they got older they realized they had more in common than they thought—they both had really shitty fathers. Cooper's took off and Ian Devlin might as well have taken off, too, for how little attention he paid to his wife, his third son, and his daughter. By the time Cooper and Jack were teenagers their lives were actually pretty similar. They were both on the football team, were both popular, both had part-time jobs, and more importantly both looked out for their mothers and sisters. Cooper was the man of his house. Jack was the only man in his house that seemed to give a real damn about his mom and sister.

As far as Cooper was concerned Jack Devlin was his brother and they had a bond stronger than most. They'd had each other's back always. Jack cried by his side at Cooper's mother's funeral and helped him take care of all the arrangements.

For Christ's sake, he'd even tried to talk him out of getting serious with Dana.

"She's no good, Coop. You keep thinking there's something deep buried under all that pretty, but that woman is as shallow as a kiddie pool."

It was the only time they'd fought about anything. Jack apologized soon after, but he'd never been very warm toward Dana.

Jack had been the truest man he knew.

Until suddenly he quit his job and started working for his old man—something he'd sworn his whole life he'd never do. Cooper knew then something was up, but Jack got distant and closed off, wouldn't talk about it at all.

And then he'd fucked Dana.

Cooper had to wonder if Jack had secretly been attracted to his wife the whole time . . . but that didn't sit right. He knew how Jack was with women he was attracted to. At least he'd thought he did.

He'd thought he'd known Jack Devlin better than anyone.

Turned out he never knew him at all.

And that was the betrayal that cut the deepest.

That was what hurt the most.

Not losing Dana.

But losing his best friend. His brother.

Pain Cooper kept buried deep shot up and across his chest.

"Fuck," he muttered, wincing.

He took a fortifying gulp of coffee and willed that pain back down.

That evening the bar was the busiest it had been in a while. It was closing in on high season and his business was feeling it. The place was filled with regulars and tourists now.

The busyness of the place was the reason he was trying to curb his irritation with his waitress as she rounded the bar from the staff room, tying on her apron.

"Lil, you're late. Again."

She flushed at his scowl and threw him a pretty, pleading smile. "I'm so sorry. I couldn't get my car to start."

Damn it, she couldn't even come up with decent excuses. "What? That brand-new Toyota you can't really afford?"

She flushed again and hurried to clear away plates. The kitchen was now closed, but an hour back they could have really used her.

"Done, boss." Crosby appeared at the end of the bar. He gave Cooper a nod, clapped Old Archie on the shoulder, and headed out. That was Crosby's way these days. He kept himself to himself. Cooper tried not to worry about his cook. Not while he was in the middle of worrying about his waitress.

She was becoming a problem. The kind of problem he liked to avoid in his life. He decided to do just that and took an order from Riley, who had been filling in for Lily out on the floor.

"Good thing I'm a multitasker," Riley said as he poured the two gin and tonics she'd ordered. "It's getting busy."

Doesn't help when you have a waitress taking advantage of you, he grumbled to himself.

Riley smirked as if she'd read his thoughts. "Boss, you do what you need to do," she said pointedly as she took the drinks.

He shot a brooding look over at Lil. She was smiling as she jotted down a drinks order.

She was a nice girl, good at the job when she actually turned up on time . . . and he hated firing people.

The door to the bar opened and in stepped the distraction Cooper needed.

The doc.

His whole being became alert at the sight of Jessica walking into the bar with Bailey and Tom.

It had been a week since he had seen her and he had to admit he'd thought about Jessica often, hoping she'd come into the bar again. The more time passed without seeing her, the more his resolve grew that if she didn't come in soon he'd go in search of her himself.

"Coop." Bailey grinned as she approached the bar with Tom and Jessica in tow. "How's it going?" She slid onto a stool. Tom took the stool on her left while Jessica took the one on her right.

As always he was happy to see Bailey. She was like a little sister to him. Sweetest, funniest, most outspoken woman he knew. His eyes slid to Tom Sutton. The guy worked for a small Web-based company in Dover. He and Cooper were different types of guys so they didn't spend a lot of time together, but he seemed to make Bailey happy, and that was all that mattered.

He nodded at Tom and he grinned back.

Then Cooper's gaze slid to the doc. His eyes drifted over her pretty face and that fantastic hair of hers, and then down.

His blood heated.

She was wearing a dark red shirt and the top few buttons were undone, showing off her cleavage. He instantly imagined what lay underneath the shirt.

Lust stirred within him, but he kept it under control when he lifted his gaze to hers. "Evening, Doc. Nice to see you again."

"You, too," she said in that soft, sultry voice.

Damn, he'd forgotten how much he liked the sound of her voice.

"What's your poison tonight?"

"I'll have a Long Island."

Bailey shot the doc an envious look. "Ooh, that sounds good. But I shouldn't. I'm technically 'on call' tonight and I'll get drunk on a Long Island. I'll just have a white wine."

"You need more staff." Tom sighed. "You need your life back." He turned to Cooper. "I'll have my usual."

He got to work getting their drinks, all the while listening in on the conversation. Mostly to hear Jessica talk.

"The inn is my life," Bailey said.

"A building is not your life."

Cooper would have to disagree with Tom on that. The bar was his life. He knew exactly where Bailey was coming from.

"Since my business is inside that building, then yes, it is my life. It's not all my life, but it's a pretty damn big part of it."

"Look at Jessica," Tom said. "I mean, she's a *doctor* and she has managed to find time to live her life."

"Uh, what do you mean by she's a *doctor*? Are you belittling what I do for a living?"

"And I should say that I take one vacation a year . . . the rest of the time I work . . . a lot . . ." Jessica added.

"No, I wasn't belittling you, sweetheart," Tom said, ignoring the doc. "What you've done with the inn is amazing. I just worry about you."

Cooper turned back with the Long Island as Bailey gave Tom a small kiss on the lips.

"I'm fine," she promised.

As they gazed into each other's eyes, seeming to share some private communication, Cooper looked at the doc and was instantly arrested by what he saw on her face.

Not only was there a hint of longing there, but also a strange mix of curiosity and sadness.

She glanced over at him, caught him studying her, and immediately wiped her expression.

Interesting.

"Your Long Island, Doc." He put it on the counter in front of her.

"Thanks." She refused to meet his eyes.

"Boss," Lily called from down the bar.

Riley was busy making up another drinks order so Cooper reluctantly moved away from Jessica to take Lily's order.

All the time he was working he shot surreptitious looks Jessica's way. From his viewpoint it would appear as if she and Bailey had known each other their whole lives. They sat close and chatted with ease and familiarity, laughing together at whatever Tom was saying to them.

Finally he got a break to move back up the bar to them.

"So, Doc," he interrupted. "You enjoying Hartwell?"

The Long Island must have hit her pretty fast because she gave him a far more open smile than the one she'd given him earlier. "I love it. Good people." She nudged Bailey with her shoulder and Bailey chuckled. "Good views. Good restaurants. Good atmosphere. I've never been somewhere that is such a close-knit community. You're all like one big family here. I feel like you'd probably do anything for each other. I'm kind of envious." She grinned. "And quite frankly this is the best Long Island I've ever had."

He nodded at the compliment. "Glad you're enjoying it. You want another?"

He was glad she was enjoying *all* of it. It felt good that Jessica liked all the things he liked about his town. But more than that, he liked that she saw beyond what the tourists saw. She saw what made this place special—the solid connection between everyone who worked on the boardwalk, which made working there feel like he was coming home every day.

"Yes, please."

Suddenly he imagined another situation in which she said "please" to him. She'd say it in pleading tones, not in politeness. And they'd both be naked.

Cooper turned away before she could see the thought in his eyes.

"Uh, I'll have another wine, too," Bailey said to his back, and he heard the amusement in her voice.

And he knew what that amusement was all about. Bailey had known him a long time. He shot her a look over his shoulder. "You'll wait your turn, B."

She gave him a huge, knowing grin. "Sure thing, Coop."

He winked at her and got back to making Jessica's drink.

"One of my guests told a really bad joke today that was so bad it was good," Bailey said behind him.

"Was it Jessica?" Tom said.

"No, it was Sherman from West Virginia," Bailey said. "Okay, here it is. A Buddhist walks up to a hot dog stand and says, 'Make me one with everything.'"

Cooper shook his head at the bad joke and glanced over to see Jessica give a loud guffaw of laughter. That made him grin.

Tom sighed. "That was awful."

"Jessica found it funny," Bailey argued. "Come on, it was cute funny."

"I'll give you cute funny . . ." Tom said. "What do you call a Christian that skips church?"

Cooper turned around to slide the Long Island over to Jess and start pulling a draft for Tom.

"I don't know." Bailey smiled. "What do you call a Christian that skips church?"

"Christian Bale."

"Oh, oh, man." His girlfriend winced as she laughed. "That's bad."

"Jessica thought it was funny."

It was true, she was giggling. "Seems Jessica doesn't have high standards for jokes."

Her eyes were bright with amusement. "I really don't."

"You tell us a joke, then, Doc," Cooper said.

She took a sip of her drink, seeming to contemplate it.

"Oh, go on!" Bailey pushed her playfully. "Anything is better than Tom's."

"My joke was better than yours, babe."

Jessica interrupted just as Bailey was opening her mouth to argue.

"Okay." The doc put her drink down. "A husband and wife are trying to set up a new password for their computer. The husband puts 'Mypenis,' all one word." Jessica grinned. "The wife falls on the ground laughing because on the screen it says . . . 'Error. Not long enough.'"

Cooper grinned at how much the stupid joke amused her. And not just her. Tom smiled. "Yours wins."

"Oh, if we're allowed to be dirty I have a good one," Bailey said.

Lily appeared at the bar so Cooper wandered away to fill her order. Still, Bailey was being loud enough that he could hear her.

"A mother is in the kitchen making dinner for her family when her daughter walks in. Her daughter asks, 'Mother, where do babies come from?' The mother thinks for a few seconds and says, 'Well, dear, Mommy and Daddy fall in love and get married. One night they go into their bedroom, they kiss and hug, and have sex.' The daughter looks puzzled so the mother continues, 'That means the daddy puts his penis in the mommy's vagina. That's how you get a baby, honey.' The child seems to understand. 'Oh, I see,' she says, 'but the other night when I came into your room you had daddy's penis in your mouth. What do you get when you do that?' The mother smiles at her and says, 'Jewelry, my dear. Jewelry.'"

Old Archie suddenly hit his palm against the bar and shouted down toward Bailey, "That was a good one!"

Jessica was wiping tears from her eyes and Tom was laughing.

"Hey." Riley grinned at Bailey as she poured a draft. "Funny and true."

Cooper's eyes moved back to Jessica. Her face was flushed from alcohol and amusement. She looked happy. It was a good look on her.

"Oh no." Bailey pulled her phone out of her purse and put it to her ear. "Hello . . . Mr. Pollock, how can I help?" She put a finger in her opposite ear and frowned. "Okay, I'll be right there." She hung up and gave Jessica an apologetic look. "I have to go. There's something wrong with the shower in one of my guests' rooms."

"Then call a plumber," Tom said, visibly irritated. "We're having a nice time, Bailey."

"I know." She stroked his cheek affectionately. "But I can't just call a plumber. I need to be there in case I have to move my guests to another room." She glanced back at Jessica. "I'm sorry. You should stay, finish your drink."

"You don't need help?"

"You're my guest. Of course not." Bailey kissed her on the cheek. "But thanks for offering. See you tomorrow."

Tom grumbled under his breath, threw money on the bar, and got up.

"What are you doing?" Bailey frowned.

"Coming with you."

"You don't have to."

"Oh, I do. You promised you'd spend the night at my place tonight. That'll only happen if I come with you."

She glowered at him.

Tension fell between them that even Cooper could feel.

Bailey started to move away from the bar. She caught his eye and gave him a wave. "'Night, Coop."

He nodded at her as she said good night to Old Archie and Riley. All the while Tom followed, scowling at her back.

Ah, the joys of being in a relationship.

Cooper pushed drinks over the bar to Lily and headed back to Jessica, who was sipping her Long Island while she played with her phone.

Her drink was almost finished.

"Another?"

She scrunched her nose, looking adorable. "I don't know if I should. I feel pretty buzzed."

"Up to you, Doc."

Jessica thought about it a second. "I better change to a chardonnay."

When he placed the drink in front of her a minute or so later she took a sip and then sighed. "I love Bailey."

Cooper grinned. "Yeah, she's pretty great."

"No, like, I *love* her. She's so kind. And so pretty. She could be a fairy."

This made him stop for a second. Had he been wrong all along about the connection between them? Was Doc . . . Did Doc play for the other team?

Disappointment started to build . . .

Jessica laughed. "Oh, you should see your face. I'm not gay. Women are allowed to show appreciation for one another without it being about sex."

Relieved, he grinned at her. "Not gay, but you are drunk, Doc."

"Tipsy, not drunk. I'm okay with that." She shrugged. "And I'm not gay," she repeated. "I've just never met anyone like Bailey before. She says what she means and how she feels, no matter what."

"And you don't?" He leaned on the bar, drawing closer to her, and her eyes flicked down to his mouth.

Heat stirred in his gut at the way she was looking at his lips.

Jessica dragged her eyes back up to his. Up close he could see the flecks of gold and green in her huge brown eyes. *Gorgeous fucking eyes.* "Sometimes," she answered and leaned in closer to him to whisper, "For instance, I'm not sure Tom is right for Bailey."

He raised an eyebrow. "What makes you say that?"

She shrugged, dropping her gaze to her drink. "Just a feeling. I can't explain it."

"Well, your secret is safe with me."

She looked up at him again and gave him a soft smile. "You have really blue eyes."

Cooper grinned. "So I've been told."

"You going to flirt with that pretty woman all night and keep her to yourself or you going to introduce her to your friends?" Old Archie called down the bar.

Sighing at the interruption, Cooper stood tall and threw his regular a look. Old Archie was grinning from ear to ear, the devious old bastard.

"Hi." Jessica waved at him.

Old Archie nodded at her. "I'm Archibald Brown, but everyone calls me Old Archie."

Doc frowned at this. "Why would they call you Old Archie when you have such a distinguished name like Archibald Brown? If it were my name, I would insist on being called Archibald Brown all the time. Not Archie, not Archibald, but *Archibald Brown*."

Cooper's grin matched Archie's. "Well, I might do that. And to whom do I have the pleasure of speaking?"

"Archibald Brown, I am Jessica Huntington."

"*Doctor* Jessica Huntington," Cooper said.

Old Archie raised an eyebrow. "Impressive, Doctor. You a surgeon?"

"I was," she said, surprising the hell out of Cooper. "I was a surgical resident—general surgery."

Jesus, a surgeon. Surgeons were their own kind of rock star.

It was hot.

"Was?" Old Archie cocked his head in curiosity.

"I decided it wasn't for me. I was good at it," she said, but it wasn't said with arrogance, just honesty. "But . . ." She shrugged. "Not for me."

Cooper wanted to know more, but he wasn't going to push for that information in front of an audience. He shot Old Archie a look, silently telling him not to, either. Old Archie got the message.

He grinned over at Jessica. "Smart and beautiful. You're double the trouble, honey."

Doc narrowed her eyes on him, but she was smiling. "You're a charmer, Archibald Brown. I bet you say that to all the girls."

"No, some of them around here are as dumb as a post."

Her jaw dropped. "That's a terrible thing to say."

"Hey, there are a lot of men around here dumb as a post, too. I wasn't being sexist."

"Just insulting."

"Honest," he argued.

"I can tell I'm going to need another drink if we're to continue getting to know each other," Jessica said, making Old Archie laugh.

Cooper took in her empty glass. "You sure you got another in you, Doc?"

She wrinkled her nose. "I hate hangovers. I'll have a water."

"You got it."

By the time an hour had passed, Old Archie was on the stool next to Jessica. The two of them kept Cooper entertained all night.

Finally, Anita called and, judging from the look on Old Archie's face, told him to get his ass back home. Cooper disappeared to take out some trash at the back of the bar and when he came back Jessica's stool was empty.

"Is Doc in the restroom?" He nodded his head to her stool.

Riley gave him a knowing smile. "Nah. She paid her tab, told me to tell you good night, and left."

"Fuck," he muttered, disappointed. And then just as quickly determination replaced the disappointment. "Watch the bar."

Riley snorted. "Like I didn't know you were going to say that."

Ignoring her teasing, Cooper hurried out of the bar, hoping to catch up with the doc before she made it to the inn. One, he didn't like the idea of her walking back there alone so late at night, and two, he'd been hoping to get some alone time with her. He wanted to take her out on an actual date and he wanted her to know that he wasn't just looking to fuck around, as if she was just another hot tourist passing through his town.

He could be a gentleman and he wanted to show her that.

Just as he was about to hurry up the boards, he felt that tingle down the back of his neck again and something drew his gaze out toward the beach.

And that was when he saw her.

Sand kicked up under Jessica's feet, her hair blowing wildly behind her as her shoes and purse dangled from one hand. It was chilly out by the water at this time of night, but it didn't look like Jessica was feeling it by the way she spun around, laughing at the way the dying waves rushed around her ankles at the shoreline.

That tingle shot down his spine.

His blood turned hot.

And suddenly Cooper wasn't feeling very gentlemanly toward the sexy doctor.

Jessica

The water was cold, but it felt great against my flushed skin. I'd been alternating between wine and water after my indulgent Long Island iced teas, so I wasn't drunk. However, my blood was still hot from the alcohol, from sitting across the bar from Cooper Lawson all night, and the chilly sea breeze was just what I needed.

I stumbled out of a tipsy spin only to stop on the shore to stare up at the sky. My feet sank into the wet sand, the squishy grain of it warming underfoot. It was a pleasant sensation, relaxing even, and that, mixed with the sound of the soft surf and the infinite darkness of the sea and sky, was soothing.

The stars were brighter here than in the city. They weren't obscured by all the city lights.

They were beautiful.

Goose bumps suddenly prickled my scalp and a little sigh escaped me.

Maybe Bailey was right. Maybe there was magic here.

"Doc?"

For a moment I thought I'd imagined the voice in the dark, attributing the phantom voice to my guilt over leaving the bar without saying good-bye to Cooper.

I was much too aware of him for my own good.

The feelings he incited in me, this stranger with his bar, well . . . it was just a complication I didn't need.

A hand touched my shoulder and this time I jumped, spinning around in alarm.

Relief and that damn awareness washed over me as I stared up into Cooper's face.

"Coop—" His name turned to a gasp because suddenly I was in his arms and my mouth was crushed beneath his.

Confusion was quickly replaced by lust as the kiss instantly turned wild. He had one arm around my back, while his other hand threaded through my hair to hold my head, to hold me to his lips.

Everything about the way he held me said he had no intention of letting me escape him.

And for a few moments, surrounded by the feel of his warm strength, my blood at melting point from his hungry, hard, wet kisses, I didn't want to escape him.

I clung to him, my fingers curled in his T-shirt as I gloried in the feel of his tongue stroking mine, the hard muscles of his chest pressed against my breasts, the tingling tightness of his fingers in my hair—

My cell phone abruptly burst into song and its unwanted shrillness jerked me back into reality.

I pulled out of Cooper's hold and he reluctantly let me go.

He stared at me with narrowed eyes, his lips deliciously swollen from our kisses.

My own lips tingled as I stared back at him, openmouthed and shocked.

"Doc," he began, but I ducked my head, fumbling in my purse for my phone. By the time I got it, it had stopped ringing.

I wasn't surprised to see a missed call from Andrew. He was the only one I knew who would think to call me this late.

Guilt suffused me. I had a deal with Andrew. I wasn't supposed to be kissing anyone else. No matter how tempting he was!

I glared up at Cooper. "What the hell was that?"

He raised an eyebrow at my tone. "Something we were both enjoying."

"It came out of nowhere!"

"I think you and I both know it didn't come out of nowhere." He took a step toward me and I stumbled back. "Doc, what's stopping you from exploring this heat between us?"

"I'm on vacation, for one thing. Nothing good could possibly come of this. And . . . and . . ."

He took another step toward me, so close his chest almost brushed my body.

My knees wobbled at his nearness. I couldn't remember the last time a guy gave me wobbly knees. I didn't think a guy ever had.

I looked up at Cooper, incredulous. How could one man incite so much sexual need in me?

"And?" he said, curling my hair behind my ear, his fingers trailing gently against my skin in a way that made my nipples tighten.

It's the sea breeze! I lied to myself.

"I'm . . . uh . . . I'm sort of seeing someone."

"*Sort of* seeing someone?"

For some reason I found myself explaining. "Andrew and I aren't in a relationship because neither of us wants that, but we have agreed that while we're doing what we're doing, we won't be doing that with anyone else."

He crossed his arms over his chest and I could see the amusement in his blue, blue eyes. "Doing what exactly?"

I gave a huff of laughter. "You know what."

Cooper gave me that crooked, sexy smile again. "Doc, you do what you do and you can't say it?"

I grinned because it seemed impossible not to when he smiled at me like that. "Fine. We are having sex, only sex, but sexual monogamy."

"You're fucking."

My cheeks turned hot and I was suddenly glad for the darkness of the sky. "Yes."

He contemplated me for about thirty seconds. And that thirty seconds felt like a really long time.

"I better get home," I eventually said, taking a step back.

He nodded slowly. "I'm walking you."

"You don't have to."

"No arguments."

And since his tone brooked no argument, I didn't. Instead I fell into step beside him, completely and totally aware of him. Before the kiss I'd been aware of him. Now I was aware in that every one of my nerve endings seemed to spark at his nearness. My body was tingling, hot, and pliant. In other words it was ready for sex.

My mind, however, was in a whole mess of confusion.

If that kiss was anything to go by, sex with Cooper had the potential to be the greatest sex ever. But Cooper . . . Cooper was a bad idea. He was a no-shades-of-gray guy. At least it seemed that way.

There was that.

There was Andrew.

Plus, I didn't want a relationship so I didn't want to complicate the situation here.

So far I loved Hartwell. What if I wanted to come back next year for vacation? If I had a one-night stand with Cooper Lawson that might make things very awkward between us. And he was Bailey's friend. The awkwardness could bleed into my friendship with her. I didn't want that!

"I can practically hear your mind whirring," Cooper murmured, sounding amused.

"It is not," I argued. "I'm too tired for whirring."

"Right." He shot me a look out of the corner of his eye. "Tired? After that kiss?"

I narrowed my gaze. "Aren't we cocky."

He smirked, staring ahead as we walked down the beach toward the inn. "I know a fantastic kiss when I share one with someone."

My insides went mushy at the compliment. I was glad he'd felt the zinging between us, too. No! I wasn't. Damn it. I scowled. "It was pleasant enough."

Cooper threw his head back in laughter. "Right. You keep telling yourself that, Doc."

I decided from there it was better if I just kept my mouth shut. Speaking to him only confused me more.

The silence was thick with sexual tension as we made our way back up onto the boardwalk near the inn. Every time his arm accidentally brushed mine it was like his touch sent signals to my breasts, and my breasts sent shooting tingles down my stomach to between my thighs.

It was ridiculous!

"I can take it from here," I said, my voice a little hoarse with desire.

Cooper's eyes swung to my face. There was a sudden tautness to his features, like he knew exactly what I was feeling, and was frustrated by it. By me.

That became clearer when he seemed to shake his head in irritation and continued on to the inn. He walked me right to the front door, and as I turned to say good night he placed two hands on the door by my head, trapping me.

I sucked in a breath, not sure I would stop him if he tried to kiss me again and wondering what the hell that was about.

Cooper leaned in, his warm breath whispering across my lips. "This isn't over, Doc."

And before I could reply to that, he jerked away from me and was striding off the porch and away from the inn.

I stared after him, in shock.

Oh boy.

How the hell was I supposed to resist temptation if temptation had every intention of being irresistible?

TEN

Jessica

It was fair to say that I was pretty worked up by the time I got into bed after my eventful evening and I had no other choice but to take care of myself.

Unfortunately, I couldn't even control my fantasies and so when I came it was to an image of Cooper Lawson thrusting inside of me.

My sleep after that was fitful and I woke up in the early hours of the morning, just as the sun was rising. Feeling restless and unsettled, I showered and dressed, deciding to take a calming walk on the beach. Kind of like the walk I'd intended to have the previous night before Cooper showed up with the intention of kissing me.

That was hot.

And romantic.

Just appearing like that and pulling me into his arms.

Nothing like that had ever happened to me before.

No! Stop! Not romantic. Not hot!

Liar.

I groaned at my increasing confusion over the situation as I departed from the inn.

The beach was quiet. In fact, I could see only one woman with her dog way up ahead.

As I strolled along the shoreline, my sandals in one hand, the breeze blowing my hair off my face and cooling the heat in my skin, I began to relax again.

My gaze was fixed on the ocean because there was something soothing about its rhythmic waves, but the dog barking brought my head around.

I saw the golden retriever bounding away from the woman in the opposite direction, heading toward a man who'd appeared around the bend in the beach. He was running along the shoreline. I smiled as he stopped running to pay attention to the dog, kneeling down to his haunches to pet and play with the animal.

Something about the guy was familiar, and the closer I got, the faster my heart started to thump in my chest.

He looked up as the dog's owner jogged over to him.

Shit.

Cooper.

I contemplated turning around, but just at that moment he looked in my direction.

My stubborn pride refused to allow me to be deterred from my calming, soothing, relaxing walk on the beach because of him.

I kept walking toward him.

The woman appeared to be chatting to Cooper as he played with her dog, and the closer I got to them, I realized there were a lot of flirty grins being exchanged.

My stomach flipped unpleasantly.

See, I told myself, *this is why you don't complicate things. It's not like you're any different to him than any other woman.*

I was nearing him when I started to panic.

Should I say hello and keep walking?

Should I stop to say hello?

Cooper looked up at me as the woman continued to talk and I couldn't work out what his expression meant so I decided to go with a nod of hello and keep walking.

As I passed I heard the woman say, "We should have dinner again. Maybe tonight?"

Disappointment flooded me as I picked up speed, not wanting to hear his answer. So Golden Retriever Woman was one of his "women." I got it. And the night before, he'd been trying to add me to the list.

Jerk.

"Well, that was a little rude."

I jumped as he suddenly appeared at my side. He wore a T-shirt and jogging pants, and the T-shirt was soaked with sweat. "Do you ever sleep?" I blurted out, thinking about how late he worked, how early he apparently rose, and the myriad of women in his bed rotation.

He ignored my question. "Why didn't you stop to say hello?"

I scowled out at the water. "You were busy. I didn't want to interrupt."

"What if I wanted you to interrupt?"

I snorted and smirked up at him. "Oh, you really looked like you wanted me to interrupt."

Cooper's blue, blue eyes lit up. "You're jealous."

Infuriated, I could barely get the words out at first. "Jealous? What? Why I would be jealous?"

"You thought I was flirting and it bothered you," he said, looking smug.

"It did not bother me."

"Leanne is just a friend."

"Yeah. Right. Like the kind of friend you wanted me to be last night."

"I had intended only to walk you back to the inn last night. What happened—"

"Shouldn't have. You're right. But thank you for seeing me home," I added, not wanting to be impolite since apparently his intentions had been honorable.

So what had the parting shot meant? *This isn't over, Doc.*

"Home?" Cooper said.

"Sorry?"

"Home. You said that last night, too. You called the inn 'home.'"

I blinked, surprised, not even realizing I'd done that. "A slip. I meant back to my room. Thank you."

"You're welcome."

He stared down at me with warmth in his eyes and with him all sweaty, his T-shirt clinging to his muscles, I was suddenly very aware of how big and masculine he was.

My fantasy came flooding back and I flushed. "You can go back to running now, if you want."

He grinned. "I will. But first . . . I was thinking just because you have a man doesn't mean we can't be friends, right?"

Confused by his sudden change of demeanor I had to wonder if this was a trick. But why would a guy like Cooper, who could get practically any woman he wanted, have to resort to tricking me into spending time with him? And if it wasn't a trick could I risk the temptation? Being friends meant interacting with him for the rest of my vacation. That wasn't a lot of days, but it was enough.

I stared into his rugged face, getting caught in those blue eyes.

"Right," I said.

Oh, crap.

"It's my day off tomorrow. Have you been to the fun park yet?"

"The fun park?"

Cooper recognized the uncertainty on my face. "We're in our thirties, not dead."

I laughed at his teasing, totally surprised that Mr. Flannel, alpha man, bar owner extraordinaire, wanted to take me to a fun park. "What about the Devlins?"

His expression grew serious and I wanted to kick myself for bringing it up. "Bailey filled you in."

"Just a little," I hurried to assure him.

"Don't worry. She didn't tell you anything the rest of the town wouldn't fill you in on sooner or later."

"Right. Small town. I just didn't think you would want to spend time at one of their establishments."

"If I made that a rule I'd have very few places to go to in this town. They own a lot of real estate."

"So I've been told." I studied him, not completely convinced by his offer of friendship. "You really want to spend the day at a fun park with me?"

"I wouldn't ask if I didn't," he said, all gruff about it.

It was kind of cute and hot at the same time. How'd he do that? Damn.

I should not spend time with this man when I was fantasizing about spending *naked* time with this man. "Great. I'll see you tomorrow then."

"Great." He threw me that sexy, crooked, and now cocky grin as he started to jog backward. "See you tomorrow, Doc."

I stared after him as he turned and began jogging in the opposite direction.

"What are you doing, Doc?" I murmured to myself.

"Thanks for letting me spend the morning here," I said to Emery as I stopped at the front desk of the bookstore on my way out.

After returning to the inn, I'd forced breakfast past the butterflies in my belly and then walked to Emery's for some much-needed quiet.

For the fourth time since I'd arrived in Hartwell I'd snuggled up on an armchair in Emery's and whiled away my time reading. As always Emery was quiet, but every time I visited with her she said a few more words. I was starting to think she was becoming comfortable with me.

"I still can't believe Emery Saunders talks to you," Bailey had said at breakfast when I mentioned where I was going. "She looks like a frightened rabbit when I try to talk to her."

I'd contemplated Bailey and her disgruntlement. "Let me guess—you brought up her shyness to her?"

Bailey had made a face as she collected my dirty plate from the breakfast table. "I only suggested she not be so shy around me. It's me. I'm not scary."

Snorting, I'd stood up to leave. "I used to be pretty shy as a teenager. I can tell you for a fact that someone as outgoing as you telling a shy person not to be shy around her just makes her even more insecure about her shyness."

Looking horrified, Bailey had whispered, "Fuck."

I'd patted her shoulder. "You meant well."

"Don't. I messed up." She'd cocked her head to the side in thought. "Maybe I should come with you and try to rectify it." She'd taken in my expression and sighed. "Maybe not."

In truth Emery reminded me of an abused animal. She'd take patience and gentle coaxing until she'd trust me enough to be a friend. Unfortunately, I wouldn't be in Hartwell long enough to do that. Or long enough to get to the bottom of why someone like Emery was so closed off.

"You're welcome," Emery said to me and gave me a gentle smile.

I smiled back, feeling a pang of longing as I wandered out of her store.

The thought of not being in Hartwell for very much longer upset me. I didn't know if it was normal to feel that way about leaving your vacation spot or if the feeling ran deeper than the usual back-to-work blues.

For now I shook it off because I had other things on my mind. Or a person on my mind. A person who was giving me prehistoric-dragonfly-sized butterflies in my stomach.

Huh. Say "prehistoric-dragonfly-sized butterflies" five times fast.

The quiet time at Emery's hadn't worked to distract me so I decided to head to Antonio's for ice cream. On the way I spotted Vaughn Tremaine standing outside the entrance to his hotel, typing away on his phone. I almost considered turning back around.

It was childish of me, but I didn't know how to interact with Vaughn, considering Bailey disliked him so much. I felt it would be better in my short stay there to just avoid him completely.

But there was no avoiding him now.

"Dr. Huntington." He looked up from his phone and I stopped to be polite.

"Mr. Tremaine."

He gave me that wolfish grin of his. "So you're Bailey's guest."

"And friend now, too." I thought I'd make that clear.

"I bet you are."

"And what does that mean?"

"Just that Miss Hartwell has a habit of turning strangers into family. That's why people return to her inn every year."

I studied him, alerted by something in his tone that he couldn't quite hide. "You admire her."

Tremaine gave me a smirk. "I'm just amazed that someone with that much apparent charm and warmth can be sharper tongued and colder than the Snow Queen."

"Descriptive," I said dryly. "But that's my friend you're talking about, Mr. Tremaine."

"Actually the woman I'm talking about is the one who has pitted an entire town against me because unlike the rest of them I refuse to divulge every aspect of my private life like we're living in an episode of *The Real World*."

"Ooh, watch, you're showing your age there."

He grinned at me. "Bailey's rubbing off on you."

"Nope, all me."

"Well, I can see why you're friends . . . but a warning, Dr. Huntington"—he stepped closer, the humor fleeing his expression—"Bailey Hartwell and her town like their openness. They don't like secrets."

Chilled, I tried to hide my sudden shiver.

Tremaine stepped back. "We city folk . . . we like our secrets, don't we?"

What the hell . . . There was no way Vaughn Tremaine knew my secrets . . . "What does that mean exactly?"

What did he know?

"It's just a friendly warning. If you have anything you don't want these people to know, then it's better not to get attached to them."

"What the hell are you talking about?" My heart was racing.

He gave me a small smile. "I don't know your secrets, Dr. Huntington," he assured me. "But from your reaction, I now know you have them."

"What kind of game are you playing?" I crossed my arms over my chest defensively, because suddenly I felt very vulnerable.

I was surprised then when a look of contrition entered his usually steely eyes. "No game. I promise. I just . . . It's easy to get swept up in the charm of this place and forget that these people are only loyal to their own. I wouldn't like to see anyone get hurt."

There was something sincere in his voice that eased me. But also something telling. Had Vaughn Tremaine been hurt by the people of Hartwell? Was it possible for someone like him to be hurt?

Just then I thought it might be.

So I nodded my silent thanks, and he nodded at me in return. I walked away feeling as if I'd just caught a glimpse of a man that Bailey refused to see.

Bailey eyed me suspiciously the next morning. "Why are you being so cagey about what you're doing today?"

Avoiding the question, I laughed. "People are right . . . you don't like secrets."

"What people?" She frowned. "Did Tremaine say that? When did he say that to you? You shouldn't listen to a man who is morally defunct. Morally defunct, I tell you!"

Covering my laughter, I just shrugged, not wanting to fuel her fire.

The bell above the front door to the inn tinkled before she could question me further, and we both turned.

I lost my breath a little at the sight of Cooper striding toward us.

Did he seem even taller today?

"Coop," Bailey said, happy to see him as always. "What brings you here?"

He cut me a look and I couldn't tell if it was annoyed or amused. "Doc didn't tell you?"

"Tell me what?"

"I'm taking her out for the day."

Bailey's eyes grew round as they swung to me. A little smirk played around her mouth. "No. The doc did not tell me."

"I was going to," I lied.

"Oh, of course . . . after all the evasion." She smiled sweetly and turned back to Cooper. "So where are you taking my Jessica?"

"The fun park."

"Good choice!" Bailey hit his shoulder playfully. "I haven't been there in an age. Tom says I'm too old."

"No such thing, sweetheart," Cooper assured her.

She flicked a glance back at me. "So this is a date?"

"No," I hurried to say, noting that Cooper hadn't denied it.

Hmm.

That made Bailey grin harder. "Sure."

"Ready to go?" Cooper asked me.

I nodded, definitely ready to get away from Bailey's teasing.

"Some advice—avoid Myrtle's Shooting Range because that's a fix." She followed us to the door. "And don't eat too much of Hilly's candy floss because I'm pretty sure there is alcohol in it—otherwise, that was the weirdest sugar high I've ever had—and don't try making out on the Shake because you'll pull something in your neck."

I felt an unexpected thrill at the idea of making out with Cooper again and shot Bailey a glower for putting the thought in my head. "It's not a date, Bailey."

Cooper smirked and gently guided me out the door.

We walked quickly down the porch, hurrying (well, I was) to get away from her.

"Sure thing!" she called, following us out. "But just in case, Cooper, don't feel her up anywhere near Old Patty's Psychic Tent . . . for an apparent free spirit she sure is a prude!"

"Is Old Patty still alive?" Cooper called back, completely oblivious to the fact that I was flushing at the thought of his big hands touching me, and plotting a thousand ways to kill Bailey without getting caught.

"She's been alive since my ancestors founded this place."

Cooper just grunted at the joke and opened the garden gate for me.

"Have fun on your date!" Bailey shouted. Really loudly.

"It's not a date," I snapped back, ignoring Cooper's laughter.

"*Right*," she said as she turned to go back into the inn.

"Are you sure she's thirty-three?" I said as we walked down the boardwalk.

Cooper shook his head. "Bailey Hartwell hit eighteen and decided she was done growing up."

I laughed lightly and we walked on in silence for a little bit.

"Wouldn't have her any other way, though," he suddenly said.

I liked that.

A lot.

"Me neither."

We shared a warm look, one that put far too much heat in my blood, and then we continued on in silence.

I felt guilty for enjoying the idea of Bailey's suggestive comments. Andrew had texted me, something that was supposed to be sexy, and I guess from the right person probably would be, but I'd felt embarrassed by it—embarrassed and guilty—and I hadn't texted him in return. I should not have been having hot thoughts about another man when I couldn't even text my current friend with benefits back.

Plus—I glanced surreptitiously up at Cooper—I couldn't let myself get carried away here. The reason this was *not* a date was because Cooper was all wrong for me.

There was no forgetting the way he'd reacted to the apology in Sarah's letters.

That reaction was still there, still bothering me, despite Bailey's explanation.

And yet . . . this . . . right then with him . . . oh, this was nice.

As on the morning we'd met, we walked to the fun park in silence and it was good. There was no awkwardness, no feeling like we needed to fill the quiet with mundane conversation. It was easy and it felt great.

Despite our hot interlude the other night, there was peace in walking with Cooper Lawson.

The truth was, my feelings for him (and despite all my misgivings I had to admit I did have feelings for him) were only compounded by how strangely detached I was beginning to feel about my life back in Wilmington. There was so much warmth in Hartwell. So much warmth directed at me.

I felt connected here.

And in all honesty I selfishly didn't want to talk to anyone back in Wilmington for fear of breaking whatever spell I seemed to be under in Hartwell.

That meant I didn't want to text Andrew back.

For that reason and another.

That being . . . that the only thing that would make walking beside Cooper better was if he were holding my hand.

Damn.

I really was all tangled up inside.

Of course I'd seen the big roller coaster and other rides towering up behind the boardwalk, but I hadn't actually gone near the park yet. The gates were old-fashioned and had a huge arch over them with *Ocean Blue Fun Park* painted on it. Ticket booths were set up on either side of the gates. Beyond the gates we could hear laughter and screams, announcing the place was already busy. The season had kicked in, so that wasn't a surprise. The smells of vendor food, like hot dogs and burgers and the sweet thickness of candy floss, were stronger here than on the boardwalk because the sea air wasn't so dominant this far back from the boards.

I had to admit I was a little excited.

"Hey, Mr. Lawson," the young girl at the ticket booth said as we approached. She was a pretty, fresh-faced blonde who looked like she was still in high school.

"Hey, Angela. How's your mom doing?"

"She's real good, thanks." She beamed at him and I'm not sure I didn't see a little hero worship there. "She was so grateful you fixed her car."

"My pleasure." He shrugged. "Two adults." He slipped money to her before I could protest.

Her eyes flicked to me and I saw the speculation. She gave him the tickets, passed him change, and wished him a good day without looking at me again.

Huh.

"Are you a mechanic, too?" I said as we walked into the park.

"I was until I was twenty-one and old enough to work at the bar."

"Is she a neighbor?"

"Who, Angela? Nah, she's my sister's best friend's kid. Her dad walked out about a year ago, leaving them in a tough place. Last thing they needed was garage bills so I helped out."

Now I got the hero worship.

"That was nice of you."

Considerate.

Thoughtful.

Damn.

He didn't respond.

"Also nice was buying my ticket, but since you bought the tickets, I'm paying for food."

"Okay."

"What? No argument?" Andrew always argued about paying for stuff. We didn't go out a lot, but there were times we had to grab food or order takeout and he always threw a fit if I tried to pay. I let him win for an easy life, but it irritated me.

Cooper stopped in the middle of the walkway. "I don't need to shoulder all the financial responsibilities of our day together to feel like a man, Doc. I buy tickets, you buy the food, seems like a fair trade. I like that you offered. Hasn't happened to me a lot."

God, did he have to be so frickin' perfect! I smirked so he couldn't see that such an innocent comment somehow had the power to give me the dirty kind of tingles. "Well, I can't be the first woman to offer to pay on a . . ." I trailed off, having almost used the *d* word.

His blue eyes brightened with humor, but he graciously let my slip pass. "Believe it or not, you are the first."

"Your wife never paid?" I blurted out before considering he might not like talking about her.

"*Ex*-wife," he said. "And I'm pretty sure Dana thought a purse was purely an accessory."

I marveled at the lack of bitterness in his voice but decided to move us off the subject anyway in case he was hiding the bitter.

"So." I stopped and gaze around us. "What ride do you recommend first?"

"I think we should dive right in." He pointed to the big roller coaster.

My stomach flipped as I stared up at it.

Suddenly Cooper was blocking my view of it and I looked up to find him frowning down at me. "We don't have to go on it if you're scared of roller coasters."

That was nice.

He was nice.

"I've never actually been on one," I said, feeling I could admit that without him asking too many questions.

Cooper looked surprised. "Never?"

"Never had the opportunity."

He contemplated me for a second or two. "Don't tell me life has been all work and no play?"

My smile was more than a little rueful. "You know, ever since I got here I'm starting to think that might be the case."

At that, Cooper took my hand in his and awareness shot through me. "Well, the only way to know if you'll like a roller coaster is to get on one." He started to lead me to it.

Following him, my hand automatically tightened in his and he squeezed it in answer. I felt a little in a daze as he led me because I recognized what I was feeling and I couldn't actually believe it. The last time I'd felt this aware of the opposite sex I'd been eighteen and crushing on a junior TA in my organic chemistry class at Northwestern. He'd been the first guy I'd slept with and the first guy I thought I could really fall for, but I . . . I wasn't in a good place back then. I was just a kid and I blew it.

It was a sudden overwhelming realization that Cooper made me feel not only like a teenager again but like a teenager in danger of falling head over heels.

Cooper, completely oblivious to my inner *Holy fuck* moment, showed our tickets to the ride operator and we stopped to wait in line.

That was when I went back to thinking about the roller coaster. I had serious butterflies.

For God's sake, you've saved people's lives . . . You can get on a freaking roller coaster!

"You sure you're okay?" Cooper suddenly asked.

"Yeah. Why?"

"Because you're cutting off the circulation to my hand."

"Oh, God." Mortified, I let go of it. "I'm sorry."

He immediately took hold of it again. "We don't have to get on it."

"I should try," I insisted.

He squeezed my hand, seeming to approve, and we waited in silence as I stewed on my nerves.

Finally the ride finished and customers got out, most laughing and happy, which put me at ease a little. Cooper helped me into the ride and we strapped in.

He chuckled as I triple-checked we were safely locked in tight.

When the coaster started to roll forward, bumping us a little bit, I wondered what all the fuss was about.

Then of course it picked up speed and suddenly it felt like I was flying through the air, rattling down steep hills at super speed and then roaring back upward and looping around and down again and up, ever faster, faster, the sea flashing into view, then the town, then the sky, then the sea again, faster, faster, faster . . .

I was air.

I was free.

I was exhilarated.

By the time the ride came to a stop my cheeks were hurting I was grinning so hard.

Cooper laughed as he helped me out of the car. "I take it you liked that."

"It was wonderful." I couldn't stop grinning.

He chuckled again and took my hand, leading me away.

"Can we do it again?"

"Yeah." His voice shook with amusement. "Let's try some other stuff, though. I'm getting the feeling you've never been to a fun park."

"You would be correct."

Next up he took me to the shooting range, the one Jessica said was a fix.

Since Cooper won me a bear the first go, I was thinking she was wrong.

"Pick what you want," the bored teenager behind the range said when Cooper told me the prize was mine.

I stared in wonder at all the soft toys. I was well past the age of wanting a soft toy, but I loved spoiling Perry, so I'd send it to her.

That was when I spotted the perfect bear. "That one."

The bored teenager handed me the purple bear.

Cooper raised an eyebrow, warmth in his eyes.

I laughed. "It's for my goddaughter, Perry. She loves purple."

"I see."

"Thank you," I said, hugging the bear close. "I will be sure to tell her that a gallant knight won it for me to give to her."

He snorted. "Glad you're keeping it real with her, Doc."

I laughed, not even bothering to pretend to put up a fight when he took my hand again.

This certainly felt like a date, and I was suddenly reminded by his warning the other night, *This isn't over, Doc.*

It was wrong and confusing for me that I was so turned on and thrilled by the idea that this sexy man might be pursuing me. I pushed the thoughts out, preferring to bury my head in the sand so I could just enjoy my time with him.

I insisted on buying Cooper an ice cream and I was glad to see he had meant it earlier. He let me pay. We strolled through the park with our cones, the sun growing stronger as the morning wore closer to noon.

"You know, I would never have pegged you as a fun-park kind of guy."

He was quiet so long I wondered if I'd inadvertently offended him, which seemed strange since Cooper didn't strike me as the easily offended type.

A few seconds later I was relieved to see my impression had been right when he said, "I have a lot of good memories from here. Spent a lot of time here as a kid. The last time I was here I was about twenty-four."

"Why did you want to come here today?"

"For you," he said, completely serious. "I can only imagine what your life is like, Doc—the kind of responsibility you bear every day. Working in a prison infirmary can't be easy on top of that. I'm sure you've seen a lot of bad shit in your time. I wanted to take you away from all that for a few hours."

"Thank you," I said, the words soft with too much emotion. "I really appreciate it."

Too much. Much too much.

I wanted to kiss the thoughtful bastard.

"Why medicine?"

I was drawn from my inner turmoil at the abrupt question. "Why did I become a doctor?"

He nodded.

Some of that warmth I'd been feeling shriveled up at the thought of telling him the biggest reason I became a doctor. But I didn't want all the warmth to go away so I found myself needing to tell him at least a little of the truth. "I guess I wanted to make enough of a difference so that whenever I leave this world, I leave it knowing I was here. Really here. Being a doctor . . . saving someone's life . . . knowing that that person will forever remember me . . . I know I've left a mark. The kind I can be proud of."

I felt his gaze on my face and looked up at him. The look he gave me made me want to jump him. "Good reason, Doc."

I smiled because he had this wonderful habit of making me feel great about myself without even trying. I looked away before he could read in my eyes what I was feeling. "What about you? Are you happy with Cooper's?"

"It's a simple life—not a noble cause—but I'm good with it."

I caught on his words "not a noble cause" and found myself wanting to reassure him that I didn't believe everyone needed to have a noble cause to have a good life or to be a good person. "Since I was eighteen years old I've been surrounded by hungry ambition. Because of that I couldn't see any other way for the longest time. Being a surgical resident only made it worse because it's a way of life. And yet . . . not even two weeks here and I'm questioning some of those people that I've worked with and I wonder if they are as content with their lives as you and Bailey seem to be with yours. Honestly, it makes me a little envious."

Cooper drew to a halt and turned to face me. He licked his ice cream as he studied me and I studied him licking his ice cream . . . naughty, naughty thoughts entering my mind and heating my blood.

I could feel the heat in my cheeks and hoped to God he couldn't see it.

I wrenched my gaze from his mouth to his eyes and found that thankfully he was too busy with his own thoughts to recognize mine had taken a wander down "dirty sexy alley."

"You're not happy."

I frowned at his words. "I'm having a great time," I insisted truthfully.

Cooper's eyes warmed. "Glad to hear that, Doc, but I'm not talking about now. I'm talking about in general."

Uncomfortable with his observation, I turned away and started walking toward the pendulum ride.

"Jess?"

It was the first time he'd ever said my actual name instead of "Doc." For some weird reason that made me feel guilty about ignoring his probing comment. "I don't know," I suddenly said, an overwhelming melancholy settling upon me. "I don't know."

And I didn't anymore.

He was looking at me again. Really looking. Before I could start squirming at the thought of being psychoanalyzed and questioned more, he said, "This is a shit ride, Doc"—he nodded to the pendulum ride—"let's try Wipeout next."

I smiled gratefully.

"I should warn you, us being here together for dinner, there will be speculation," Cooper murmured in my ear as Iris led us to a booth in the back of Antonio's.

By the way Iris grinned at us and said, "Well, well, well," as we wandered in together I was already getting that. I gave him a look to tell him so and I saw the humor in his eyes.

"Here you go," Iris said as she laid down our menus.

We slid into opposite sides of the booth and looked up at her. She was grinning at us. Her eyes landed on Cooper. "Moving on and moving *up*, son."

Cooper didn't say anything to correct her. I didn't say anything to correct her because what she said was so nice I was internally *aww*-ing too much to do so.

"Drinks?"

"Water," Cooper said.

"Same."

"Okay. I'll be back to get your orders in a bit."

Cooper recommended the Italian hot dog so that was what we got.

"They should name this 'Dogs Go to Heaven,'" I moaned after swallowing a mouthful of deliciousness.

Cooper shook with laughter as he ate. He swallowed and said, "Ira will love that. You should suggest it for real."

I chuckled. "Will do. Once I eat this mother-effing goodness."

"Mother-effing?" He grinned.

I shrugged. "It would be inappropriate to use the actual word in a family place."

He shook with more laughter as he chewed and I felt a rush of something warm and fuzzy go through me. I liked making him laugh.

"So did you enjoy returning to the fun park?" I said.

"Yeah." He wiped his mouth with his napkin and sat back against the booth, looking content in a way a person does when he's just eaten really good food. "Because I was with you. It loses something, though, when you get older."

"I don't think it loses anything. It's us that lose something." I wondered what it was that he had lost that made the place special. Was it his ex? And why did that thought make the hot dog in my stomach turn to ash?

Cooper nodded. "You're right."

When he didn't elaborate I felt a surge of disappointment. I hoped to God he wasn't talking about his ex.

"So tell me about the bar," I said, changing the subject.

"What do you want to know?"

"How did you come to be the owner of a bar on the boardwalk? From what I hear that's prime real estate." I grinned cheekily.

He chuckled. "You been talking to the Devlins?"

"No. Bailey."

"But she's been talking about the Devlins. Everything she said is true. They're a pain in the ass."

"Have they been bothering you about the bar?"

He shrugged. "Nothing I can't handle, Doc."

I frowned at that because I hated the idea of anyone trying to disrupt the contentment Cooper seemed to have.

"The bar used to be called the Boardwalk and it was owned by my mother's brother. My great-grandparents owned it and it's been passed down since. My uncle died in a car crash when I was just a boy and he left the bar to my mom. She kept the same management on to run the place for her and then when I was twenty-one she gave it to me. I wanted to make it my own. The place was dog tired, needed a face-lift. I did all that and renamed it Cooper's. I added a menu and hired a cook and the place is doing well."

"It's hard work owning a bar."

"It's hard work owning any establishment, but at the same time I get to hang out with people I like every night."

I grinned at the way he looked at it. "So no downsides?"

"Oh, there are a few."

"Such as . . ."

He ran a hand through his hair, suddenly looking uneasy, and he leaned in closer, his voice quieter as he said, "I currently have a waitress who is constantly late for work. She's a good girl, though, just a bit of a flake. I don't want to fire her, but my bar staff has to carry her weight. I'm stuck on what to do. I've fired waitstaff before if they weren't keeping up, but Lil is different. She's a good worker when she is there, and she gets great tips. I keep going back and forth on it because I hate the thought of taking away anyone's livelihood—especially a kid who does do a good job when she actually makes it in on time."

At that moment I found myself completely lost in the blue of his eyes.

Physically this man was the most masculine, rugged man I'd ever been around. He was the complete opposite of the slim, athletic, perfectly coifed Andrew.

In more ways than one.

Andrew would fire that girl without even thinking about the consequences for her. I'd seen him make both male and female interns cry at the hospital.

Cooper didn't want to fire a girl who was hurting his business in case it hurt *her*.

God, I liked this man. I *really* liked this man.

I didn't think I kept a very good job of keeping the admiration off my face, because Cooper's eyebrows suddenly shot up in question.

I pulled back a little, clearing my throat, as I tried to regain focus. "How many times has she been late?"

"Every shift for the past two weeks."

"And she was never late before that?"

He thought about it. "Not continually like this."

"Okay, then something may have changed in her personal life. Figure out what that is and then make a decision from there."

He contemplated this. "How so?"

"Well, if she's late because she has . . . say . . . a new boyfriend or girlfriend that is distracting her, then you may have to fire her or issue a warning that she's going to get fired if she doesn't clean up her act. If there's something more serious going on—an illness in the family—then you help her work something out. It's all about context."

Cooper stared at me a moment too long . . . so long I felt myself growing warm all over. The warmth in his eyes didn't help. In fact, it was the cause of the flip low, low in my belly. "Right you are, Doc," he said, his words coming out a little thicker, a little deeper.

Quite abruptly, inexplicably, sexual tension hung in the air as we stared at one another, and I wanted to wrench myself out of the sudden spell but couldn't.

"Can I get you anything else?" Iris suddenly appeared at the booth, shattering the moment.

I breathed a deep sigh of relief and gave her a shaky, grateful grin. "All good here."

"The check, please, Iris," Cooper said.

"I'm paying," I said, reminding him.

"I know, Doc." He grinned. "Don't get your panties in a twist."

I flushed at the mention of the word "panties."

He grinned knowingly and I threw him a dirty look that only made him laugh harder.

Not five minutes later we were back on the boardwalk.

He grabbed my hand before I could stop him and the slide of his callused palm against my softer one sent a rush of images through my brain.

Those hands skimming my bare arms, fingertips tickling my spine, thumbs brushing my nipples . . .

"Let's take a walk, Doc, before I have to get you back," he said, either oblivious to what he was doing to me or deliberately prolonging my torture.

I was struck dumb by my intense sexual awareness of him, realizing the physical attraction was only growing stronger the more time I spent with him and the more I got to know him.

While I was freaking out, Cooper seemed just as at ease in our silence as always.

And then he brushed his thumb over the top of my hand and I involuntarily squeezed his in return. He looked down at me in question.

We stared at each other in silence for a few steps and I saw the heat start to darken the blue of his gaze.

His grip tightened and he bent his head closer to mine. "What's life like back in Wilmington? You got a nice place? Friends?"

"Yeah," I said. "Nice apartment. Good colleagues. Long hours, though." I looked out at the beach where people were just starting to pack up. I smiled, watching them. "It must be so nice to work all week and then head to the beach on your day off, or even head to the beach for a walk after work. Unwind."

"Yeah. I run on the beach every morning. It's a nice way to start the day," he agreed.

A pithy comment about it being a nice way to pick up women, too, trembled on my tongue, but I swallowed it, not wanting him to tease me again for being jealous.

"And then there's Emery's," I said instead. "Now that is a place to unwind."

"Emery's?" He looked surprised. "The bookstore and coffee place next to mine?"

"Yup."

"Unwind . . . there?"

I laughed at his confusion. "Yes. Emery is a very soothing person. I've been going there a lot to curl up and read and drink her amazing coffee."

"Does she talk to you?"

"Yes."

"Really?"

"You sound as surprised as Bailey."

"I am. Emery Saunders is so shy it's painful to be around her."

I noted his discomfort at even just the mention of her name. It surprised me. He seemed like the kind of man who was just cocky enough to be comfortable around all women. "She just takes a little time to come around. But her place is wonderful."

"Her coffee is definitely good, I'll give you that."

"Her coffee, Antonio's hot dogs, Bailey's view, and your Long Islands." I tallied them.

"What's that?" He grinned curiously.

"My favorite things in Hartwell so far."

"Not the people?" he teased, squeezing my hands.

I laughed because I liked how he teased me, even if it did complicate my feelings, and I teased back by not giving him an answer.

ELEVEN

Cooper

All was going according to plan.

Although Cooper hadn't intended to walk out on the beach the other night and take the kiss he'd been itching for since he'd met Jessica, he was glad he'd done it. That kiss lived up to all his expectations and not even this fuck-buddy situation she had going on with some other guy was going to stop him from getting to know her.

And while he was getting to know her, he was crumbling her defenses.

Cooper planned to seduce Jessica right out of friendship and into his bed. Permanently.

She was smart; she was sassy; she was fun and cute and sexy all wrapped up in one irresistible package. And, Jesus, she could kiss. If the kiss was anything to go by, sex between them would be explosive. More than that, Cooper liked her. He liked how he'd shared a problem with her about work and not only had she listened, she'd even given him advice.

He liked that, despite how strong she appeared, he now knew there was something really vulnerable about her. He didn't know what it was, except he'd caught a glimpse of it when he'd realized she wasn't happy. It made her less perfect, more human.

He liked how protective he'd felt in that moment and how he'd wanted to change the subject to take the sadness out of her eyes.

The strange thing was Jessica had seemed startled to consider whether or not her life made her happy.

"*I don't know*," she had said in answer to his question. "*I don't know*."

Well, Cooper knew. The doc was not happy. He could see something was missing for her. Every time she talked about her life in Wilmington she was factual, disconnected, and she quickly changed the subject. But when she spoke about Hartwell she was animated and happy.

Cooper was suspicious that Jessica Huntington was falling in love with his town—a whirlwind romance—and she didn't even know everything about it yet.

He found himself at Bailey's place a few blocks from the inn, on the north side. Bailey had arranged a big dinner for Jess since it was one of her last few days in Hartwell. Ira and Iris had joined Tom, Jess, Bailey, and him.

"When you said we were having salad I nearly died," Ira cracked at Bailey. "But this is damn good."

Bailey beamed from the head of the dining table. "I'm glad you like it, Ira."

Ira was right. The crab and apple salad with the crab cake fritters Bailey had put together for the main course was a hit.

"You have to give me the recipe for this," Jessica said.

She'd moaned at the first bite and put heat in his blood, but Cooper was getting used to that feeling around her. That last walk they'd taken on the boardwalk had been so thick with sexual tension it had taken everything within him not to throw her over his shoulder and carry her back to his place.

"Sure," Bailey agreed.

"I mean . . . not to use," Jessica said. "Just to pin it to my fridge and pretend that it's a possibility I could ever make anything this good."

"You can't cook?" Iris said, frowning at the thought.

The doc flushed a little. "Not really."

"You can save lives, but you can't cook?"

"You can cook, but you can't save lives?" Jess countered.

Iris's frowned turned to a grin as her husband chuckled at her side. "I like you. You remind me of my Ivy."

"That is a compliment of the highest order," Bailey assured the doc.

Jessica smiled that pretty smile of hers. "Thank you." But when her eyes met Cooper's across the table, that pretty smile wilted a little.

Cooper didn't take it negatively.

He knew by the jealousy she couldn't hide on the beach when she thought he was going to take Leanne up on her offer, and by the way she'd rushed to get into the inn and away from him after their nondate, that she was feeling exactly what he was feeling. She was scared shitless about it.

He thought maybe he should be, too.

But she had fired something in him, and he couldn't ignore it.

"So, Jessica," Tom said, "are you planning on returning to our little town anytime soon? I know Bailey would love that."

She gave Bailey a wistful smile. "I will definitely be back, but I work such long hours I couldn't say when. I do know that my phone bill is about to go sky-high."

Bailey gave her a sad smile. "I'm going to miss you being at my inn every day. I feel like you've been there forever."

"Me, too."

Cooper watched the friends share a long look.

It was the way of it sometimes. Like it had been for him and Jack as kids. They were friends from the moment they met.

He immediately threw the thought away.

"Coop, I went into Dr. Duggan's office the other day to see if they were looking for anyone after his daughter left. They are," Bailey said, her eyes round to playact a *Help me!* look. "And he said he'd be happy to talk to Jess about it."

The doc groaned across from Cooper. "We talked about this all day yesterday."

Cooper frowned at her downcast expression and looked sternly at Bailey. He didn't want Jess to feel coerced into staying somewhere she'd only been vacationing for three weeks. He wanted her to stay longer in Hartwell because—even if a little crazy—it felt right. "Don't."

Bailey opened her mouth to protest, but Iris cut her off. "I want the recipe for this, too. We could add it to the menu."

"You're not stealing my recipe for the restaurant," Bailey said, sufficiently diverted.

"What if we called it Bailey's crab apple salad and fritters?" Ira offered.

Bailey considered it and then shook her head. "Sorry, no. We serve this at the inn. I can't have my competition serving the same dish." She frowned. "Anyhow, it's not Italian."

"Oh, right." Iris grinned mischievously.

"Coop, I saw Cat the other day with Joey. That boy is getting bigger every time I see him," Ira said.

He felt the doc's curious gaze and answered her silent question. "My sister, Cat, and her eight-year-old son, Joey."

"Oh."

He looked back at Ira. "He's skipping a grade, did she tell you that?" he said proudly. Unfortunately, Joey's dad had been a one-night stand, a tourist whose name Cat couldn't even remember. Not so unfortunately for Cooper, that meant he got to be the man in Joey's life and it filled a hole in his own in a way that he'd be forever grateful for. His nephew was the nicest kid and he was smart as a whip.

"She did." Ira grinned. "Proud as punch. And she should be. That boy is being raised right. All 'yes, sirs' and 'no, sirs.' You don't hear that much anymore."

"And he is your spitting image, Coop," Iris said. "I swear that boy has got more of you in him than his own mother."

It was true. Joey had inherited his and Cat's blue eyes and dark hair, but he looked just like Cooper had when he was his age. Except Joey was smarter and more talented.

"Cat was saying he's doing really well with his piano lessons," Ira said.

He nodded even though that was an understatement. The kid was a little virtuoso. When he was four Cat had the piano she'd inherited from their mom tuned and refurbished because Joey was so fascinated by it. He just took to it. Cooper had offered to pay for piano lessons, and the teacher had just recently suggested Joey audition for a private tutor in Dover who had once been a tutor at the New England Conservatory and had a high success rate of getting his kids into the best music schools in the United States.

He was very picky about who he worked with and he liked to start with them when they were young like Joey.

He also didn't come cheap.

But Cooper had promised Cat he'd do whatever it took to make it work if this guy took Joey on as a student.

"Plays 'well'," Bailey scoffed at the word choice. "Ira, you should hear him play. He's eight and—" She made an exploding noise as she made a bursting gesture with her hands near her head. "Seriously. Blows my mind."

"He sounds amazing," Jessica said quietly and Cooper's gaze got all tangled up in hers again. "You must be very proud."

"The proudest," he said gruffly.

"They make everything better, don't they?" she said.

He guessed she was thinking about her goddaughter and he found himself wanting to know more about the girl, whose kid she was, and why those people meant so much to her. "Yeah," he answered instead. "They do."

"Thank you for dinner," the doc said, giving Bailey a hug. "And for everything. Best vacation ever."

"It's not over yet," Bailey said, sounding almost panicked about it. "We still have a few days."

The doc grinned at her. "That's true. We'll make the most of them."

"I'll walk you back, Doc," he offered.

Her grin wilted a little. "We all will." She gestured to Iris and Ira.

Iris smirked. "Oh, we just live a block over. We don't live at the boardwalk."

"Right. Of course." She turned back to Cooper. "You don't either, right? So I don't want you to go out of your way."

"You're not walking back to the inn alone at night, Doc. We've been over that." He grinned as she flushed at the reminder of their make-out session on the beach.

She huffed. "I'm perfectly capable of doing so."

"Not arguing about it."

"What happened to the enlightened gentleman who let me pay for dinner the other day?"

"Splitting the cost of a date is different from seeing to your safety."

"Date?" Bailey's ears perked up.

"Fine, you can walk me home," Jessica said abruptly, cutting off Bailey's curiosity. "'Bye, all!" She hurried out of the house.

Cooper was met by four amused stares. He smiled back at them and Bailey looked ready to burst with delight. She thought they were a tag team.

They weren't.

Cooper still wanted the doc to make up her own mind.

Didn't mean teasing her wasn't fun as hell.

He hurried to catch up with her outside. "Hold your horses, Doc."

She turned to wait for him. The sadness he caught on her face kicked the amusement right out of him.

They walked together toward the inn in silence until Cooper couldn't take it anymore. It needed to be talked about. "You happy back in Wilmington, Doc?"

He felt her tense beside him. She suddenly threw her hands up in seeming frustration. "I don't know, okay? I don't know. But I do know that my life *is* back in Wilmington, Cooper. My job is there. And I'm good at my job. Those women need someone like me. I made a commitment to my job that I can't just break."

"And what about you?" he argued. "What about what you need?"

Her only answer was this pained expression he didn't quite understand.

It was full of so much hurt he decided to drop it.

Silence fell between them, but the usual camaraderie he enjoyed so much between them was gone. As the moments passed, he was aware of everything about her. The heat of her body close to his, the quick rise and fall of her chest that told him she was just as affected by his closeness, the little tremble in her full bottom lip he didn't think she was even aware of.

The previous night, he'd dreamed about her.

She was in his bar like the day they'd met. No one else around but them.

He'd fucked her on top of one of the tables.

Fast. Furious.

So hot.

Cooper had woken up only to jump into the shower. He'd closed his eyes and remembered the dream as he took care of himself.

It was empty, so fucking empty, in comparison to what reality could be.

His dick tightened in his jeans thinking about it, his gaze shooting to Jessica's mouth. It was time to remind her what was possible between them.

Cooper grabbed her wrist and pushed her up against the side of Dahlia's gift shop. The alley between it and George's place was dark and silent except for their heavy breathing. He pinned her in, his hands braced on the wall at either side of her head.

Jessica stared up at him with those big, dark eyes. "Coop—"

He cut off her coming question with his mouth just like last time.

She tasted of the mint ice cream they'd had for dessert and something else. Something all Jess.

She whimpered against his kiss a second before he felt her tongue touch his and that was it.

He was lost.

His kiss turned hungry as a feeling of desperation came over him and he pressed his body down the length of hers. The lush feel of her mouth mingled with the weight of her breasts pressed to him was enough on its own to fire him up, but when she wrapped her arms around his neck and tightened her fingers in his hair to draw him closer, he was done for.

He gripped her ass in his hand, urging her closer, his dick straining against her belly. His hand slid down to the back of her thigh and he hiked one of her legs up against his hip so he could be where he needed to be, fitting snugly between her thighs.

Fuck, he wished she were wearing a skirt.

"Cooper." She breathed out his name, breaking the kiss. Her head fell back and her eyes fluttered with the sensation of him rubbing against her, mimicking sex. Her cheeks were flushed as she moaned and dug her hands into his shoulders to hold on. She flexed her hips against his and he felt his nerve endings catch fire.

He needed to be inside her.

The soft skin of her throat called to him and, as she gyrated against him, he tasted her, pressing kisses down her neck and across her collarbones. He moved his other hand down her back as his mouth reached the rise of her breasts. He brushed his thumb over the thin shirt and bra that hid them from him and groaned as her nipple visibly pebbled through the material.

If they didn't stop soon he was going to take her right there.

"Fuck." He pulled away from her abruptly and she stumbled back against the wall, looking as dazed as he felt.

All he'd wanted was a taste of her.

Now he knew for certain that just a taste would never be enough with this woman. "Tell me," he said, a little breathless, "tell me you've got this back in Wilmington, Doc."

He watched the muscle in her jaw twitch as she clenched her teeth.

She couldn't tell him.

He knew that. Because what they had between them didn't come around very often.

"Doc?" he persisted, and he learned in that moment that Jessica Huntington was not only smart and sassy but stubborn as hell.

"I can't do this"—she gestured between them—"not with you."

And she walked away.

Gutting him.

He was just asking her to think about making room in her life for him. The fact that she wouldn't even contemplate it for a second, when his blood was on fire with need for her and his mind was on her most hours of the day, was like a gaping wound.

Strangely, the pain fired his determination. Jessica Huntington was lying to herself. Cooper didn't know why, but he was going to find out.

By then the doc would be in his bed.

Right where they both knew she belonged.

TWELVE

Jessica

"Are . . . are you okay, Jessica?"

I glanced up from staring at the unlit hearth in Emery's bookstore to find Emery standing over me, staring down at me with concern in her eyes.

"I don't know," I answered honestly.

She looked away, seeming uncertain, and then she drew in a huge breath and turned back to me. "Do you want to talk about it?"

I smiled at her generous offer. "It's about a man."

Her eyes lit up with curiosity. "A love affair?"

"Maybe."

Emery sat down across from me, looking more eager than I'd ever seen her. "Unrequited love?"

"Nope." I shook my head. "I walked away from a man last night who wants to explore the chemistry between us."

"Is he a not good man?"

"He appears to be a very good man." *Too good for me.*

"So what's the problem?"

"Well, there is the fact that I don't live here and he does. But the biggest problem is that he doesn't know me like I think he thinks he does. There is this possibility that he has built me up in his head as something I'm just not and if he ever found out who I really am"—my chest hurt at the thought—"I'd lose him." I immediately braced myself. I hadn't meant to say so much and I didn't want to answer the inevitable questions.

Yet, I shouldn't have been surprised when Emery just nodded. "You think that if you leave now before things between you get more intense, then it won't hurt as much as it would if he left you down the line."

I relaxed at her complete understanding of the situation. "Exactly."

She gave me a sad smile. "I wish I could give you a huge dose of encouragement, but I think it would make me too much of a hypocrite. I'd probably do exactly what you're doing."

In that moment I temporarily forgot my own problems as it occurred to me this was the most I'd ever gotten out of Emery. My curiosity, as always, was piqued. What was it that she was hiding? I felt a kinship with her I couldn't explain and my fear for her was that our kinship came from a similarly dark place in our pasts.

God, I hoped not. Emery Saunders seemed like such a sweet soul.

"When do you leave?" she suddenly asked.

I felt a pang in my chest again, this one at the thought of putting Hartwell behind me. "In a few days."

"You like it here," she observed.

"Very much."

"What do you like about it?"

That was something I found difficult to put into words. Finally I said softly, "I feel at peace here."

Emery gave me a slow, sad smile. "That's why I like it, too."

The poignant moment between us was broken when the bell over her door jingled and Bailey was suddenly there, hurrying up the steps to the reading area. Her eyes widened a little at the sight of Emery sitting with me. Emery immediately popped up from her seat.

"Emery," Bailey said with a soft smile. "How are you?"

Emery returned her smile with a shy one of her own. "Good, thank you. And you?"

Bailey tried to hide her surprise. "I'm good, too. It's nice to see you."

"Oh. You, too."

Bailey threw herself down on the sofa beside me as Emery hurried off, busying herself down in the bookstore. "Wow. She actually responded to me."

I smiled as if to say, *I told you so.*

She scowled at me suddenly. "What happened last night between you and Cooper?"

What the hell? How did she even know something had happened? I sighed heavily. "I had the most intense make-out session of my life."

"Well . . ." She made a face. "Isn't that a good thing? The 'most intense make-out session' thing . . . that's good, right?"

"No. That's not good. I'm going back to Wilmington in a few days."

Bailey narrowed her eyes on my face. "Do you realize you never call it 'home'?"

"What?"

"You never say, 'I'm going home.' You never call Wilmington *home*."

When I didn't say anything, because I wasn't sure what I could say, Bailey continued. "I don't think you're happy there, Jess."

Not this again!

Was I wearing a neon sign that said, "I'm Jessica Huntington and I'm incredibly unhappy!"?

"I'm not moving to Hartwell for a guy I barely know," I said defensively and as a diversion tactic.

It didn't work.

She glowered at me. "This isn't about Cooper. If Hartwell is a big old cake you want to eat but are denying yourself, Cooper is just the cherry on the cake."

"What?"

She sighed dramatically. "I'm not saying this because I found a good friend I really don't want to lose. I'm saying this because in the short time that we've gotten really close you hardly ever talk about Wilmington or about your job there. Most people I know talk about their job nearly all the time or about where they live. Not you, Jess. It's like it makes you sad to even think about it. So my questions are: Are you happy there? And are you happy being a doctor?"

Fear made my chest tight and I felt my breathing come short and fast. I lay back against the sofa and started breathing slow and easy.

"Jess, are you okay?"

I waved her off. "I'm fine. I'll be okay."

Bailey waited patiently by my side. When I finally felt like I'd gotten over my minor panic attack, I looked at her and gave her the same honesty I'd given Cooper. "I don't know if I'm happy. But I'm good at my job. Plus I made a commitment there. I need to go back."

She looked suddenly outraged. "Even if you're not happy?"

"Bailey, we aren't kids anymore. Sometimes we have to do things that we don't like. That's life."

"No, that's being a martyr," she argued. "We all have to do things we don't like, you're right. And a lot of people don't have a choice. They work crappy jobs and live in crappy homes because that's all they'll ever have and they don't have the strength or the opportunity to reach for more. But you're not one of those people, Jessica. You're educated. You're strong. You have friends here. You have options. You don't have to work in a prison infirmary if you don't want to. You don't have to live in a town you don't like if you don't want to. So tell me this: why do you feel like you don't deserve to be happy?"

I sucked in a breath, shocked as hell at her perceptiveness.

I swallowed hard because now that Bailey knew I had a secret, it was game over in Hartwell for me. I would never be able to withstand interrogations about my personal life.

I shook my head, trying to keep the pain out of my eyes.

Whatever Bailey saw there made her expression soften. "It is never too late to change the road that you're on. I have never believed that you need a fancy-ass career and a fancy-ass house to be happy.

In fact, if Vaughn Tremaine is an example of that, then I'm right. Good people, Jess, good people are what makes somewhere a home. I don't know your story and frankly I really don't need to because I know *you*. I also know you don't have a home and there is absolutely no shame in wanting that more than anything else. No matter what age you are."

I fought the tears burning in the back of my eyes at her kind words.

They confused the hell out of me. More than that, they put me at war with myself.

"Your fuck buddy is currently sitting in my reception area," Bailey said abruptly.

Confused, it took me a moment to make sense of what she'd said. Then a jolt of surprise, and not pleasant surprise, had me on my feet. "Andrew is here?"

"Yup." She stood up to follow me out. "By the way, what do you see in that guy?"

"Emery, I've got to go," I said, ignoring Bailey as we passed the bookstore counter.

Emery frowned and asked, "Will I see you before you leave?"

Warmth supplanted some of the unpleasant surprise from its hold on my chest. "Definitely. I promise."

We shared a smile and said good-bye. Two seconds later I was hurrying up the boardwalk.

"Wow, she really does talk to you. And likes you. See! That there is a sign, Jessica Huntington. Emery Saunders has owned that place for seven years and has never befriended any of the locals. But you . . . you she befriends. That's a sign!"

I found myself chuckling because as confused as I was about my life, I couldn't complain about the fact that Bailey and Emery liked me enough to want me to stick around.

"Back to my earlier question: what on earth do you see in that Andrew guy?"

"It's as simple as his hot body."

"I'm not sure even that's worth having to deal with him."

"We understand each other." That was partly true. The bigger truth, I realized, was that Andrew kept me tied to something safe and cold.

I felt comfortable in my unemotional relationship with him. Whereas true contentment was never something I had allowed myself to strive for. It all came down to protecting myself—and not allowing anything else to throw my world into chaos.

A few hours later I found myself walking down Main Street with Andrew at my side. When I'd gotten to the inn I wanted to stomp my foot like a small child and demand to know why he was infiltrating my vacation. I didn't do that, but I wasn't exactly offering a warm welcome.

Instead I was shocked by the way he hugged me and said, "I was worried when you didn't answer my text. I have no surgeries today or tomorrow so I thought I'd come check on you."

In other words he wanted to get laid.

But the simple idea of having sex with him left me uncomfortable.

And I couldn't shake that feeling.

Plus the more time we spent together in Hartwell that day, the more annoying he became.

"I can't believe you came here for a vacation." He made a face as we walked down Main Street. "Seriously, Jessica . . . if you wanted a real vacation I would have taken you to Bora-Bora."

In order not to have a public fight, I kept silent as he suggested we walk back to the inn. Obviously he was done seeing the sights of Hartwell.

And that was when things went from bad to worse.

As we were walking by the park my eyes swung past the shirtless guy who appeared to be replacing the steps up to the bandstand. And then they swung back because I recognized his profile.

Shit.

Cooper.

He stood up, grabbing a bottle of water, and my throat went thirsty just watching him drink it. Holy crap.

Shirtless Cooper with his impressive abs was a sight to behold. And then there was the way the tool belt around his hips dragged a little on his jeans, but not quite enough to give me a glimpse of his ass. That was a shame. A crying shame.

His Adam's apple bobbed as he drank the water and I became mesmerized by a bead of sweat that rolled down his neck and over his chest. I had the sudden urge to run my hands all over him.

I hadn't thought it was possible to get that turned on just looking at a man.

"Do you know him?" Andrew's curt voice yanked me out of my lust fog.

"Oh . . . Well—"

"Doc?"

I froze at Cooper's voice and nodded at Andrew. "Yup," I said before looking back over at Cooper. He stood with a hand above his eyes, shading them from the sun so he could see me.

Caught, I had no recourse but to walk over to him with Andrew at my side.

Cooper's gaze flicked to Andrew and as we came to a stop in front of him he dropped his hand. His eyes remained narrowed on my companion.

"What are you doing?" I gestured to the bandstand steps.

He continued to stare at Andrew, who was eyeing him with suspicion. "Last time the bandstand was used they dropped a piano they were trying to remove. Piano was busted and so were a few of the stairs. I said I'd fix it. So I'm fixing it."

Bartender, mechanic, carpenter . . . was there anything this man couldn't do with his hands?

Stop thinking about his hands.

I cleared the lust out of my throat before I said, "You're very handy, aren't you?"

What?

Why would you mention his hands?

I flushed immediately when Cooper looked at me, eyes bright with amusement and not a little bit of flirtation. "You have no idea."

And . . . mini orgasm.

Andrew cleared his throat in an attempt to break the staring match between me and Cooper. It worked. I turned to him, shamefaced.

"Aren't you going to introduce me?" he said.

No.

"Cooper Lawson." Cooper held out his hand to him.

Andrew stared at it a moment and I swore right then I'd slap him across the head if he didn't take Coop's hand. I sighed inwardly when he did. "Dr. Andrew Livingston."

I saw Cooper visibly tense before he shot me a now very *not* amused look out of the corner of his eye. I felt guilty even though I hadn't invited Andrew to Hartwell.

"Well, it was nice to meet you," Andrew said, sliding his arm around my shoulders. "But Jessica and I really need to be going."

I allowed him to lead me away, guilt churning in my stomach. That feeling only worsened when I looked back to find Cooper staring after us. And he was definitely not a happy handyman.

As Andrew and I strolled back to the inn I had to fight the urge to run back to Cooper, to explain, even though I knew it was for the best if he started to hate me.

But I didn't want him to hate me.

Yet he was probably back there fixing those steps, frustrated with me, while other women drooled over him. They were probably all way less complicated than I was and—

Stop!

I was in knots. And it had to stop. First I had to deal with Andrew.

"Why are you really here?" I finally got up the courage to ask as we walked up the porch steps to the inn.

He pushed open the door but stopped to face me as we stood inside the empty reception area. "It's time we changed our relationship. Into an actual relationship. No more messing around, Jessica. This time apart has given me perspective. We're getting too old for our ridiculous behavior. It's time to settle down."

The thought made me feel equal amounts of panic and irritation. It was just like him to make this momentous decision without me.

I'd just opened my mouth to say so when Bailey came hurrying in from the dining area. "Mona is going to cover for me this evening so I thought you, Tom, and I could take Andrew out for drinks at Cooper's."

The thought made my stomach churn. I glowered at Bailey. Why was she doing this? "I don't think—"

"I need a scotch after the day I've had," Andrew said, apparently not registering Cooper's name in what she'd said. "Why don't we take a *nap* before that?"

As in sex.

Nope.

I just couldn't, I realized.

"Why don't you go *nap*"—I handed him my room key—"and I'll meet you back here in a bit. I promised I'd help Emery out with something at her store."

I was gone before he could protest.

In fact, I'd never moved quicker in my life.

While I was pulling my phone out of my purse, I noted that the gift store owned by Bailey's friend was open. It hadn't been open that morning when I'd passed.

Dahlia must be back.

As soon as I could, I really wanted to meet her. Bailey spoke so highly of her.

Except you are leaving soon. So why does it matter?

Slipping my shoes off, I walked down from the boards onto the beach. I didn't stop until I'd found a quiet spot on the south end of the mile, away from the view of the inn and from other tourists.

I sat down on the sand and pressed speed-dial number 1 on my phone.

After a few rings, Matthew picked up. "Jess, everything okay, sweetheart?"

I immediately relaxed at his voice. "Is this a bad time?"

"No, I'm just finishing up for the day. You don't sound so good. What happened? Last time we spoke you were having a great time."

"What if being a doctor doesn't actually make me happy? What if I've just convinced myself it does? What do I do?"

"Oh, God, Jess . . . I've told you before . . . you do what makes you happy."

"Isn't it ridiculous, though, to be questioning this at thirty-three years old?" I laughed at the absurdity of it. "I feel so fucking lost, Matthew."

He was silent for a while and then: "You've been lost for a long time, Jessica."

The mere mention of the past made me clam up. I didn't talk about it, not even with Matthew, the only person who knew the truth.

He sighed at my silence. "Tell me what's going on."

"I need to know," I said, the words coming without me even realizing it was what I was going to say, "that if I decide to start over somewhere new, you won't think that's crazy. Because right now I feel crazy even considering it."

"Okay . . . are we talking about starting over in Hartwell?"

I shrugged and then remembered I was on the phone and he couldn't see me. "Maybe. I guess what's important is that I've come to realize I'm not happy in Wilmington. I keep fighting with that truth . . . except it is the truth. I thought things were going the way they should"—the way I deserved—"but maybe it's time to grow the fuck up and live the life I want, right?"

"Yes," he said vehemently. "God, yes, Jess."

"I mean, I hate the idea of leaving the women in the prison, because I'm a good doctor to them."

"I know it."

"But maybe it's time to put myself first. Maybe?"

"Not maybe, Jess. Definitely. I cannot tell you how happy I am to hear you say this."

"So you don't think it's crazy and irresponsible and immature and—"

"No. None of that. Sometimes life just doesn't work out the way you hoped and no matter what age you are there comes a time to change it. I have a forty-year-old man working as an intern in my office. He was a dentist for fifteen years and he decided one day he was miserable and that he wanted to start over."

"Really? You're not making that up to make me feel better?"

"His name is Mike Lowery. I can put him on the phone if you want."

I laughed. "Okay, I believe you."

We were silent for a while.

"I can hear the waves," he said softly.

I stared out along the stretch of sand. "It's beautiful here. Peaceful."

"You do what you need to do, sweetheart. And when you're ready I'll bring Helena and Perry out to see you so we can check that you're doing alright."

I swallowed the lump in my throat. "No one will ever care about me like you."

"Jess . . . they will if you give them the chance."

"This is a bad idea," I hissed into Bailey's ear as we followed Tom and Andrew into Cooper's.

"I think it's a great idea. It'll clear a few things up for you." She smiled. "Oh. Dahlia's back," she said, changing the subject deliberately. "She's got some stuff to do, but she promised to meet us for drinks before you leave. I can't wait for you to meet her."

"Nice try," I said.

She just smirked and then that smirk wilted a little when her attention moved to the bar.

I followed her gaze.

Andrew and Tom were standing at the bar and I suddenly wanted to rush over and take Andrew away. Cooper's expression was completely blank as he looked toward Bailey and me.

"This was a bad idea," Bailey muttered. "Shit."

"Oh, what makes you say that?"

She ignored my sarcasm. "Because I was thinking about helping you. I thought if you could see Dr. Arrogance next to the amazing Cooper Lawson it would finally pull your head out of your ass. But I don't want to hurt Cooper to help you. Shit."

"Uh, they met today already," I said, and then her last sentence penetrated. "Hurt Cooper?"

But she was moving forward before I could get an answer.

"This is Doc Andrew"—Tom was introducing Andrew to Cooper by the time I got over there—"Jess's . . . friend."

Cooper nodded at my . . . friend. "Yeah, we've met."

"Tell me you stock Macallan," Andrew said in lieu of hello.

Cooper just nodded.

"I'll have two fingers on the rocks."

"Let's sit over at a booth." Bailey tugged on Tom's hand.

Confused, he frowned. "But we usually sit at the bar."

"I feel like the moody atmosphere of a booth tonight." Bailey smiled brightly. Too brightly. "Come." She pulled harder on him. "Give me a little romance."

"You are acting weirder than usual," Tom said, following her.

Andrew took my hand. "Are you coming?"

I was too busy staring up at Cooper, who was staring at me with expressionless eyes. But I knew him a little better now. There was a hint of heat there. And not the good kind.

He was still pissed at me.

That made me want to shrivel up and find a hole somewhere to hide in.

"Cooper," I said, suddenly needing him to be nice to me.

All I got was a nod and—"Lil will take your order."

Deflated, I started to follow Andrew. He let go of my hand only to wrap his arm around my waist and I wanted desperately to pull out of his hold. But I wasn't a teenager anymore.

I'd put myself in this position and I needed to act like a mature adult about it.

I brushed off the move as inconsequential by quickly slipping into the booth beside Bailey so Tom and Andrew would have to sit opposite us.

So much for being mature.

But not hurting Cooper trumped being mature.

Bailey leaned into me as if she was giving me a one-armed hug. "I'm sorry," she whispered in my ear.

I forgave her childish stunt immediately because I knew her motives were pure. I squeezed her hand in reassurance.

"This place is . . . *quaint*," Andrew said, looking around at the bar.

Tom and Bailey shared a look that clearly said they were not impressed by Andrew's pretention. I wanted to kick him under the table.

"I love it here," I informed him.

He gave me a patronizing smile. "Darling, there are plenty of nice bars back home. You've never tried them so you don't know the difference."

"That is incredibly condescending," Bailey said.

I almost burst out laughing.

Andrew seemed surprised by her outburst. "It wasn't meant to be."

"Right. I'm going to need a drink." Her arm shot up in the air. "Lil, over here. Pronto!"

Lily jerked in surprise at Bailey's yell and quickly finished scribbling down the order she was taking to hurry over to us.

She gave us a huge grin. "What can I get you?"

"Two fingers of Macallan on the rocks," Andrew said before anyone else could speak. "And a glass of your best red."

He'd ordered for me.

I wasn't surprised.

Bailey, however, looked like she wanted to slap him.

Tom choked back laughter as he ordered. "Beer, Lil."

"Bailey?" Lily said.

My friend shook herself. "Long Island. And cancel the red wine." She turned to me pointedly. "What would you like to drink, Jessica?"

Now it was my turn to struggle with holding in laughter. I turned to Lily, avoiding Andrew's gaze. "I'll have a Long Island, too."

I had a feeling I was going to need it.

"Sure thing. Oh"—she dipped her head down to me—"I wanted to thank you. Cooper said it was you who told him to talk to me about what's been going on . . . I should have spoken to him earlier. Anyway, thanks. I really need this job."

Warmth spread through me. "You're welcome. I hope everything is okay."

"It will be. Helps I have an awesome boss." She grinned and trotted away.

My gaze moved past her to Cooper. He was laughing with Old Archie about something and my belly flipped. I loved his crooked smile.

I loved that he had taken my advice and made whatever was going on in Lily's life better for her.

"Are you alright?" Andrew said, drawing my attention back to him.

"Dr. Jess!"

I jumped at the shout that had everyone turning in the bar to look at Old Archie. "Yes?" I called back, a little worried about what he was going to say, considering he'd just been talking to Cooper.

"My old lady, Anita, she's got a problem with her neck. I said I'd ask you to have a look at it. And while you're at it, will you give her something for that damn flu she's got? She keeps trying to work through it."

Everyone turned to stare at me, waiting for a response. "Um . . . doesn't Anita have a doctor here?"

"Ah, she hates going to the doc. Hates waiting in that creepy waiting room place, you know. I said how nice you were and she finally said she'd get it checked."

I sensed concern in Old Archie and so I found myself saying, "Tell her to pop by the inn tomorrow morning."

"She works. Eight a.m. okay for you?"

"Sure."

"Great. I'd buy you a drink, but I've only got enough on me for four more beers."

Amused, I grinned. "That's quite alright."

I turned back to find Andrew frowning at me.

"What?" I shrugged.

"House calls? Really?"

Lily arrived and put our drinks on the table. I picked up my Long Island and said, "He's a friend."

"You've certainly made a lot of those here," he said stiffly.

"Yes. I have."

There were other tourists in the bar, at Bailey's inn, at Emery's, at Antonio's, and although they were treated with cordiality, they were not treated by the business owners like friends.

The real truth, I suddenly realized, was that the people here recognized something I was too stubborn to admit. They recognized the connection that I had made to their town.

And that made me something more than a tourist to them.

That made me connected to *them*.

I slid out of the booth, no longer able to pretend the situation was any different from what it was. "Come outside," I said to Andrew. "We need to talk."

"We just got our drinks," he argued.

I didn't argue back. Instead I turned on my heel and strode out, knowing he would follow because he hated to make a scene.

The waves crashed onto the beach, the surf lit up under the moonlight, and I leaned against the boardwalk railing, knowing in that moment that I was about to do the exact right thing. Maybe the first right thing I'd done in a long time.

"What the hell is going on?" Andrew said behind me.

I slowly turned to face him, not nervous, not uneasy. Calm. And resolute. "I need to be honest. I don't want to be in a relationship with you, Andrew. I'm sorry."

He raised an eyebrow in surprise. "Why didn't you say anything before?"

"I never had a chance to."

"Well." He laughed shortly. "This is preposterous. It's this place. The people. That woman"—he jerked his thumb over his shoulder—"so aggressive. You'll feel differently when you're away from her and at home."

I bristled. "No, I won't . . . because I'm not going back to Wilmington. I'm staying here."

Relief moved through me as soon as I said the words out loud.

"Are you insane?" he snapped, striding toward me. "Seriously?"

"I'm not happy, Andrew. I haven't been happy . . . well, I can't remember the last time I was happy," I admitted sadly.

He scoffed at that. "And you think you'll be happy here? You've been here all of five minutes."

"I know. And maybe I won't be happy here, either, but I know for damn sure that I am not happy working in that prison—"

"I've been telling you that for two years!"

I ignored his interruption. "I'm not happy in my empty apartment and I'm not happy with a fuck buddy anymore."

"Which is exactly why I'm changing our situation to a relationship," he insisted, taking hold of my upper arms.

He gave me a coaxing smile.

"No."

"Yes."

"No."

"No?"

How could I do this without being mean? "Um . . ." I didn't think there was really a way to be not a little mean unless it meant being dishonest, and really at this point I didn't think anything else but honesty would convince him. "I don't want to be in a relationship . . . with *you*."

"But you just said—"

"I said I've come to want more than to be someone's casual sex partner. But that doesn't mean that I want more with *you*."

He let this sink in and then his eyes narrowed. "That Neanderthal bartender you were making moon eyes at this afternoon? You want *him* over *me*?"

Hot anger fired my blood. "He *owns* the bar."

"Oh, well, that makes it so much better."

Arrogant asshole!

"It's not even about him," I said and that was the truth. "It's about me. I like it here."

"With the shirtless bartender?" He guffawed.

"Ugh, you actually think you're better than him."

"I *know* I'm better than him."

"You know what, Andrew, here's the truth. I liked having *sex* with you, but I have never liked *you*. I respected you because you're a great surgeon and you save lives and I found that hot. But that's all it was. Because as wonderful as it is that you do all that . . . you are quite possibly the most selfish, inconsiderate, arrogant asshole I have ever met."

His lips parted in shock at my brutal honesty.

And somehow I still couldn't shut up! "Cooper is not selfish. Not arrogant. He's just a good man. And you are so far up your own superior ass that you can't see what's important anymore."

"You know all this about a man you've known two seconds?" He completely ignored the part about him, not wanting to hear it and so pretending he hadn't.

"I know this because of the way the people here are around him. They all respect him. They genuinely care about him. That says more about him than anything else does."

Andrew shook his head and heaved a sigh. "Oh, Jessica . . ." He stared out at the water. "I'm going to forgive everything you just said because"—he turned back to me—"I'm worried about you. I think you're going through something. That's alright. But when you get out of whatever midlife crisis this is, you will realize that you've just thrown away me and your career. You might get your career back. But I won't be waiting."

I didn't know whether to laugh or cry at his pomposity.

"I don't want you to wait, Andrew."

His expression turned cold as he studied me for what felt like forever. Finally he gave me a clipped nod. "Good luck, Jessica."

I watched him walk away, disappearing out of sight, and felt nothing but relief. I took a few minutes in the fresh night air to gather myself to go back into the bar.

I didn't know what my sudden decision to stay meant for me and Cooper or if there was even a chance for me and Cooper. Somehow he had the power to make me want to give up the autonomy I'd enjoyed for so long, and that scared the shit out of me. Because I was terrified that somewhere down the line he'd find out something about me he didn't like and I'd lose him.

But I realized right then that I was equally afraid that he wouldn't even want to give me a second chance to explore what was between us. I knew if I walked back into that bar and he turned away from me, I would regret my actions from the other night for the rest of my life.

Because what Cooper had said to me that night was true. I'd never felt anything like this before.

Gathering my courage, I strode back inside and headed straight for where he stood at the bar. He was pouring a draft and he looked up from between his lashes as I came to a stop across from him.

Quickly he looked back down at what he was doing, but his tone gave him away when he asked, "Where's the surgeon?"

I perched on the stool and leaned over a little closer to say, "I told him to leave. I also told him it was over between him and me."

He stopped what he was doing and put the draft on the bar without looking at me.

"I also told him I wasn't leaving Hartwell anytime soon."

His head jerked up at that and he stared at me in surprise.

"You were right." I shrugged. "I wasn't happy."

Cooper just continued to stare.

Uncertainty moved through me. "Do you think I'm crazy? Was it a bad call?"

His answer was to wrap his hand around the nape of my neck and pull me across the bar into his kiss.

It wasn't any ordinary kiss.

It was hot and hungry.

I immediately melted into it, just like I had the night before.

I'd never met a man whose kiss could make me burn for so much more.

Whoops and catcalls suddenly met my ears and Cooper pulled back just enough to murmur against my mouth, "Good call, Doc."

THIRTEEN

Cooper

The energy in the bar went up a level after he impulsively kissed her in front of everyone. The tourists had no idea what was going on, but his regulars did. Even if they didn't know the doc too well, they knew him. He wasn't one for kissing random women in public.

They understood there was something different about Jessica, and because his regulars were good people he knew they were happy for him.

So the mood was light, it was fun, and it was helped along by Bailey, Jess, and Tom having a riot at the bar with Old Archie as they celebrated Jess's decision to stay in Hartwell.

"Ooh, I just had a thought!" Bailey clapped her hands together excitedly. "You'll be here for the pumpkin festival—we have a mini punkin-chunkin' world championship, and—"

"Wait." Jess held up her hand, grinning. "What on earth is punkin chunkin'?"

"You've lived in Delaware how long and you've never heard of a punkin chunkin'?"

Cooper chuckled at Bailey's shock and explained for Jessica's sake, "It's a sport where people see how far they can hurl pumpkins. They can use all kinds of devices to do it. There is actually a world championship."

"Huh." Jess nodded. "Can't wait to see that."

"Oh, there's more than that," Bailey continued excitedly. "We have a chicken festival, too, to celebrate our majestic state bird—the blue hen."

"And what exactly is involved in a chicken festival?" The doc looked genuinely interested and excited by the prospect of a chicken festival.

He guessed she was just excited about being part of something.

Cooper wanted to kiss her.

"It's really just an excuse for us to take over Main Street at the beginning of October," Tom said. "Locals enter a competition to see who comes up with the best chicken dish. We get a band for the bandstand. We sell crafts and homemade baked goods."

"It sounds fun," Jess said wistfully.

Bailey threw her arm around her and gave her a squeeze. "It is fun. You know what else is fun? The gay pride parade at the end of the summer."

"I thought gay pride parades usually hit the bigger cities."

"They do. This is little in comparison, but Hartwell is very popular with the LGBT community and Kell Summers and his partner, Jake, organized the parade about eight years ago and it's gotten more popular every year. It's a blast. I'm so excited you'll be here for it!"

"Me, too. You guys certainly have a lot going on here."

"Don't forget the music festival," Tom added.

"Oh yes! Next month. We get bands from all over. Kell Summers is actually a councilman and he's head of a whole bunch of organizations so he's, like, the official event planner for the town. Ooh, and you should probably know that our mayor is Jaclyn Rose—she's a friend of my mom's. Very cool lady. And our vice mayor is Paul Duggan, the doctor I mentioned. And, ugh, Ian Devlin is a councilman—"

"Bailey, give the doc a chance to take it all in," Cooper said, amused. "She's got more than a night to get to grips with town politics."

"Right." Bailey laughed. "Sorry."

"It's fine. I'm sure I'll remember none of it in the morning," Jess cracked.

"Speaking of." Tom glanced at his watch. "I need to head back, babe."

Bailey took hold of his wrist and squinted at the time. "Ah, hell." She turned from him and threw her arms around Jess. "Gotta go, but so glad you're staying."

Jess squeezed her and then pulled back. "We'll talk in the morning."

"Yay," Bailey said softly.

They said good night and Tom led Bailey out of the quieting bar. She kept waving the whole time, making Jess giggle in an adorable way that held Cooper transfixed. There were so many layers to this woman and he'd only spent just a little time with her. He couldn't wait to learn everything about her. She was complicated, but complicated in a way that was exciting.

"I should really go, too," Jess said, turning back to him. "I'm so wired, though."

He glanced over as the last of his regulars called out good night as they left the bar. There were only a couple of tourists and Old Archie still sitting there. It was final call in five minutes. He looked at Jess and found she was watching him in an intense way he liked a lot. "Stay after closing."

She raised an eyebrow.

"No funny business." He grinned, reading her mind. "I'll make you a decaf coffee and you can talk it out."

Because, as much fun as she'd had with Bailey and Tom, they hadn't really discussed why she'd made the decision to stay and what she was going to do here. This was a huge move for her. Some people, maybe most, might say it was quite impulsive after so short a time here. It couldn't have been an easy decision and Cooper wanted to make sure her head was in the right place.

Twenty minutes later the bar was closed, and he'd sent Lily and Riley home early.

He locked up and made decaf coffee for himself and Jess and led her over to a booth at the back of the bar.

They sipped at their coffee in silence for a moment and then he finally said, "So . . . what happened today?"

She heaved a huge sigh and relaxed back into her seat. "Today was a culmination of a lot of things. For a start, you were right about me not being happy. I . . . I convinced myself that I was content with the situation I'd carved out for myself back in Wilmington. It was easy to convince myself while I was there because I didn't really know what I was missing out on. I've spent so much of my life wrapped up in the world of medicine that I didn't have time to notice.

"And then I get here and the pace is so different . . . you guys love your jobs and you work hard . . . but it feels slower and more laid-back here."

"It is," Cooper said.

"Good." She gave a shaky smile. "I'm glad I'm not wrong about that because it's a huge part of the appeal of living here . . ." She looked down into the coffee in her hand. "I can't even explain it, Cooper, I just feel . . . I feel connected to things here. I've never felt connected to anywhere before."

"And that's why you're staying?" He wanted her to say yes; because the truth was, as good as he felt about her staying, Cooper had been worried all night that she'd made this huge decision based on him. He liked the doc too much for her to throw away what she'd already built for the possibility of what was between them. He would have been happy to try a relationship with a commute while they were still testing this thing out.

"Yes," she said, and he felt the relief sweep through him. "This is all about what I want. Don't get me wrong—the people here are obviously a factor. Everyone is warm and friendly and accepting . . . Well . . ." She laughed. "Of me. Not everyone, I guess."

"You thinking of Vaughn?"

"Andrew actually. But I guess Vaughn, too."

"That was because of the hotel. The council approved planning before Jaclyn became mayor. She became mayor in the middle of the hotel's construction and with the help of Bailey, who was especially pissed off by Vaughn's arrival, tried to put a stop to it. Legally they couldn't do anything, but their public disapproval of his hotel has left some negativity around him. He's not a bad guy, though, as far as I can see."

"Yeah?"

"Yeah. Anyway, you were saying . . ."

"Oh. Right. I was saying that I've never connected with strangers the way I've connected with the people here. Bailey, Emery . . . you. I already had this all going on in my head and then suddenly Andrew turned up."

Cooper scowled. The moment he'd met him at the bandstand Cooper could practically smell the arrogance on him. When he'd put his arm around the doc, Cooper had wanted to punch something. He'd also wondered how the hell she could see something in him when this surgeon guy was the kind of man she was used to dating.

In fact, that still bothered him a little.

"I didn't invite him," she said. "I was shocked when Bailey told me he was here. He and I . . ." She shook her head, looking annoyed. "We were never in a relationship and I won't go into it—"

"I'd appreciate that."

She smirked. "All I will tell you is that I respected him and even admired him professionally. He's a great surgeon. But—and this sounds awful—I have never actually *liked* him very much."

It didn't sound awful. It filled him with a sense of relief, in fact. "So why have anything to do with him?"

Jess shifted uncomfortably. "I didn't want a relationship with anyone . . . at least I didn't think so. But I'm still a woman."

As relieved as he felt that she wasn't the kind of woman who'd fall for a guy like that arrogant prick, Cooper also wasn't particularly happy talking about her getting her needs met by the asshole, either.

"Gotcha," he bit out.

"Anyway, when he showed up here suddenly announcing that he missed me and how we were too old to mess around and we needed to start getting serious about one another . . . I was stunned." She scrunched up her nose in irritation. "Typical Andrew, making decisions for the both of us. It got me really thinking about what I wanted and I called an old friend for advice. That, plus Andrew's behavior in here tonight, made me realize what I didn't want. And what I didn't want was him—and the really scary part . . ." She looked up at Cooper with big round eyes, dark with true uncertainty that made him want to reach over and comfort her. "I don't know if I want to be a doctor anymore."

Surprise stopped him from reaching for her like he'd intended.

He didn't know what to say at that point.

Her profession . . . well . . . Cooper saw that as being a part of who she was. He knew that was strange since he'd never actually seen her practice medicine, but he still sensed that her calling to heal was a big part of her character.

"I'm not sure I'm following."

"I'm not sure I am, either." She gave a huff of sad laughter. "It's just that . . . there is a possibility I went into this career for the wrong reasons."

"What wrong reasons?"

Jess looked down. "I can't fully explain it. Just . . . maybe I was trying to make up for something, and maybe that isn't a good enough reason to be a doctor."

The silence fell between them.

He didn't want her to hide anything from him because, hell, he felt like he could tell her anything. But it was still new between them and there were certain things about him that he would wait to tell her. That went both ways.

He didn't need to know what the doc wasn't telling him. Not yet.

He remembered something she had told him, though. "What about what you told me? About making your mark?"

Cooper's reminder of their conversation pulled Jess's gaze back to his. "I don't know. I don't know if that's all mixed up with something else." She sighed. "I know I'm not explaining myself very well."

They were quiet awhile as they drank their coffee. Cooper thought over her dilemma. It concerned him. Clearly, Jessica was in a mixed-up place in her life—she wasn't the wholly self-assured woman he'd thought she was when she first walked into his bar. He'd been attracted to that aspect of her personality. But knowing differently didn't make him any less attracted to her. It made her less than perfect, it made her more real, someone who might need him after all, and to his surprise, Cooper liked that. He liked that a fuck of a lot. He wanted to help her find what it was she was looking for.

He had to hope he didn't get trampled in the search.

For now, he focused on making her feel better, because lots of people reached their thirties and realized they weren't happy with their career or their life in general. She wasn't the first.

"You know what, Doc, your degree isn't going anywhere. No matter what, you're a doctor. So why not take some time out from it and try to find if there's something else out there for you? If you decide you want to go back to being a doctor, then I'm sure that won't be a problem."

Jess smiled brightly at him, relief visible in that pretty smile. "You really think so?"

"Yeah. Nothing is set in stone, right?"

"Right."

He watched her whole body seem to melt as the pent-up tension left her. She was studying his face in that intense way again, like she was memorizing him.

"What?" he murmured, his blood turning more than a little hot as he thought about memorizing her all over in return.

"Tell me about your family," she suddenly said.

Cooper stared into her big hazel eyes and saw longing in them. It wasn't the kind of longing he'd been feeling a second before and he was suddenly really curious to know about *her* family. If that meant talking about his, then that was an easy way to get the info he wanted out of her. He realized he wanted to tell her about them anyway. Maybe it was stupid of him to trust a woman so soon after one had betrayed him, but Cooper didn't ever want to get twisted and bitter over his ex's behavior. He certainly didn't want to mistake a good woman for another Dana Kellerman.

"My dad left when I was twelve" he said.

Sympathy brightened her eyes. "I'm sorry."

"No need to be. The guy was an asshole. An abusive asshole."

Jessica flinched. "Then I'm even more sorry."

"I bet you've seen a lot of that in your line of work."

"Unfortunately, yes. Quite a bit at the prison, actually. Old fractures, scars so multiple it's a history of abuse mapped out on the body—the truth right there for me to see and yet they still lie to me about it." She shook her head sadly. "I can't tell you how sorry I am that your family ever had to deal with it."

"My mom mostly," he said, the familiar anger licking at his nerves. "She did the right thing, though. She got help. The sheriff at the time was a man who'd been really good friends with my grandfather. He, uh . . . well . . . let's just say he did what he had to, to get the message over to my dad that he was no longer welcome in Hartwell." He narrowed his eyes, remembering their conversation about his mother's cousin. "There were options open to my mother. She made the right choice."

Understanding instantly dawned on Jessica. "I get you," she whispered.

He continued, "After he left, things got better. But they were also hard. It was just me, my mother, and my baby sister, Catriona.

Mom had inherited the bar from my uncle who'd passed, and she never liked it much. She kept the management on and they ran it for her, but it wasn't what it could be. For a place on the boardwalk it was kind of a dive. I was always trying to find ways to make money and so I worked a lot and missed out on a lot of school. Graduated with my GED and got a job working as a mechanic in Uly's Garage. Mom worked as a grocery store clerk. We worked our asses off so Cat didn't have to. Mom gave the bar to both of us, but Cat let me buy her out years ago. She had no passion for it. She wanted college. She was a smart kid. We wanted college for her, too. She wanted to be prelaw and, smart cookie that she is, she got into UPenn."

"That's amazing. And partly because of you." There was open admiration in Jessica's expression.

He liked that, but he wasn't taking credit for Cat's hard work. "It was all her. She worked hard in high school and didn't have much of a social life. But she got to college and . . . I don't know." He sighed. "I don't know if it was too much pressure or what . . . She got a little wild. She called me about a pregnancy scare her freshman year and I hoped the scare and my reaction to the scare would be enough to keep her on the straight and narrow."

Jess made a face. "It didn't."

"It didn't." He still remembered how he'd felt when she told him she had to quit college because she was pregnant. "She was twenty years old. She came home for the summer. Got shit-faced and knocked up by a tourist whose name she couldn't remember."

"Oh boy."

"Yeah. But I had to come around fast because our mother was so disappointed she didn't speak to Cat for the first five months of her pregnancy."

"Double oh boy."

He gave a huff of laughter. "Yeah."

"But then Joey came along."

"Joseph Cooper Lawson." He grinned just thinking about the

kid. "Even smarter than his mom. And you can bet his grandmother was more gaga over that kid than anyone. She got over her disappointment quick first time she held him in her arms."

Jessica was quiet a moment as she studied him. She said, her voice soft, "And how long did she get to enjoy him?"

That sharp sting of sadness pricked him. "Not long, Doc. Only a few years before the cancer claimed her."

"You were close."

"Extremely. It was like the world ended for a while."

Her eyes suddenly shone with tears and that sting got a little sharper at her genuine sympathy. "I'm sorry you lost her."

He nodded, unable to speak for the emotion that was thick in his voice. Sometimes the grief could hit him hard out of nowhere, even after all these years.

"But you know what?" she said. "I'm even happier that you had her."

And just like that her words took away a bit of the sting. He cleared his throat, but it was still thick when he said, "Me, too, Doc."

Jessica

I discovered something new about myself right then. I discovered that my emotions *could* be connected to my sexual attraction to someone. Because right then, emotionally tangled up in this man, I had never been more attracted to a guy in my life.

I wanted Cooper Lawson.

Badly.

I wanted to launch myself across the table at him.

To hold him.

To kiss him.

To rip his clothes off after the embracing.

Very inappropriate, considering what we'd just discussed. I'd never met a man like him before, though. How he could be so many things . . . so goddamn rugged and masculine, honest and open, and even showing a little of his vulnerability . . . it was unreal. He hadn't hidden his emotion, his grief over his mom. He'd given that to me. And that meant so much more to me than anything else could.

And for the first time in a very long time I wanted everything with a man.

And for the first time *ever* I was going to see if it was possible to have everything with *this* man.

"So what about you?" Cooper said after a moment of comfortable silence. "Tell me about your family."

His question dropped down in my stomach like a lead weight, sending up a flurry of butterflies in its wake. Anytime someone asked me a question about my family I physically trembled before shutting the line of questioning down. This time was no different—Cooper's question made me shake—but it was the first time I'd ever contemplated giving someone at least part of the truth as an answer to that question.

This would be a day of a lot of firsts because I knew it would be unfair not to give Cooper anything after he'd given me something of himself. Something so real.

I took a deep breath and watched Cooper frown as he watched my reaction to his question. "It's not an easy question, is it?" I said.

"For some people it is."

"Well, that's true," I said. "I'll amend that. It's not an easy question for me."

"You don't have to tell me anything you don't want to."

He meant that. However, I could see the light of something in his eyes and I thought it might be disappointment. I felt completely anxious at the thought. I didn't want to disappoint him and miss my chance to explore this connection with him.

"It's just not a pretty story . . ." I took another slow breath, trying to find the words and all the while willing the painful images to stay out of my head. "I don't really ever talk about it. My sister . . . uh . . . my sister, Julia, committed suicide when I was nineteen. It was only a few days after her sixteenth birthday."

Cooper looked stunned. "Fuck, Doc . . . you don't have to—"

I waved away his concern with a confidence I didn't feel. "It's alright. She . . . had her issues that I won't go into. But we were really close. Our parents . . . um"—at the mention of my parents, the old hurt gripped my chest hard like it always did—"they completely disconnected from me when she died. I mean, I tried. I tried for years to reconnect with them, but they're not interested. I only have my best friend, Matthew, back in Iowa, and his daughter, Perry, is my goddaughter. They're about the only family I have left now." My mouth trembled, but I wouldn't cry. A long time back I'd shut that part of my emotions off. It protected me from the worst of the pain.

Suddenly Cooper's hand covered mine, his fingers wrapping tight around my hand. The gesture made me look up.

His expression was fierce. "If you need to cry, Doc, you can cry. You don't have to hide that from me."

I covered his hand with my other one and gave him a grateful smile. "I'm okay, Cooper. It's a hard story to tell. But I'm okay."

"It means a lot to me that you told me," he said gruffly.

And there. There it was.

What I'd been thinking about him, he'd just said it right out in the open.

No bullshit.

God, I liked this man.

I squeezed his hand and then let go and watched him as he slowly withdrew his hand from mine. "You don't have any other family?" he said, frowning. "No aunts or uncles, cousins or grandparents?"

"My mom's sister. Theresa. We were close. But after . . ." I'd feared she'd want nothing to do with me, just like my parents, and somehow I knew her rejection, her blaming me, too, would hurt worse, so I'd left her also and never looked back. "We haven't spoken since . . . then . . ." I shook off the thought of her. "Tell me about growing up here," I said, changing the subject to something a little less heavy.

"Let me get you another coffee, and I'll do just that."

Five minutes later he was back and sprawled in the booth, relaxed and at ease with me as he'd been from the moment we met. "This is a great place to raise kids," he said immediately. "Even with all the shit going on with my family, I had a great childhood here. It's got that small-town thing where nearly everyone knows your business, and that has its ups and downs, but for the most part it's good. Thing about Hartwell is, although you've got your small pocket of hard-core conservatives, this is a friendly, open place. We've moved along with the times pretty well." He gave me a crooked grin.

That grin hit me low in my belly.

It was starting to do that every time.

"You grow up somewhere like here and I like to think it gives you good values, makes you a better kind of person."

"From what I've seen I would say so," I said. "You have all charmed me."

"And thank fuck for that," he said forcefully.

I crossed my legs under the table at the heat in his eyes, and that smolder in them only darkened at whatever he saw in my own.

"Idyllic, then," I murmured, a little dazed from the intensity of the rush of desire pumping through my veins.

"What?" he murmured back, still staring at me like he wanted to devour me.

"What?" I said as my thoughts grew increasingly lust fogged. I suddenly had a vision of him throwing the table between us across the room like Superman, and then scooping me up in his arms and hurrying me home to his bed at the speed of light.

Oh boy.

"Idyllic?" he said, pulling himself out of the sensual moment and thus pulling me, too. "Yeah. This place is pretty idyllic for a kid."

I nodded and recrossed my legs.

Cooper's eyes narrowed on my body. "You okay there?"

I knew by the purr in the back of his throat that he was plenty aware I was not "okay." "Fine," I lied.

He smirked and looked down into the coffee mug. "Tell me about medical school."

"You weren't done telling me about Hartwell."

"Tit for tat, Doc. You tell me something, I'll tell you something."

That sounded fair. "Okay. Medical school was grueling. My medical residency was worse. Working twenty-four-hour shifts is pretty hard."

Cooper winced. "Twenty-four-hour shifts? Are you kidding?"

"Nope. Once you hit second year you're legally allowed to do twenty-four hours. It's hard-core."

"How did you cope?"

"Adrenaline mostly. Most people who are cut out to be surgeons . . . I think that's what gets them through it. And mixed in with the high you get from saving someone's life is that feeling of power. We can't always control life or death, but we can do our damn best to. And that's what it's like being a surgeon. It's taking back a little of that control. The high is phenomenal. It's even better when you get to tell a patient's family that the person they love is going to be okay."

"But equally shitty to tell them the opposite."

There were actually no words for how shitty that was. I would always remember the first surgery I'd participated in as an intern when the patient died on the table. I was with the attending surgeon when she told the family. On top of the overwhelmingly raw grief that emanated so powerfully from them that I couldn't escape feeling it, I couldn't see past the look in their eyes . . . this angry disappointment in us that went beyond any description.

It had never left me.

I tried to compartmentalize it, and the deaths that came after, in order to do my job. I just couldn't. I could handle giving a patient bad news, knowing the person could still fight to survive or, selfishly, knowing I wouldn't have to be there to see it if he or she lost that fight. But watching a patient die and then telling the loved ones that the person was gone started to wear on me. And that was when I knew I couldn't be a surgeon. Even if the good days far outweighed the bad, it was the bad days that haunted me long after.

Cooper saw the answer in my eyes.

I changed the subject. "A growing-up-in-Hartwell story," I prompted.

He immediately went with it. "You want to hear about the time I held up Lanson's grocery store?"

Shock ran through me. "What?"

"I was eight and my gun was a toy."

I laughed. "Oh, my God."

"My mom regretted letting me watch that marathon of western movies, but old Jeff Lanson got a laugh out of it. Thankfully."

I laughed harder, imagining a cute little version of Cooper holding up the supermarket. "What happened?"

We sat there for the next few hours, exchanging stories, until my eyes started to grow heavy.

"Come on, Doc, we better get you home. You've got an appointment with Anita in a few hours."

Oh, crap. I'd forgotten about that.

After Cooper had locked up the bar, he walked me back to the inn along the darkened boardwalk. The whole way there I had my head on his shoulder. He held up my tired body with his arm around my waist and I held on with my arm around his.

It felt easy and right.

And so goddamn beautiful I could have cried.

To cap off the best night I could remember in a long time, Cooper brushed his lips over mine to say good night. Just a whisper of his mouth, a tease of the taste of him, and that touch zinged through my blood.

"I'll check in with you in a while." He whispered his promise against my lips.

There was so much emotion rising up out of me that it got choked up in my throat and I couldn't speak. I could only nod, hoping he saw everything I felt in my eyes.

And, judging by the small, sexy smile he gave me, he did.

FOURTEEN

Jessica

Less than fifteen minutes before, I'd been exhausted, splashing cold water on my face and downing coffee to feel just awake enough to see Archie's partner, Anita.

The previous night had been worth the lack of sleep, though.

The last time I'd sat all night and talked with someone had been with my college roommate, who I lost touch with when we went to separate graduate schools.

Life just got in the way sometimes.

Anyhow, I'd never spent all night talking with a man about everything and nothing. It felt as though my finding those letters from Sarah had been kismet.

Bailey had led Anita up to my room, and within only a few moments I was wide awake . . . and my happy mood had taken a turn.

"I didn't want to worry Archie because I knew it was probably nothing. I'm a bank teller and have been my whole life so I sit in that seat bent over a computer half the time," Anita said.

She was a tall woman with tired brown eyes and a pale complexion. I could see from her high cheekbones and still-full lips that she'd once been a beauty.

"So you haven't told Archie about the back pain?"

"No." She scrunched up her face.

When I'd examined her neck I found her lymph nodes were swollen. And when I'd examined her lower back she cried out from the pain of my touch.

"Anita, have you experienced any other symptoms?"

She nodded cautiously. "Yeah . . . my legs feel funny sometimes. Kind of weak, even numb sometimes, but I've been fighting off this flu for a while so I'm guessing it's just part of that . . ."

"Flu?" My unease increased by the bucketload, and I suddenly remembered Archie had mentioned it the night before.

"Yeah."

"Your symptoms?"

She made a face. "The usual. I've been throwing up, got a fever, chills, and can't eat much so I've lost some weight, which is a plus." She gave me a shaky grin.

I hoped she'd take me absolutely seriously when I said, "Anita, I'd like you to visit your own doctor. And I'd like you to make that appointment today."

Anita's eyes held worry. "You don't think I've got the flu?"

I didn't want to scare her in case I was wrong. "I'm concerned that there is a chance something else other than a flu is going on here. I'd like you to make an appointment with your doctor so he can take a look."

She nodded, seeming dazed. "Okay."

"Anita?"

She looked up at me. "Yeah?"

"You will make the appointment?"

"Sure." She didn't meet my eyes.

Hmm. "Why not make it now while you're here?"

"Seriously?"

I gave her my most serious face as an answer.

She huffed but opened her purse and pulled out her cell. Her eyes on me, she pressed a button and held it up to her ear. "Hey, Liv," she said and had to clear her throat when her words came out in a croak. "It's Anita. Has Doc Duggan got time to see me today? . . . Oh . . . No . . ."

I made a face.

She understood what that face meant. She took a deep breath.

"It's kind of important, Liv . . . I got . . . I got some symptoms that're worrying the new doc . . . Yeah, that's her . . . Yeah, I'm guessing that's true . . . You can? Okay . . . No, I'll be there right away . . . See you in ten." She hung up. "She's squeezing me in now." Anita stood up and gave me a shaky smile. "Thanks for looking at me. Apparently your reputation precedes you. Liv knows who you are."

"Liv is the receptionist?"

"Yeah, at Dr. Paul Duggan's practice on Main Street."

I nodded. I remembered Bailey had mentioned talking to Dr. Duggan about me. I guessed that was a good reminder that staying in a small town meant having to put up with people being in your business. I felt a moment of panic at the thought.

"Thanks again for looking at me. I don't like the doctor's office . . . I was hoping you'd tell me it was nothing so I didn't have to go." She laughed humorlessly.

"I just want a second opinion," I assured her.

"Yeah." She nodded, but her eyes filled with the fear I dreaded seeing in a patient's eyes.

I walked her out of the inn and wished her well, knowing that Hartwell was a small enough place that if she didn't keep me in the loop herself, I'd find out anyway.

"You look worried," Bailey said as I stepped into the dining room, where she had breakfast waiting for me. Morning breakfast was in full swing and the room was noisy with guests.

Patient-doctor confidentiality stopped me from telling her just how worried I was that Anita's symptoms were a sign of something serious. "It's just . . . Anita might be my last patient for a while. Maybe ever."

Bailey's eyes widened. "Okay, after you eat, you explain." Her expression told me I had no other choice and I chuckled to myself as she reluctantly moved away to see to one of the guests.

Breakfast helped wake me up a little, although it took me a while to eat because not only did I have that weird, nauseous, empty feeling you get when you haven't slept much, but I also had pangs of concern for Anita and Archie.

Two hours later I was up in my room trying to figure out where to start first. I had my job to quit, my apartment to give up, a job to find here, and a new place to find to live.

Just as I heard a knock at the door I got a text.

From Cooper.

How are you feeling this morning, Doc?

I smiled and quickly texted back as I wandered over to open my door.

Tired. But last night was worth it. ☺

"Explain," Bailey said, striding into my room upon my opening the door.

My phone binged.

Glad you think so. I plan to give you more sleepless nights in the future.

I grinned, feeling a surge of tingles between my legs.

My phone binged again.

Believe me. It'll be more than worth it.

I felt a little breathless just thinking about it.

I have no doubt. Can't wait, I texted back.

"Would you stop flirting with Cooper and explain what you said," Bailey said, crossing her arms over her chest in a huff.

"How did you know I was flirting with Cooper?"

"The goofy grin on your face."

Damn. I blushed. "He is making me act like a teenager."

"Good." She grinned and flopped down on her bed. "Feeling like a teenager is good."

I laughed and sat down next to her. "I feel all light-headed around him."

"I'll bet you feel more than light-headed around him. You know, in high school his classmates called him the Panty Melter."

"They did not." I guffawed.

Bailey chuckled. "Nope. But if I'd been in his class they would have. When he was a junior I was a lowly freshman. I called him the Panty Melter, but it only caught on with me and my friends."

"Did you have a crush on him?" I could just imagine Bailey crushing on the older, popular Cooper.

"He was the senior high school quarterback, he had those eyes, and on top of that he's always been a good guy. Jack Devlin was the same. Every girl I knew, and a few guys, too, had a crush on Cooper and Jack."

"Does Cooper know this?"

She made a face. "What do you think?"

I laughed, knowing how open she was. "He knows."

"It was probably the love letter I sent him at the beginning of freshman year. And the flowers and invitation to homecoming in sophomore year. Or the time I got shit-faced at the fun park in my senior year and declared my love for him in front of everyone at the Ferris wheel. He was twenty years old and on a date with Brandi Sommers from New York. Her parents owned a house on the south boardwalk and they visited every summer. She was beautiful and classy, and there was no way I stood a chance with her around."

I frowned. "What happened?"

"He was worried about me because I was so drunk. He and Brandi took me home."

"God!" I threw my hands up. "Is he perfect?"

Bailey laughed. "No. He's just a really good guy."

"Two questions: when did you get over your crush and what happened to Brandi?"

She gave me a knowing look. "No need to worry. Cooper is more like a brother to me now. I just grew up, I started falling in actual love instead of lust, and over time he became a friend. A good friend. As for Brandi . . . she was Cooper's summer girl for four years. Until Dana came along."

"He stopped seeing Brandi for Dana?"

Bailey's mouth twisted. "Hmm." Her expression suddenly turned careful when she studied me. "Look, back then I could see it.

Dana . . . she was a year younger than me so Cooper didn't take much notice of her. Also she'd been dating this kid from Dover all through high school. She went to college, dropped out, and came back to Hartwell and she caught Cooper's attention . . . because . . ." She winced. "As much as I hate to admit this . . . Dana Kellerman is outrageously gorgeous."

Now it was my turn to wince. "Gorgeous?"

She nodded. "Like, could have been a model."

"Ouch."

"Hey, but she's a bitch," Bailey hurried to assure me. "Cooper knows that now. I'm just saying, when they were young, I get it . . . he probably got caught up in how beautiful she was and that's how she managed to tie him down."

None of that made me feel any better.

I had my insecurities about my physical appearance, like most women, but in general I didn't have any big complaints. I felt confident I was attractive. But I wasn't "outrageously gorgeous."

"Huh."

"I shouldn't have said anything. I was just . . . You're staying now and I wanted to prepare you for meeting Dana. Because that's inevitable. And I didn't want you to see her and feel threatened, because you shouldn't. All that beauty is hiding something ugly. You . . . you're beautiful all the way through, Jessica. Cooper sees that."

I heaved a sigh. "You're sweet. And thanks for the heads-up." Now, though, I wished I knew what Dana looked like, because she'd turned into Kate Upton in my mind.

"So back to the matter at hand . . . explain what you meant by 'Anita might be my last patient for a while. Maybe ever.'"

I told her about my decision to take a break from medicine.

Unlike Cooper, who'd wanted all the details behind my decision, Bailey just accepted it. That surprised me, considering how little she accepted Vaughn Tremaine's "mysterious" decision to stay in Hartwell.

"Okay, so you can of course say no, but how would you feel

about working for me while you try to figure out what it is you want in life?" She grinned and nodded excitedly at the idea.

I was surprised by the offer. "Work for you how?"

"Tom is on me about getting someone to help out—to split my responsibilities with. You'd pretty much be doing most of what I do. The pay won't be what you're used to, though." Then she told me how much I'd be making and it was considerably less than my pay at the prison.

"You do realize that I've never worked in hospitality before?"

"You've been a doctor, Jess, which I'm guessing means you're hella smart. I'm pretty sure you can handle running an inn."

I felt a little bubble of excitement at the thought. After all, Bailey loved her work here at the inn. And I did love the inn. Maybe this was what I was looking for. "Okay." I grinned. "Okay, I'll do it."

"Yay!" Bailey bounced on the bed. "Right. Your vacation ends in a few days, so we'll start then."

"Brilliant. Thank you."

"What are friends for?"

"I've got so much to do. I need to quit my job for a start."

Bailey frowned. "What if they don't give you a reference for quitting without notice?"

"They probably won't give me a reference." I knew I should be worried about that, considering there was a chance I might need to return to medicine, but I was suddenly terrified of the prospect of returning to Wilmington. If I went back to work out my two weeks' notice, I knew there was a chance I'd convince myself all over again that my life there was all I deserved. I'd chicken out and I wouldn't come back to Hartwell.

"Maybe you should go back for a few weeks. I'll hold your job here."

I shook my head, adamant. "I can't go back."

My friend suddenly took on this fierce expression. "Is something going on that I don't know about? Are you *afraid* to go back there?"

Yes. But not for the possible reasons she was conjuring in her head. So I gave her a little truth. "If I go back, I know I might chicken out. If I go back, I might not do it. Quit, I mean. There's a possibility I'd stay."

Bailey relaxed. "I get it. I know I've been all blasé and excited about you staying, but I realize what a huge decision this is. It's only natural that there is a part of you questioning if this is a crazy move. So I get it. And I wouldn't go back, either."

"Thanks. I feel terrible letting them down at the prison, but I'm not the only doctor working there . . ."

"Sometimes you have to be a little selfish in life."

Guilt swirled in my belly. "Right."

"What the hell do you mean you're not coming back, you quit your job, and you want me to pack up your apartment for you?" Fatima yelled through the phone at me a few hours later.

I'd already called the hiring manager to let him know I was faxing through my resignation. He hadn't been too pleased, but I tried to ease my guilt by reminding myself that there were two doctors at the prison who could step up while they found a new primary physician. In fact, Dr. Whitaker would probably be gleeful about it.

Still, it didn't leave me feeling good. I'd never acted irresponsibly in my entire adult life.

"What the hell do you mean?" Fatima repeated at my silence.

I cleared my throat. "I mean that I'm staying in Hartwell."

"What the hell for?"

"I like it here. I like the people. The lifestyle is very different from what I've been used to in Wilmington. I've made fast friends here. There's this crazy lovable inn owner; and Emery the sweet, shy bookstore owner; and this really hot, sexy, nice—so goddamn nice—bar owner. And there's Old Archie, and Iris and Ira, and Tom, and Vaughn, who is a very interesting character, and I want to meet Cat and Joey and Dahlia and—"

"Jesus, woman, is this place trapped in a time vortex or something? Has three weeks to me been three years to you?"

I laughed, but it came out sounding sad. "You are the one person I am going to miss, Fatima."

"My God, you are serious, aren't you?"

"Before I got here, you were trying to tell me something. You were trying to tell me that my life was empty. And it turns out you were right. I can't do anything about it back in Wilmington. But I think I've got a chance of filling my life up with good things here in Hartwell."

She was quiet a moment as she thought about this. "You've got a job at the inn you're staying at, you say?"

"Yes."

"Think maybe you can get discounts?"

I smiled and my mood lifted. "Probably."

"Then I'll pack up your apartment for you. But this isn't goodbye, Jess. When I get vacation time I'm coming to see what's so great about this place that has won you over."

"That sounds great."

"Quitting your job and moving to a new town after only three weeks for a hot guy—yeah, I heard that part—you're a crazy woman. The craziest. How come I never knew how crazy you are? You are a riot. A frickin' riot . . ."

I let her babble on, laughing to myself the whole time.

I'd surprised her.

But more than that, I'd surprised me.

And it felt good.

"Uh-oh," Bailey said as soon as I came downstairs to the kitchen.

It was my first time in there, but I figured since I was going to be working there I should get to know the workings of the place.

A curvy woman with black hair stood beside Bailey, staring at me. This was Mona, the chef, and we'd met briefly a few times over the course of the last few weeks. Mona was hard to miss. Every time I'd seen her she'd been wearing a head scarf with a large knot in the top. She wore oversized black-framed glasses and bright red lipstick, and when she wasn't in her chef's whites, she wore overalls. She was like a 1940s war propaganda poster for female industrial workers.

And the look worked for her.

Also in the kitchen were Nicky and Chris—her sous chef and junior chef.

"She's in my kitchen," Mona said, looking affronted. "There's a guest in my kitchen."

"Chill," Bailey said. "I told you she's going to be working here."

"But until then she's still a guest and she's in *my* kitchen."

I was getting the vibe Mona was a little particular about her kitchen and the rules of her kitchen. "Maybe we should step outside?"

Bailey rolled her eyes but followed me out of the room before speaking any further. "You know, I'm trying to break her of her obsessive rules and regulations. We should have stayed. You're going to work here now and the staff need to get used to you."

I stopped at the reception desk where we had some privacy. "That may or may not be a problem. I'm unsure at this point."

"What do you mean?"

"I've been looking at real estate here and, um . . . it's pretty expensive."

Bailey made a face. "Seaside town."

"Right. Well, you'd think as a doctor I'd have put some money away, but the truth is I'm still paying off my student loan debt and, um, that, versus salary here—I'm not sure I can swing it." It took a battering to my pride to admit that, because for the longest time the most positive thing I could say about myself was that I was a successful career woman. There would be no more nice jewelry or designer handbags for me for a long while.

"Oh." Bailey's eyes widened. "Right. I didn't think of that."

"I can't afford the apartments here." I slumped down into a chair. If I wanted to stay in Hartwell, I would likely have to stick to doctoring after all.

"Maybe not . . ." She suddenly grinned at me. "But it's not a problem. You could stay with me. I have a pullout."

"No," I said, despite feeling grateful for the offer. "I appreciate it, really. But Tom is at your place a lot and it . . . I'm not going to intrude on the two of you like that."

Bailey sighed heavily. "Okay. Well, I keep a room at the inn open for myself in case I need to crash here. It's not as big and it doesn't have a view, but it's a room with a bathroom, and it's yours for free if you want it. I'll show you."

She led me to the back of the inn, to a modest but pretty room. One window looked out to the garden at the side, and I caught a sliver of the beach and water at the corner. The other window looked out on the parking lot at the back.

But it was free, and it would certainly do until I could come up with something more permanent.

"Are you sure?"

"Absolutely."

I hugged her hard, making her stumble back and laugh in surprise. "Thank you."

Bailey squeezed me tight. She gave good hug. "We're going to make this work for you, Jess. Just you wait."

Despite her reassurances, a while later, back in my current room upstairs, I felt more than a little panicked by all the decisions I'd made that day.

I was exhausted from lack of sleep, so my anxiety was worsened by it, and I guess that was how I sounded when Cooper called me late in the afternoon.

"So Fatima is packing up my apartment for me, and Bailey has given me a job and a room here until I can figure out something else, and the prison isn't too happy with me, but it's done, so I guess . . . Oh, and I'll need to find somewhere to store all my stuff. I hope I can find a cheap storage place and—"

"Doc," Cooper interrupted, "you sound like you're freaking out."

"I'm a little on edge," I admitted.

"Look, it's done, it's scary, and now it's about living with those decisions. As for storage, I've got a big secure shed on the outskirts of town. I used to work on cars there, but I haven't had the time lately and the place is lying practically empty. You can put all your stuff there."

"Really?" God, I liked this guy.

"Really. Now get some rest. Things will look better after a little sleep."

"Okay. Thank you."

"No problem. I'll see you soon."

As I hung up and lay down on the bed, all I allowed myself to think about was his voice, his reassurances . . . and just like that I was out like a light.

FIFTEEN

Jessica

I awoke with a start, momentarily disoriented. The room was pitch-black.

To me it felt like it had been daylight only minutes prior.

Sitting up with a groan, still fully dressed, I caught sight of the clock on my bedside table and winced.

It was almost one o'clock in the morning.

Flipping on the lights, I then swung my legs over the bed. I felt weird. One, I was now all over the place with my sleep because I'd slept during the day, and two, my whole body felt hot and needy.

Suddenly I remembered why.

I'd been dreaming.

It had been a *good* dream.

And Cooper had the starring role.

Thinking of him, I realized Cooper would just be closing up the bar. I wanted to see him. Moreover, I was such an uncertain mess over making the move there that I needed to see him. It scared me to give him this much power, but I knew that if I saw him I would feel better about everything.

A piece of paper on the carpet by the door caught my attention.

It was a note from Bailey.

Left some food in the fridge for you in the kitchen, Sleeping Beauty. See you in the morning. B. xoxo.

God, I loved her.

I thought about going downstairs and getting the food, but I wasn't really that hungry. Looking back at the clock, I considered my options. If I was quick, I could probably catch Cooper as he was closing up. We didn't need to do another all-nighter, but maybe we could talk a little until I felt better.

I considered my wardrobe. The dress I'd been wearing was wrinkled badly from sleep.

"Screw it." I didn't have time to change.

Instead I threw on some flats and a sweater, grabbed my keys, and dashed quietly out of the silent inn. I hurried along the boardwalk, loving the soothing breeze that moved through my hair and caressed my flushed skin. The waves lapped gently to shore, and with them a sense of calm whispered up toward me.

I already felt better about my decision.

Seriously, the boardwalk was like some kind of seductive sentient being.

I laughed softly at the thought and tried to ignore the couple who looked at me like I was crazy as they strolled by.

There weren't many people about at this time and it was more than kind of nice. The past few days, the boardwalk had been packed with people as the high season kicked in and, as cool as it was to see it so alive, I'd also missed the quiet.

My heart sank as I approached Cooper's. The lights on his signage were switched off and the blinds were down on the windows and door.

Had I missed him?

I picked up my pace, hurrying to the front entrance.

I knocked hard. "Cooper, it's me!" I called.

At the sound of heavy footsteps beyond the door, I relaxed. When he unlocked the door and opened it for me I relaxed even more.

I remembered back to when we first met and how I hadn't seen him as the kind of guy I'd be attracted to. Sure, I'd thought, *Wow, amazing blue eyes,* but I hadn't thought, *Wow, he's the most beautiful man I've ever met.*

Now I was thinking, *Wow, he's the most beautiful man I've ever met* ever.

Cooper gave me a bemused look but stepped aside to let me in. "You okay?" he said as he locked up behind me.

Most of the lights in the bar had been turned off.

I suddenly felt bad for imposing on him. "You were heading home. I should let you head home. You'll be tired."

"I'm fine," he said. "Are you?"

"I just woke up."

"You want a drink?"

"Water, please."

All the chairs had been placed on the tabletops. I pulled one down and sat up on the table with my feet on the chair. Less than a minute later I had a glass of water in my hand and Cooper was leaning against the bar, watching me.

"It's been some day for you, Doc."

I gave a little laugh. "I'll say."

"You still freaking out?"

Staring at him, just being with him, I had the overwhelming realization that I wasn't freaking out and all evidence was suggesting his presence was the reason. "I was. Until I got here."

Cooper's eyes warmed.

I smiled before taking a sip of my water, studying him as he studied me. Those blue eyes of his traveled over me, lingering on my legs awhile, before slowly making their way back up to my face.

My breasts suddenly felt too tight against the fabric of my dress.

I finished the water and moved to get up.

"Don't move." The way his voice had turned suddenly deep held me captive.

He approached me slowly, carefully, and I felt my heart rate start to speed up as I waited for his next move.

I knew what move I wanted him to make and also suddenly realized that I'd come here for more than reassurance. I'd come here because I'd woken up turned on after a sexy dream about him.

Cooper gently took the water glass from me. "Stay right where you are," he demanded.

His tone brooked no argument and the heat in his eyes and his serious expression were an incredibly hot combination.

My breathing grew shallow as he strolled casually back to the bar to deposit the glass and then he turned back, his gaze burning through me.

"Cooper?" I whispered, somehow unable to raise my voice, fearing if I did I'd put a stop to whatever was about to happen.

He prowled toward me, his eyes never leaving my face. He stopped, his body pressed against the back of the chair my feet were on. "I had a dream about you a few nights ago."

There was a flip deep and low in my belly and an answering tingle between my thighs . . . because there was no mistaking what kind of dream he'd had. The sexual hunger in his expression told me everything.

My God.

I'd *never* had a man look at me like that before.

He made me want to strip off my dress then and there and let him feast on me.

"We were alone. In my bar," he continued, carefully moving the chair out from between us so that I had no choice but to scoot forward and plant my feet on the ground. "And you were on a table just like this." He moved closer and goose bumps rose up all over my arms as his fingertips trailed across the bare skin of my thigh. Cooper gently pressed against the inside of my legs there and moved into the space he'd created.

"Cooper," I murmured, my chest rising and falling quickly. I stared up at him, completely open to whatever he wanted to have happen next because at that moment my body was on fire for him. I wanted him to help me escape all the seriousness of the decisions I'd made that day.

His eyes dropped to my breasts, where he could plainly see how much his proximity was affecting me—my stiff nipples peaked against the fabric of my dress, begging for his touch.

Cooper's lips parted on an exhalation at the sight and he suddenly gripped the backs of my thighs, tugging me with a hard jerk against his straining erection. I grabbed on to his arms to steady myself and our eyes locked.

Mine told him how much I wanted this.

His were fierce with how much he wanted to give it to me.

I felt the bite of his fingers on my bare skin as he rocked me against him, the denim of his jeans catching on my thin, now damp, panties. I whimpered, pushing against him for more.

"Doc, in my dream," he said, his voice guttural, "I fucked you on the table. Hard. Fast."

The flip in my lower belly this time was bigger and as he moved me against him again I felt the slick wetness of my reaction to his words. I'd never liked Andrew talking to me during sex. It distracted me. But Cooper's blunt hot words were like foreplay.

Cooper bent his head to brush his lips gently against mine, and in the process he pressed his cock harder against me. "You up for making a man's dream come true?" he murmured against my mouth.

Fuck, but he was good with words!

My answer was to kiss him, my tongue flicking against his in a wet, erotic kiss that mimicked everything I wanted our bodies to do. I pulled back, breathless and excited and more alive than I could ever remember feeling.

"Thank God," Cooper muttered, nipping at my lips as I helped him remove my sweater. Once it was gone he slipped two fingers under each thin strap of my dress and smirked at me. "How come this is the first time I'm seeing you in a dress, Doc?"

"Today was too hot for pants." I was surprised I managed a coherent sentence while I was so freaking dazed by the lust roaring through my veins.

"Well, now it's too hot for clothes, period." He grinned at me, pulling the straps down my arms until my breasts were bared. His smile disappeared and I felt his cock grow impossibly hard between my legs. "Fuck me," he breathed, cupping my breasts in his big, warm, callused hands.

I whimpered, arching into his touch as he gently squeezed them and then brushed his thumbs over my nipples.

"You're beautiful, Jessica," he said gruffly, and something about him using my name instead of the nickname he'd given me made my sex throb even harder.

My fingers curled tighter around his biceps. "Cooper, please . . ."

At the hot, wet sensation of his mouth closing around my right nipple, my thighs automatically clamped against his hips. He sucked hard and lightning streaks of delicious heat seemed to score down my body to where his cock was currently rubbing against me.

Usually I loved the foreplay. I needed the foreplay.

I was never in an impatient rush to get to the main event.

But I was so unbelievably turned on that all I could think about was getting him inside of me.

"Fuck me, Cooper," I whispered, straining against him.

He lifted his head to stare at me, breathing fast. "Say it again," he demanded.

I slid my hands up his arms and behind his neck, my fingers curling in his soft, dark hair. I tugged him close to kiss him again because he was freaking fantastic at it. "Fuck me, Cooper," I repeated against his lips.

His hands were on my ribs and his grip tightened there. "You have no idea what it does to me when you say those words."

I smirked, hitching my legs higher against his hips and, in doing so, creating more friction between us. He was going to burst the zipper on his jeans if we didn't do something about it right then. "I think I do."

He kissed me again, this time sweet, slow, and languid, and it only fired my impatience.

Cooper abruptly stepped back from my body and I watched in wonder as he pulled his T-shirt over his head, throwing it at a nearby table.

"Holy . . ." I murmured, that impatience I'd been feeling quadrupled at the sight of his taut abs and big, strong shoulders. His tanned skin emphasized his muscled physique.

I'd wanted to explore every inch of him with my mouth and fingers since I'd seen him shirtless at the bandstand.

He really was the most ruggedly beautiful man I'd ever known.

A prick of emotion clogged in my throat as I drank in the sight of him.

He didn't take time to notice that my drooling over him was mixed with mooning over the fact that we'd found each other just when I most needed it—he was too busy staring at my body. That was okay. If he stared at me like a starving man for the rest of his life I'd be happy.

When he stepped back into my space I reached for him, caressing his stomach, and my fingertips followed his happy trail to the top button on his jeans.

I slipped the button out, but Cooper stilled my hand.

"Me first," he said.

I got what he meant when he grabbed hold of my ass and lifted me as if I weighed nothing until I was balanced precariously on the edge of the table. Eyes holding mine he hooked his fingers under my panties and began to draw them down my legs.

Cool air caressed me along my naked skin and I felt my core pulse.

My legs automatically opened for Cooper as he stepped between them to slip his fingers into me. "Oh, God," I groaned.

"Fuck, Jessica, I can't wait," he growled as soon as he felt how wet I was.

When his fingers slipped out of me my eyes popped open and I watched impatiently as he pulled a condom out of his wallet, threw the wallet aside, and then unzipped his jeans.

My gaze zeroed in on his thick, long dick, which stood at throbbing attention for me.

Yes, please!

It was like I was a teenager again. Or what I thought I would have felt as a teenager if I'd ever found a boy to love—impatient with emotion and, more urgently, hormones.

"Cooper," I said, and he heard the urgency in my tone because he was rolling the condom down his cock in seconds. He took hold of my thighs, parted them, and thrust inside of me. "Oh, God—" My breath caught at the sensation of him filling me.

All I could feel was him pulsing inside of me, and his heated skin under my fingertips. All I could smell was him—the woodsy cologne with a hint of spice he wore, and now the added base note of sex.

He was everywhere and everything.

His mouth came down on mine as he started to move in fast, hard thrusts. It was sensational. The desperateness to his kisses; the hurried, frantic rush for ecstasy.

"Jessica," he groaned, breaking our kiss to press his face against my neck, "Fuck, Jessica, yes, Jess, Jess . . ." He said my name every time he pounded into me.

I could only hold on for the ride, pleasure sparking me ever closer to igniting every time my inner muscles squeezed his cock.

I slid my hands down inside his jeans to grip his firm, muscled buttocks, urging him against me. I wanted it even harder, faster.

Cooper pulled back, his expression fierce as he got the message, and he tilted my lower body so he could slide into me at a different angle.

Lights exploded behind my eyes.

No joke.

I think I might have screamed.

"Oh, God!"

And suddenly everything was harder, faster, deeper, dirtier.

It was rough, unadulterated, fierce, raw sex.

I came hard, and the pulsing waves of my orgasm tugged Cooper's cock so intensely I took him over the edge with me.

"Fuck!" he growled, his hips jerking against mine as my body demanded his climax from him.

I rested my forehead on his strong shoulder and tried to catch my breath. If it wasn't for Cooper still holding me against him I think I might have melted right off the table onto the bar floor. My muscles were languid, like I'd just had a deep-tissue massage. Except sex with Cooper was better than any massage I'd ever had.

By a mile. By a thousand. Okay, a million.

My cheeks turned hotter than they already were because I suddenly wasn't sure if I should be embarrassed that it had taken me until I was thirty-three years old to have the best sex of my life.

As a doctor I knew that that was entirely normal. There were some women who couldn't orgasm from penetration alone and I was one of the lucky ones who could. There were some women who would go their whole lives having mediocre sex.

I should feel lucky.

But I was embarrassed to have climaxed so fast.

I was willing to bet Cooper had never been with a woman who had lit up and exploded that quickly. Usually, I made Andrew work for it and that got him all worked up and he *loved* that.

Likely Cooper's "outrageously gorgeous" ex-wife had made him work for it.

What if I seemed gauche and inexperienced in comparison?

"Doc," he murmured against my cheek, "I can practically *feel* you overthinking this."

I slowly pulled my head from his shoulder and looked into his face.

The low-lidded relaxed expression of satisfaction he wore eased my concerns a little. Cooper caught my lower lip with his thumb, his eyes steady as he said softly, "You've got the prettiest mouth I've ever seen in my life."

God! He was so charming. He'd literally charmed the panties right off me.

I suddenly remembered the woman on the beach and Bailey telling me he'd dated a lot of women before me. Practice made perfect after all, huh.

I froze.

How many women had he screwed in his pub?

He sighed and squeezed my waist as he slowly pulled out of me. "Wait right there."

He turned and walked toward the staff room, pulling up his jeans to cover my delectable view of the top of his muscular ass. Denied said view, I looked elsewhere and found myself mesmerized by the delicious V of his torso. I remembered what it felt like to cling to his big, broad shoulders as he moved in me.

Needing to occupy myself in some way, I hopped off the table, pulled the straps of my dress back up, grabbed my sweater, and searched for my panties. I couldn't find them.

"I thought I told you not to move." Cooper reappeared, his jeans refastened.

"No, you just said 'wait right there.'"

"On the table." He smirked at me as he reached for his T-shirt.

I wanted to pout when he put it back on.

But I didn't have any time because Cooper wrapped an arm around my waist and hauled me up against him. With his other hand he cupped my nape and drew me to him for a long, sweet, deep, intimate kiss that had me clinging to his strong shoulders again.

When he eventually broke our embrace he stared into my eyes as if he were searching for something. "You're not regretting this, are you, Doc?"

Why did it feel like having sex had complicated things so much? Usually sex was complication-free for me.

But before that night I'd been completely sure that Cooper was interested in exploring something more with me, and now I was freaking out that his interest would wane now that he'd had me.

I shook my head slowly. "No. It was good."

He scowled, his arms tightening around me so much there wasn't an inch of space between us. "It was better than fucking good, Jessica."

I scowled back and pushed at his chest for some breathing space. "Well, I'm sure you'd know all about that."

"What the fuck does that mean?"

"You use the word 'fuck' a lot."

"It's a good *fucking* word."

I was tempted to laugh at how disgruntled he sounded and he seemed to catch my amusement because his hold on me eased.

"What's going on in your head, Jess?"

I thought about evading this conversation. I'd never had to have an adult, open conversation with a man about sex. However, I realized, somewhat reluctantly, if I wanted something more with Cooper Lawson I was going to have to give him more than I was used to giving.

I couldn't change his past, but I could figure out what it was he wanted in the future by just being honest and asking the question.

"You still want something with me, right? This"—I gestured behind me to the table—"it wasn't just about sex."

"No," he said. "It's not just about sex."

As I heaved a sigh of relief, he let go of my waist to cup my face in his hands, dipping his head down to mine so our noses almost touched. He stared deep into my eyes and I shivered. I felt like he was trying to see right into my soul.

"I'm in this for the long haul, Doc. I was before you walked into my bar tonight, but now, after the best fucking sex of my life, after how wild that was, there's no way I'm letting you walk out of here without me."

And there he went doing it again.

His words resonated deep within me along with giving me that deep, sexual belly flip of arousal.

My fingers curled into the top of his biceps. "Best sex of my life, too," I murmured. "It stunned me a little. Confused me . . . I thought maybe . . . you . . . this was old hat for you . . ."

He gave me a crooked grin. "You think I make a habit of fucking women in my bar."

"You could," I said. "You are definitely a man who could pull that off."

Cooper threw his head back in laughter and I pressed my body deeper into his to feel his joy.

And then he wrapped his arms around me and hugged me.

Just as I'd suspected, he was a really good hugger.

When he pulled back he was smiling gently at me. "You're the only woman I've had in my bar." He let me go only to take my hand in his. "No one sits at that table anymore." He gestured to the scene of the best sex we'd both ever had. "It's now a shrine."

"You can't do that!" I was mortified at the possibility of people finding out why there was a table in Cooper Lawson's bar that no one was allowed to sit at.

"I can. It's my bar. I think I'll even carve 'Coop and Doc were here' on it."

Finally getting that he was joking, I made a face. "Funny."

"You're slow on the uptake tonight," he teased.

"My brain was just frazzled by the orgasm to beat all orgasms."

He squeezed my hand. "You up for more brain frazzling?"

I shivered at the thought. "Definitely."

His eyes darkened. "Let's go back to my place."

Exhilarated by the prospect, I followed him, and it wasn't until we'd stepped outside the bar into the cool night air that I said, "I don't suppose you know where my panties are?"

"I do, actually." He led me to the back of his bar to the parking lot. A dark-colored GMC was the only truck there.

"Um . . . could I have them, please?"

He stopped me at the passenger side of the truck, pressing me up against the car. "Why?" he whispered against my lips before he kissed me deeply. He came up for air a few seconds later. "You're not going to need them where we're going."

The nagging pressure between my legs increased. "You are so very, very good at stringing the exact right words together."

He kissed me again.

"You're just good with your mouth in general," I murmured.

Cooper grinned and brushed his lips over mine. "In the truck, Doc."

SIXTEEN

Cooper

The sound of his phone binging on the bedside table woke Cooper from a sound sleep. He was just about to reach for it when he became aware of the heat of her body and the smell of her perfume.

Jessica.

He opened his eyes to find her soft blond hair spilled out over the pillow in front of him, a few strands tickling his nose and chin. He couldn't see her face, but her shoulders were bared, the sheet on his bed covering them both only to the waist.

One of his arms was stretched out along the pillow by her head, and his other was curled tight around her waist. His left leg was insinuated between hers, and his cock was pressed against the round cheeks of her ass.

He'd never slept with a woman like this before.

Not even Dana.

Dana had hated spooning—said it made her too hot, too uncomfortable.

That had never bothered him.

But that was because he didn't know what he was missing until now.

Cooper buried his nose in Jessica's neck, biting back a groan as the blood rushed to his dick. The night before, he'd fucked this amazing woman in the pub, then brought her home to his place, where he'd made love to her in his bed. The sex had been great, but it brought out something vulnerable in her and Cooper found he didn't like how uncertain she'd seemed about him. The doc was sexually confident at first and he liked that about her. He didn't want to be a guy who took that confidence from her. He wanted to be the guy she felt free with—not insecure about—and he had a feeling Bailey had been filling Jessica's ears with rumors about his behavior over the past eighteen months.

He wanted her to know that she wasn't just some woman he wanted to fuck.

And so he'd taken his time when they got back to his place, exploring every inch of her curvy, gorgeous body . . . making love to her.

Hopefully she was more sure of him now.

Because he didn't want to ever leave this bed as long as she was in it.

He heard her little gasp as she woke up to feel his erection pressed between the cheeks of her ass.

"You've got me addicted, Doc," he murmured in her ear.

Jessica turned to face him and as she did he curled his hand around her full breast, his thumb catching her sweet nipple when it peaked against his touch. She gave him a sleepy, sexy smile as she hitched her leg over his and his cock strained further against her. "Morning," she murmured, sliding her arm around his shoulder and moving in closer for a soft kiss.

"I can't remember the last time I woke up to something this sweet," he said, caressing her body as he moved his hips into her.

She gave a little gasp again, her neck arching slightly, her full lips parting.

Sexy as hell.

He slid his hand over her soft stomach and down between her thighs. His thumb pressed in, catching her clit, and she moaned. He played her until her hips were undulating against him for more and then he pushed two fingers inside her, groaning at the feel of her wetness.

"Jessica." He didn't know how to explain how much he loved being with her like this without sounding like a lovesick schoolboy.

Her fingers dug into his back as her panting increased.

She was ready.

Cooper wanted inside her, with nothing between them.

"You on the pill, Doc?" he said, his fingers moving faster, pushing her toward orgasm.

"Ah," she whispered, her grip digging deeper, "Cooper, ah . . ."

"Doc. Pill?"

"Yes, yes . . ." She shook her head. "But . . . not . . . not been checked. Condom."

Fuck.

She had to go and be sensible about it. "We both get checked ASAP, Doc. I want nothing between us. Just you and me."

Her inner muscles rippled around his fingers and he savored the sight as she came around him. Jessica gave everything over to it. There was no bullshit posing, no fakeness, no shyness. Jess let go completely. And when she did it was sexier than anything he'd ever seen.

Her eyes closed; her cheeks flushed; she cried out—she let it take over as she arched her back into the sensations, thrusting her beautiful tits up in invitation.

Cooper took what she offered.

Cupping her breasts, caressing and memorizing the soft, gorgeous globes, he wrapped his mouth around one dark, flushed nipple and sucked at it.

"Oh, God!" Jess cried again, her hips jerking against his as he sucked and licked her nipples, one and then the other.

"You taste so fucking good," he growled, pulling away only to push her gently onto her back.

He grabbed a condom from his bedside drawer and ripped it out of the wrapper.

"Let me." Jessica sat up, reaching for the condom.

He pulled the sheet back, revealing his dick, and it jumped at the way she licked her lips like she wanted to eat him.

"Can't wait much longer, Jessica," he warned her, his voice guttural with need.

She stopped ogling him and started rolling the condom down his swollen cock.

Heaven.

Fucking heaven.

She made it even more heavenly by taking him between her fingers and thumb and giving him a hard jerk.

"Jesus, Jess." He grabbed her wrist and pushed her back on the bed with his body. "Another time." He kissed her hard, deep. "Definitely."

Wrapping her arms around his back, she lifted her hips into him and gave him a smile of hunger and anticipation. "I can't wait to taste you."

He shuddered at the thought and gripped her by the hips, positioning himself at her entrance. "Tit for tat, Doc. You suck me off, I promise you I'll make you come harder than you've ever come, just using my tongue."

Desire flared in her eyes and she made a little whimpering noise that killed him. "I think I just came right now."

"Not without me this time." He drove into her, her snug channel clamping down on his dick, so hot and wet and tight . . . fucking perfect.

Fucking heaven.

"I'll be right back." The doc pressed a kiss to his lips before darting into his bathroom with her dress bundled up in her hands.

He supposed he should return her panties to her.

Grinning at the thought of her having to ask him for them, Cooper turned to pick up his phone. He'd just remembered it had binged before he and Jessica got carried away with unbelievable morning sex.

He was happy—and he couldn't remember the last time he'd felt this alive.

Sure, he had moments of enjoyment—usually when he was hanging with Joey—but contentment wasn't the same as out-and-out happiness.

The doc made him happy.

He swiped the screen on his phone and just like that the grin was knocked clean off his face.

We have to talk. Dana. xx.

Cooper cursed and deleted the text. He'd blocked her number from his phone, so either she had gotten a new number or she was using someone else's phone to contact him.

Damn it. He'd thought she'd gotten over harassing him after last time, but obviously someone had told her about Jessica.

Shit.

"Hey, you okay?"

He glanced up from his phone. Jessica was leaning against the doorjamb of the bathroom, makeupless, dress wrinkled, hair wild from his hands, and she was still the most beautiful thing he'd ever seen.

No way was Dana taking this happy moment away from him.

"Everything's great, Doc." He threw off the sheet. "Let me have a quick shower and I'll get you back to the inn." She was far too tempting standing in his doorway. He pressed into her instead of passing her by and stole a sweet kiss from her. Cooper loved how she just melted into him at the first touch. "You sure you don't want to shower with me?"

She caught her bottom lip with her teeth and reluctantly shook her head as her hands explored his chest. "I shouldn't."

"You should do whatever you want."

"If I get in the shower with you, I'll make us late."

That sounded too good to pass up.

Cooper took hold of the hem of her dress and drew it up over her head. Jessica raised her arms to help him relieve her of the fabric.

He threw the dress in the direction of the bed and then scooped her up into his arms.

Jessica whooped with surprised laughter and wrapped her arms around his neck.

Pure joy shone out of her big hazel eyes as he carried her back into the bathroom and placed her gently on her feet in his shower.

When he got in beside her, moving her out of the way of the water—because it came on freezing cold before it turned hot—and conveniently placing her up against the wall, she said, "Best morning ever, Coop."

Those four little words made his chest go tight with a warm ache.

"Yeah," he murmured against her mouth. "Not going to argue with that."

There were only a few occasions when Cooper had been late getting to the bar to open up, but each of those times he'd been able to rely on Jace to open the place. Jace had worked as a bartender at the pub for the last five years and had a key.

Sure enough, after Cooper dropped off Jessica at the inn and then pulled into the parking lot behind his bar, he saw Jace's and Crosby's trucks parked there.

He was really late.

But damn it had been worth it.

He grinned as he walked around front instead of going in the back door through the kitchen. When Crosby was setting up he liked peace and quiet. In fact, Crosby liked peace and quiet, period. His least favorite time of year was the current busy season because Cooper always hired another cook to help him out.

The grin Cooper wore immediately died when he stepped inside his bar. Dana was sitting on a stool, smiling and talking to Jace. They both looked up at his entrance, Dana's eyes lighting up at the sight of him like they used to when they first started dating.

Jace had the good sense to look concerned.

"Back room. Now," Cooper said to him, ignoring Dana completely.

His bartender reluctantly followed him into his office.

"Look, Coop, before you saying anything, you know I was angrier than anyone for what Dana pulled on you, but I found her outside and she was crying, man. She really seems like she knows she's fucked up."

"Jesus Christ, Jace." Cooper glowered at his idiocy. "That woman is the most manipulative person I've ever met. Do you want to know why she's really here?"

Jace crossed his arms over his chest, looking uncomfortable.

"She's here because word reached her that I'm seeing Jessica. She knows I've moved on and she's not too happy about me doing that first."

"Fuck," Jace muttered, running a hand over his head, looking more than a little sheepish.

Cooper walked over to him and clamped a hand on his shoulder. "I'll forgive you once for letting her into my bar, because you're young and when I was your age I was stupid enough to let my cock do my thinking, too. Warning, Jace: Dana is beautiful and she can be sweet . . . but then she gets her hooks in you and that all turns to shit pretty quick."

"Coop, I'm sorry, man."

"Wait here while I get rid of her." He sighed, not looking forward to that task, especially pissed that she'd have to ruin the best morning he'd had in a long time.

"Cooper," she said breathily as he walked back into the bar. She stood up from her stool and he took in what she was wearing with more than a little annoyance.

It was a tight-fitting white summer dress that contrasted with her even tan. She wore it with wedged heels with white ties that wrapped around her slim ankles. The first day she'd walked into their kitchen wearing that outfit he'd been so taken by her beauty he'd made love to her right there and made her promise to wear that dress only for him in the future.

But that was back when he thought the passion between them was enough.

Now the sight of her left him cold. Like he was staring at a pretty doll and nothing more.

He ignored her intended manipulation with the dress. "You need to leave. Right now."

Dana hurried over to him, stopping just short of touching him when he warned her with his stern expression to not even dare. "Look . . . I stopped coming around because I knew you needed more time . . . but I can't wait any longer. Cooper, you have to know how deeply sorry I am for what I did. I was feeling adrift from you and instead of being mature about it, I got mad and stupid and did a thing that I can't even believe that I did." She begged him with her eyes. "Please forgive me. Please. I miss you so much."

Cooper wasn't sure he didn't believe her. The missing-him part. After all, he had taken care of her. Dana didn't have to worry about being an adult with adult responsibilities when he was around. He felt almost sorry for her now. She was a woman who needed to be taken care of completely. And right now she was so busy seething at the idea of someone else having what she considered hers she couldn't see far enough in front of her to realize there were any number of stupid men out there who would take care of her.

"I thought we were finished with this, Dana," he said. "I told you before that I'm done. You need to respect that."

"You're not done. *We're* not done."

He saw the glint of anger she was trying to hide and that did it for him. "The only reason you're back bothering me is because you heard something in town that you didn't like."

"About your doctor." She jumped on it immediately, as he'd known she would. "Not exactly your type, Cooper," she sneered.

"You think you're my type, Dana?"

"Yes, I am. I am not threatened by this doctor, whoever she is." She huffed, crossing her arms over her chest as she glared up at him.

"She's just one more woman in a long line of women. You've been sticking your dick in anything that moves since our divorce."

"Christ." He breathed out in disbelief. "You have no class."

"Oh, and *she* does, does she?"

Dana wasn't even in the same league as Jessica. He'd known the doc only a few weeks, but he'd learned the hard way how to tell a good woman from a not so good one. "In spades. And she's not just some woman. She's *my* woman. You stay out of our way, Dana," he warned.

Her lips parted in shock. "You don't mean that," she whispered.

"Every fucking word. Now get the hell out of my bar."

And finally she left, but not without giving him the kicked-puppy look that used to work on him all too well.

She might have retreated, but Cooper knew it was only so she could plan a new strategy.

SEVENTEEN

Jessica

Bailey had given me a knowing grin when she saw me hurrying into the inn in the wrinkled dress I'd been wearing the day before. She was too busy talking to a guest to give me crap about it, but I knew I didn't have long to wait until she did.

I'd just finished dressing when I heard the knock on the door, and I had to shake myself out of my stupor. Even dressing had become erotic to me. It was like Cooper had awakened something in my blood, and just the whisper of my fingers across my skin, the brush of fabric as it touched my body, set off memories of his mouth, his hands, *him* thrusting inside of me.

Oh boy.

I knew I must be flushed and by the look on Bailey's face when I opened my bedroom door I saw I was not wrong.

"Tell me everything," she said, striding into the room.

I closed the door for privacy and gave in to the fact that I really had no choice in the matter but to tell her. Not that I minded. I'd never had a girlfriend to talk boys with. I'd never had a boy to discuss. I grinned, giddily.

"Oh, my God." She gave a bark of laughter at my expression. "You've got it so bad."

"You would, too," I said defensively. "If you'd just had the night I had."

Bailey's excitement level went up tenfold as she clapped her hands in delight, looking more like a teenager than ever. "Tell me everything."

"I went to see him last night when I woke up because I just . . . I don't know . . . I guess I needed to. When I got there . . . well . . ." I grinned, getting hot at the memory. "We had sex on a table in his bar."

"No way!" She slapped my arm, laughing. "Which table? Because, as hot as that is, I would like to avoid it."

I shook my head, chuckling. "I'm sure he's already taken care of it."

"Sex on a table in his bar. That's hot."

"Oh, you have no idea."

"That good, huh?"

"Best I've ever had."

"Holy shit. Then what happened?"

I told her about going back to his place, where he made love to me. How we fell asleep in each other's arms, how safe but turned on I felt to wake up in his arms, how he made love to me again, and then fucked me in the shower.

When I was done, Bailey was looking at me with undisguised envy. "Holy shit."

I frowned, a little surprised by the depth of her envy. "You and Tom have great sex, though, right?"

She hesitated a second before nodding too fast. "Of course."

Hmm.

I wasn't convinced.

And that surprised me because they seemed really in love.

But maybe you could be in love and not have great sex.

"What you and Cooper have, though, sounds like higher levels of hot," she said, a little in awe. "It sounds very special."

I smiled. "I think it is. I hope it is. Anyway, I'm too wired to just hang around today so I was hoping you might want to show me the ropes."

"You want to start early?"

"If you don't mind."

"Of course not." Bailey jumped to her feet. "Let's get you started."

First we started off in her small office, where she showed me how to use their booking system. Bookings came in online through hotel sites, trip comparison sites, and her own website. Then we moved on to reception, where she had another computer with the same booking system on it.

"I'm going to go talk to Mona first, make her aware I'm bringing you into the kitchen to go over the menu, our dining schedule, blah-de-blah-blah. We have guests arriving this afternoon: Mr. and Mrs. Urquhart. Greet them in a friendly manner, casual; just be yourself. Book them in using the computer, get their key"—she pointed to the locked cabinet with keys in it behind the reception desk and handed me the master key to the cabinet—"and then show them to their room."

It was pretty straightforward so I wasn't concerned I'd mess it up.

"I'll just be five minutes while I speak with Mona."

I was looking over the booking system, familiarizing myself with how it worked and when new guests were arriving (and sneaking a peek at what lucky devils would be taking my room when my vacation officially ended), when the bell over the door jingled.

I glanced up, smiling to greet the new guests.

However, a lone woman stood in the entrance, sweeping her gaze around the inn. When her eyes fell on me she tensed.

I walked around the desk. "May I help you?"

The woman walked toward me, drinking me in from head to toe, examining every inch of me with a scrutiny that immediately rubbed me the wrong way. She was a very beautiful woman, and it pained me to be openly measured by anyone, let alone someone so gorgeous.

That irritation only grew when she gave me a satisfied, smug smile. The smugness, however, didn't detract from her beauty. She was a little taller than me, slimmer, with a tanned, toned athletic body. Her shoulder-length brown hair framed her face attractively in waves and was lightened near the ends with caramel-blond streaks. Her eyes were ice blue and had an exotic tilt to the corners. A perfect little nose matched symmetrical perfect lips and went well with her high cheekbones. I didn't think I'd met anyone quite as beautiful as her.

She stood in front of me in a white summer dress that clung to her toned curves and showcased long, lean legs. I suddenly had this horrible feeling in my gut.

"Are you the doctor?" she said.

"I am."

Her gaze narrowed. "I'm Dana. Cooper Lawson's wife."

That feeling in my gut worsened.

This . . . this was Cooper's ex?

Bailey had not been lying when she described her as outrageously gorgeous.

Holy crap.

I felt a wave of insecurity roll over me and instantly resented it.

"Ex-wife, you mean." Bailey appeared, striding out of the dining room into reception. She did not look happy, and that was putting it lightly. "What the hell are you doing here, Dana?"

Dana flicked Bailey a dirty look before turning back to me, all wide-eyed with faux innocence. "I'm just here to warn Dr. Huntington away from Cooper. It's a friendly warning, believe me, because he'll only break your heart."

I narrowed my eyes on the she-witch. She was everything I'd heard and more, and I couldn't believe she'd had the audacity to show up to spook me. "And why is that?" I said, making sure I sounded bored.

"Because he and I have unfinished business. I made a mistake and I'm going to try to make up for it. If you were any kind of good person you'd take a step back and let me fix my marriage."

She said it like it was completely reasonable.

I was shocked. Beyond shocked. Plus, I was growing more than a little concerned this woman was going to be a problem for us.

Bailey, however, opened her mouth, looking so outraged, I knew the put-down of all put-downs was about to come out of her. I gave her a quick shake of my head, a silent warning to leave this to me.

She clamped her mouth shut.

I stepped toward Dana and she took a step back in surprise, before trying to cover her surprise with a look of feigned nonchalance.

Hmm.

She was hoping I was going to be a pushover.

Well, I'd faced bigger and badder things in this world than Cooper's ex-wife and there was no way I was giving him up so easily. Not when there was so much possibility between us. Cooper made me happy and right now I was too invested in that happiness to have it taken away from me.

"Let me get this right: you cheated on a good man—with his best friend in the whole world, no less, thus stealing that friendship from him as well as betraying him—and you come here warning me away from him? If you have any decency left in you, you'll let Cooper be happy and leave him alone."

"Cooper loves me." Dana tilted her chin up in defiance. "We have history. You can't beat history. I want him back and I warn you, I *always* get what I want." She smirked at me. "Final warning: I am going to get Cooper back and I also don't care what I have to do in order to get him."

Fury rushed through me, not only at what she was suggesting but at the idea of her hurting Cooper. My protective instincts had me facing up to her in a way I knew she hadn't expected. "Are you threatening me?"

Something like uncertainty flashed in her eyes before she quickly hid it. "Just a warning." She shrugged and then gave me a sharklike grin. "May the best woman win."

The bell tinkled above the door as she swooped out of the inn.

Bailey and I stood in shocked silence for a few seconds.

Then . . . "What. The. Hell?" Bailey said.

I felt more than a little sick at the thought of already having an enemy in my new town.

"You're not going to break things off with Cooper, are you?" Bailey said, visibly concerned.

"Heck no." I screwed up my face, feeling the stubborn determination fire my blood. "That horrible witch hurt someone that I care about and there is no way she's going to do that again on my watch." My voice softened as I thought of him. "The truth is that I really believe there's something special between us and I really believe he thinks that, too. I won't take this away from him because of one spoiled little brat."

Bailey grinned. "Good."

"There's a childish part of me that wants to flaunt our relationship all over town," I admitted.

She laughed and threw her arm around my shoulders. "Oh, my God, we are *so* soul sisters."

Cooper

Laughter drifted over from the crowd of women around his pool table and Cooper did his best to ignore it.

He wouldn't give her what she wanted.

She wanted his attention.

When Dana had walked into the pub earlier that night overdressed in a short black dress, along with a bunch of her girlfriends, all overdressed, too, he knew he couldn't make a scene. If he made a scene then it was like he was proving she bothered him.

As it was, all his regulars kept glaring over at her, struck by disbelief that she had the audacity to turn up there.

Cooper had spent the previous night in bed with Jessica, wiping away the annoyance of Dana showing up.

Now she was back to fuck with him and he wasn't quite sure what was the best way to handle it.

"This is unbelievable," Ollie said as he pulled a draft for a customer. Ollie had been working nights with him for a while, and like anyone who lived in Hartwell he knew the full story about Dana.

"Just ignore her," Cooper said.

"You should throw her out."

"I'm not giving her the satisfaction."

"You got more cool than me, boss." Ollie sighed.

Cooper grunted, finished making the cocktails for Dana and her crew, and passed them to Lily.

She was not happy. "Do I really have to serve her?"

"Yes. But you don't have to do it with a smile."

Mischief glinted in her eyes. "Sure thing, boss."

He shook his head in amusement, his attention then immediately caught by the bar door as it opened.

Anticipation lifted his mood as Jessica walked in with Bailey at her side. Jess wore jeans that were molded to her long legs and a black sleeveless shirt that showed off a generous amount of her cleavage. It also wrapped over and tied at the side in a big bow—practically an extended invitation for him to pull the damn thing open.

He'd definitely be doing that later.

She walked straight to him, grinning at him the whole time, and he could feel the huge smile on his face in return.

"Hey," she said, slipping onto the stool in front of him.

"Hey back." His eyes dipped to her mouth. "Is that all I'm getting?"

"Hmm." She considered him. "Have you been good today?"

That ache he felt for her got bigger. "Not really, Doc," he murmured, leaning over the bar so only she could hear. "See, I've been having all sorts of dirty thoughts today."

Jessica bit her lip to try to stem an excited smile. "About me, I hope."

"Every. Fucking. One."

"Dirty is good," she murmured back and leaned in to meet him.

Her kiss was soft, sweet, just the tip of her tongue touching his before she pulled back.

"Tease," he murmured, grinning.

He heard a throat being cleared. Loudly. And that was when Cooper remembered where the hell they were.

Shit. The doc had a way of making everything in the world disappear but her.

Bailey was the throat clearer. "Just thought I'd remind you that you have an audience." She gave him a girlish finger wave.

"Bailey," he said in acknowledgment.

She grinned at him. "How's it going?"

"It's been better," Ollie said, sidling up to them from the other end of the bar. "We have company." His eyes flicked to the pool area.

Cooper sighed, bracing himself for Bailey's reaction. As soon as she saw Dana, she'd explain to Jess who she was. And Cooper wasn't looking forward to that.

To his surprise both Bailey *and* Jessica looked shocked when they turned to view the pool area.

What the hell . . .

"Dana?" Bailey whipped her head around to glare at him, but Cooper was too busy studying Jessica, who had paled.

"Doc?" he said, an ugly suspicion creeping into his mind. "Please tell me you haven't met Dana before."

Bailey frowned. "Of course she has. Yesterday. When the bit—"

"Bailey." Jessica hushed her.

Instead of hushing, Bailey glowered at her. "You didn't tell him?"

"Tell me what?" he snapped.

"I didn't want to stress him out," Jessica hissed.

"Stress him out? He has a right to know she threatened you."

"What?" His voice was louder this time, drawing attention, but Cooper couldn't give a fuck. His blood was quickly turning hotter than sense could handle.

Jessica looked at him, reluctance in her gorgeous eyes. "She came to the inn yesterday to warn me to back off—she promised that she was going to do whatever it takes to get you back and that I was only going to get my heart broken in the end when she won."

"Oh, and she also referred to herself as your *wife*," Bailey huffed. "Present tense."

What the fucking fuck!

The idea that Dana would try to take Jessica from him, after everything she'd already taken, ripped through him.

There was no way he was going to sit back and let her get away with that shit.

"Hey, guys." Dahlia suddenly appeared beside Bailey, smiling broadly at them all.

Cooper barely even registered her. He couldn't see anything past his anger.

Storming around the bar, he threw up the counter with so much fury he almost ripped the thing off its hinges. He was vaguely aware of his name being called, but he wasn't stopping for anybody.

Dana looked up from taking a shot at the pool table and her girlfriends turned to watch him storm toward them.

He saw uneasiness in her expression as he approached.

Good.

He pushed past two of her friends and leaned on the pool table so his face was level with Dana's. He wanted this to truly sink in at last. "You listen to me, and you listen good. You and I are over, Dana. *Over.* I don't want you. I'll never want you again and I don't know how many ways I can say that before you get it. So . . . you threaten Jessica again or harass me again, I will go to the sheriff, because you're acting like a fucking crazy person."

Dana flinched.

"Do you understand me?"

She stared at him in shock.

"Do you understand me?" he yelled.

The whole bar silenced behind him.

Dana swallowed and straightened away from him. She nodded slowly.

Cooper stood up.

He couldn't stand the sight of her.

Calming a little as he sensed he'd finally gotten through, he said, voice soft but no less angry, "Now get the fuck out of my bar and don't ever come back."

Some of her friends looked embarrassed as they grabbed their purses, but not Dana. She held her head high as she strode out of his bar, refusing for even a second to be humbled.

When he was younger he'd thought she possessed sexy confidence. Now he knew it as blind, ignorant arrogance.

Cooper looked out over the crowd. Everyone was staring at him. His regulars wore looks of sympathy, while tourists looked unsure.

God damn it.

"Sorry about the interruption," he said, striding back to the bar. "Next round is on the house."

That should settle the tourists.

As for him . . . his blood was still pumping. His eyes fell on Jessica. He knew exactly how he wanted to work out the adrenaline racing around his system, but the look of worry she was wearing warned him off.

He slipped behind the bar.

"It had to be said, Coop." Ollie clapped him on the shoulder.

He gave him a nod but made his way over to Jessica.

He didn't know what to say.

He wanted to know what she was thinking.

She looked like she wanted to know what he was thinking.

But there were too many people around for that conversation.

"Um . . ." Dahlia said, "what did I just walk into?"

Bailey grinned up at her friend. "Dahlia, meet Jessica. Jessica is Cooper's new girlfriend and our new best friend."

Dahlia laughed as she gazed at a still shell-shocked Jessica. "Ah. Now everything makes sense."

"What makes sense?" Vaughn was suddenly there, slipping into the space between Jessica and the customer on her left.

Bailey glowered at him. "What are you doing here?"

"I'm here to give you all the good news," he said, his tone suggesting it was anything but.

"And what good news is that?" Dahlia said.

Vaughn looked at Cooper and the uneasiness in his eyes made Cooper still, distracting him from the bad scene with Dana. "George Beckwith is selling up. Ian Devlin is gloating all over town about how he's finally going to have a spot on the boardwalk."

"Fuck!" Bailey snapped.

Vaughn flicked her a rueful look. "For once, Miss Hartwell, we are in absolute agreement."

Jessica

I was still so stunned from watching Cooper throw his ex-wife out of the bar that I got whiplash from Vaughn's change of subject.

It was like he'd appeared out of nowhere.

"Wow, things have gotten exciting around here," Dahlia said beside me. "Never let me go on vacation again."

"Exciting? This isn't exciting," Bailey huffed. "This is horrifying."

Confused, I held up a hand to stop anyone from saying anything else. I understood no one liked the Devlins, but they were acting like this news was Armageddon. "Okay, I know Ian Devlin is unscrupulous, but why exactly is it *such* a bad thing for him to have a place on the boardwalk? Won't it mean he'll finally stop harassing you guys?"

Bailey sighed. "As businesses we work closely together. Well"—she shot Vaughn a suspicious look—"most of us work closely together, and none of us want to work with Devlin."

Vaughn leaned on the bar beside me and I was suddenly caught in his pale gray eyes as they focused on me. "Despite Miss Hartwell's lack of enthusiasm for me, there really are no issues between any of us. We understand one another's place here. Devlin, however, is the kind of man who likes to stir up trouble and he has a certain vision for the boardwalk. All of this—Cooper's bar, Bailey's inn, Dahlia's gift store, Ira and Iris's place, the bookstore next door—doesn't fit Devlin's vision. He wants to bulldoze it and create something sleek, modern, and shiny in its place. Think European designer stores and five-star restaurants."

"Your hotel fits that description," Bailey said.

Vaughn flicked his gaze to her. "I'm aware. But my hotel is successful because Hart's Boardwalk is popular. As it is. Rule of thumb in business and life, Miss Hartwell: if it ain't broke, don't fix it."

From the sound of Ian Devlin's vision for a new boardwalk, he wanted to destroy everything I loved about this place. He wanted to take away all of its character and authenticity and make it something for just the elite. "He can't do that," I snapped.

Cooper suddenly reached over and took my hand. "The problem is, we don't know what Devlin is really capable of. He's shady. Ruthless. If he becomes part of this community, throwing his weight around, at the very least our lives will be more stressful."

"Surely George won't sell to him," Dahlia said, sounding worried.

Vaughn straightened from his spot beside me. His look was grim. "Beckwith is moving to Canada permanently. He'll sell to the highest bidder."

Bailey made a face at him. "George isn't just a businessman, Tremaine. He's a Hartwell man. He won't sell to Devlin."

His answer was to grunt in disbelief.

"Worst-case scenario . . ." Cooper said. "He might."

"Well, you've got a ton of money," Bailey said, gesturing to Vaughn. "You buy it."

"I *am* a businessman. I'm a hotel man. I don't need a second hotel here. I don't go after what I don't need."

"What about going after what you want?" she huffed.

Those steely eyes of his suddenly narrowed on her and his tone turned low, sexy, and more than a little dangerous. "Oh, Miss Hartwell, you don't ever want me going after what I want."

My eyes bugged out at the insinuation and I tried to peek at Bailey surreptitiously. For once he'd completely silenced her. Her lips were parted in shock and I could tell she was trying to work out what the hell he meant by that comment.

I looked at Cooper, who was looking down at the bar, wearing an amused smirk. Feeling my perusal, he glanced up at me, caught my bugged-out expression, and grinned.

"Um, the point, anyway"—Dahlia threw Vaughn a bewildered look—"is that we need to do something to stop this. Ideas?"

"And that's my cue to leave," Vaughn said.

"Of course," Bailey bit out. "Of course you'd leave."

"I just came as the messenger."

"Well, messenger of doom suits you. Good job," she said sarcastically.

He rolled his eyes toward Cooper and gave him a beleaguered look.

Cooper struggled not to laugh. "Thanks for the heads-up."

Vaughn nodded before turning to me. "Good night, Dr. Huntington."

"You know you can call me Jessica," I said.

I heard Bailey squeak in indignation behind me.

He heard it, too, and smiled. "Jessica." He flicked his gaze to Dahlia. "Miss McGuire." And without looking at her, Vaughn began walking away and called over his shoulder, "Good night, Miss Hartwell."

"Tremaine," Bailey growled under her breath.

It took everything within me not to burst out laughing.

"Well, hell," Old Archie suddenly called from the other side of the bar, pulling us all out of the moment. "That put a damper on things. But I still remember you said next round on the house, Coop."

"You would, Archie," Cooper drawled as he headed over to serve him.

As soon as Archie spoke, I immediately thought of Anita and wondered how she was doing. Archie didn't seem too perturbed so I guessed her results weren't back yet.

"Hey, Archie." Dahlia slid onto the stool beside Bailey. "How's Anita?"

"Oh, she isn't feeling so good. The doctor is doing some tests or something, but I'm not worried." He gave a tired smile. "You know Anita. That woman is made of steel. She's with me, isn't she?"

Dahlia smiled at his crack. "Tell her I'm asking for her."

He nodded and took the draft Cooper shoved toward him.

"Okay, ignoring for a second the dramatic bombshell Tremaine dropped," Bailey said, still sounding aggravated, "proper introductions are in order."

Sitting between us, she touched my arm and looked at Dahlia. "Dahlia, meet Jessica." She looked at me and touched Dahlia's arm. "Jessica, meet Dahlia."

I grinned and reached past Bailey to shake Dahlia's hand. "It's nice to finally meet you."

She grinned at me. "Same to you. Looks like you've sparked some excitement around here."

Dahlia McGuire, I soon noted as we all began to chat, was an intriguing mix of an adorable personality and beautiful features. For the most part she was cute because there was a slight goofiness about her manner—the way she pulled exaggerated faces whether she was laughing or pretending to be horrified or surprised—but when she was still and serious she was beautiful. Her hair was the stuff of envy. It was thick and black and fell down her back in luscious waves. Thick bangs (adding to the cuteness) framed her large crystal-blue eyes. She had a delicate nose and lush mouth, and that with her big eyes reminded me of the Bratz dolls my goddaughter loved collecting. Dahlia and Bailey shared a similar peaches-and-cream complexion—except Dahlia didn't have cute freckles over her nose like Bailey did.

What added to Dahlia's cuteness was her height. She was a couple of inches shorter than me, but like me she was curvy. My height stretched out my curves. Dahlia's height seemed to emphasize hers and she was dressed in a tight summer dress that captured her sensuality. I wondered if there was a man alive who didn't drool when Dahlia McGuire walked by.

"Jess has been wanting to get into your store since she got here. I told her about your jewelry."

"You're welcome anytime," Dahlia said.

I'd been staring at her earrings for a while. Each was a large hammered copper heart with a smaller hammered silver heart layered over it. "Did you make those?"

She fingered them. "Yup."

"Those are beautiful. Are you open tomorrow?" Not that I had the extra cash to spend on jewelry . . .

Dahlia laughed and nodded.

Cooper had been busy at the bar, but I was aware of him the whole time I spoke with Dahlia. When he stopped by us, I looked up at him and immediately got ensnared in his gaze. "You ladies come up with any solutions to the Devlin problem?"

"No," Bailey said. "We've been talking about Dahlia's jewelry."

"I thought you were worried."

Clearly *he* was.

I frowned, wanting to comfort him.

"I am," Bailey insisted. "But solutions don't come to me at the end of a long day. My brain works better first thing in the morning and I promise if I think of anything I will let you know."

"I think our best bet is George," Dahlia said. "We just need to talk him out of selling to Devlin."

I felt a sudden flurry of butterflies at the mention of George. After all, he was the reason I had ever discovered Hartwell. Well, Sarah and her letters were. If George returned, I'd finally get to give him Sarah's letters. "Do you think he'll come back to finalize the sale?"

"Probably." Bailey said and then realization lit up her eyes. "Oh, Sarah's letters."

"What?" Dahlia frowned. "What am I missing?"

Without saying a word Cooper disappeared to the other end of the bar, and I knew it was because we'd mentioned his mother's cousin. I frowned, uneasiness settling over me at his continued reaction to the woman.

She had died young. Of cancer. In prison.

Hadn't she served enough penance to be forgiven?

". . . so Jess brought the letters here to give to George." I caught the tail end of Bailey explaining the situation to Dahlia.

"Oh, my God, that's so sad," Dahlia said. "And so kind of you, Jessica."

I gave a strained smile, unable to get that feeling of foreboding out of my chest.

"I think that's the plan," Bailey said. "We find a way to contact George. Get him back here. We stop him selling to the Devlins and Jess can give him the letters."

The two friends nodded triumphantly at each other, happy with their plan. I, however, suddenly wondered if I wasn't setting myself up to fail here in Hartwell . . . and setting myself up for heartbreak over Cooper Lawson.

There was no need for me to worry about Cooper questioning why I was quiet as he drove me to his place that night. There was no need to worry because he was too busy stewing quietly over his own thoughts to notice I was doing the same.

My worries about what that meant for us dissipated a little when he got out of the truck and came around to take my hand as I got out. He absentmindedly brushed his thumb over the top of my hand as he led me into his house. He liked me enough to still want to touch me.

So maybe he wasn't thinking about his anger toward Sarah or my compassion for her, and why I was so compassionate about her . . .

Fingers crossed.

When he said, "You should have told me about Dana," I wondered if this conversation was any better than a convo about Sarah.

I sat down on the sofa, breaking his hold, but Cooper sat on the coffee table so that our knees touched, not allowing me physical space in the hopes, I thought, of me not creating any emotional space between us.

And I really, really wanted emotional space when it came to the topic of his beautiful ex-wife and his heated reaction to her earlier that night.

"Jessica," he prompted.

He usually reserved my name for when we were having sex. I took the dropping of my nickname to mean that he meant business. "I honestly didn't want to stress you out about it. I didn't think she was worth it."

"Anything she says to you is my business," he snapped.

More worry needled at me. I didn't want to come off as some jealous girlfriend, but the truth was . . . I'd felt a surge of possessiveness over him when I realized Dana was in the bar. The feeling scared me. I'd never felt possessive or jealous over a man in my entire life.

"What is it?" he said, leaning closer to me.

The worry I felt was mirrored in his expression.

"You've got this look in your eyes . . ." He took hold of my hand and squeezed it. "You've been wearing it since I threw Dana out of my place."

"Your reaction tonight . . . all that *heat* . . . Do you still have feelings for her?" I blurted out.

Cooper dropped my hand, shock in his eyes. "What?"

Oh boy.

This conversation could go downhill really fast, I knew that, but I also thought the best policy at that point was total honesty. "The way you reacted to her . . . there was a lot of passion there, Cooper." Silently, I thought to myself: *And she's drop-dead gorgeous.*

I knew that last part was particularly unfair because it suggested

Cooper was a shallow man. And that was not how I intended it. But he was a *man* . . . and I couldn't imagine many men not succumbing to someone as beautiful as Dana.

He surveyed me a moment and then he drew his hand over his mouth, looking suddenly tired. "I've been ignoring her," he said softly. "When she first started popping up after the divorce, asking me back, I got pissed. And then I realized getting pissed was giving her what she wanted. She thought my anger *meant* something. All it meant was that I couldn't believe that the person who'd taken away a man I considered a brother had the selfish audacity to show up bothering me again.

"That's what I feel, Doc, when I see her. I don't see her betrayal anymore. I see *his*. I see Jack's. She could have cheated with anyone. Any asshole. But she did it with him and she knew, she fucking knew, that man was like a brother to me."

I heard the venom mixed with deep pain in his voice and I reached for him, gripping his hand tight as tears stung my eyes. There was so much pain there. So much pain buried down deep.

And I could see, I could recognize now, that it wasn't for Dana. It was all for Jack Devlin.

"We were friends since we were kids." He squeezed my hand so tight it was almost painful. "Closer than that. Brothers. Every shitty thing I ever went through, Jack was there by my side. There after my dad left. There when my mom died. Cried at my fucking side at her funeral," he muttered.

I wanted to cry for him right now. "I'm sorry."

His blue eyes pierced through me when he suddenly refocused. "Tonight I was ignoring Dana like I always did because I didn't want to give her what she wanted—my attention. But threatening you . . . trying to fuck up what we have the way she fucked up my friendship with Jack . . ." He leaned in, his voice thick. "That heat I gave her wasn't about *her*, Jessica, it was about *you*."

His words drew me forward until my mouth hovered near his, and just like that the uneasiness that had resurfaced earlier at the mention of Sarah's letters was shoved back down by my undeniable attraction to him. "Dana's threat did the opposite," I whispered, brushing his lower lip. "It just made me more determined to explore this connection between us . . . to make you happy."

Cooper groaned and captured my mouth with his. It was a slow, languid kiss, but it was also deep and drugging, pulling my body under a now familiar sexual spell. He gently broke the kiss, leaning his forehead against mine. "You're doing a great job, Doc."

"Hmm?" I said, confused and dazed by the lust pumping through my blood.

He smiled knowingly. "Fuck, you're adorable."

"I'm doing a great job of what?"

"Of making me happy."

A thrill zinged through my whole body, a thrill mixed with warmth and tinged with fear. "Oh."

"Yeah." He grinned. "Oh."

EIGHTEEN

Jessica

"You know my vacation officially ends tomorrow," I said after swallowing a bite of the pancakes Cooper had whipped up along with bacon and scrambled eggs.

Cooper had made me breakfast.

I'd *never* had a guy make me breakfast before.

I'd never stuck around long enough to give a guy time to make me breakfast.

"How do you feel about that?" Cooper said, sitting across from me, sipping his coffee. He'd already finished his food.

I was savoring mine.

Savoring the moment.

"It's scary," I said truthfully. "Not the new job. Bailey showed me the ropes and anything I don't know I can learn as I go along."

"So what's still scaring you, Doc?"

"Well, that, for a start." I gestured to him with my fork. "The not-being-a-doctor part. That is scary."

"Remember, there's a position open at Paul Duggan's office. His daughter used to work for him, but she moved up to New Jersey with her husband. He needs another doctor in there. Some might call that fate."

I gave him a wry smile. This town and its belief in fate.

Although, to be honest, I was tempted by the offer and tempted by the thought that maybe it was fate. It would make life easier to believe that, because it was a job I did well and one that had meaning for me, and the money would be better than what I'd make working for Bailey. However, I still wasn't sure why I'd chosen to become a doctor. I used to think I knew. But everything had flipped on its head since I'd arrived in Hartwell, and I still wasn't sure that being a doctor wasn't repentance rather than a dream.

"I just . . . I need some space from it." I shrugged.

"Sure that's all it is?" he said.

I tensed at the suspicion in his voice. Looking at my plate, I shrugged again. "Sure."

Silence fell between us and it didn't feel as comfortable as usual. I had to fill it before he spoke up with more questions I didn't want to answer. "What do you want to do today?"

Bailey had told me to enjoy my last day of vacation so I was doing that, and Cooper didn't work the bar on Sundays. He left the management of it to Ollie on Sunday since it was one of the days he didn't serve food, and things were a little easier to handle.

Cooper had just opened his mouth to reply when there was a loud bang at the front door two seconds before a tall, pretty brunette strode in with a young boy at her side.

His house was on the north side, a few blocks from Bailey's small home, and it was very similar in style to hers. Everything was open plan. You walked in off the porch into the main room. There was a staircase in the middle of the space leading up to the second level. To the left of the staircase was a sitting area, to the right a dining area, and at the back of the room was a large kitchen.

We were currently in the dining room being stared at by the brunette and child.

"Oh." The brunette was visibly confused. "Coop, I'm sorry. It's . . . just . . . Sunday."

The boy looked just as confused, his blue eyes boring into mine.

Cooper stood up and I found myself doing the same. I'd already guessed who the intruders were and now I had nervous butterflies in my belly. "Cat, Joey, this is Jessica. Jessica, this is my sister and nephew."

I stumbled against the leg of a chair trying to round the table to get to them. I flushed, wondering why I was acting like such an idiot over meeting his family. I laughed, a little embarrassed, and held my hand out to Cat.

She stared at it with eyes as blue as Cooper's, and I felt her hesitation. Finally good manners forced her to shake my hand.

"Nice to meet you," I said, although now I was thinking not so much as she gazed at me with polite coolness.

I turned my attention to the boy and my heart almost melted. Iris was right. Joey was Cooper's spitting image. I cast a glance back at Cooper, my expression clearly giving away my thoughts because his eyes warmed. When I turned back to Joey I found him studying me.

"Are you Uncle Cooper's girlfriend?"

"Um . . ." I didn't know what to say because Cooper and I hadn't labeled our relationship yet.

"Yes," Cooper said from behind me.

Okay, then.

Yay!

I grinned. "Yes."

Joey grinned back at me. "That's nice. Not for Sadie Thomas, though. She likes my uncle Cooper a lot."

"Joey." Cat shot him a look of warning.

His eyes went round. "What? It's the truth." He looked at his uncle. "I asked her why she was kissing you and she said it was because she liked you a lot."

I raised an eyebrow at Cooper and mouthed, *Sadie Thomas?*

"That was a while ago," he assured me. "And Sadie will be fine, Joe."

"Yeah . . . she seems to like *a lot* of people a lot." He nodded sagely. "You're not the only one I've seen her kissing."

"I'll bet," Cat murmured, smirking.

Who the heck was Sadie Thomas?

"Okay." Cooper moved toward his nephew. "Beach today, Joey?"

"Yup!" He started bouncing on the balls of his feet. "I have my drawing in my backpack." He looked at me and went on to explain, "We're building the biggest sand castle ever today! We're going to break our own record."

I almost melted at the hero worship in the kid's eyes. He loved Cooper. Seeing that kind of adoration for him only increased my own, in fact. I seriously needed to start finding some imperfections in this man; otherwise, I was going to start to worry that I was merely infatuated rather than actually falling—

I cut that thought off abruptly.

Too soon, Jess; too scary!

"So what do you think?" Cooper slid an arm around my waist, drawing me close. "You up for the beach today?"

"Oh, I don't want to intrude."

"Okay, then." Cat gave me a smile that didn't reach her eyes. "We'll see you some other time."

Ouch.

Cooper gave her a dirty look. "No. Jessica is coming with us if she wants to."

I wasn't sure that I wanted to join them. I'd never really liked hanging out with someone who didn't want to hang out with me. I didn't know many people who did like being in that situation.

As if he sensed my thoughts Cooper squeezed my waist. "I want you there. I want you to get to know Joey."

"Yeah!" Joey cried enthusiastically. "Uncle Coop said you're a doctor, which means you're really smart, and engineering a large sand castle isn't easy."

Engineering a large sand castle . . . "I don't think you need me," I said, blown away by his vocabulary. "You are clearly wicked smart."

Joey beamed. "I have an above-average brain, yes."

I laughed and caught Cat's eyes and she softened a little. "You must be really proud of him."

"More than," she said and then heaved a sigh. "Okay, if we're all going, let's get this show on the road."

"Three weeks?" Cat said.

She was sitting beside me on a towel, staring down the beach to where Cooper and Joey were starting their sand castle.

"Excuse me?"

When she turned to look at me I couldn't read her expression because she was wearing big black sunglasses. Thankfully she didn't have me at a disadvantage because I was also able to hide my thoughts and reactions behind my sunglasses.

We'd taken Cooper's truck to the beach, parking at his bar. The whole drive there and the whole time we set up our towels and picnic area, Cat didn't say a word to me.

When Joey pulled Cooper away to get to work on the sand castle, Cat asked me to stay just as I was about to follow the boys.

So out of politeness I'd stayed.

Even when I didn't want to.

Because I could feel a lecture coming on.

"You've known each other three weeks. *Three weeks*."

I was right. Lecture.

"I'm aware."

"Are you?" She cocked her head to the side. "Because from where I'm sitting you're not exactly screaming 'stable, responsible adult.' You meet my brother on vacation and then you give up your whole life? After three weeks?"

Alright, so I got her point. From the outside looking in, I probably seemed crazy.

"It's not just about your brother." I tried to explain what I had discovered about myself since coming there. "I wasn't happy where I was. This trip and the people I've become close to in Hartwell have made me realize what I was missing for so long. Friends, relationships . . . peace."

"A woman doesn't start over after three weeks unless she has nothing to lose. And a thirty-something woman who has nothing to lose concerns me. Because someone like you could easily pick up and leave again, and my brother has lost enough people in his life."

The bite of pain in her voice actually soothed my ruffled feathers. It reminded me that Cat was a sister who loved her brother and she was just looking out for him. "I'm not going to hurt him, Cat."

She looked back toward her boys, not saying anything for a while.

My whole body was tense, waiting for her to decide if she was going to accept me in Cooper's life or not.

Finally she said, "Sadie Thomas was in my year at school. She likes sex and doesn't care what anyone thinks about that."

"And Cooper was with her," I murmured, feeling sick at the thought of him being with someone else. It was ridiculous! It wasn't as if I hadn't been with other men.

"One night." She sighed. "Unfortunately I don't get the same privilege as other siblings of not knowing anything about my brother's sex life. We live in a small town. After Dana he went through a lot of women. Mostly tourists who didn't stay in town for long. I thought for sure you were going to be just another one of those women." She lowered her sunglasses so I could see her eyes. "You're not, though. He talks about you a lot."

Warmth suffused me. "Yeah?"

She smiled reluctantly. "Yeah."

"I really care about him. I just want . . . I want to give him a little happiness. He deserves it."

"He deserves someone who will be open and honest with him." She gave me an assessing look that turned a little sad. "There's something about you. I can't put my finger on it . . . but it just doesn't sit right. I don't trust you."

Well, crap.

That stung more than I was expecting.

I blew out a shaky breath. "What can I do to change your mind?"

She shrugged. "Stick around. Only time will tell."

"So Uncle Cooper says you were a surgeon?" Joey said around a mouthful of sandwich.

He and Cooper had returned from building their sand castle. They had a ton of pictures to capture the moment they broke their sand castle record (it was a pretty epic sand castle), and finally they came back to relieve the tension between me and Coop's sister.

"I was," I said in reply to Joey's statement.

"A head surgeon or a heart surgeon?"

I smiled at his inquisitive question. Was I really talking to an eight-year-old about this? "Neither. I was what you call a general surgeon."

He scrunched up his cute little face. "What's that?"

"It's a surgeon who helps fix problems with the stomach, esophagus"—I pointed to all the places on my body, deciding not to dumb it down for the kid—"small bowel, liver, bile ducts, gallbladder, and pancreas."

"Huh." He frowned in thought. "I don't know what some of those are." He seemed put out by this. "What's an eso . . ." He trailed off.

"Esophagus."

He repeated it until he felt it sounded like what I was saying.

"It's the tube that connects our throats to our stomachs."

"Oh." He nodded. "Was it yucky? Being a surgeon?" He made a face at the thought.

Cooper chuckled beside me and I laughed. "For some people it is a little yucky. But it never bothered me."

Joey shook his head. "I once saw the inside of a dog. I didn't like it."

I raised an eyebrow.

Cat gave me a sad look. "Our neighbor's dog. She got run over last year. Joey found her."

"Oh no." I was a dog lover. We'd had a beautiful Lab, Hazel, when I was a kid and I was heartbroken when she died of old age. I hated any sad stories about dogs.

"You like dogs, Doc?" Cooper said softly.

I nodded.

His eyes smiled at me. "Me, too."

"Why don't you have one?" I remembered him playing with that woman's dog on the beach. I could see him with a big dog, accompanying him on his morning runs along the shore.

Cat grunted beside me. "One guess."

Confused, I shrugged at Cooper and waited for him to fill me in. He sighed. "Dana. She hated dogs."

"And kids," Joey said, piping up.

Cooper and his sister tensed on either side of me and I wondered what that was about. I wasn't going to ask, however, with Joey around.

"So"—I hurried to change the subject—"I hear that you are something of a musical genius."

He shook his head, very serious and grown-up. "I am very good, though."

I bit back my laughter, nudging Cooper with my shoulder. He grinned at me, pride practically bursting from him. "Well, I would love to hear you play. You know, Bailey has a piano at the inn."

"I know." He nodded, his eyes lighting up. "She lets me play on it."

"Well?" I looked to Cat and Cooper. "Would you mind?"

It turned out they didn't mind at all and were, like any proud family, excited for me to hear how good Joey was.

"Well, this is a surprise," Bailey said as we strode into the inn. She moved from behind the reception desk and immediately hunched down to hug Joey, who patted her on the back like a forty-year-old man.

When he pulled back he grinned at her. "Jessica would like to hear me play."

Bailey smiled. "You know I love listening to you, kid. The

piano"—she gestured to the Steinway upright she had in the front room of the inn—"is all yours."

"You're in for a treat," Cooper said, taking my hand as we followed Joey around the corner.

"What would you like to hear?" Joey said to me.

"You pick."

When the first strain of Tchaikovsky hit my ears I couldn't believe it. And when I recognized it as the music from the dying swan scene in *Swan Lake*, every muscle in my body locked.

There was a part of me dealing with the awe of watching an eight-year-old play Tchaikovsky.

But a much bigger part of me was thinking of my little sister and the fact that the anniversary of her death was only a mere thirty-one days from now.

I'd been trying to push it aside, hoping that my new routines here, the excitement of settling into a new place, would help me forget. However, it was like someone didn't want me to. Someone didn't want me to finally have peace after all these years.

Tears welled in my eyes as the memory of my sister dancing the dying swan rushed me. Julia had loved dancing since she was a kid, and she'd been a talented ballerina. She'd danced until the end. She'd finally gotten an audition for the School of American Ballet. She didn't get in.

It was the one thing that had kept her focused. Kept her going.

Everything fell apart after that moment.

Bailey wrapped her arm around my shoulder and gave me a hug, pulling me back into the present. "I know, he's that good."

I could feel Cooper staring at me, but I refused to look at him. I didn't want him to know my emotion wasn't over Joey. "He's amazing," I whispered.

Because, despite what his music choice had done to me, the kid *was* amazing.

A warm, strong hand curled around mine. At Cooper's touch I couldn't help but look up at him. He stared back at me, concerned.

He saw far too much.

I squeezed his hand and smiled to cover up what I didn't want seen. "You must be so proud," I whispered.

His answering nod was slow because he was still scrutinizing me.

Thankfully, Joey finished and I was able to avoid Cooper by whooping and clapping along with Bailey and Cat.

"So?" Joey turned around on the seat to grin at me. "Did you like it?"

I returned his grin. "Like it? I loved it! You, Mr. Lawson, have the hands of a world-class surgeon."

Joey's whole face lit up at the thought before it quickly turned crestfallen. "I find insides yucky, remember."

Cat laughed and moved over to her son to hug him against her waist. "I guess you'll just have to stick to being a piano prodigy."

He grinned at his mom and then jumped off the stool to hurry over to me. He tilted his head back to look up at me. "What next?"

My melancholy began to slip away. Joey was adorable and it was heartwarming that he seemed to like me. "Hmm." I tapped my chin, thinking about someone I hadn't seen in a few days. "Do you like books?" I had a suspicion he did.

I was right.

His blue eyes grew round. "I love books!"

"Yeah? What's your favorite?"

"I can't choose just one, silly," he scoffed.

I laughed. Oh yes. He definitely had to meet Emery. "I know someplace where there are lots of books." I looked up at Cooper and Cat. "And coffee for us."

Cooper shook his head, but he was smiling. "You can't be serious, Doc. She'll have a heart attack if we all walk in together."

"I don't think so." I looked down at Joey. "Trust me."

Not too long later we found ourselves at Emery's. The place was much busier than I was used to, with tourists looking for a coffee and a good book to read on the beach. There was a girl behind the coffee counter I'd never seen before, while Emery was helping a customer in the bookstore. The reading area itself was empty—I guessed because it was so nice outside.

Emery shot me a smile as soon as she saw me and, finishing up with her customer, came toward me. Her footsteps faltered as she realized Cooper was with me.

"Hey." I grinned at her. "Guess who decided to stick around?"

"I heard," she said, her smile shy now. "Iris told me."

"You talk to Iris?" Cat said, not hiding her surprise.

Emery immediately blushed.

"I brought someone who loves books," I said as a distraction, nudging Joey toward Emery.

As for Joey, he was staring up at Emery with his lips parted in wonder.

As for Emery, when she looked down at Joey all her timidity seemed to disappear. "Hey there."

Joey just blinked at her.

I covered a chuckle and placed my hands on his shoulders. "Why don't you go with Emery and she can help you pick out a book? My treat."

He nodded, still staring at her, that wonder only increasing when Emery held out her hand to him. "So what kinds of stories do you like?" she said as they walked away together.

"Your treat?" Cat said. "If the plan is to buy my kid's affection with books and a woman who looks like a character from *Frozen*, then well done." She grinned at me and strode toward the coffee counter.

Confused, I turned to Cooper. "*Frozen*?"

"The Disney movie."

"I don't watch a lot of movies."

He wrapped his arm around my waist and shook his head in disbelief. "Jesus Christ, Doc, I'm a thirty-six-year-old bar owner and even I've heard of *Frozen*."

"That's just depressing." I sighed. "Is it good?"

"Not after the fifty-sixth time, no."

I threw my head back in laughter. "Clearly Joey thinks it's good."

"Yup." He looked over at his nephew, who was laughing at whatever a surprisingly animated Emery was saying. "She likes kids."

"I thought she might." I studied her. "So, she looks like a character from *Frozen*, huh?"

Cooper smirked. "Actually, yeah. I didn't see it until now."

I chuckled and burrowed closer to him. "I like your nephew, Cooper."

"He's easy to like."

After a moment of silence, he said, amused, "What about Cat?"

Hmm.

It wasn't that I didn't like her. "She doesn't trust me. But it's only because she loves you."

"She'll come around." He kissed the side of my head. "Just give it time."

The scary part was that for him . . . I was ready to give it all the time in the world.

NINETEEN

Cooper

Jess laughed at something Dahlia said and Cooper watched the two women together, transfixed. She laughed with her whole body. Pure joy.

It made standing in the middle of Main Street, holding shopping bags, surrounded by a ton of tourists, a lot easier to handle.

Two weeks had passed, and he and Jess had spent every spare moment together. Same as he'd done when he was married to Dana, he'd given Jace and Riley more management responsibilities so he could have time off to spend with Jess. It was music festival day in Hartwell, and Main Street was filled with stalls—people were selling music memorabilia, food, and arts and crafts, while band after band each did a set up on the bandstand.

Cat and Joey were with Jess at Dahlia's jewelry stall, Joey standing in between his mother and the doc, holding their hands. Cooper couldn't even put into words how much it meant to him that Joey had taken such a shine to Jess. And it meant a lot to him that Cat was at least trying, despite her reservations over the good doctor.

Not that Jess was a doctor anymore.

And that still didn't sit right with him.

For the past two weeks she'd been working closely with Bailey at the inn, but Cooper could feel her floundering. Jess loved the inn, but he didn't believe it was her calling in life. He was just waiting for her to wake up and realize it.

As for her new boss, Bailey loved music festival day, but she'd given Jess the day off so she could enjoy it with him and his family.

And Jess was more than enjoying it.

She was coming alive here. In his town. With him and his people.

A rush of possessiveness moved through him.

Cat broke away from Joey and Jess and sauntered over to him, smiling. "Thought I'd come and relieve you of those." She took her shopping bags back, leaving him with Jess's.

They both watched in silence for a moment and he shot his sister a look out of the corner of his eye. She was wearing a soft smile as she watched Jess hug a laughing Joey into her side.

He grinned.

Then she shot him a look out of the corner of her eye when she caught his expression. "What?"

He shrugged.

She turned to him, wearing an exasperated look. "What?"

He gave her a grin that said, *You know what.*

Cat huffed, rolling her eyes, but he caught the smile quirking the corners of her mouth. "Okay, okay. I like her."

"I know you like her."

"I'm still cautious, though," she warned. "I don't want you and Joey getting attached to someone who might pick up and leave."

Feeling affectionate, he hooked an arm around Cat's neck to draw her close. He kissed the side of her head. "Okay, Mom."

She pushed him away playfully, huffing the whole time. "Whatever. You know, Aydan's pretty annoyed at you. Apparently you told her you weren't interested in dating her because you weren't interested in dating anyone. She was surprised to hear about Jessica."

"Jessica was a surprise to me, too." He searched her eyes. "Aydan's not really pissed, is she?"

"Nah." She shrugged. "You know Aydan. And anyway, I told you before that you were the last on her . . ."

But Cooper didn't hear the rest of what she had to say because he felt an odd sensation on the back of his neck and turned around to look for whoever was staring at him.

Through the crowd of tourists and locals his gaze collided with Dana's. She was standing with her sister. Watching him.

Fuck.

He whipped back around, his whole body tensed. Since the night he'd thrown her out of his bar, he hadn't seen or heard from his ex-wife. Cooper thought that meant he'd finally gotten it through to her that they were over.

Now she was watching him with those goddamn puppy dog eyes again.

"Shit."

"Jesus Christ," Cat snapped, glowering over his shoulder. "Has she been bugging you again? Because if she's bothering you again, screw it. I'm throat punching her."

Cooper grunted, knowing his sister was only half joking. "You cannot afford to get arrested. You have responsibilities." He pointed to Joey, who was now standing at the next stall from Dahlia's, laughing hysterically up at Jessica, who was currently sporting a long, curly wig for his amusement and making devil horns with her hands.

"God, she's a goof." Cat smirked.

He grinned, his annoyance with Dana far outweighed by the tenderness he felt for Jess. "Yeah, and she's all mine."

"Ugh, when did you become such a sucker for romance?" She nudged him, feigning disgust.

He shrugged. "I have no qualms admitting I like the woman who shares my bed."

"No talk of beds." This time she shoved him.

"What? Are you five?" He laughed because as hard as she shoved him he hadn't budged.

She huffed and crossed her arms over her chest as she scrutinized Jess and Joey again. "She's really good with him. Does she know?"

"Know what?"

"The rest of the story? Yours and Dana's?"

"No."

"Huh. I'm surprised this lot have managed to keep their mouths shut about it."

"Sometimes they know when to be discreet."

"Apparently."

They both chuckled as the stall owner demanded the wig back from Jess, gesticulating at her, presumably asking her to pay for the thing if she was going to insist on wearing it. Cat sobered quickly as she turned back to him. "Are you going to tell her?"

"I'm sure it'll come up." He didn't see the point in laying out all the problems he'd had with Dana. Not yet. Not until it was time for that conversation.

Jess and Joey were moving back toward them, having to push through the small crowd around Dahlia's stall, when Jess, who was too busy yapping to Joey, was suddenly knocked back by a man who hadn't been looking where he was going, either.

The guy gripped her arms, steadying her, and as they turned to apologize to each other, Cooper's blood immediately overheated.

Jack Devlin.

And he was smiling down at Jessica.

Cooper was moving before he could stop himself, ignoring Cat saying his name urgently behind him. As soon as he reached them, he shoved in between them, gently pushing Jess and Joey behind him.

"Cooper," Jess said, surprised. And annoyed.

He ignored her annoyance and stared at Jack.

Don't you even fucking think about it.

Something flashed in Jack's eyes. If he were the old Jack, Cooper would have recognized that "something" as regret. But he didn't know this Jack. This Jack lifted his hands in surrender and stepped back. "I was just apologizing for bumping into her."

Cooper kept a tight lid on the desire to punch the guy, unable to speak for fear he'd say more than the current situation warranted.

Jack's gaze moved over Cooper's shoulder. "I heard you'd moved on. I'm glad for you."

Choked with anger, Cooper stayed silent.

His old friend gave him a taut nod of his head and just walked away.

What the hell?

He stared after Jack, wondering if he'd make sense of that particular Devlin ever again, and as his gaze moved past Jack, Cooper caught sight of Dana.

She was too busy watching Jack to notice Cooper watching her.

"What was that?" Jessica was suddenly in his face, scowling at him.

He glanced to his side to see Cat had Joey in hand. His sister was visibly concerned. "I'm fine," he told her.

"Cooper?"

Jessica stepped into him, touching his chest to get his attention. He curled his hand around her wrist and brought her knuckles to his lips for a kiss. "It was nothing."

"It was Jack Devlin," Cat said.

Jess's mouth formed an O shape and sympathy he couldn't bear to see lit her eyes. "Coop," she whispered.

He pulled away, not wanting sympathy from anyone. In that moment he regretted admitting to her how much it had stung to lose Jack. He handed Jess her shopping bags and turned to his nephew for distraction. "How about some ice cream from Antonio's?"

"Yeah!"

He swung Joey up onto his back and the boy wrapped his arms around Cooper's neck and held on.

Relief moved through him as they walked through the crowds, his nephew's chatter filling his ears, and helping him forget the fury that had scored through him at the mere sight of Jack talking to Jessica.

TWENTY

Jessica

The inn was a beautiful place to work. It could be peaceful. It could be busy and fun. There were downsides—where customers were involved there were always downsides. Some people weren't as friendly or as easygoing as others. Some made being particular into an art form. But it was nothing I couldn't handle. And I liked working with Bailey, although to be fair we actually saw less of each other now that I was working for her.

Another downside.

The biggest downside, however, the one that scared me, was the niggling voice in my head that whispered that hospitality really wasn't what I wanted to do with my life.

Okay, so I knew that running an inn probably wouldn't turn out to be a permanent thing, but knowing only two weeks into it that I didn't have the passion for it that Bailey did was scary stuff. Because that meant I needed to start thinking about what the heck I was planning to do with the rest of my life.

Trying my best not to think about that, I was in the middle of helping Mona close up the kitchen for the night when my phone vibrated in my pocket.

Cooper's name flashed on the screen and with it came the butterflies.

Still.

I wondered if and when the excitement of being with him would go away.

I was hoping never, because it was a pretty awesome feeling.

"Hey, you." I smiled as I answered the phone.

"Doc, I got a problem," he said without saying hello.

I immediately went on alert. "Oh?"

"Archie is here. He's not drinking, though. Just sitting at the bar, looking depressed as all hell. It's something about Anita, and I'm guessing you have an idea what's going on. Any chance you could get away to come down and talk to him?"

Obviously things with Anita were as I'd suspected. "Of course. I'll be right there."

"Everything okay?" Mona said as I got off the phone.

"I'm not sure. Do you mind if I head out for a bit?"

"No problem. I'll get finished here and lock up front for you."

"Thanks, Mona." I gave her shoulder a squeeze. Despite her control-freakery in the kitchen, she'd turned out to be a pretty cool lady.

I hurried out of the inn and down the boardwalk, my heart pounding faster the closer I got to Cooper's. My fear was that nothing could be done for Anita, that her cancer had progressed too far, and Archie was in the first stages of grief.

Inside the dimly lit bar, my eyes met Cooper's first and he gave me a tender look before nodding his head toward Archie. The place was packed, but unlike most nights, when Archie found someone to chat with, he was huddled up on a stool in the corner, staring forlornly into a full draft of beer.

My stomach twisted with sympathy for him as I slowly made my way over to him. When I placed a hand on his shoulder he turned to look at me.

His gaze softened. "Hey, Doc."

"Hey, Archie." I leaned in to him. "Do you feel like taking a walk with me? It's a beautiful night."

He shot Cooper a look. "You called her?"

Cooper didn't say anything.

"You called her." Archie heaved a deep sigh and then to my

surprise moved off the stool with little prodding. "Alright, Doc, let's take that walk."

He walked close by my side and it was the first time I'd really noticed much about him. Although it would be fair to call Archie an alcoholic, he was certainly a functioning alcoholic. He was immaculate, for a start. From head to toe. The crisp, fresh scent of soap clung to him, his hair was combed and styled, his shirt and pants ironed with perfect crease lines, and his black leather shoes were gleaming they'd been shined so well. I wondered if it was all Anita's doing.

Looking at him, at his well-trimmed gray beard and warm brown eyes, I could see he'd been a handsome man, and by some miracle he'd escaped the wrath of alcohol on his physical appearance.

I stopped us near the bandstand by leaning on the railing to look out at the dark waters. "So . . ."

Archie came to a halt beside me, his sad gaze following mine to the gentle surf. "I guess you know about Anita."

"I don't. I just know what I suspected when I told her to go see her doctor."

"Cancer." He looked at me now, anguished. "It's not good, Doc. They told her weeks ago. She only just got up the courage to tell me."

Sorrow for him and Anita tightened my chest and I couldn't help but reach for his hand. "I'm so sorry, Archie."

"They say she's got a chance. But it's going to be a tough fight."

"Anita seems like a tough woman. If anyone can do it, I'm sure she can."

"Ah, Doc." Archie sighed heavily. "That woman is the strongest woman I have ever met. But that doesn't mean she hasn't got lots of soft in her. She's cut up about this. She needs me."

"So you'll help her." I squeezed his hand.

In answer he yanked away from my touch. "She needs me," he snapped. "And do I look like the kind of man she can depend on? I'm all she's got and I'm going to fail."

I considered my options. I could pander to him, tell him everything would be alright. Or I could be blunt.

I went with my instincts.

"The next year is going to be the toughest year of Anita's life. From what I've heard she's a good woman. You need to step up, Archie."

"How can I look after her when my priority has been the drink this long?" He shook his head. "I've had a lot of shit happen to me . . . and the drink has always been there for me. Now it's going to cost me."

"Anita gets that, doesn't she? About you and the drink. She's never tried to change you or take it away from you."

He turned his head to stare at me, surprised perhaps by my understanding. "Never, Doc. Not once. She took me as I am."

"Then you owe her. She needs you. Don't take *you* away from her. Not now."

Fear darkened his face. "I'd need to kick it—to really be what she needs. How the hell can I do that in time, Doc? There's no way."

It was true that rehabilitation was an extremely hard and long road for addicts, but sometimes things happened in life that made us more capable than we'd ever imagined. According to Cooper, Archie hadn't drunk a drop all night. Anyone would reason that the first thing Archie would have done was drown his sorrows in the drink.

He didn't.

I leaned in to him, speaking from my heart. "People can do extraordinary things to save the ones they love."

Watching Archie walk away, I was suffused with melancholy. Archie had accepted my comfort, and I'd like to think I helped a little.

For a start he was going home to Anita, rather than returning to the bar.

But he had a hard road ahead. They both did. And I was sorry for them.

A pall hanging over me, I decided to head back into the bar to tell Cooper I'd sent Archie home, but also because I needed a Cooper hug.

I was not amused, then, upon strolling back into the pub to find a woman in jeans so tight they looked painted on sitting up on the bar counter, her red stilettos settled on a stool. She had her fingers curled in Cooper's shirt and was looking at him with sex in her eyes.

Cooper had been trying to gently loosen her grip on him.

When Ollie clapped him on the shoulder and gestured to me, Cooper scowled and yanked the woman's hand off him.

She pouted and tried to grab a hold of him again.

I could feel the regulars' eyes on me, obviously excited for a show, as I hurried over to Cooper. Of course I wasn't going to give them a show, but I was going to get this stranger out of my man's bar.

"Come on, Coop, why you acting so tense?" I heard her say, and I bristled at her familiarity with him.

"May I help you?" I said, stopping at the bar.

Cooper sighed. "Doc, it's not what you think."

I raised an eyebrow. "I think this woman is coming on to you and you want her to go away."

"Then, yes, it is what you think."

The woman turned to look at me, her eyes growing round. "Oh. You're the doctor."

"That's me."

"So . . ." She gestured between me and Cooper. "You two are serious?"

"Who are you?" I said.

She grinned at me. "I'm Sadie Thomas."

I cut Cooper a dark look and he winced and scrubbed a hand over his face.

I ran my eyes over her revealing shirt and big hair.

She was attractive in a very obvious way.

And my total opposite.

Yet he'd had sex with her.

Jealousy bubbled up and I hated it.

"Sadie"—I stepped closer, hoping to reduce the number of people who'd overhear me—"in answer to your question, yes, Cooper and I are dating, and if you don't get off his bar and keep those well-manicured fingers to yourself, I may have to forget that I'm a lady."

I heard Cooper snort and shot him a killing look.

"Oh, honey." Sadie shook her head, somehow getting off the bar with a grace I did not expect. "You don't need to threaten me. I didn't realize you two were serious, that's all. Cooper and I flirt. No big deal. But if you two are together, then I respect that."

Surprised but gratified, I nodded. "I appreciate that."

"Sure thing. I'm going to go shoot some pool." She waved her long red fingernails at me and sashayed over to the pool table to flirt with one of the regulars, Hug.

I shot Cooper a look.

He stood, bracing himself, it seemed.

And so he should. "Archie's gone home. I'm going back to the inn."

"Jess." He darted his arm across the bar and stopped me as I turned to leave. "Don't leave angry."

I narrowed my eyes on him. "Why didn't you tell her we were dating and that she needed to get her hands off you?" I hissed.

"I was trying," he said through gritted teeth. "You walked in just as she was starting that shit."

With a harrumph of annoyance, mostly at myself for my jealousy, I pulled my arm away. "I need to go. We'll talk later."

"Jess," he called, but I was already halfway across the bar.

I was lying in bed, reading—or trying to read—when my phone buzzed on the bedside table. Picking it up, I felt a flip in my stomach at the text from Cooper: I'm right outside.

This flip was different from the usual.

It was a sensation caused by worry.

This man was tangling my insides up in knots, and sometimes I loved it, but tonight I'd found it unsettling.

I'd been angry with Sadie for touching Cooper because I thought of him as mine. It had been a long time since I'd thought of anyone as mine. To feel that way meant that person was in my blood.

There was no way to get people out of your blood once they were in.

Even if you lost them.

But I wasn't going to avoid Cooper because I was scared of how he made me feel. The scariness was accompanied by an addictive thrill and a sense of connection I didn't want to shake.

Hurrying to pull on a pair of yoga pants, I moved quickly through the inn to reception, to open the door for Cooper. He crowded me immediately, his hand on my hip, and turned to take over locking up for me.

Without saying a word, he led me by the hand to my room. He closed the door softly behind us and then pulled me into him for a hug.

That was all I'd wanted earlier.

Cooper hugs were all-encompassing and warm and safe, and I felt utterly cared for and protected when he hugged me.

My arms tightened around him and I mumbled into his shoulder, "Not that I mind at all, but what are you doing here? You know I'm technically still working, right?"

Cooper moved me back to arm's length. He curled my hair around my ear and then trailed his fingertips along my jaw. I was utterly disarmed by the warmth in his expression. "I wanted to sort out our earlier misunderstanding. Also I *needed* to see you, make sure you were okay. I found out about Anita's diagnosis. I know she has cancer."

"Oh," I whispered.

"One of her friends came in tonight to tell us."

"I'm sorry, Cooper."

"You've known for a while."

"I suspected. That's why I insisted she see her doctor right away."

He brushed his thumb over my mouth and then leaned in to rest his forehead against mine. He sighed heavily. "Must be hard, Doc. Telling people they've got a battle ahead of them."

"It's not easy."

He slid his nose along my cheek and pressed a kiss to my earlobe. "You know what, though?" he whispered, and shivers cascaded down my neck. "You gave her a better chance of survival by getting her to the doctor right away."

I pulled away to stare into his eyes and saw deep admiration.

"Cooper," I whispered, unsure what to say, "I'm sorry about the whole Sadie thing. I know you weren't flirting with her. I guess I got a little jealous."

He opened his mouth as if to say something and then immediately seemed to think better of it. Instead his hands slid under my shirt as he drew me back against him. "She doesn't matter to me. You do. And right now I'm reminded how we should grab what happiness we have by both hands while we've got the chance."

When he kissed me slowly, in an embrace that was both sweet and hungry, I forgot about everything else but grabbing that happiness with him.

My bed at the inn was smaller than Cooper's, but we were cozy and satiated after Cooper's tender lovemaking. I was happy.

He lay on his back, staring up at my ceiling with his arms tucked behind his head, and I was on my side, my head resting in my hand, as I stared at him.

I could never get enough of staring at him.

"You never talk about life in Iowa," he suddenly said.

Surprised, and not in a good way, I didn't say anything for a minute.

The truth was that I'd hoped my telling him about my sister

committing suicide would be enough to keep him off the subject of my past for good.

He turned his head on the pillow to look at me.

I tried not to shift uncomfortably. "There's not much to say."

"Well, what was it like growing up there?"

I knew there had been good moments in my childhood, but after everything my family went through it was pretty hard to remember them. There was one bright light back in Iowa. "Well, I met my best friend, Matthew, when I was eight years old."

Cooper turned onto his side to face me, relaxed, clearly happy I was sharing something. "Yeah?"

Guilt suffused me.

I was so closed off about this stuff. I worried it would start to bother him.

"Yeah. His family moved in next door and we bonded over a shared love of *Thundercats*."

He chuckled. "You've been friends ever since."

"We've been friends ever since." I smiled.

His gaze turned curious. "Nothing more than that?"

I shook my head and then laughed as I remembered something. "We were each other's first kiss, though. We both had a crush on other people but decided to get the nervousness of a first kiss over with by kissing each other."

"Cute." Cooper smirked.

"It was weird. We're too much like brother and sister. Although our friendship did cause problems. My date to junior prom dumped me because I got pissed he'd booked a hotel room. He said, in front of everyone, that I was an ice queen and we were over, and he walked out of the prom with Jessie Young, who happened to put out." God, I'd been humiliated. "Matthew insisted we leave and his girlfriend at the time, who hated me anyway, dumped him for choosing me over her. Before we knew it, a rumor started that we were secretly having sex behind his girlfriend's back. Then from there the rumor took life. By the end of the week I was pregnant with Matt's love child."

"High school." Cooper heaved a sigh. "Who the fuck would ever want to go back?"

"I thought you had a good time in high school."

"It was good. But it was also filled with drama. I don't do drama."

I snuggled closer to him. "That makes two of us."

He skimmed the back of his hand down my arm, following his touch with his eyes. "Tell me more. About home."

Damn.

"There's not much else to say."

His gaze flicked back to mine and his hand stilled against my arm. "What about your other friends? Your parents? Your kid sister?" He leaned in. "I know it isn't easy for you, Jess, but you must have good memories, too."

I could feel an uprising of familiar panic inside of me, the kind of panic that turned to trembling, and I didn't want that. I didn't want Cooper to see how I reacted to the mere idea of him, or anyone, finding out the truth. "I don't talk about them." The words came out icier, sharper, than I'd meant. I hurried to warm the sudden answering coolness in Cooper's eyes and said, "You tell me more about yours."

Instead, he sighed, dropped his hand, and rolled onto his back. "Actually, it's getting late. We should try to get some sleep."

Shit.

"Okay," I said softly.

As he closed his eyes, I felt the panic I'd been feeling transform into a new kind of anxiety. Usually we curled up with our arms and legs all tangled before we fell asleep.

He was frustrated with me.

Double shit.

After a while his chest rose and fell in steady breaths as sleep took him. Sleep didn't take me, though. Instead I watched him sleep, hoping that I'd get to watch him sleep for a long time to come, and worrying that it just wasn't in the cards for me.

I wished that I hadn't spent years building so many defenses against the pain of the past that it was almost impossible now for me to face it.

I wished that I were brave enough to tell him all about it.

To tell him that once upon a time I did an extraordinary thing to save the one I loved.

An extraordinary and terrible thing.

TWENTY-ONE

Jessica

The music swelled up from the orchestra pit, sweeping the dancer onstage into the air. I watched her, my chest bursting with pride.

Julia.

The happiness, the relief, the overwhelming urge to rush up onstage and grab hold of her, surprised me. It was as if I hadn't seen her in years instead of weeks.

I felt tears in my eyes as she created beauty, and told a tragic story, with her whole body. She made an ethereal, compelling Odette.

No one could look away from her.

My urgent need to see her, hold her, pulled me out of the spell, and I sat impatiently in the audience waiting for the curtains to fall for the end of the first act.

I found myself pushing rudely past people, ignoring their annoyed mutterings as I hurried backstage. Julia had left word to allow me access, and soon, though it felt like ages, I was trying to weave through the dancers in the corps to my sister's dressing room.

I took a huge breath when I got to it, my whole body trembling.

Why did it feel like I hadn't seen her in forever?

"Jules?" I said softly, as I opened the door.

"Come in."

Pain scored deep across my chest at the sound of her voice.

I felt like weeping with agonized joy.

Inside the small dressing room, she stood up from a chair. I stared at her feet, knowing that inside the shoes they were red and hard. I winced. I didn't know how she'd put up with the pain over the years.

Julia floated toward me.

That was how it seemed to me.

That was how it had seemed to me for years.

Ballerinas walked differently from the rest of us, gliding, graceful, tall, straight backed. It was confident, regal, strong. So incredibly strong.

My eyes roamed over my beautiful sister. She had soft features like me but hers were buttonlike. Button nose. Rosebud lips. The only similarity was our big hazel eyes.

But the softness of her face, the vulnerability in her round eyes, was in opposition to the strength in her body. There wasn't an ounce of fat on my sister's body. She was incredibly slim, every limb shaped by muscle.

Julia had the strongest body of anyone I knew.

After . . . well . . . she became so focused on dancing and her body changed as the music made her stronger and stronger.

But I only had to look deep in her eyes to know her soul was weak and hurting behind its steel cage.

I pushed the thought out of my head and rushed at her. She laughed and immediately held me close. She was taller than me. Always had been, from the age of twelve. It was a running joke between us that I was technically her *little sister and not the other way around.*

I felt inexplicable anguish choke me, and my grip on her tightened.

"Hey." She squeezed me back. "Are you okay?"

"You're beautiful up there, that's all," I said, pulling back to memorize her face. It was currently caked in stage makeup. I frowned. "You should take that stuff off as soon as your performance ends."

She grinned and nodded, pulling away to look into the mirror to check that her makeup and hair were still in place. Once her back was turned to me she asked, "Are Mom and Dad here?"

Anger, hurt, and disappointment were not new feelings to me, but still those feelings chafed as I said, "No, sweetheart. Not this time. But Aunt Theresa is."

Our parents had never been very involved in our lives, but we both knew they were proud of Julia because they'd actually attended some of her performances. This night was the biggest performance of her life, the night that people from the School of American Ballet were in the audience. This was Julia's audition for the school of her dreams.

I wanted to tell her I was sorry our parents couldn't get their heads out of their asses to be there to support her, but I knew that would only make her feel worse. At least we had Theresa, my mother's little sister. She was always there for us, even when our parents weren't.

Julia turned to me, love shining out of her eyes. "Thank you for being here. I know how busy you are at school."

"I wouldn't miss this for the world."

"I know." She rushed toward me and hugged me hard. "You know I love you the best, right?"

I held her tighter. "I love you the best, too." I reluctantly moved out of her hold. "I better get back to my seat."

She squeezed my hands. "Do you think I'll get in?"

Hearing the anxiety in her voice always made me uneasy. Part of me hated that she was so consumed by dance, but the other part of me was grateful that it had been the thing to get her through her trauma. "I know it."

She gave me a shaky grin and I left her to prepare.

Ignoring the scowls from the people I'd pushed by earlier, I took my seat in the audience again and waited anxiously for the curtain to go back up. I wished I knew who the heck were the representatives from the ballet school.

My heart fluttering in my chest for my sister, I sat tense as the music rose up again and the second act started.

Julia was a perfect ballerina.

I had no doubt of that.

So I didn't expect it.

I didn't see it coming.

I'd later learn from her teacher that she'd faltered on a sequence of steps, something I hadn't noticed, and that had seemingly messed with Julia's head.

From what we could tell afterward, when we discussed it in the aftermath, the mistakes threw her completely.

I watched with horror as she stumbled on the landing of her grand jeté. The people beside me gave little intakes of breath as she righted herself and pushed through into her next movement. My fingernails curled into the arms of my chair.

And then it happened.

Julia had a difficult move where she was supposed to lower her front outstretched arm while in arabesque until her hand was almost touching the ground in high arabesque. I knew from her talking about it that it took a lot of core control and strength.

My stomach flipped as she teetered, lost balance . . . and fell.

I wanted to cry as I watched my sister just sit there on the stage, looking horrified and broken.

When she showed no signs of moving, one of the other dancers rushed over to her. She didn't seem to hear her. Her dance partner, Micah, picked her up and hurried offstage with her.

I was vaguely aware of the rumbling murmurs of the audience, but I was too busy hurrying out of the theater to pay attention.

I had to get to my sister.

Heart pounding, I rushed through the back hallways of the theater, pushing past people to get to my sister's dressing room.

I barged inside, the door slamming shut behind me, but she wasn't there.

Fear, this inexplicable fear, gripped my chest and I spun around, yanking the door back open. But as I stepped out I fell, my stomach dropping as I plummeted into darkness, screaming.

My body slammed hard into something solid, but I didn't feel any pain.

Until I opened my eyes.

I was in my parents' basement.

No.

They'd never moved even though they should have.

So I'd never returned to the basement.

Until now.

That fear I'd been feeling paralyzed me.

But then I heard this ominous creak.

Not wanting to, but needing to, I turned slowly around.

And my whole world shattered.

The creak came from the rope tied to a pipe that ran along the ceiling of the basement. My sister's body swung from it, making it creak with movement.

I stared at the rope around her neck, at the blue around her lips.

And I screamed.

I screamed and screamed until my voice couldn't scream anymore and all I heard was the screaming in my head.

"Jessica."

I flinched at the voice.

No.

NO.

NO, NO, NO!

I squeezed my eyes closed, feeling his breath on my ear.

"Now she's mine for good," he whispered.

My eyes flew open.

I stared up at the ceiling of the room I was in, the distant sound of the surf aiding me in remembering where I was, that I was safe.

That years had passed.

Tears stung my eyes as I sat up. I was covered in sweat, shaking with adrenaline from the part memory, part nightmare.

Part memory, part nightmare. "It was all a nightmare," I whispered.

Picking up my phone on the bedside table, I lit it up: 4:44 a.m. And the date . . . the anniversary of Julia's death.

Like clockwork. My nightmares were like clockwork.

My sister committed suicide a number of weeks after the performance that ruined her chances of getting into the School of American Ballet.

I was home from college and I found her in my parents' basement.

Every year since, on the anniversary of her death, I had the same nightmare.

And usually for a week or so after, I'd have that nightmare every night.

I thought of Cooper.

If I spent the day ahead with him, he'd know something was wrong. Thankfully, I was working all day. I could convince him I was tired and that we could see each other the next day.

Having never slept in the same bed as anyone before Cooper, I didn't know if I made noises during the bad dreams. I should avoid Cooper completely until it passed.

Yet, to my surprise, I didn't want to.

I wanted to go to bed with him beside me, feeling safe.

Maybe with him beside me the nightmares would disappear.

I was willing to chance it, hoping that his presence would chase away my sister's ghost.

"*You know I love you the best, right?*" I heard her say. I heard her say it all the time.

"I love you the best, too," I whispered into the dark of my room.

TWENTY-TWO

Cooper

Her whimpers seeped into his subconscious first, slowly waking him like they had for the past four nights she'd spent in his bed.

Just as Cooper was opening his eyes he felt the bed shake with her legs thrashing.

"No," she moaned, the pain in that one word piercing his chest.

He sat up and quickly turned on the lamp on his bedside table. The room was illuminated and so was Jess. Her body was covered in a light sheen of sweat and her face was contorted in agony as she whimpered and moaned her anguished noes.

"Jess." He curled over her, his hands tight on her biceps as he spoke into her ear. "Jess, wake up."

When she didn't immediately, Cooper shook her a little, and her eyes suddenly popped open. They were rimmed with red, like she hadn't slept at all.

This was getting out of hand.

"Coop," she murmured, her chest rising and falling fast like she'd been running.

He pushed her sweat-soaked hair off her face. "Another one."

Jess didn't spend every night in his bed. The times she worked the evening shift at the inn she usually spent the night there. Sometimes he'd go to her; sometimes he didn't. Most times she came to him, though. And for the past four times that she'd spent the night with him in the last week she'd had nightmares.

Nightmares she wouldn't talk about.

Well, Cooper was done not talking about it. "Tell me what's going on."

To his disappointment and frustration Jess pulled away and sat up, running shaking hands through her hair. "Nothing is going on."

He tried not to let that burn.

But fuck, it burned.

The only spare time he hadn't spent with Jess since she'd moved to Hartwell permanently was when she insisted on him having his alone time with his nephew. The kid had been despondent since his audition for the fancy tutor in Dover hadn't gone so well. To all their surprise Joey had gotten a severe case of stage fright and mucked up his piece. The tutor had been kind, told Cat that he saw great potential, but said that Joey needed to be exposed to more public performances to build his confidence. They were to bring him back to the guy in a year.

But kids were kids and they were impatient. Joey was crushed.

Joey needed him—Jess saw that and was happy to step aside even though things between them were intense and it was hard not to want to spend every moment with each other.

It just reinforced everything Cooper already knew: Jessica Huntington was the opposite of his selfish ex-wife in every way. She was kind, considerate, and generous.

And he'd never felt this way about anyone before.

He couldn't stop thinking about her, he wanted to touch her all the time, and he just felt . . . *full* of her.

The problem was that the independence and self-reliance that he'd so admired in her was now the thing that was keeping her from him. He'd thought when they first started seeing each other that not having to be responsible for her would be refreshing. Now Cooper realized he was just *that* guy. Caretaker guy. He didn't want her to give up who she was, but he wanted her to let him at least look after her a little. To let him in so he could help with whatever the fuck it was that was bothering her.

But she wouldn't let him.

And that shit stung.

He tried to rein in his annoyance. "It's not nothing, Jessica. I make that the fourth nightmare in a week. And that's only when you're with me."

She glanced over her shoulder at him, her expression completely closed off. Her voice was flat when she said, "I told you I'd stay at the inn tonight, that I didn't want to bother you."

His annoyance hit full-on anger. "It isn't about fucking bothering me. It's about what's bothering you." People didn't have these kinds of continued nightmares over nothing. He already knew there was something in Jess's past that she was hiding, but now he was really starting to worry about it. She'd refused to be emotionally involved with a guy before him; she'd had nothing to hold on to back in Wilmington; her empty life . . . her secret past . . . *that* was starting to bother him. He feared there was something big she wasn't telling him.

"Nothing is bothering me," she said in that same flat tone.

"You're lying."

She sighed and looked away. He saw the muscle in her jaw flex. "Fine. It's something." She stared back at him, her eyes hard. Anytime he probed about her past she got cold and hard and he didn't like it, not one bit. "Not something I want to share with anyone."

"Fuck's sake, Jess." He threw off the covers and got out of bed. "I'm not just anyone." He reached for his underwear and sweats. He needed space. He needed to run.

"Coop." He heard the desperation in her voice, felt her hand curl around his wrist to stop him. She looked up at him then with big, sad, tired eyes. "I . . . It's just about my sister, okay?"

At the confession, relief began to move through him. "What about your sister?"

She tugged on his wrist and he lowered down onto the bed beside her. Jess immediately melted against him, pressing her cheek to his bare chest.

Just like that, all his anger drained from him when he felt how badly she was trembling. Cooper held her close, brushing a thumb over the silky skin of her upper arm. "What about your sister?" he repeated.

"I . . . I get these bad dreams around the anniversary of her death. But I don't want to talk about them."

"Come on, Jess, you're a doctor. Surely you know talking about it might help with the nightmares."

She shook her head against him, her hair tickling his chest. "I don't want you to think I'm shutting you out. I don't talk about this with *anyone*." She pulled back to look at his face, her expression pleading. "Please . . . the nightmares will go away. Trust me."

Disappointment flooded him. And he couldn't hide it. The problem wasn't *him* trusting *her*. If *she* couldn't trust *him*, they had big problems. He let her go, brushing off her touch as she tried to pull him back. "I'm going for a run."

"Cooper," she pleaded.

It took everything within him not to look back at her.

Jessica

Overwhelming panic.

That was what I felt as I watched Cooper walk out of his bedroom.

I didn't want to lose him over this, over my secrets, but I felt him slipping away every day I held things back from him.

If he knew the truth . . . I could lose him anyway.

The past seven weeks I'd spent getting to know this man had been the best of my life. And the last month of getting to be the woman who curled up in his arms at night had been absolute heaven.

I was way past falling.

I'd fallen.

Hard.

The idea of losing him was crippling.

"No." I threw back the covers and snagged one of his T-shirts off his bedroom chair. Hurriedly pulling it on over my head, I dashed out of the room.

"Cooper!" I stormed down the stairs, catching him as he was halfway out the door.

He looked back at me, his expression cold. "Go back to bed."

"No." As soon as I reached him I took hold of his arm and pulled him inside with one hand as I tried to shut the door with the other. "Please."

To my relief he came back inside and closed the door, but he was rigid under my touch.

Desperate to soothe him, to melt his resistance to my affections, I slid my arms around his neck and pressed a kiss to his mouth. He stayed rock solid, unyielding, no matter how many kisses I laced along his jaw, or how my fingers tightened in his hair the way I knew he liked.

"Cooper," I murmured against his mouth. I felt an ugly knot in my stomach at his cold distance. "Don't."

"Why not?" he said, his voice gruff. "This is what you do to me."

Pain shot across my chest. I pulled away, horrified. "No." I shook my head.

"Yeah." He nodded, his expression like granite. "Anytime I try to even mention your family or your past you lock up and lock me out. You think telling me that you don't talk to anyone about this is supposed to make me feel better? I'm not supposed to be just anyone to you. Not when you are what you are to me."

I felt the panic tighten my chest. "Why?" I said, my breathing coming fast and shallow. "Why do you need to know about that stuff? Why can't you just have this?" I gestured to myself. "This. Right now. You . . ." I pressed his hand to my chest, over my heart. "You have more of me than any man has ever had. Please just want me. Just me. The me you have right now."

Cooper didn't move, but I saw the spark of heat in his eyes.

That was enough.

It could be enough.

I took advantage of that heat and stepped back into him, pressing my body flush against his. I brushed a kiss against his throat, inhaling the musky, earthy scent of him. "Cooper," I whispered.

He cupped my breast, his thumb dragging over my nipple.

"Yes." I kissed his throat again as I trailed my fingertips up his arms. "Coop—"

He crushed his mouth over mine, swallowing my moan of relieved need. I could taste and feel the anger and lust in him as he gripped the back of my neck with one hand and turned and pushed me against the door with the other.

Despite the volatility I felt in him, I held on for more, because it was emotion and I needed him to feel for me. I didn't ever want him to look at me the way he looked at his ex—like I was nothing to him after once being so much. My fingers dug into his back, as he tugged my thigh up so he could press deeper between my legs. My lips parted on a whimper of lust and desperation. Cooper growled. The sound caused a ripple of arousal in my lower belly and I rubbed against him for more.

His kisses grew more demanding, turning into desperate, hungry kisses that were almost punishing. "What you do . . ." he said against my mouth, his fingers biting into my waist.

When I whispered his name again, something dark and fierce flickered in his gaze. A mere second later he'd pulled his T-shirt off of me, his hands running all over my body. "Is this enough?" he said, his voice thick as he began maneuvering me from the bottom of the staircase into the dining room. "If this is to be it, I want it all."

I didn't understand what he meant until I found myself bent over the dining table, my breasts crushed to the cool wood. I gasped at the suddenness of it, and then at my vulnerability when he spread my legs apart by pushing his feet against mine.

He bent over me, his chest to my back, and his fingers caressed my inner thigh on a path toward my sex.

I elicited another strangled gasp when he pushed two thick fingers inside of me.

"Soaked," he grunted in my ear, satisfied. "At least I have that from you."

He pulled up off of me, his fingers sliding out of me. His cock was suddenly hot and throbbing against my core, and his hands were gripping my hips.

He slammed into me.

The impact stunned me for a second, only to be replaced with the rush of pleasure as he dragged his cock out of me and then thrust back into me.

My upper body slid back and forth on the table, my nipples catching against the lacquered wood as Cooper slid in and out in fast, deep drives. The sensations mingled together until I was immersed in lust, immersed in one thing—him fucking me.

There was no other word for it.

It was rough and hard.

Not like our first time together.

That had been an explosion from pent-up sexual frustration.

This was frustration.

This was Cooper's frustration.

His disappointment.

His hurt.

His need to have at least something no one else had from me.

I felt claimed.

I felt needed.

And it exhilarated me.

I cried out his name, begging for more, and his grip on my hips turned bruising.

The delicious pressure built and built inside of me until with one more deep thrust it could no longer be contained. My orgasm exploded through my whole body in floods of hot light, and my inner muscles squeezed around Cooper's dick.

"Jessica," he gasped, his hips stilling for a second before I felt his release as he came inside me, his hips jerking against my ass in tight shudders.

My brain was still playing catch-up with what had happened and as the desire faded out enough for reality to seep in, despite my languid muscles, I shivered against the table.

Cooper covered my back, his hands moving up my hips to my waist in soothing caresses. "Jess," he said softly against my ear. "Fuck, Jess."

I pushed up against him and he pulled back and out of me. With what little energy I had left I pushed up off the table and turned to him. Cooper immediately settled between my legs, his hands squeezing my ass as he lifted me up so I could wrap my legs around him. I circled his shoulders with my arms and held on as we stared at one another.

Cooper looked as shell-shocked as I felt.

"Don't leave me," I said, my words barely above a whisper. "I just found you."

He closed his eyes, like my words hurt him, and then he buried his face in my neck and held on tight.

We stayed like that for what seemed like forever before finally he kissed me softly, sweetly . . . reassuringly.

And then he carried me back to bed.

TWENTY-THREE

Jessica

"So I suggested he move into Ocean View, the room I had while I was on vacation, and he had the audacity to complain about that room, too," I huffed, still not over meeting the most particular son of a bitch I had ever had the misfortune of meeting. "I'm telling you, I don't know how Bailey does it. She was so cool and calm, and actually friendly to him."

Cooper squeezed my hand as we strolled down Dover Street together. This meant he was listening to me ramble on about the latest annoying guest at the inn.

"And then, *then* he said—right to Bailey's face—'The whole décor is far more schmaltzy than it appeared online.' I mean, what the hell does 'schmaltzy' mean? I mean, I know what it means, but how in the hell can décor be sentimental? And what exactly is wrong with sentimental décor? But the *final straw* was when he called Bailey 'grating' and said that he should have booked at Paradise Sands—'but this place was cheaper and what a hell of a mistake that was.' I could tell she was going to be all diplomatic about it, but I'd had enough because if he didn't get out of the inn I was going to strangle him."

Cooper chuckled, shooting me this look I didn't quite understand out of the corner of his eyes.

"What?"

"You've been hanging out with Cat too much."

I grinned. "She has a feistiness that this situation called for. I just channeled her."

"Now I'm worried. What did you do?"

"I kicked him out," I said, trying not to feel bad as I remembered the look on Bailey's face. "I told him if he was going to be insulting to the owner he could pick up his bags and get his pompous ass off the property and check into Paradise Sands after all. He said he would. Now Bailey is mad at me."

"Jess . . ." He grinned, shaking his head at me. "It's nice you stuck up for Bailey, but I can understand why she's pissed at you. You kicked out a guest. As far as I know she's never, not once in her whole career, kicked out a guest."

The guilt I was feeling increased. "But surely this was a situation that called for it, wasn't it?"

He shrugged. "I would have kicked him out of my bar, but that's different."

"I never thought Bailey would be the kind of person who would take crap from anyone."

"She works in hospitality. It comes with the job. Why do you think she has such a low tolerance for bullshit in her personal life? She's storing it up."

I laughed, cuddling closer to him. "Do you want to hear the best bit? The bit Bailey doesn't know."

His eyes smiled at me so I took that as a yes.

"She has Vaughn's direct number. Apparently they exchanged numbers for business purposes—"

"We did that, too. Most of us on the boardwalk did it."

"Oh." And there I'd been hoping they'd exchanged numbers for a different reason. Still . . . it didn't take away from what Vaughn had done. I grinned again, thinking about it. "Well, in my adrenaline rush of anger at the guest and admittedly wanting to be annoyed at Vaughn because I could tell the comparison to his hotel had hurt Bailey, I called him. Vaughn. I told him everything and that he could expect the pompous ass on his doorstep any minute and he was welcome to the idiot, with his nonschmaltzy décor and overpriced hotel."

"Jesus, Jess," Cooper muttered.

"I know, it wasn't fair. His hotel is not overpriced. But that's not the part that's important. Vaughn got all growly and wolfy on the phone."

"I don't even know what that means."

"Never mind. Anyway he asked me to repeat what the guy had said to Bailey and when I did he got all quiet and intense."

"You could feel that on the phone?"

I shoved him playfully for making fun. "*Yes*. Anyway, he asked for the guy's name. You know why?"

He rolled his eyes but played along. "Why?"

"Because he was going to refuse him a room."

That got Cooper. I saw the question in his eyes.

"Really," I said. I squeezed his hand. "He likes her, Coop."

"Maybe. Or maybe he just respects her. He was also raised in a world where manners are everything. Maybe he just doesn't take too kindly to someone insulting a woman that he knows."

"I imagine it's all of those things. And more," I insisted.

"Why do you care if Tremaine likes Bailey? Bailey has Tom."

This was true. And she seemed to love him . . . but there was something lukewarm about what they had. I couldn't put my finger on it. Also, I didn't think he was as supportive as he could be about the inn. Bailey was under pressure as it was and he compiled it by making her feel guilty for working hard.

All I knew was that Bailey Hartwell was one of the most special people I'd ever met and I wanted her to have what I had with Cooper.

Excitement.

Thrill.

An adventure.

I didn't know how to answer his question without saying all of that to him, so I wrapped my other hand around his elbow and leaned my head on his shoulder as we walked. We were heading to the music shop to price guitars for Joey, who wanted to branch out after the failed piano audition a few weeks back.

I felt the soft touch of Cooper's kiss on the side of my head. "Leave them be, Doc."

Doc.

He hadn't called me that in a while.

I nodded, smiling.

"Cooper." An older man had stepped out of the doorway of a fish and tackle store and was now striding toward us. "How are you?"

"Dr. Duggan." Cooper nodded. "I'm good. How are you?"

I tensed against Cooper. I'd met a lot of people over the past few weeks, including the mayor and Kell Summers and his partner, Jake. I had not, however, met the local doctor.

"Oh, trying to sneak in the hobby while I can. It's not easy what with the practice the way it is." He smiled at me and held out his hand. "Paul Duggan."

I shook his hand politely. "Jessica."

He nodded and his hand tightened ever so slightly. "The doctor who sent Anita to me."

"Yes. How is she?" Archie hadn't been into Cooper's much, and I took that as a good sign for him, but had no idea what it meant for Anita.

His expression turned grim. "It's a hard battle for her, but it would have been even harder if you hadn't gotten her to come see me when you did."

I was struck mute at what to say because the topic of medicine wasn't exactly an easy one for me at the moment.

"Actually"—he stepped a little closer—"I'm sure you've heard, but my daughter left my practice recently and we are in need of another doctor. You are more than welcome to apply, Dr. Huntington."

My pulse started to race at the offer.

I was not going to lie, I was tempted to jump up and down and scream, "*Yes!*"

The inn was fun. On good days. But I missed being challenged, and having to deal with obnoxious customers wasn't the same thing as being challenged with complex medical ailments. Of course I'd had to deal with obnoxious patients (mostly their families, actually), but I could handle that because of the bigger picture.

The problem was I didn't know if I missed the challenge of doctoring or just being challenged in general. Did I miss the fact that practicing medicine made me feel less guilty about my past or did I just miss being someone who helped people?

"Thank you, Dr. Duggan," I said finally. "I will keep it in mind."

"Good." He gave me a sharp nod and smiled at Cooper. "I'm pleased for you, son." He clapped him on the shoulder and nodded his good-bye.

As we watched him stride away, I leaned in to Cooper. "People are nice here, Coop."

"Yeah." He looked at me in a way that I knew meant he wanted to ask me if I was seriously considering the job offer.

However, he didn't ask.

In fact, since our argument and the resultant passionate encounter afterward, Cooper hadn't asked me any questions that might lead to me closing up on him.

The questions might not be asked, like right then, but they might as well have been, because all that the silence did was remind us of my secretiveness. And just like that, the thick tension crept up between us.

When we reached the music store, Cooper took the opportunity to let go of my hand.

I tried not to be paranoid about it.

He needed his other hand to look at guitars, after all.

But the sudden emotional distance between us made me want to freak out.

So I followed him around the store as he looked at the guitars without acknowledging my presence. Finally, done with being ignored, I caught his hand in mine and leaned in to him again.

I waited, anxious.

He turned to look at me, and as he studied me, a familiar heat began to creep into his eyes. "After this, we're going back to my place."

My breath grew suddenly shallow. "We are?"

"Yeah." He leaned down to murmur in my ear, "I want you on your hands and knees."

"My hands and knees," I whispered. This was also becoming a familiar response to my emotional distance. Sex.

He pulled back and there was more than a hint of the devil in his eyes. I wondered if this was his way of punishing me for not opening up to him.

"Soaked . . . at least I have that from you."

It was possible this was Cooper's way of controlling a situation he had no control over. If he couldn't have my secrets, he'd have my desire. And I was helpless against my passion for him.

Suddenly Cooper was striding out of the music shop, his hand still holding tight to mine. "Cooper?"

He didn't answer as he marched us briskly down the street to his truck. "Get in," he demanded as he yanked open the passenger door.

I didn't argue.

Within seconds the truck was pulling away from the street as he headed toward his house. However, to my surprise, not a minute later, Cooper swung the truck into the dark alley between the ten-pin bowling building and the movie theater. The truck just fit behind the trash cans in the sunless space. "What are you doing?" I said, dumbstruck as I watched him unbuckle his seat belt in the dim light. Quickly realizing he meant for us to have sex here, I gasped, "Cooper . . . anyone might see us."

"No, they won't." His voice was gruff as he unbuckled my seat belt. "And I can't wait for you, Jess."

Our eyes met and I flushed hot from the hungry need in his tone. But still . . . "Cooper . . ."

His hand slid under my dress, pushing my thighs apart, and my hips jerked as his fingertips brushed over my underwear.

My very damp underwear.

Satisfaction hardened his gaze. "Get in the back, Jess."

I was about to combust. "Okay," I whispered, clambering over the middle console, feeling like a naughty teenager as I collapsed against the backseat.

Cooper was there with me in seconds, grasping my hips and pulling them toward him so I slipped down the leather onto my back. Our ragged breathing filled the car and I watched as he shoved my dress up and yanked down my panties.

Next I heard the zipper on his jeans and anticipation rippled through my lower belly, making me past ready for him. "Coop," I found myself pleading, suddenly as desperate as he was. We'd both been checked out; I was on the pill—there was no reason not to give in to the need for instant gratification.

He gripped my left thigh, holding it high and tight against his hip, and then he thrust inside of me.

Lights exploded behind my eyes as my inner muscles clamped around him, an unexpected orgasm shaking through me instantly.

"Jess!" he grunted in surprise, slamming into me in deep strokes, stoking another fire inside of me. He braced his hands by my head, his thrusts slowing to hard pumps as his mouth crushed over mine.

I kissed him back, desperate for the taste of him on my tongue.

His lips trailed from my lips along my jaw to my ear. "Come for me, Jess. Again," he demanded with a thrust that made my back arch with pleasure.

I wanted to. I was hungry for it . . . but it was just out of reach, and I knew Cooper was close to coming.

He slipped his hand between our bodies and pressed his thumb down on my clit. A jolt of hot pleasure zinged through me. "Yes!" I cried, arching against him as he circled my clit while his cock moved inside of me.

Another climax tore through me.

Cooper's hips tensed against mine. "Jess." He gave a long, low groan and his hips jerked against mine as he came.

Gripping my thigh against his hip, he rested his forehead on my chest as he tried to catch his breath.

Reality began to seep in as the heat of satisfaction cooled. "We just had sex in an alley," I said, stating the obvious.

"Couldn't wait," he murmured, lifting his head to look at me. "And that was over too fast. We're not done."

Unbelievably, I felt desire stir within me again. "Can we make it to your place this time?" I teased.

"Oh yeah." He sat up, pulling gently out of me. "I still want you on your hands and knees."

Oh boy.

There were worse ways to pay for being emotionally distant from him, I thought, pretending even to myself that I wasn't scared that what we had between us was becoming too fragile to stay in one piece. "You got it," I promised.

I stared at the two bestsellers, trying to make up my mind which one I wanted to borrow. It was my morning off from the inn, and like many a morning since my arrival in Hartwell, I was spending it at Emery's.

A few weeks before, we'd stumbled over the awkward subject of finances. My finances. My now limited finances.

Emery, because she was kind and did it without hurting my pride, offered to let me borrow books from her instead of buying.

"I need your help," I called to her after the only other customer in the store had left.

It was still early in the morning. Not Emery's busy time.

A few seconds later she was by my side. "You can't choose?"

"These two." I pointed to the books on her bestsellers chart.

She contemplated them. "That one." She pointed to the one on the right. They were both thrillers. "It's smarter."

"Cool." I took a copy down off the shelf and hugged it. "Thanks again."

She shrugged, wearing her usual shy smile. "Do you want a coffee?"

"I sure do." I followed her to the counter. "So what's new with you?"

"Um . . ." She frowned, thinking about it, and then her eyes lit up. "I ordered a new espresso machine."

I opened my mouth, not even sure how I was going to reply to that, when my phone rang, saving me. It was Bailey. She was, thankfully, over being pissed at me. "What's up?"

"George Beckwith isn't selling to Ian Devlin!"

I winced at her excited, shrill cry. "What?"

"George Beckwith! We just got word. He refused to sell his building to the Devlins."

I grinned as she laughed. "Good news. So who is he selling to?"

"Not a clue. But who cares? It isn't Devlin! Oh, and he is furious." She tee-heed.

Emery gave me a quizzical look as she watched me chuckle. I mouthed, *Just a sec.*

"Ooh, and another positive! George is coming back to town to deal with everything. You can give him Sarah's letters."

Sarah's letters.

Wow.

Like everything about my old life, I hadn't thought about those letters much in the past few weeks. I guessed because I didn't really want to think about them or the connection I felt to the woman who had written them.

They were tucked away in a drawer in my room at the inn.

But George deserved to see those letters.

"That's great."

"Look, a guest just walked in. Gotta go. But spread the good news!" She hung up.

I grinned at Emery. "George Beckwith isn't selling to Ian Devlin."

She smiled. "That's good."

To be fair, Emery hadn't seemed as concerned about Devlin buying property as everyone else, and I'd put it down to the fact that she wasn't as big a part of the boardwalk community. I had learned that she and Iris were friends, but I worried that Iris and I were the entirety of Emery's social circle.

"Bailey is ecstatic."

"I could hear." She laughed a little.

"Yeah, she can be loud," I said, affection clear in my voice.

Emery gave me a rueful look. "I wish I had her confidence."

I wanted to ask why she didn't have that kind of confidence. She was smart, she owned her own business, and she was beautiful. What was there not to be confident about? Before I could slip in a sneaky, prying question, the bell above her door jingled and we both turned our heads.

My heart immediately shriveled up at the sight of Dana Kellerman.

As per usual she was stunning and perfectly put together. I'd learned she was a hairstylist at the best salon in town. For that reason (and monetary reasons) I hadn't had my hair trimmed since I got to Hartwell.

Her cat eyes widened at the sight of me, suggesting she was just as surprised to see me, but I couldn't tell if it was an honest reaction or not.

She sauntered up to the counter, giving me a sharp nod, before turning to Emery. "Skinny latte," she said.

Emery nodded and proceeded to make her the latte.

The most awkward, awful silence fell between the three of us, broken only by the sound of the coffee machine.

"So . . . you and Cooper are for real after all?" Dana said suddenly.

I didn't say anything.

It was a known fact that vipers could inject as much venom as they wanted depending on the circumstances. I wasn't prey and I wasn't predator, but I had the feeling this viper saw me as both. I didn't want to help her out in deciding which one I was more of to her.

She sighed. Heavily. "Look, I'm not trying to cause trouble. I'm just saying, I get it now. You two are obviously solid. I mean, you'd have to be." She threw me a wry smile. "Other women might have left over the whole kids thing."

"Kids thing?" Damn. It was out of my mouth before I could stop it.

"Yeah." She leaned in closer. "I know Cooper likes to tell people that my infidelity was the end of our marriage, but everyone knows the truth—I couldn't have children and he resented me for it. And me . . . well, I was stupid. Instead of discussing adoption like he wanted, I let my hurt over his attitude get the better of me. But he was in the wrong, too. He . . . he's not a very forgiving person and when you don't act a certain way he . . . just shuts down. And kids . . . well, of course you know how important they are to him. He wants to be a father more than he will ever want you or me."

"Your skinny latte." Emery slammed it down on the counter, momentarily pulling me out of my increasing panic.

I'd never seen her glower at someone before.

Dana seemed just as surprised. She sniffed haughtily, threw a few dollars on the counter, grabbed her coffee, and walked out before anyone could say anything else.

"You're not going to listen to her, are you?" Emery said.

"Is it true?" I said, feeling this growing, horrible tightness in my chest. "Did that happen? Between them?"

She gave me an apologetic look. "I wouldn't know. I'm sorry."

"I know she's a snake . . . but . . ." I'd seen something in Dana's eyes—a flicker of real pain. "There was a kernel of truth in what she was saying. I could tell."

"Don't jump to conclusions. Talk to Cooper."

I nodded.

I would.

If only to get this sudden feeling of dread out of my stomach.

TWENTY-FOUR

Cooper

"I'm telling you I like the menu just fine," Cooper said, trying not to get exasperated with his cook.

Crosby frowned at him. "So you're sure you're not telling people that you're worried customers are bored with it? That it's not fancy enough?"

Patience. Give me fucking patience.

"Crosby, this a fucking bar." *So much for patience.* "I don't want fancy-ass food on my menu and people don't expect it."

"Well, I heard—"

"I couldn't give a shit what you heard." Who the hell was riling his temperamental cook? "You add anything to the menu, you and Dean won't be able to cope."

"I could cope on my own if he wasn't in my way."

"Is it him?" Cooper sighed. He hated this crap. "Is he fucking with your head?" He'd hired Dean as an extra cook to help out during high season.

"He thinks it isn't fancy enough." Crosby rubbed his forehead, looking at the menu. "I started to think maybe he was right."

"The menu stays as it is. And when Dean gets in today I'll tell him the same thing, and if he doesn't like it he can leave."

Crosby nodded, looking relieved. "Okay. Sorry, boss."

"Jesus," Cooper muttered and strode out of the kitchen. His cook needed to get a social life. Making his job his life was turning him into an even bigger nut than he already was.

"Hey."

The familiar soft voice shot through him and he looked over toward to the door to see Jess stepping inside the bar. He immediately crossed the room to her, his irritation dying on the spot. "Hey, yourself." He wrapped his arms around her waist, drawing her to him for a kiss.

"It's good to see you." He looked into her eyes as he pulled back and his happiness at seeing her dimmed. "What's going on?"

"I . . . uh . . ." She sighed, her fingers tensing against his shoulders. "I just had an encounter with Dana."

And this morning just keeps getting better. "What now?"

"Oh, she had something very interesting to say." Jessica pulled away, only to take a chair off a table and hop up onto the space it had made. He tried not to be distracted by the reminder of the first time they'd had sex together.

He crossed his arms over his chest, willing the memory out for now. "Hit me with it."

Jessica gave him an inscrutable look. "She said that you want kids more than anything and that when you found out she couldn't have them, you resented her for it, that you were cold and distant and she got hurt, that she wouldn't talk about adoption and then took her hurt out on you by cheating on you . . ."

His gut tightened.

His blood heated.

For a second he couldn't even speak, he was that mad.

"Cooper?"

He held up a hand, needing a minute.

Finally, when he felt like he wasn't going to throw a table through the window, he choked out, "*She* would tell it like that."

Jessica hopped off the table and came to him, sliding her hands up his arms and around to clasp the back of his neck. She stared up into his eyes, showing him all the things she felt for him but had never said. "I'm sorry she's such a bitch, Coop."

And just like that he found himself laughing.

Calling Dana a bitch at this point was such a goddamn understatement.

He wrapped his arms around her, pulling her close. "Don't you think if I wanted kids more than I wanted to have them with someone who meant something to me that I'd have started on that as soon as my divorce finalized?"

She gave a soft smile. "Yes."

"So do you want to hear the real story?"

"If you're willing to tell it."

"It's just another example of what an idiot I was to marry her." He nudged her back over to the table and lifted her onto it. He wrapped her legs around his hips, keeping them connected. "I want kids. Back when I thought I knew her, I wanted them with Dana. We talked about it; she said she wanted kids, too. Outright said it. So as far as I knew we were trying. A few months went by and nothing happened, and I discovered why when I found the damn pill in her purse."

Jess gasped. "She was still taking the pill?"

"Yep." He no longer felt the betrayal and confusion he'd felt back then. But he remembered the ugly feelings. There was nothing worse than the realization that you didn't know the person who lay in your bed as well as you thought you did. "I confronted her and she cried a lot, promised me that she just got scared and that she really did want to have children. She said that. She said it straight to my face: 'I want kids with you, Cooper.' So I forgave her and we tried again.

"Nothing happened again and we argued because I thought she was still on the pill. She denied it and said we needed to go to the doctors to see what was wrong. Turned out this time she wasn't lying. She'd had something called an ectopic pregnancy just after high school that I didn't know about."

"Jesus," Jessica muttered.

"I learned that was partly why she'd been afraid to get pregnant to begin with. But she could have told me that."

"She could have," Jess agreed.

"I think she was ashamed." He shook his head, not understanding that shit. "The problem pregnancy damaged one of her tubes. Significantly. We couldn't afford IVF so adoption was our only option. Dana didn't want to adopt. In fact, she was relieved about the whole thing. Turned out she didn't want kids after all. We argued a lot. All the time, in fact. And then she cheated."

"I'm sorry," Jess whispered, her fingers tangling his hair the way he liked. "I'm so sorry."

"Done now, Doc."

"Yeah." She frowned.

"What is it?"

"It's just . . . Dana seemed . . . She really seemed to regret how she acted. She said that she acted out of hurt."

"That might be true. I tried to understand where her head was at about the whole kids thing because she'd been through a lot, but she wouldn't talk about it. She just got defensive and argumentative. Who knows with Dana what the truth is anymore? She has gotten pretty good at constructing fairy tales."

"So." Jessica dropped her gaze. "That does mean kids are important to you."

He felt something an awful lot like fear at her refusal to meet his eyes. He and Jessica were already in a fragile place. With her refusing to share whatever was haunting her, and him getting increasingly frustrated by it, he'd been using sex as a way to keep them close. It felt a little like the past repeating itself, but he was hoping this time if he fought hard enough he'd wear Jess down. But if she didn't want kids, that was a whole issue he might not be able to fight. "Like I said, I want them with someone who means something to me. But I do want them. They're a deal breaker," he said, giving her his honesty and dreading her answer when he followed it with, "You want kids, right?"

After a few seconds she lifted her head and stared into his eyes. He saw the truth in them when she said, "I really do," but for the life of him he couldn't understand the darkness that mingled with her honesty.

"And you can have kids, Doc?"

"As far as I know. But if I couldn't, I would do whatever it takes. Adoption, IVF, surrogacy . . ."

Relief moved through him. "Good." He lifted her chin because she'd dropped her gaze again and he kissed her.

He kissed her hard.

Then harder, longer, deeper.

He did it to shove out the voice niggling at his conscience to question her more.

Because he was gone for her.

And he needed to believe that everything was going to work out for them.

Jessica

Standing on the balcony of the ocean-view room that had been mine for my first three weeks in Hartwell, I searched for that peace that had come over me when I stood there the first time.

But it wouldn't come to me.

My phone buzzed in my pocket and even as I dreaded looking at the caller ID I did it anyway.

Cooper calling.

I hit the red button and shoved my phone back in my pocket.

For the past few days I'd been avoiding him because I felt like just as big a liar as Dana. I hadn't lied when I told Cooper I wanted children. I did want kids. I did.

But how could I even start talking about a future with our kids in it when Cooper didn't even know the whole truth about me? There was no way I could tie him to me forever like that without him knowing *everything.*

I guess I just hadn't really thought about that until the subject of kids came up.

My phone vibrated again and when I pulled it out I had another text from Cooper.

What the hell is going on?

I blanched, squeezing my eyes closed. If I didn't answer him soon he was just going to show up.

Busy, I texted. I'll call you later. x.

"Jess. Earth to Jess."

I spun around, surprised to find Bailey standing by the bed with her hands on her hips. "Hey."

"Hey. I've been calling your name from the doorway for the past thirty seconds."

"Oh." I was so out of it. "Sorry."

Bailey frowned. "What are you doing in here?"

I shrugged. "I just like it in here."

"Well, the new guests will be checking in soon, so we better skedaddle."

I nodded and followed her out.

"Are you sure you're okay?" she said as we walked downstairs.

"I'm a little preoccupied," I admitted.

"You don't say."

"Do you and Tom ever talk about having kids?" I blurted out.

Bailey almost stumbled on the last step. She shot me a look of surprise over her shoulder before marching toward reception. "What makes you ask?" She spun around, eyes wide. "Are you pregnant?"

"God, no," I assured her. "I just heard about Dana and Cooper's situation before the divorce. So we had a talk. About kids."

"You want them, right? Cooper wants kids."

"I'm well aware." My voice sounded really high-pitched.

Bailey cocked an eyebrow. "You okay?"

"I want kids, too. It's just . . . I've never had to discuss the idea with someone. It's a little . . . intense."

"Yup." She made a face and then looked at the computer screen. A little too intently.

"So you and Tom?"

"Hmm?"

I was the mistress of avoidance and I knew another mistress when I saw one. I leaned on the desk, ducking my head so she had no choice but to look at me.

"What?" She sighed dramatically and rolled her eyes. "Okay. Fine. Every time I bring up the subject he gets cagey. He's cagey about marriage and children in general. For Christ's sake, he still has his own apartment."

"How long have you been together?"

"Coming up ten years. But that's his point." Now it was her voice that was getting all high-pitched. "He says that we don't need a piece of paper to tell us that we're together. While I say that if we're going to have children then we need to protect them and each other legally by getting married so that if anything happens to either one of us, the other and the kids will be okay financially."

"Good point."

"I know!" She threw her hands up in exasperation. "But then he gets all mumbly and immature because the subject of children has been mentioned. He tells me that he does want kids but not right away. And he's been saying it for eight years! Come on, Jess, I'm thirty-three years old. I hit *thirty* and started panicking about it being too late to have kids. Can you imagine how I feel now?"

I flinched at her yell. It appeared I had unwittingly awoken a dragon. "I can." I'd also had similar periods of panic since turning thirty. I hadn't wanted a relationship until Cooper so my future plan had been to be artificially inseminated or to adopt, but the timing had just never felt right. But both Bailey and I were only two years away from mature pregnancy age. I knew all the possible risks and complications that might come with pregnancy in the mid to late thirties.

So yes, I could imagine how Bailey was feeling and more.

The bell jingled above the front door just as Bailey opened her mouth to fire a second launch of pent-up frustration. Her eyebrows immediately slammed together and she snapped, "What the hell are you doing here?"

At this, I half expected to turn and find Vaughn standing in the hallway but was surprised to find an older, very distinguished-looking gentleman. He was tall, fit, and had strong facial features. He was dressed immaculately in a three-piece suit.

Cold, dark eyes narrowed on Bailey. "Do you speak to all your guests like that?"

"No, but then, my guests are not Ian Devlin." She huffed and rounded the desk to stride over to him. "That was my roundabout way of saying *get out*."

He gave her a blank, cold look. "I'm not here for you. I've come to speak to Dr. Huntington."

I'd been so busy studying the villain I had heard all about, but had yet to meet, that I was shocked out of a daze at him saying my name.

"What do you need from Jess?" Bailey got all mother hen on me.

"That's a matter for Dr. Huntington and me only."

"I don't—"

"Bailey, it's fine," I interrupted, striding over to him. "Whatever you have to say, just say it."

Something smug entered his expression. "Believe me, Dr. Huntington, you'll want to discuss this in private." He gestured to the front door. "Take a walk with me."

"Don't, Jess."

But I was curious and more than a little worried that I'd caught the attention of this man. And I didn't like the look in his eyes.

"It's fine. I'll be right back." I squeezed her shoulder, ignoring the concerned look on her face.

Following Ian Devlin outside and onto the boardwalk, I didn't like the feeling I got off this guy. He might look distinguished and well coiffed, but there was a slickness about him, and something

I couldn't quite put my finger on. Maybe it was just because my friends had filled my head with stories about him, but this guy immediately rubbed me the wrong way. I just wanted out of his presence. "Well?"

He moved over to the railing to look out over the beach. "Do you like it here, Dr. Huntington?"

"If I didn't, staying was asinine."

He flicked me an unimpressed look. "May we continue without the immature smart-ass comments?"

I huffed, "Only if we may continue without all the cloak-and-dagger crap. Get to the point, Mr. Devlin. What do you want?"

In answer he pulled out a piece of paper from inside his waistcoat. He handed it to me.

Bemused, I took it; and when I unfolded it, it felt as if the boards beneath my feet had suddenly given way.

Blood rushed in my ears and I couldn't quite catch my breath.

"I have your attention. Good."

I looked up from the paper, feeling it tremble in my shaking hands. "How? How did you get this? This was sealed by the courts."

He shrugged nonchalantly. "Money goes a long way in this world."

No. *No. NO!*

The worst thing about myself, the one thing I didn't want anyone to know, the thing I couldn't even tell the best man I'd ever met, and this son of a bitch knew it.

I started to tremble, visibly, and I hated that this asshole could see what he'd done to me.

"Have you told anyone?" My voice shook, too.

"Why would I do something that's not in my own best interests?"

Ugly understanding dawned. "What do you want?"

The muscle in his jaw ticked for a moment, his eyes hardening. "I'm sure you've heard I lost out on the Beckwith property."

I nodded stiffly, my thoughts all over the place, as I imagined him telling Cooper, telling Bailey, telling everyone and ruining my new life here.

"As you can imagine, I'm getting a little frustrated. But then I came across this little nugget"—he tapped the record in my hand—"and thought, *How can this benefit me?*"

"And how can it?"

He turned to face me fully. "I want Cooper's pub and he won't sell. And it looked like he never would . . . but everyone is all atwitter over how cuckoo he is for Dr. Jessica Huntington." He gave me a shark's smile. "The wonderful thing about small-town life, Doctor: everyone knows everyone's business. And what everyone knows is that Cooper Lawson is in love. And he'd do anything for the people he loves."

Disbelief struck me dumb.

Was he actually suggesting what I thought he was suggesting?

Was this blackmail?

"You're going to convince him to sell that bar to me."

My breath finally gusted out of me. "Are you nuts? This isn't an episode of *Dynasty*, Mr. Devlin. This won't work. Cooper would never give up his bar. Not even for me."

"A man like Cooper will do it if you need him to. Tell him you're in serious financial trouble. You do have student debt and I doubt working for Miss Hartwell is putting much of a dent in that debt. Or tell him you have an ill family member who needs the medical bills paid. Say whatever you need to. Stick to those kinds of things, though. Cooper likes to be a hero. He can't help himself. Press that hero button and he'll sell his bar. I'll swoop in and make him a very generous offer. That's a promise."

"There's no way I'm doing this." I was in shock.

I couldn't actually believe that real people pulled this kind of underhanded, ignoble shit.

"You'll do it." He leaned in to me and there was a new hint of menace in his voice. "Or I tell Cooper the good doctor's dirty secret."

I stared at him, not hiding my revulsion.

He must have considered my silence agreement, however, because he gave me that smug smile, nodded his head, and turned on his heel.

I watched him walking away, feeling as if the world had suddenly ended.

In a way it had.

At least my new life in Hartwell.

With Cooper.

I pressed a hand to my chest.

When my sister died, a piece of my heart broke. When my parents refused to have anything to do with me after it, another piece snapped apart.

What was left of it shattered into a million little pieces because I suddenly knew what I had to do.

"Jess?"

I glanced over my shoulder. Bailey stood studying me, concerned.

"What did he want?"

She can't know. She'll tell Cooper.

Think. Think. Think!

I cleared my throat, trying to rid myself of any semblance of the agony that was pressing down on my chest and making it hard for me to breathe. "I . . . uh . . . I guess I should feel flattered, feel like one of you."

"Why?" She stepped toward me. "What did that bastard say to you?"

"He thought somehow he would be able to convince me that Cooper should sell the bar." I gave her a wry look as I moved toward her, calling on all my acting skills. "He gave some bullshit about Cooper being in financial trouble and said that I had to help him make the right decision."

Bailey's cheeks flushed red with anger. "That is bullshit. Cooper is doing fine."

"I assumed, or he would have told me." I let some of my pain leak through for the next part of my deception. "Anyway, even if he weren't, Cooper and I are nowhere near a partnership. His bar has nothing to do with me." I started walking back to the inn.

"What does that mean?" Bailey hurried to catch up to me.

"We just have a lot to talk about."

"You mean the kids thing?"

"That and other stuff."

"That doesn't sound good."

I sighed, heavily, shakily, desperately holding on to my refusal to burst into body-shuddering sobs. "I'm not sure it is. That's why I've been out of it all day."

"Are you breaking up with him?" Bailey grabbed my wrist, looking horrified.

I shook my head. "I just . . . I just really need to talk to him, sort things out."

She studied me carefully. "Jess, you look really upset and worried."

I shrugged.

"Okay." She squeezed my wrist. "I'll be a pal and be on call tonight so that you can talk to Cooper after he closes up the bar."

My stomach flipped, and not in a good way, as I imagined that very thing. "Thank you."

"It will all be okay." She gave me a reassuring smile. "Communication is the key."

I felt sick.

"Right," I muttered.

My heart was pounding so fast I was sure I could see my racing heart beat through my shirt.

And I felt like I was going to be sick.

Shivers moved through me and my teeth were chattering. I wrapped my arms around my body, feeling cold even though it wasn't all that cool on the boardwalk.

If I didn't make a move soon I'd miss Cooper.

I already miss Cooper.

God, I couldn't catch my breath.

The front door to the bar suddenly opened and Cooper's head popped around it. "Hey," he called to me, "what are you doing out here?"

My feet started moving toward him as if of their own volition since my brain wanted me to run in the opposite direction. Or maybe that was my heart.

"Hey," I said, but it sounded croaky. He stepped aside to let me in and I muttered my thanks.

"I was about to leave," he said as he started closing all his blinds.

"Yeah."

"You here to talk about why you've been avoiding me for the past few days?"

He had his back to me.

It would be so much easier to say it to his back.

Don't you dare. You are not a coward.

I snorted.

Yes, you are.

"What's funny?" Cooper said as he finished up and walked back over to me. He assessed me as he stopped at a table, leaning on it. He crossed his arms over his chest and one ankle over the other and just stared at me.

Clearly he was already pissed at me for avoiding him.

I knew because Cooper touched me all the time.

It made me feel cherished.

And I hated when he didn't touch me.

I blinked back the sting of tears, but Cooper caught sight of the shine in my eyes and I saw him visibly tense. "What's going on, Doc?"

As I drew in a breath, my chest shuddered and I exhaled shakily. So shakily he heard it.

"Okay, I'm worried now." He stood up straight, coming for me.

I raised a hand to ward him off. "Don't."

Cooper stopped. "Jessica?"

I flinched. "I . . . Oh, God." I pressed a hand to my forehead, feeling like I was going to be sick right there.

"If you don't tell me what the fuck is going on I'm coming over there."

"Don't." I shook my head. "Believe me, after I say what I have to say you won't want to."

Silence fell fast and thick between us and then he saw something in my eyes.

"Jesus," he choked out, sounding winded, like he'd just been punched in the gut. "Are you breaking up with me?"

I covered my mouth with my hand, my skin clammy. The tears I'd been trying to hold back spilled down my cheeks as I nodded.

His face hardened. His hands clenched into fists at his sides. "Why?" he bit out.

"I'm . . . I'm not happy here," I lied.

"Bullshit!"

I flinched again at his tone, and my whole body locked with tension as he suddenly strode over to me. He didn't touch me, although he looked like he wanted to wring my neck. "It's not," I lied.

"It's a fucking lie. For once, Jessica, tell me the truth."

I shook my head, the tears coming fast, too fast to keep up with.

Cooper glowered at me. "Look at you. Your whole body is telling me you're lying, so fucking tell me the truth!"

I couldn't. Literally. My throat was choked with sobs that wanted to break out.

"You owe me," he said, his voice lowered, so deep and thick with his own emotion that it made me cry harder. "You owe me that much."

At my continued silence he gripped my arms and pulled me close, his lips just a whisper from mine. Everything he felt for me shone in his eyes and I'd never felt such a strange mix of exultation and agony in my life. "You told me," he whispered. "You told me when we met that the reason you became a doctor was so you could leave this life saying, 'I was here,' because someone out there that you'd helped would never forget you . . . and you'd made your mark on the world. Well"—his grip on me tightened to painful as he leaned his forehead against mine—"Jess, you can rest easy . . . because you've made your mark. You made your mark on me. No matter what happens between us now or in the future, I will never forget you. You're inside me. Always will be." He pulled back just enough so I could see his love for me, open, beautiful, and so incredibly heartbreaking that the sobs I'd been holding in burst out. "So you owe me."

Needing to feel him, needing him to feel how I felt in return, even if I couldn't say it, I buried my face in his chest, my sobs muffled against his shirt as I wrapped my arms around him and held on tight.

He held me just as tight. No hesitation.

I memorized the moment. The feel of his hard, strong body against mine, the musky, earthy scent that would forever make me think of him and what it was like to hear him whisper my name. I tried to trap the sound in my mind, praying that time would never take it from me.

"You're still leaving me," he choked out.

I sobbed harder.

He gently but firmly pushed me away.

I thought my heart couldn't break any more but then the look on his face. The pain. All those shattered places in my heart, they shattered some more.

"Tell me why."

I swiped at my tears, trying to get a hold of myself. He was right. I owed him that much. "I don't deserve you."

"That's not an answer."

"I can't tell you. That's the point. You'll never really know me.

I'd just be another Dana, Cooper. Just another woman in your bed that you don't really know."

This time it was his turn to flinch.

"I'm sorry."

Anger hardened his expression. "That's fucking up to you, Jess. You could let me know you. What happened in your past? Does it have to do with your family? Your sister?"

Just like that my blood went cold, and I started to tremble harder. My tears dried up, and I wrapped my arms around my body in an attempt to control the shaking.

"It is," he said. "Every time I mention them you change."

And that was why I was leaving.

I couldn't physically or emotionally bring myself to tell him the truth. I'd never been able to unburden myself with anyone.

Not even him.

If he knew the truth . . . well . . . he'd never look at me the same way again—my black-and-white kind of guy.

It was my own fault.

I'd seen it coming weeks before.

But I just couldn't resist getting close to him and exploring the connection between us.

Now . . . now I'd hurt us both.

Not so smart for a smart girl.

Finally Cooper turned away, unable to look at me. "I should have walked out that last night you had a nightmare. I should have kept going."

"Yes," I whispered.

"*You* begged me to stay."

"It was wrong of me."

He looked back at me. "What the hell are you hiding?"

I dropped my gaze. "I should go."

He was silent for what seemed like forever and then he said, his voice hard, "You go now, you don't ever come back."

His warning moved through me and chilled my body to ice inch by inch.

And, like the coward I knew I was, I didn't look at him again as I hurried from the bar. As soon as the door slammed shut behind me, I ran.

I ran and ran until the boards came to an end and there was nowhere else to run.

TWENTY-FIVE

Jessica

Only an idiot would have stayed in Hartwell.

I was a damn idiot.

Bailey hadn't thrown me out. She'd been confused and upset by my breakup with Cooper and hurt when I refused to tell her why, but she hadn't thrown me out. Instead I quit and packed my things.

Now she was mad at me.

I watched the porch door slam behind her as I stared up at the inn from the boards, my suitcase by my side.

I should leave.

I knew it.

But tucked into my pocket were Sarah's letters to George, and George was apparently due back in town at the end of the week.

What the hell I was going to do until then I had no clue.

I'd have to find somewhere cheap to stay because cash flow was kind of a problem.

And it turned out news traveled really fast.

Walking down the boardwalk, suitcase in hand, trying to figure out what to do, I saw Iris opening up Antonio's and I waved to her.

She glowered at me, stuck her chin in the air, and turned her back on me.

Hurt, I almost stumbled over my own feet.

"What did you do?"

I jerked my head around from Iris to find Vaughn in my path. He kept doing that. Appearing out of nowhere.

"Huh?"

"Well, even I get a hello out of Iris." He smirked at me. "What did you do?"

"Cooper and I broke up last night."

He raised an eyebrow. "And you're still here? Everyone will know by tonight."

"I . . . I can't leave just yet." My mouth trembled as I tried to hold in my tears. I'd already cried more than I knew I had in me. Enough was enough. I cleared my throat. "I have some business with George Beckwith. As soon as he gets here, that gets done and I'll be gone." To what and where . . . I had no idea.

Vaughn scrutinized me for a moment and then his eyes dropped to my suitcase. He frowned. "Miss Hartwell kicked you out?"

I heard the disbelief in his voice. "No. I left. She's pretty mad at me right now."

He looked at me again. "Where are you planning on staying?"

It occurred to me that Vaughn probably had a good idea about local rates. "Do you know where the nicest but cheapest place is?"

He made a face. "Ouch, no time for pride, huh?"

"If you're going to be an asshole, get out of my way."

Vaughn chuckled. "I'm not being an asshole. I've just . . . I've been there."

"Oh, I'm sure with all of your money, you've been there. Yeah, I can see that."

He tsked me. "And here I'm trying to help."

"By making digs at me about my lack of pride?"

"No." He stepped closer to me, his eyes losing some of their usual glacial superiority. "You can stay at my place."

I shook my head. "I'm not staying on the boardwalk." I didn't want to chance bumping into Cooper.

"My place, not my hotel. And my place isn't on the boardwalk. It's on the outskirts of town."

Confused by his generous offer, I said suspiciously, "Why?"

"I spend most of my nights in my suite at the hotel. My house is just lying empty."

"But why? Why are you helping me?"

My question made him look away. He stared out at the water. "Let's just say I know what it's like to be the heartbreaker, the villain."

I sucked in a breath at the label. "How do you know *I* broke up with Cooper; that it wasn't him who did the heartbreaking?"

Finally Vaughn looked back at me. The shrewdness in his eyes had never unsettled me more. "Because any fool can see he's in love with you."

I winced.

"Doesn't mean he couldn't have let me go."

"When the woman you love lets you into her bed, you don't let her go unless she wants to leave."

I surveyed him, happy to be distracted from my own heart for a second. "Speaking from experience?"

"Didn't I just say *I* was the heartbreaker?"

"That doesn't answer my question."

"Do you want a free place to stay or not?"

I thought about it. It would be incredibly helpful not to have to pay for accommodation. Plus, he'd said his house was on the outskirts. It sounded far enough away from town to be perfect. "Yes. Thank you."

"Where is your car?"

My car.

Right.

"Oh. Um . . . in Bailey's parking lot."

"So you're wandering on the boardwalk, why?"

Feeling sheepish, I shrugged. "I wasn't thinking."

Something akin to concern flickered over Vaughn's features. "You sure you're up for driving?"

"Yes." I nodded quickly. "Honestly, I'm fine."

"Well, a bigger lie you've never told," he said dryly and then gestured over his shoulder with his thumb. "Meet me in my hotel parking lot. You can follow me out to the house."

"Okay."

He gave me a sharp nod and then turned, swiftly striding away.

"Vaughn!"

He stilled, shooting me a look over his shoulder.

I swallowed past a new lump of emotion in my throat. "Thank you."

If I wasn't mistaken, Vaughn Tremaine looked uncomfortable with my thanks. He made no reply and instead just walked away.

Some of my worries eased, I turned around to head back down the boardwalk to my car. Iris was standing in her doorway, arms crossed over her chest, frowning at me.

She was probably wondering what I was doing talking to Vaughn.

I didn't attempt to wave again, knowing it wouldn't be welcome.

Instead, I dropped my gaze and hurried away from her.

The sight of Emery standing on Vaughn's porch gave me the first moments of lightness I'd felt in a few days.

I had not been surprised to find that Vaughn's home was on an isolated patch of land right on the waterfront. It was down the coast from the boardwalk, out of sight, and private. Architecturally it was like most homes in Hartwell but on a larger scale. White cladding, wraparound porches on the first and second floors, pretty garden. But inside it was anything but traditional.

It had a huge chef's kitchen with high-end appliances, glossy floors, and contemporary furniture, all black, chrome, and white with splashes of color in the artwork and minimal soft furnishings.

It was beautiful but cold.

It was a bachelor's house.

But it was my safe haven until George got into town.

No one had called. And only Emery had texted me to see if I

was okay. Glad for a friendly face, I'd asked her to come out to Vaughn's to see me.

"You came," I said, opening the door for her.

"Of course." She gave me that quiet smile of hers and walked in, her gaze moving around the open-plan space. "Wow."

"I know."

"It was very kind of Mr. Tremaine to let you stay here."

"Yes." It was. And I wouldn't forget it. "He's never here."

Tension I didn't even know Emery was carrying seemed to melt out of her. "Oh."

Damn, but I wished I'd be sticking around to help her get over her timidity with men.

I wished I'd be sticking around, period.

Suddenly I found myself under Emery's scrutiny. Her face fell. "You've been crying."

Every damn day. I shrugged, feeling silly. "I can't seem to stop."

Then, to my surprise, she hugged me.

I immediately hugged her back, my face crumpling as she set off more tears with her kindness.

She held me until my crying subsided. "Let's make some tea."

Thankfully, Vaughn had partially stocked the kitchen, but I was running out of food, and I was getting sick of takeout. At some point I was going to have to make a run to the grocery store in town.

Once we had our mugs of tea, we settled on the porch.

"Wow," Emery said again. "He's right on the water."

"It's beautiful, isn't it?"

"Why doesn't he stay here more often?"

"No clue." If it were my house I'd stay there all the damn time. Of course, I'd have to redecorate.

We were silent awhile as we sipped our tea and enjoyed the view.

But I was only half enjoying the view. I needed to know—"Is Cooper okay?"

She gave me a strained smile. "I spoke to Iris this morning."

"And?"

Emery winced. "She's quite mad at you."

"I know." I tried to ignore the ache in my chest, remembering the way she'd looked at me the other morning. "Did she mention Cooper?"

My friend nodded. "He put someone in charge of the bar . . . he went on a fishing trip."

"Fishing trip." I was confused. "Cooper doesn't fish."

"I think he just needed to get away for a few days. Small town. Gossip—"

"Not wanting to run into me until I'm gone," I whispered hoarsely.

"I'm sorry."

"Don't be, sweetie. It's my own fault."

"Bailey came to see me."

The thought of my friend caused another deep ache inside me. "And?"

"She's worried about you, Jessica, but she doesn't feel like she can reach out to you without being shut out. Perhaps you should call her."

"No." I shook my head stubbornly. "It's better this way."

My phone started ringing inside the house and for a second we looked at each other before I was up on my feet and hurrying inside for it.

The anticipation I'd felt disappeared at the sight of the caller ID.

Matthew calling.

I had no intention of answering. If I answered, he'd know something was wrong, and when I told him what, he'd only be mad at me and try to convince me I was insane.

"Not Cooper?" Emery said softly from behind me.

I turned slowly around and gave her a sad shrug. "I don't even know why I want it to be him. It's not like it'll change my mind."

She sighed and gave me a look that made me tense.

"What?"

"Well . . . there are rumors . . ."

Fear shot through my blood. Had that bastard Devlin gotten his revenge on me for breaking up with Cooper instead of doing his bidding? "What . . . what kind of rumors?"

"Rumors . . . rumors that . . . rumors that you were cheating on Cooper with Vaughn."

Oh. My. God.

"Are you kidding?" I growled.

"No. I'm sorry."

"Because I'm staying here? They . . . idiots!" I threw up my hands in disbelief. And then something worse than the town of Hartwell's stupidity occurred to me. "Does Cooper believe this?"

"No. Bailey said no. And she doesn't, either."

How can they still have faith in me after what I've done?

"So . . ." Emery shrugged. "What are your plans?"

Thankfully distracted by the question, I slumped down on the nearest chair. "I contacted an old professor of mine and he thinks there might be a position for me at a teaching hospital in Illinois. It's not definite, but I think I'll head out that way anyway. I know Chicago well. It's as much a home to me as anywhere."

Lie, lie, lie.

Hartwell is my home.

Emery gave me a sad smile. "I'll miss you."

That made me tear up all over again. "I'll miss you, too."

Later that night, I was sitting on Vaughn's couch, sipping a glass of wine and staring dazedly at a movie on the television. All day I'd been plagued by thoughts I tried so hard to shut out. I couldn't stop thinking about my sister. I couldn't stop thinking about how much she'd like Cooper. He was everything that was rare in our lives growing up—supportive, kind, loving. Mostly I thought she'd have liked how safe he made me feel. He would have made her feel safe, too, I was sure of it. I thought she'd have been angry at me for leaving him.

No. I *knew* she'd have been angry at me for leaving him.

If Julia had overcome her depression, how differently might my life have gone? Maybe I wouldn't have shut down so much about what had happened. Maybe I'd have been able to talk about the pain without feeling like I might genuinely die if I did.

If she'd lived, would I have gone down the same path without the grief weighing me down? Would I have still wanted to be a doctor?

Yes.

Tears burned in my throat as I imagined that life and I could clearly see myself practicing medicine.

It wasn't just about penance.

"Shit," I muttered.

Before I could think about my own stupidity over the past few weeks, the doorbell rang. My heart jumped in my chest as I looked at the clock on Vaughn's mantel. It was nearly midnight. I placed my wineglass on the coffee table and got slowly to my feet, my heart racing harder when the doorbell rang again. Cautiously, I tiptoed out into the hall and put my eye to the spy hole in the door.

Standing outside was an abstract version of Cooper.

My breath caught.

Hands trembling, I unlocked the door and pulled it open to find Cooper glowering down at me. Joy rushed through me at the sight of him.

I opened my mouth to ask him what he was doing there, but the words were silenced as he pressed his mouth down on mine without missing a beat, wrapped an arm around my waist, and pushed us both inside. Shocked, I grabbed on to his shoulders for balance.

And then, like always, the taste of his drugging kisses overpowered me and I was kissing him back before I could stop myself.

I suddenly found my feet off the ground as Cooper lifted me onto the sideboard in Vaughn's hallway. He pressed himself between my legs and I wrapped them around his hips, arching into him and his hard, desperate kisses.

He broke the kiss, pulling back only to grab the hem of my nightdress in his hands and start tugging it upward.

"Wait," I said, out of breath. "What are you doing? Why are you here? I thought you were fishing."

His fingers tightened in the fabric, and there was something dangerous in his eyes as he said, his voice gruff, "All I could think about was the fact that when we last fucked I didn't know it was going to be the last time. So I came back."

A shot of pain lanced across my chest. "To punish me?"

He gave a sharp shake of his head. "To give us one last time, Doc." He began to yank on my shirt again. "You know you want it."

I did.

As stupid as I knew it was, as much as I knew it would only hurt even more in the end, I lifted my arms so he could take off my nightdress. My bra was quick to follow.

I shivered, my nipples turning to hard pebbles, drawing Cooper's attention. He cupped my breasts and I arched my back on a sigh as he kneaded them, his touch sending sparks down my belly and between my legs.

"Now I get to remember you like this," he said.

I saw the anger, the ice and the accusation, in his eyes and closed mine against it.

All I wanted was to feel how good it was between us. I didn't want reality to intrude.

"Open your eyes, Jessica," he growled.

They immediately snapped open for him.

His were narrowed on me. "Don't you fucking shut me out for this. Not for this."

"Not for this," I promised softly.

Cooper wrapped his fingers up in a handful of my hair and pulled gently, arching my neck and back to lift my breasts closer to his mouth. He bent his head and closed his hot mouth around my right nipple.

I whimpered as my lower belly rippled with pleasure. He sucked hard, sending a sharp streak of desire to my core, and then he licked the swollen nipple before moving on to the other.

Needing to feel him against me, I began tugging on Cooper's jacket. He stepped back from me and hurriedly removed it. He whipped his T-shirt off over his head, throwing it by my nightdress on the floor. As soon as he stepped toward me I grabbed on to him, yanking him back to me, our kisses growing frantic with need. With one hand I caressed his strong back, with the other his hard chest before sliding it down over his abs. At the feel of his abs rippling under my touch, arousal throbbed in my breasts and between my legs.

Cooper pulled back from my kisses, sliding his hand along my inner thigh. "Will I find you wet? Do I still have that from you, Jess?"

I looked directly into his hurt, hungry eyes and whispered, "Always."

Pain flared in his gaze and suddenly he was kissing and biting at my mouth, his fingers bruising as he gripped my thighs in his hands. All I could do was hold on for the ride.

As he pressed hot kisses against my jaw and my neck, his tongue flicking against my skin as he did so, I rubbed my thumbs over his nipples, scored my nails lightly down his stomach, and panted with excitement when his fingers curled in the fabric of my panties. I stopped touching him only to brace my hands on the sideboard at either side of my hips so I could lift my bottom to allow Cooper to pull them off.

Once they were gone he gripped the backs of my knees in his hands and wrapped my legs around him so his jeans-covered erection pushed between the folds of my sex, brushing my clit in a way that made me lose my mind. I tried to press harder against his erection, my fingers digging into the muscles of his back.

Cooper groaned against my mouth and I was vaguely aware of the sound of him yanking his zipper down. And then he pulled me to the edge of the sideboard. I immediately put my hands at either side of my hips to brace myself.

I recognized the harsh passion on Cooper's face and I knew—

I cried out as he slammed inside me.

"You've always been mine, Jess," Cooper said, his voice guttural with desire and emotion. "Remember that."

Tears pricked the corners of my eyes, but I wouldn't stop this for anything. He was right. Always his. And I'd always want him. I arched into his deep strokes, the orgasm building in me, my arousal only increasing at the way he was watching me as he thrust inside me.

His grip on my legs became almost biting as his thrusts came faster. "Come for me, Jess. Come hard on me, beautiful."

And just like that the tension he'd built in me cracked. I tensed, frozen for a second, and then it all shattered apart. My cries filled the room as I shuddered against him. He continued to pump into me, my inner muscles squeezing around him, until finally he stiffened. Cooper was staring deep into my eyes as he gritted his teeth. "Jess." His hips jerked against me, and I felt his release inside me.

I was holding on to his forearms as the heat slowly died and the lust gave way to reality.

We stared at each other for what seemed like forever, until finally Cooper pulled out of me and away from me.

I watched, frozen, as he zipped his jeans up and bent to pick up his clothes. Without looking at me he pulled on his T-shirt and shrugged into his jacket.

The tears that had pricked my eyes earlier began to cloud my vision as he strode to the door and yanked it open. But before he moved to leave he stopped, his back still to me, and said, voice hoarse, "One last time will never be enough. For either of us."

And then he left me.

Sometime around three o'clock I eventually cried myself to sleep.

The next day I had no choice but to make the grocery run I'd been dreading, since I was out of essentials like toilet paper and food. I put a ball cap on to hide my face, hoping to disappear among the tourists after parking on the west end of Main Street. Inside the grocery store I kept my head down as I walked through the aisles, hoping and praying with each step that I wasn't going to bump into anyone I knew. Like Cooper Lawson.

The cashier, Annie, recognized me because I'd been in the store a lot with Cooper over the past few weeks, and anyone with Cooper seemed to become famous in Hartwell.

"Thought you left." She had her eyebrows raised at me.

"Soon," I muttered, hurrying to pay for my stuff.

I was practically fleeing for my car, my heart pounding as I loaded the last shopping bag into my trunk. Hurrying, I pushed the cart back under the awning outside the store and as I turned to head back to my car I smacked straight into Catriona Lawson.

"Cat." I'm pretty sure I went a pale, ghostly color at the sight of her.

Those blue eyes, just like Cooper's, narrowed on me. "You had the better idea when you were hiding out at Tremaine's place."

"I needed food," I said dumbly, looking away.

"Oh, my God, look at you," she snapped, drawing my startled gaze back to her. "You've lost weight, you look like shit, and you're acting like a victim. Lots to be proud of there, Jessica, considering you're the one that broke my brother's heart." She gestured behind her.

Panic had me looking over her shoulder, my gaze zeroing in on Cooper. He was parked a few spots up from me, leaning against his truck, talking to Sadie Thomas. Sadie was leaning into him, laughing up into his face. He wasn't pushing her away like the last time.

My heart twisted in my chest as though the bitch had shoved her fist in there and squeezed.

Cooper stared down at Sadie, expressionless. He was so handsome. I remembered the anguish in his eyes, the anguish he couldn't hide behind his desire the previous night. I should have pushed him away, instead of giving in to what we both wanted. I'd only hurt and confused him more.

"What?" Cat brought my gaze back to her. "You don't want him but you don't want anyone else to have him?"

"It's not like that," I muttered, moving to go around her.

Cat blocked my path. "I started to trust you. That you weren't going to hurt him. You know, I don't even think Dana was the one who hurt him last time. That marriage was ending. Nah. It was Jack who hurt my brother."

I had to agree. I was also confused about where she was going with this.

"But you . . ." She laughed bitterly. "Oh, you've shredded him."

Pull out my heart, why don't you, and stomp on it.

I didn't need to hear this!

"It's for his own good," I said, my voice stern in the hopes his sister would get out of my face. "Believe me."

She shook her head, looking so disappointed in me I could add it to the ever-growing list of things to self-flagellate about. "How dare you decide that for him."

"Cat—"

"No." She shoved a hand up between us to shut me up. "He told me you're hiding something, something you're obviously ashamed of. But you know what you should really be ashamed of? How much of a coward you are right now. And how little you've actually gotten to know my brother . . . because if you knew him, you'd have a lot more faith in him than you do."

"No, he would never understand." I shook my head, wrapping my arms around myself.

Cat huffed and glanced over her shoulder at Sadie and Cooper. Sadie was touching his arm now, tilting her head in her flirty way, giving him her come-hither eyes. "As far as she's concerned, he's fair game."

I got a sudden unwelcome image of him kissing her . . . touching her . . . and it felt like poison sliding down my throat.

"Not now, but at some point"—she turned back around to give

me a hard look—"he will be fair game. Have you really thought about that?"

I squeezed my eyes closed. "Cat."

"Jesus, Jessica, look at how much pain you're in. Will Cooper knowing the truth about you be any worse than how you already feel?"

My eyes flew open at that, her words reverberating around and around my head.

Will Cooper knowing the truth about you be any worse than how you already feel?

Will Cooper knowing the truth about you be any worse than how you already feel?

WILL COOPER KNOWING THE TRUTH ABOUT YOU BE ANY WORSE THAN HOW YOU ALREADY FEEL?

I flinched away from her, needing space, needing to think. "I have to go."

This time she didn't stop me, but as I moved to my car my eyes were drawn to Cooper, despite not wanting to see another woman flirting with him.

As I opened my car door, he seemed to sense me, his head jerking in my direction, those blue, blue eyes focusing in on me.

His whole body tensed.

And then he pushed away from his truck as if he were going to come to me.

Will Cooper knowing the truth about you be any worse than how you already feel?

I didn't know!

I didn't know, but I couldn't figure that out in the ten seconds it would take him to get to me. Fumbling with my car door, I practically threw myself in, started the car, and reversed back so fast my wheels spun.

Before he'd even made it to me I was out of there, the blood whooshing in my ears at the galloping of my heart.

TWENTY-SIX

Cooper

For once Cooper liked the bar better empty.

He cleaned down the bar top, wishing like hell he could afford to just shut the place down for a few days. Of course Ollie could keep running it for him if he decided to take off again, but he knew he couldn't run from his life.

Or the pain.

Being with Jessica the other night . . . that was like having a stinging cut for days and then suddenly someone slathering cool balm over it.

His head was all fucked up about her.

Part of him felt betrayed by her, angry, furious, resentful. That part wanted her to get the hell out of his town and never come back. But unfortunately there was this bigger part of him that felt like if he could only find out what the hell it was she was hiding, then maybe they could work this shit out. That part of him was responsible for the fear he felt, and Cooper hadn't felt fear since his mom got diagnosed with cancer.

He feared Jessica packing up from Tremaine's and leaving Hartwell for good.

When the rumors hit that Jessica and Vaughn were having an affair, he didn't even entertain it, which was surprising, considering Dana. But he didn't believe that of Jess. What she was hiding wasn't an affair. No. He was worried it was much darker than that.

In fact, he was worried that if he did find out, Jessica's fears would be proven right; that in the end the truth would be too much for him to handle.

Yet the idea of not wanting to be with Jessica for any reason seemed absurd to him. He couldn't seem to stay away. And so he'd taken what he'd wanted from her . . . and like he'd told her, it wasn't enough. If anything, the taste of her only made her leaving him burn harder. Yet, he knew he wasn't above making that mistake again. In fact, he was itching to find her and repeat the other night.

His head was all fucked up.

The knock on his bar door was like a shot of adrenaline through him. The knock reminded him of all the times these past few months that Jessica had come to him before the bar opened.

He braced himself for finding her on the other side of his door.

The disappointment he felt was mixed with a whole lot of anger at the sight of Ian Devlin on his doorstep.

"You do not want to be here right now, believe me," Cooper warned.

His warning went unheeded as Devlin pushed past him, striding into the bar like he owned the fucking place.

"Bad mood, Cooper?" Devlin shot him a smirk over his shoulder before he perused the bar with his greedy eyes.

Cooper kept the door open. This asshole was leaving. Now. "Worst ever. Which means I'm not in the mood to deal with your shit."

"You heard about Beckwith selling to some rising star chef from Boston?" Devlin sneered.

He had to admit this part of their conversation lifted his spirits a little. "Didn't know who he sold it to. Just knew it wasn't you."

"And you loved that, didn't you?"

"Not going to lie, it didn't suck."

Devlin narrowed his eyes. "I'm not the one that screwed your wife, son."

Dick.

Cooper kept his expression blank, not willing to give him a reaction.

"And now another woman has messed with you. I heard the good doctor is shacked up with Vaughn Tremaine." His eyes glittered with malice as he ran his fingers along the top of Cooper's bar. "Admittedly that makes more sense. A woman of Jessica Huntington's caliber . . . Anyone who was smart enough to recognize what she is would know a small-town bartender wouldn't keep her happy for long."

Do not rip his fucking face off.

Do not.

I'm going to rip his fucking face off.

Cooper found himself leaning toward him and stopped just in time, reining in his anger, forcing his features clean of reaction, because that would be what the prick wanted.

"I met her, you know." Devlin sauntered over to him. "Interesting woman. And very attractive. Although she's no Dana Kellerman." He smirked. "I always thought you were a lucky son of a bitch to have caught that woman's eye. But . . ." He sighed. "Maybe it's the bar, Cooper. Have you ever considered that? All those long hours. It doesn't really give you much time to look after your women the way they obviously need. Otherwise they wouldn't keep leaving you." He gave him a small smile that Cooper guessed was supposed to look fatherly. And it did. If fathers ate their offspring. "I will make you a very generous offer on the bar. It will be enough to start fresh, do something that isn't killing your time the way the bar does."

Jesus Christ.

Cooper crossed his arms over his chest, studying him. "Is it stupidity?"

Devlin frowned. "What?"

"You and your fucking persistence. Is it stupidity or just sheer arrogance? I don't know how many times I have to tell you that I am not selling my bar. I'm telling you now"—Cooper lowered his voice in warning—"I've just about reached the end of my tether with this shit."

Devlin gave another heavy sigh as he walked casually over to him, stopping mere inches away. "I came here to give you one last chance to accept my offer."

"And what exactly does that mean? Are you threatening me like you've threatened all the other people whose places you've stolen out from under them?"

"I have no idea what you're talking about. And this is just a friendly warning."

What the hell was he up to?

Uneasiness settled over Cooper, but he didn't let it show. "You come after me, Devlin, you'll have the biggest fight of your fucking life on your hands."

"Somehow I doubt it." Devlin leaned in to say quietly, "What you haven't seemed to grasp is that money makes the world go around. And I have it, Cooper. You don't."

It took everything within him to keep his fists at his sides as every nerve ending he possessed screamed at him to deck the bastard. Instead he stood locked in place, fighting for control, watching Ian Devlin swagger out of his bar with a smug smile on his face.

He was still standing staring out the door when Tremaine appeared in it.

Eyebrows raised as he strode inside, he said, "Was that Ian Devlin I just saw?"

Cooper nodded tightly.

Tremaine's cold eyes narrowed. "What did he want?"

Finally, Cooper managed to unlock his muscles enough to walk back behind the bar. He touched the bar top, worrying now about his future with it.

"Lawson?"

He looked up at his neighbor. "What the hell is Jessica doing at your place?" he blurted out.

Tremaine sighed as he slipped onto a stool at the bar. "Don't tell me you believe those ridiculous rumors?"

"No, I don't."

"Good."

"That doesn't answer my question."

"The doctor said she had some business with Beckwith before she could leave. She doesn't have much money so I offered her my place to stay until she's ready to leave. I spend most of my time in a suite at the hotel, so it wasn't a big deal."

"I still don't get why."

Tremaine shrugged. "It gave her time."

"Time for what?" Cooper scrutinized him. Cooper had realized a while back that Tremaine wasn't just the cool businessman he portrayed himself as to everyone else, but it shocked the hell out of him that Tremaine may actually be trying to play Cupid here. "To come back to me?"

His neighbor didn't give him the truth one way or the other. Instead he said, "What did Devlin want?"

The fury returned. "It was a warning. He gave me one last chance to accept an offer on the bar."

"One last chance? What does that mean?"

"He's coming after me."

Tremaine studied him, surprise lighting his eyes. "You're worried."

"He's got the kind of money I don't. I'll fight him, with everything I have. But that sneaky bastard is underhanded, and if he greases the right palms—"

"Cooper."

He stilled at the quiet way Tremaine said his name.

He gave Cooper a dark smile. "Don't worry about it."

"Why?"

"Because I've got more money than *ten* Ian Devlins. And I like my boardwalk the way it fucking is."

A slither of reassurance moved through Cooper. "*Your* boardwalk?"

Tremaine smirked. "Better the devil you know, Lawson. Better the devil you know."

TWENTY-SEVEN

Jessica

Number 131 Providence Road was on the south side of Hartwell and it ran along the coastline. The homes varied from moderate to large there, and 131 was somewhere in between. It was a smaller version of Vaughn's in style. The gardens and driveway were well maintained, and the white cladding had been repainted recently, because it was pristine and fresh.

I'd passed a For Sale sign as I drove up the driveway.

One thirty-one Providence Road.

George still lived in the same house.

One half of the double front doors swung open before I could knock and I found myself staring into the warm brown eyes of a tall, older gentleman. "May I help you, miss?"

Oh, my God.

Butterflies raged in my stomach as I clutched the purse that contained Sarah's letters. "Mr. Beckwith. George Beckwith?"

"Yes?"

I thrust out my hand. "Jessica Huntington."

Bemused, George shook my hand. "Pleased to meet you, Ms. Huntington. Now, how can I help?"

"This is strange," I said softly. "I . . . uh . . . I guess I'll start off by saying that up until a few months ago I was a physician at the women's correctional facility in Wilmington."

Immediate understanding dawned on him and I saw the warmth overshadowed by pain. "Is this about Sarah?"

Like the emotional nutcase I'd become, I had to fight back the strong urge to burst into tears. She was the first thing he considered.

He'd never forgotten her.

"Yes."

George opened the door wider. "Then you'd better come in."

"So . . ." George said a few minutes later, as he put down a tray of tea and biscuits on the coffee table in front of me.

I was sitting in a large, comfortable lounge, the furniture dated but of a quality that put my stuff now stored in Cooper's garage to shame.

Shit. My stuff. Getting that back would be awkward.

"What do you have to tell me?" George said, pulling me from my thoughts.

He sat down on the sofa across from me as I reached for my cup of tea.

The letters were by my side. I'd gotten them out of my purse while he was making tea. Shaking a little— for him—I handed them over. "I found these, Mr. Beckwith."

"Please call me George," he muttered as he took the letters from me.

"They were sealed inside a library book. They've been there for forty years."

His eyes washed over his name and address, and I heard the pain in his voice when he whispered, "This is Sarah's handwriting."

"She wrote to you . . . but unfortunately she passed away on the same day she wrote the last letter. She never got the chance to send them." The tears I'd been holding back sprang free and I swiped at them, embarrassed.

George's gaze turned kind at my show of emotion. "I'm almost afraid now to know what's inside, if it has caused such a reaction in a stranger."

"You need to know."

"And you came all the way here to give these to me?"

I nodded.

He studied me. "How extraordinary," he murmured.

Not really. Not if he knew me. He'd get it then. He'd understand why Sarah's story had gotten under my skin.

"I can leave," I said, "if you'd like to read them in private."

"That's alright."

So I sat there, watching George read Sarah's words, and my heart broke for him as he reached the last and his own tears began to fall. I watched him as he read them all over again.

And again.

Finally he looked up at me, his eyes shining, and he whispered, "I already knew. I already knew. God damn it, Sarah."

With my chest aching so much for them both, I moved to sit beside him, to clutch his hand in comfort. "I'm so sorry."

After a moment he took a shuddering breath, his fingers tightening so hard around the letters they began to crumple. "I found out about my father's criminal activity a few years after Sarah married Ron. I was disillusioned, yes, but I still loved him. I couldn't betray him. All I could do was stay out of it, let it all die with him." He looked at me, regret in his eyes. "She should have trusted me. She should have trusted me enough to tell me."

"Was I wrong to give you these? Have I made it that much worse?"

"No," he said. "At least this way I know that she loved me like I loved her."

A little sob escaped my mouth before I could stop it.

Looking concerned, George slid an arm around my shoulder. "Why does this touch you so much?"

It took me a minute before I could speak properly. "I feel like I understand her."

His expression fell. "For your sake I hope that's not true," he said kindly.

I had to ask, had to know . . . "Do you still love her? Despite what she did? Do you forgive her? Do you still love her?"

George gripped my hand tighter and leaned in to me so I could see the absolution in his eyes. "I loved my wife. I did. But Sarah

Randall was the love of my life, Ms. Huntington. Yes. Yes to all of the above."

I swiped at my tears and gave him a shaky smile. "You can call me Jessica."

George smiled back. "Jessica. Somehow I think there is more to this story for you."

I nodded and looked at Sarah's crumpled letters. "You know, she doesn't say it, but I think maybe she didn't fight her life with Ron because you were lost to her once you married Annabelle."

"Why do you think that?" he said hoarsely.

"Because you were her whole world, George. Maybe it wasn't right, maybe it was stupid, but she made you her whole world. Once you were gone, she stopped fighting . . . until she realized not fighting was going to kill her."

"She was my whole world, too," he said quietly. "I thought she knew it."

I gave him a sad smile. "Sometimes women in love are fools."

"Not just women, Jessica. *People.* People in love can be fools." He gave a heavy sigh. "Well, I need a stiff drink after all of this. What do you say?"

I nodded again, smiling through my tears. "That sounds just about right."

The trendy bar just off Main Street was nice, but it lacked the coziness of Cooper's. George had first suggested that we go to Cooper's and as soon as he saw my face, realization dawned. "You're the *doctor*?"

See—small town.

"And it all begins to make sense," he'd said, giving me a smile.

So we'd ended up at Germaine's. For obvious reasons I'd never been there before.

And by the time I'd made it on to my second Long Island (nowhere near as tasty as Coop's), I'd made up my mind to tell Cooper the truth.

Cat's words the other day had played a part in the decision. My thoughts of Julia and how much she'd like Cooper were part of the decision. So I'd already arrived halfway to the decision when George Beckwith's love for Sarah saved me.

Yes.

I did consider it saving me.

Because even if I did tell Cooper and I lost him, at least I wouldn't have to live with the kind of regret that Sarah had lived with. A regret that she found peace from but George never did.

I couldn't do that to myself or to Cooper.

But I was terrified. I'd spent all these years creating barriers between me and everyone else, even Matthew, and I wasn't sure what would happen to me once I tried to take those barriers down.

Without telling George the details I gave him the gist of my inner turmoil, while he regaled me with his fond memories of Sarah. He also talked about Annabelle, his late wife, and the fond memories he'd made with her, too, including their beautiful daughter, Marie. It was for Marie and his grandchildren that he was packing up his life in Hartwell and heading to Canada.

"Oh, excuse me." George slid off the stool at the high round table we were sitting at. "Bladder isn't what it used to be." He winked at me, making me laugh.

I watched him walk away, still straight-backed, tall, and strong for his age, and I saw what Sarah had seen in him.

Only a few hours.

That was all the time I'd spent in George's company, but I knew instinctively that he was a decent man, a kind man. A good man.

Like Cooper.

Suddenly the vision of George walking away was blocked by a man.

I blinked, as the man slid onto George's stool.

I was about to tell him politely that I wasn't interested, when I froze in recognition.

Jack Devlin.

Bailey hadn't been exaggerating when she'd first told me about Jack. He was a handsome devil. The day I'd bumped into him at the music festival I couldn't help but smile at him in return, he was so charming.

Of course I lost my kind thoughts as soon as I realized who he was.

Right then he wasn't smiling at me.

He wore a cold, blank expression that I found more than a little concerning. "What do you want?"

He shrugged. "Just saying hello."

"Hello. Now you can leave."

That earned me a hint of a smirk. "Last I heard, you and Cooper were broken up."

"So?"

"So that means we can talk."

"No, it doesn't."

"You're still loyal to him?" He scrutinized me.

"So loyal that if you don't get your ass off that stool I'm going to make you." I didn't know how I was going to make him, since he had half a foot on me, but I'd try!

Jack took a swig of his beer in reply, looking around the bar casually as if I hadn't just threatened him with bodily harm.

"Well?"

He flicked his gaze back to me. "You know, Dana came to me a while ago. Just after the music festival, actually."

"I don't care what you and Dana get up to," I snapped.

He shrugged again. "Just thought you might find it interesting that the reason she came to me was you."

"Oh?" I said, dryly, still not giving a shit.

"She wanted me to seduce you." His eyes hardened with dark humor. "Seduce you. Those were the exact words she used."

Fury moved through me, but before I could react he said, "My father isn't going to use what he knows about you."

I tensed, thrown by the sharp subject change. And then by the knowledge that *Jack knew, too.*

I started to tremble.

Shit. I had to get to Cooper. I had to tell him.

"And why is that?"

"You broke up with Cooper. You're no longer of any use. That doesn't mean my father doesn't know a good resource when he sees it. He'll keep that information on a back burner until it proves useful again."

Disgust roiled through me. "You son of a bitch. Both of you."

Jack shrugged, his eyes narrowing in the direction where George had gone.

Relief moved through me as I saw George making his way back to me.

Jack got off the stool but rounded the table to face me.

I tensed as he studied me, and then he offered quietly, "Cooper's liquor license."

"What?"

He gave me a pointed look, his face hard with frustration. "Cooper's. Liquor. License."

And that was when understanding dawned.

Jack was warning me.

He was gone before I could say anything else.

"Jessica, are you okay?" George said upon his return.

I shook my head. "No. I have to get to Cooper."

You know that scene in the movies where someone who has done another someone wrong walks into a room and everyone in it goes quiet and glares at the first someone?

No? Yes?

Well, anyway, that was exactly what happened to me when George and I walked into Cooper's bar twenty minutes later.

Every regular, every townie in the place, stopped talking and glowered at me.

I stared back, stunned.

Until I felt George nudge me forward and my eyes flew to the bar, where Cooper was staring at me, looking as frozen and shell-shocked as I felt.

I wanted to run at him.

I wanted to launch myself over the bar at him.

I did neither of those things.

"Come on, Jessica," George said in encouragement, "you can do this."

With his hand pressed to my lower back, George led me over to the bar. My eyes were locked with Cooper's the whole time, his head moving as I made my way closer to him. Until finally I was standing across the bar from him.

Neither of us said a word, just drank the other in like it had been years, not days.

"Jessica," George urged.

"We need to talk," I blurted out.

Cooper didn't give me much. "About?"

"Two things."

"Being?"

I swallowed hard at his flat tone. "Devlin."

His eyes narrowed.

"And the truth."

"And what if I don't care anymore?"

My insides twisted at the thought, but I pushed through, thinking of George and how hurt and angry he'd been with Sarah at first, and how that anger had ruined any small chance he'd had of getting her away from Ron.

And then I remembered how lost in me Cooper had been the other night when he'd turned up for his "one last time" with me. "I don't believe that."

Something shifted in him and that was when I saw it.

I saw the pain he'd tried to hide behind lust at Vaughn's place. But he couldn't hide it from me.

I wanted to do everything I could to fix it, and tried to convey that with my eyes.

Finally he nodded. "Riley, watch the bar."

"Sure thing, boss," she said quietly.

Relief mingled with terror shook through me as Cooper strode out from behind the bar.

George squeezed my hand. "You can do this."

I gave him a grateful, shaky smile, and then made myself move toward Cooper. I followed him out of the bar. We were silent as he led us to the parking lot at the back. I got into his truck without saying a word, then endured a very tense five-minute drive to his place.

He threw his keys in the bowl on his side table as we walked into his house and I was suddenly flooded by memories of our time together in here.

Such a short amount of time.

But it was filled with so much.

I didn't want it to end.

I wanted to be brave with him.

"Devlin first," Cooper said as he walked into his kitchen to pull a beer out of the fridge. He offered it to me, but I shook my head. In answer he twisted off the cap and took a slug before staring at me, waiting.

"Okay." I took a few tentative steps toward him. "I was out with George at Germaine's. Jack was there."

"And?" he bit out.

"Two things. One: apparently Dana tried to encourage him to seduce me while you and I were still together."

Something sharpened in Cooper's eyes. "Why did he tell you that?"

"I thought at first he was just being an ass until . . . he told me the second thing."

I was silent for a minute, lost in studying him. I'd missed him so much.

Cooper huffed, "Well, don't keep me in suspense."

"He brought up the subject of his father and he said three words to me before he left. 'Cooper's liquor license.'"

Cooper frowned. "What does that mean?"

"It was a warning. Devlin is going after your liquor license. If you can't get your license renewed, you're out of business."

His eyes narrowed and then he turned and dumped the beer bottle in his sink with a clatter. "Son of a bitch," he muttered harshly.

I wished we were in a place where I could just wrap my arms around him to soothe him. "Cooper—"

"He came to me." His eyes blazed hell fury as he turned back to me. "He fucking threatened me and this is what it was about."

"He can't get away with it. We won't let him."

Just like that Cooper stilled, his voice still icy as he said, "We?"

My stomach roiled.

Do not upchuck.

Do. Not. Upchuck.

Be brave, Jessica.

"That is . . . if you . . . I need to tell you the truth about why I broke up with you."

I waited until he snapped impatiently, "Well?"

I almost laughed nervously but managed to stifle it. "It's not an easy story to tell. I just . . . It never occurred to me that I had to until you mentioned kids. I knew then . . . I knew I couldn't tie you to me like that forever without telling you, but I was so scared that if you knew the truth you wouldn't want anything to do with me. I thought it would be better to walk away than have your feelings for me *go* away."

"What the hell did you do?" he whispered hoarsely.

"You have to understand," I pleaded. "The way you reacted to Sarah's letters, to what she did . . . I thought for sure that you would react the same to me. And I . . . I mean it when I say I haven't spoken to anyone about this. I've spent so long not thinking about that time, not wanting anyone to know, that anytime someone asked about my family, about my past . . . I felt like I might die if they found out. If *you* ever found out."

"Jesus, Jess . . ." His eyes softened.

"But Cat said something and then George . . . and I realize now—and I'm so sorry, Cooper, because you were right, I *owe* you this."

"Then just tell me because I'm going out of my fucking mind here."

I dragged my hands down my face and let out a shaky sigh as I tried to tamp down the wave of nausea.

"Are you going to be sick?" he said, taking a step toward me, unable to hide his concern for me.

God, please don't let this take away that concern.

I pushed through, forcing the words out. "I didn't just take the position at the prison because I wanted to help the women," I said, my words stilted, fragile with fear and pain. "I took it because I felt a little like one of them; like they understood me without even knowing it."

Cooper paled. "Jess . . ."

"I was fourteen."

His eyes turned dark, hollowed. Mirroring mine, perhaps, as I went back there, to that place; that horrible, tormented place.

"My parents were always busy with work and each other. The only time they ever seemed to get it together for us was for some of Julia's performances. They liked to watch her dance. We all did.

"She was eleven years old." My chest tightened at the memory, just like it had the day I found them. "I'd been out with friends. My parents used to leave us alone a lot so I was the one who looked after Julia. There was my aunt Theresa, we were close to her, but she was at school and we only ever saw her during school breaks, and she'd look after Julia if I couldn't. So the only time I got to myself when she wasn't around was when my dad's kid brother, Tony, came around. He'd lived out of state for most of our lives, but he'd moved back a few years before. I remember being glad. I liked him. I was grateful to him for being interested in us." I curled my lip in disgust at my naïveté. "I didn't sense anything bad from him."

"Jesus Christ," Cooper breathed.

"I would go out with friends when he came around because he watched Julia." I looked over at Cooper through blurred vision, begging him to believe me. "I didn't know. I didn't know what he was doing to her until that day. I came home early and I couldn't find them . . . but I heard something . . . down in the basement, in our games room. And what I saw . . ."

"Fuck, Jessica." Cooper strode over to me, pulling me into his arms.

I held on to him for dear life. "I just flew at him," I said, lost in the memory. "This rage just came over me. It startled him enough that I was able to grab Julia. We were running up the stairs"—my grip on Coop tightened—"and he caught hold of her and there was this look in his eyes . . . God, it was like staring straight into evil." The words tumbled out of me. "And I just—I just had this overwhelming sense that he wasn't going to let us out of there alive." I pulled back. "I don't know if it was just the fear of a kid or if I felt something instinctual, but whatever it was . . . I managed to pull Julia away from him, but he came at me at the top of the stairs. He got me on my back and it was a blur . . . he just kept punching me until suddenly he wasn't on me and I heard my sister scream. When I got up, when I could focus, he had her pinned against the wall, and he was choking her. I had to stop him. My father's golf clubs were there. I took one. I swung." I closed my eyes, still remembering the shudder of impact up my arms, the sickening thud of it against his head. "He fell down the stairs. Broke his neck."

I found the courage to look up at Cooper. He stared down at me, looking tortured. "I killed my uncle."

His eyes shone for me. "Jessica."

"Julia told our parents what had happened. What had been happening. For two years." My face crumpled again. I'd failed her. "I wasn't sentenced. The police considered it self-defense—I was badly beaten and my sister bore physical evidence of everything we'd said had happened. But we were both put into therapy for a long time. It helped." I let out a long breath. "For me. But then Julia just . . . she focused in on dancing. To an unhealthy degree. And when she didn't get into the school of her dreams, she hung herself in my parents' basement. I was the one who found her.

"My parents blamed me. They refused to believe that she killed herself because of what Tony did. They said she couldn't live with the memory, the horror, of watching her sister kill a man right in front of her. And me . . . well, I let them get away with it because the truth is, I failed her."

I saw Cooper's face transform, the fury burning in his blue eyes. "No. Your parents failed Julia. You fought for her." His grip on me tightened as he tugged me close. "Jess, what you did . . . it was brave. You know that, right? And every day since has been brave. Why are you punishing yourself? You killed a man defending yourself and the person you loved. Horrific for you, yes. But I cannot say I wouldn't have done the same fucking thing."

I sobbed, relief rocking through me. "Really?"

"Yes."

My tears came faster as hard, wracking shudders moved through my body. I fell into Cooper and accepted his compassion, his understanding. Suddenly I was swung up into his arms and I clung to him, burying my face in his neck as he climbed the stairs.

He settled on his bed, tucking me into him, holding me tight and letting me cry all the tears I'd kept bottled up for years.

Cooper

Jess's tears subsided after a while, her body stopped moving in little juddering jerks against his, and her shallow breathing eased out.

Cooper held her so tight, wishing like hell there were magic words or actions that could take away her traumatic past.

Fuck.

He'd known she was hiding something, and he'd known for her to break up with him that it had to be bad, but he'd never have been able to imagine it was as bad as it was.

The things she'd seen as a kid . . .

And all Cooper could think was that no one would ever know it—that she was haunted like she was. She'd become a doctor, she practiced kindness in every way, and she loved to laugh and make other people smile. There was so much light in her, despite the dark trying to snuff it out.

"I wish I hadn't reacted the way I did," he suddenly said into the quiet of his bedroom, "about Sarah."

Jess's fingers curled into his T-shirt. "What do you mean?" Her voice was scratchy from all her crying.

He squeezed her closer, not ever wanting to let her go. "If I had been more compassionate about her letters, you might have had the courage to tell me about this sooner."

She pulled away so she could look at him.

He drank in her red-rimmed, puffy eyes and blotchy cheeks and felt an overwhelming surge of tenderness for her.

"Cooper, no." Jess shook her head. "Even if you had, there's no guarantee I would have felt brave enough to tell you. It took losing you, as horrible as that is; it took losing you. But you . . . I know you." She pressed her hand over his heart. "I should have trusted in you and I am so sorry."

"Jess," he whispered, brushing his thumb over her damp cheek, "you've got so much to work through. But I'll be here while you do it. Never doubt that."

She bit her lip in thought and after a while she nodded. "Matthew is the only person still in my life from then who knows what I did. But I wouldn't talk to him about it, either. Ever. The records are sealed. I was scared to tell anyone because of how my parents treated me. Even before Julia died, they wanted nothing to do with me. To them I was monstrous for what I'd done. I was scared everyone would feel the same way. Even Theresa. I shut her out, too. I haven't spoken to her since Julia's funeral. I couldn't stand it if I found out that she, of all people, thought I was a monster, too."

Indignation raged through Cooper. "Your parents are the monsters, Jess. They didn't protect you. Either of you."

"Rationally I know that." She nodded. "But their rejection left its mark. My whole life I've been terrified to let anyone in. But everyone needs to feel needed and being a doctor gave me something I just wasn't getting in my personal life. It also felt like redemption."

"You don't need to be redeemed."

She gave him a grateful smile. "I thought I did. I didn't realize until I got here just how empty I'd made my life. On some level I guess I knew that I was still punishing myself, but coming here . . . I felt this peace I can't explain. I've never felt any kind of peace before and I didn't want to lose it. It made me question everything. About why I was really a doctor, why I didn't have anyone in my life . . ." Her smile turned open and warm. "And you and Bailey—you liked me. Me. Not the doctor part."

"I liked that part, too," Cooper said honestly, "because I think it is a part of you. It's not just a way to be redeemed. You save people, Jess. You've been doing it since you were fourteen. It's *who* you are."

Fresh tears slipped down her cheeks, but she was smiling. "You really think so?"

Cooper needed her to understand this once and for all. He sat up, cupping her face in his hands, and he said, "It hurts like hell knowing you've seen what you have, done what you have, but it came from a place of survival, strength, bravery, and loyalty. I don't see anything but beauty in that."

Jess stared at him in astonishment, in wonder. Finally she whispered, "Where did you come from, Cooper Lawson?"

She loved him.

He knew it without her having to say it.

Relief poured through him as he wrapped his arms around her and held her tight. "I love you."

Her fingers dug into the muscles in his back. "I love you, too."

"Thank fuck for that." He closed his eyes in relief, smiling at her answering giggle.

A little while later Jessica eased back from him, worry shining in her eyes. "We have two problems."

Cooper felt his irritation return. "Devlin and Dana."

She nodded. "I hate them to ruin this"—she gestured between them—"but we have to do something. Dana . . . I guess we just keep an eye out for her troublemaking."

"I saw her at the music festival"—he knew she was up to something then—"eyeing Jack. That's when she came up with the plan to get him to come on to you."

She curled her lip in disgust. "She must think every woman is exactly like her."

"She's an idiot. And an annoyance. But I don't think we should give her any of our time. Like you said, we just need to watch out for her."

"But your license—Cooper, we need to do something about that now. Devlin . . ." She sighed, giving him a wary look. "Ian Devlin approached me the day I broke up with you."

What the . . . Cooper tensed.

"He knows about what I did to my uncle. Like I said, those records are sealed because I was a juvenile, so he must have paid off someone to get his grubby hands on them."

"What are you talking about?" he bit out, trying for her sake to hold on to a semblance of calm.

"He tried to blackmail me. He said he'd tell you what I was hiding unless I convinced you to give up the bar."

He was going to kill him.

He was going to fucking kill him!

His anger exploded and he pushed off the bed with every intention of finding the piece of shit and tearing him apart.

Who the fuck used something like what Jess had been through against a person?

"Coop!" Jess threw herself at his back as he was storming out, wrapping her whole body around him like a monkey. It would have been funny if he weren't so mad. "No!"

He trembled with his fury. "Get off me, Jessica."

"No! He is not worth it!"

"You're worth it!"

Her arms tightened around his neck. "Coop," she whispered. "Calm down."

He closed his eyes and took a deep breath, his blood still too hot. "He can't get away with this."

"Sweetheart." She slid off him and moved around to face him, cupping his face in her hands. "The only way to defeat someone like Devlin is to save your bar and to stop him from getting his hands on anything on our boardwalk."

Cooper considered her words and slowly he started to tremble a little less. He nodded. "Tremaine said something."

"Yeah?"

"He *really* doesn't want Devlin getting his hands on boardwalk property. We can use him. Maybe he can help put a stop to whatever Devlin is planning."

"Good." Jessica gave him a relieved smile, pressing her body into his. "Now promise me you aren't going to go after Devlin. With your fists."

He wanted to punch the smug look off the conniving, soulless bastard's face.

But for her . . . "I promise."

She relaxed against him. "Good." She pressed her cheek against his chest. "I'm so tired, Coop. Do you think we can start fighting him tomorrow?"

A rush of love crashed over him, washing every other feeling away. He kissed the side of her head and then turned to lead her back to his bed. "Anything for you, Doc."

And he meant it.

But best of all it no longer made him uneasy to mean it.

He was sure.

He was certain.

Because the doc was a good woman and Cooper was wise enough now to know that a good woman was the most beautiful woman any man could have for his own.

TWENTY-EIGHT

Jessica

Bailey stared at me, her face pale, eyes gone round with a sadness that turned to tears as I told her my story.

Cooper had assured me that I didn't owe my story to anyone—but also that he knew Bailey and he knew Bailey loved me. He said if I told my friend, all she would do was accept me and help me realize that I wasn't destined to spend my whole life being rejected by the people I loved. He'd also urged me to contact Theresa.

"She's your family, Jess. Give her a chance."

I'd decided to be brave and take his advice.

First, I was starting with Bailey.

When I was done telling her everything I had gone through, she just shook her head, tears spilling down her cheeks, and then she reached for me, hauling me close for a hug so tight I almost couldn't breathe.

Bailey pulled back to cup my face in an almost motherly way. "How?" she whispered. "How can someone like you have been through so much?" She gave me a watery smile. "Bravest person I know, Jess. Bravest person I know."

Relief poured through me. It was my turn to hug the oxygen out of her. "Thank you," I choked out.

"I can't believe you've been holding on to this so long." She pulled back. "I wish you'd come to me sooner just so I could knock some sense into you about Cooper."

I laughed. "Yeah. I'm an idiot. But I'm over that now."

She grinned. "Good. So . . . about the inn? Does this mean I've got you back?"

I gave her a shaky, apologetic smile. "Actually . . . I was thinking about applying for the position at Dr. Duggan's clinic."

"Really?" She grabbed my hands in hers, looking genuinely delighted.

I laughed again. "Yes. I'm guessing you're okay with that?"

"Of course I am. Jess! You're a doctor! Not an innkeeper. Not that I won't miss the help," she hurried to assure me, "I'll just need to find someone else I can trust."

"You will," I assured her back.

"So this is exciting." She gave me a wicked smile. "You have no idea what you're in for as a small-town doctor."

"What do you mean?" I said, concerned by the mischief in her eyes.

"Being a small-town doc is being a full-time doc. No matter where you are—out for lunch, canoodling with Coop on the beach—people will come up to you with all their ailments, expecting a diagnosis."

Not sure I liked the sound of that, I made a face.

"You just have to be firm from the get-go," she said. "You tell them, 'Come see me in my office; I'm not working right now.'"

"Okay." That still didn't make me feel any less worried about it.

"And of course if I'm with you, you won't have to say a thing because I'll tell the idiots to fuck off."

I snorted because I knew she meant it and that she would.

"So," she said, letting out a sigh, "you and Coop are going to be okay?"

The truth was, I would never forget the way he'd looked at me or the beautiful words he'd said to me the night before.

It hurts like hell knowing you've seen what you have, done what you have, but it came from a place of survival, strength, bravery, and loyalty. I don't see anything but beauty in that.

I didn't think it was possible to love him any more than I already did.

"We're going to be great . . . but Cooper has a problem." This was the second reason I'd come to Bailey. Cooper had said he would talk to Vaughn, but I was thinking I might already have an idea how to stop Devlin from going after Cooper's liquor license. The only way his liquor license wouldn't be renewed was if Devlin had bribed someone on the city board of licenses. I had an idea how to change the mind of the person who had been bribed. I laid out what was happening to Bailey and what my idea was. "Can you get everyone to meet at Cooper's place tomorrow morning before it opens?"

Bailey nodded her head, looking fierce and determined. "You bet your ass I can. There is no damn way Ian Devlin is getting away with this shit."

I nodded back, feeling just as fierce. Cooper loved his bar and I loved Cooper.

There was a snowball's chance in hell of me letting anyone take what he loved away from him.

Loading the last of my stuff into my car, I turned in surprise at the sound of gravel crunching under wheels.

Vaughn's beautiful but conspicuous dark blue Aston Martin Vanquish was heading up his driveway toward me. I leaned against my car and waited for him.

He got out, dressed as always in a tailored three-piece suit. He slipped off his sunglasses as he walked toward me and I wondered at how much in love with Cooper I had to be for Vaughn Tremaine not to affect me.

I smiled at him, perfectly at ease around him now that I knew he wasn't the cold, hard businessman he seemed to want everyone to believe he was.

"You're leaving," he said, gesturing to the suitcase that was now in my trunk.

"Yeah. I was going to swing by the hotel to say thank you again. I really appreciated you letting me stay."

He waved me off. "Cooper told me you two have reconciled. He also told me about the little problem with Devlin."

"About that—"

"I'll take care of it."

"Actually, I'd really rather you didn't until we try out my plan first."

Vaughn frowned. "Cooper didn't say you had a plan."

"Because Cooper doesn't know about my plan."

"And why is that?"

"Because Cooper won't want to bother anyone else about 'his' problem. But Devlin is a problem for everyone on that boardwalk. So . . . tomorrow . . . be at Cooper's at ten a.m."

"What are you up to, Dr. Huntington?"

I crossed my arms over my chest, feeling quite pleased with myself. "A little something called community backbone."

Cooper had made space in his closet, and in his bureau, for me.

God, I loved that man.

But it wasn't enough space for all my stuff, I mused. He was still holding all my furniture and clothes in the garage he owned on the outskirts of town. I'd like my clothes, but that meant possibly converting his second bedroom into a dressing room.

Hmm. I wondered how he'd feel about that.

As for the rest of my stuff . . . well, I liked Cooper's place as it was, but maybe we could take a look at my stuff and see if anything would fit.

The rest we could sell.

"You're moving in with him?" Matthew had said, sounding a little shocked, after I'd called to give him a rundown on what was going on in my life. He sounded relieved when I told him that I'd confessed my past to Cooper.

"He asked me to move in. I know it sounds fast, maybe even crazy, but for us . . . it's not, Matthew. It feels right. I don't want to waste any more time. I just want to be with him and by some miracle he wants to be with me."

"Of course he does. He's a lucky bastard to have you."

"And he believes that."

"Good." Matthew sighed. "Well, now I really need to come out there and meet this guy."

"You do. And you are welcome anytime. I'd love to see Perry and introduce her to Coop's nephew, Joey."

"Definitely. I'm happy for you, Jess. You have no idea."

That got me all teary eyed because no matter how happy or sad I was, this guy was always there for me. "Yeah, I do. Come see me soon, Matt."

"I will, sweetheart. I promise."

"I'm going to try to find my aunt Theresa," I told him. "Cooper thinks I should give her a chance."

Matt was silent on the other end of the line.

"Matt?"

"You don't have to look very far," he finally said. "I have her number."

Shock froze me to the spot. "You do?"

"When you shut her out, she came to me. I've been keeping her up to date on your life over the years. I wasn't trying to betray you, Jess. I was just . . . She loves you. She misses you."

Tears clogged my throat. "My God," I whispered. "I've been such a fool."

"You were scared. She understands that."

"Will you . . . will you text me her number?"

"Right away."

And he did. But I didn't call Theresa immediately. I had to build myself up to that. So I spent the rest of the day unpacking, then I dropped by Paul Duggan's office to submit my résumé, and now I was back, hanging around Cooper's. Well, technically, I was hanging around my and Cooper's place.

Cooper and Jessica's place.

It had a great ring to it.

Lying on the couch, reading a book, trying to stay awake until Cooper came home from closing the bar, I thought about how much more amplified my feelings for him were now that he knew everything.

I'd been in love with him before.

But now what I felt was so powerful it was a little overwhelming. There had not been a second of the day that I hadn't thought about him, and those thoughts put good butterflies in my belly.

At the sound of a car pulling into the drive I sat up, waiting in surprise as I heard the heavy footfalls that belonged to a tall, rugged, flannel-wearing, blue-eyed guy.

I grinned as Cooper stepped inside the house.

He stopped at the sight of me, seeming just to drink me in.

"You're home early," I said softly.

Cooper walked toward me and I recognized the heat in his eyes. "Got Riley to cover again."

I felt that familiar luscious flip in my lower belly and the answering tingle between my legs. "Needed something, did you?" I whispered.

His answer was to take hold of my hand and pull me up off the couch. And then he was leading me by the hand, hurrying us up the stairs and into his bedroom. He spun around and I couldn't even speak, I was that lust dazed already, as he stripped off his clothes and then came at me. I was naked before I could even manage to whisper his name.

And then Cooper shoved me gently on the bed and the breath whooshed right out of me as I lay back in anticipation, watching him as he got on the bed and settled his knees on either side of my waist. I looked up at him and in that moment he was my entire world.

The heat in Cooper's eyes flared to tenderness as if I'd said what I was thinking out loud. Hands braced on the mattress on either side of my head, he bent to graze his lips over mine. Soft, teasing kisses that grew deeper, longer, sweeter. Kisses that dissolved everything else around us, until we were just lips and breath and love. And that love sparked what it always had between us:

Passion.

I gripped Cooper's waist as the kiss turned rough, breathless, desperate; I sighed into his mouth with pleasure as his erection stroked my belly. His lips drifted from my mouth and he whispered my name before lacing kisses across my chin, down my jaw. He kissed his way down my body, his mouth hot, hungry, as though it had been more than a week for us. It was as though it had been years.

I held on, caressing his muscled back, sliding my hands up into the silk of his hair.

When that hot mouth of his closed around my left nipple, my hips undulated against him. "Oh, God." My thighs gripped him as I urged him closer, my back arching for more as he licked me and then sucked hard, all the while pinching my other nipple between his forefinger and thumb.

"Cooper," I moaned in delight.

He lifted his head, watching my reaction as he moved against my hips, his dick sliding against my sex, shooting off sparks of sensation. I whimpered. "Cooper," I begged.

He groaned and dipped his head again, licking my other nipple now, knowing how sensitive I was there. As he continued to suck and tease and torment me, I felt the coil of tension tighten in my lower belly.

I was panting hard, my fingers tugging his hair and making him grunt with desire, and the noise vibrated against my areola. "I want you inside me," I gasped.

But Cooper wasn't done making love to every inch of me. He moved down my body, his lips trailing wet kisses over my stomach. I shivered at the touch of his tongue across my belly and melted, knowing his destination was my clit.

He kissed me there. Licked me. Sucked me. Until I was shivering and trembling, my orgasm building to its height as he lapped at me.

I lost my breath as the tension tightened inside of me, my hips stilling against his mouth momentarily as I balanced on the precipice of explosion.

And then one more lick.

Over the edge I went as my climax blasted through me. I pulsed and pulsed against his mouth until I was limp with satisfaction.

Satisfaction.

The word just didn't suffice for how much pleasure this man could give me.

Cooper moved back up my body and when I opened my eyes I stared straight into his. He had his hands braced on either side of my head, his lower body pressed to mine.

I melted all over again at the love in his eyes. Somehow I found the strength to draw him to me and I kissed him, still hungry, as I tasted myself on his tongue.

I broke the kiss before he did, eager to love him back just as much. Gently, I pressed my fingers against his shoulder and pushed him onto his back. Lust flared in Cooper's eyes as he lay back on the bed for me, his cock straining toward his belly. I needed it inside me. But I fought for patience, wanting to enjoy him.

I lowered my head and Cooper groaned before I even touched him. When I wrapped my mouth around him, the muscles in his abs contracted and his hips flexed against me. "Jessica," he huffed out, as his fingers threaded through my hair. "Fuck, Jess."

I licked along the underside of his cock first, teasing him for only a few seconds before I began to suck, tasting the salty heat of him. At the same time as I moved my mouth, I pumped the root with my hand.

His pants of excitement filled my ears, making my nipples pebble with desire. I grew slicker, my hips moving of their own accord with need, as I turned relentless in my urge to pleasure Cooper.

I looked up at his face from under my lashes, loving the worshipful look in his low-lidded eyes. The color was high on his cheeks and his chest rose and fell in shallow breaths as I chased his orgasm for him. I slid my free hand up over his lower abs, feeling the sheen of sweat on his skin.

I groaned and he squeezed his eyes shut, his teeth gritted together as he choked out my name.

"I'm coming," he warned, but instead of jerking back like I usually did I stayed put, hungry for everything from him.

I sucked him through his climax, something I'd never done before, and he shuddered in aftershocks for a while.

When I felt him relax under me, felt his cock soften, I pulled back to stare at him.

He stared back at me in wonder.

Feeling smug, I hopped off the bed, putting a little more swing in my naked hips as I strolled into the bathroom.

Freshened up, I returned a minute later. Cooper watched me, like a hunter, as I sauntered back out, his eyes dropping to my breasts as they bounced with my movement.

Mine dropped to his dick, excited and impressed as the blood began to surge back into it.

Smiling, I crawled onto the bed and back up his body.

He moved, quick like lightning, and I let out a yelp of laughter and surprise as he flipped me on my back. My laughter was swallowed up in his deep kiss and I wrapped myself around him. There was no high like the high of knowing the guy you loved wanted you with a ferocity that showed no sign of dying.

Cooper broke the kiss to put his lips all over me again, loving my breasts, my stomach; and where his mouth went, his hands followed, squeezing my breasts gently before skimming down to my waist. He rested on his knees and I gazed down at him, breathless with anticipation.

I cried out, feeling sensitive when his thumb pressed down on my clit.

And then he pushed two fingers inside me and I arched my back, spreading my legs to take him deeper.

He was in the mood to tease, torment, but I was so turned on from sucking him off that my patience was nearing its limit.

"Jess," he groaned, thrusting his fingers in and out of me. "You're soaked."

"I like you in my mouth," I groaned.

"Heaven," he said, his eyes dark. "Fucking heaven sent."

I bit my lip at his sweet words, trying to suppress my smile and failing. "Coop . . . come inside me. Please."

He could never resist my "please."

He gently eased his fingers out of me and then coasted both hands up my body as he moved upward.

"Now." I tilted my hips against him.

Cooper narrowed his sensual gaze, and excitement volleyed through me as he roughly pushed my legs farther apart and then slammed inside of me.

My back bowed as I cried out in pleasured relief. I loved the swelling, overwhelming thickness of him inside of me. When we were like this, nothing else existed.

To my surprise, since I'd assumed he was going to take me hard and fast, Cooper dragged almost all the way out of me in a slow, torturous stroke, before pressing back in, in an equally torturously slow thrust.

My eyes were locked on his face, mesmerized by his expression, by the mixture of primal sexuality and love in his eyes. Every muscle in his body was locked, tensed, as he strained to love me gently, slowly, tenderly.

His eyes moved over me, watching my lips shape his name, watching my breasts quiver against his thrusts, and I saw his control begin to wane.

"Jess, fuck, I love you," he choked out as if he was in pain.

"I love you, too. I love you more than anyone," I told him, needing him to know he wasn't alone in this. Not ever.

My words snapped what little control he was holding on to and suddenly he was pushing harder, moving faster, deeper inside of me. "Come for me, Jess," he commanded, his voice guttural. "Give me everything."

"I am. I will," I promised, pumping my hips into his strokes. "Always."

His lips parted and he faltered for a second. "Jess," he choked out on a harsh pant and I felt his cock throb hard inside me before his release triggered my own.

My inner muscles pulsed around his throbbing, straining cock and we shuddered together in climax.

Cooper collapsed against me and I somehow managed to find the strength to wrap my arms around him.

I felt his awe without him having to say a word because I was feeling the same awe.

We'd never climaxed together like that before.

In fact, I'd never experienced anything like that before.

"Wow," I finally whispered.

His body shook against mine, his cock twitching inside me, and warmth suffused me at the feel of his amusement all around me. Cooper lifted his head, his eyes smiling into mine. "Understatement, Jess." He murmured against my mouth. "Wow is an understatement."

I laughed, the sound joining his laughter.

And that was how we began our new life together.

TWENTY-NINE

Cooper

"You can do it," he whispered, giving her waist a squeeze.

They were lying in bed, a little sleep deprived after the best night of his life, and Jessica had just told him about Matthew giving her Theresa's number.

He'd suggested she call while he was there to support her.

"Maybe it's too early." Jess stared at her phone. "It's only six o'clock there."

"I don't think she'll mind."

She heaved a shaky sigh and pressed the call button. Her hazel eyes flew to his, wide with fear. He squeezed her waist again, wishing he could take the fear away.

But only the woman on the other end of the line could do that.

"Hello." Jessica suddenly tensed, alert. "Theresa?" She grabbed Cooper's hand and held on for dear life. "It's Jessica." Whatever her aunt said to her in return made tears well in Jess's eyes.

He held his breath, worried he'd done the wrong thing in encouraging her to contact her family.

But then Jess smiled, and the tears spilled down her cheeks. "It's good to hear your voice, too."

Cooper grinned and relaxed, lying down, his head on the pillow, to watch his woman's face light with joy and relief as she talked softly with her aunt.

Joey was sitting in a booth at the back of the bar, watching the cartoons Cooper had put on the television for him.

It was never an inconvenience for his sister and nephew to drop by to see him, at home or before the bar opened, but the morning after he'd had the best night of his life, on the morning when he'd sat with Jess while she had an emotional talk with her aunt, Cooper wasn't really in the mood for a lecture from Cat.

And the look she was giving him screamed lecture.

She glanced over at her son to make sure he was happily preoccupied before turning to scowl at Cooper. "You're back with her?" she hissed.

"Yes." His tone told her not to argue with him.

It only made Cat narrow her eyes. "Did she tell you whatever the hell it is she's hiding?"

"Yes."

Surprise flickered over her expression, softening it. "Really?"

Cooper sighed and leaned toward her. "Really. And believe me when I say I understand why she was so fucked up about it. But we're all good now."

"Well, what was the secret?"

He loved his sister, but sometimes she was a nosy brat. "None of your damn business."

"You're my brother. Of course it's my damn business."

"You shouldn't be using the word 'damn'!" Joey called over to them, his eyes still on the screen.

Amusement flooded Cooper and he saw the laughter mirrored in his sister's gaze. Her amusement fled as she continued to study him. "I'm glad Jessica told you what was going on with her . . . but she knows she can't pull this crap again, right?"

The only thing that stopped him from getting impatient with her lack of faith in Jess was the fact that it came from a place of absolute love. And the truth was that if their roles were reversed and some guy had messed Cat about, he probably wouldn't exactly be forgiving. "I don't think she will, but that doesn't mean there might not be speed bumps along the way. Jess has been through a hell of a lot."

Sympathy softened Cat. "Is she okay?"

"She will be," he promised.

"I really wish I knew what she's been through. I'm imagining all sorts of horrible things."

He remembered Jess's words from the other night. "You couldn't imagine how horrible the truth is."

Cat flinched. "God, Coop," she muttered.

"Maybe one day she'll tell you her story—but it is her story to tell."

His sister heaved a sigh but nodded. "It's hard to imagine she's been through anything that horrible. She hides it well."

"She's tough. She's . . . amazing."

Cat suddenly smiled at him. "You really love her."

He nodded. No point bullshitting about it.

"You never spoke about Dana the way you speak about Jess."

"Dana and I were just kids. We didn't know what love is—confused sex for love."

Her nose wrinkled. "Right."

He grinned. "Conversation over."

"Yup. Once my brother utters the word 'sex' I go temporarily deaf." She glanced over at Joey. "He'll be glad. He likes Jessica a lot."

"Always trust a kid's instincts."

"Or at least my kid's instincts."

They shared a proud smile just as a knock came at the bar door, seconds before it was pushed open. The sight of Jessica brought on a flood of memories of their night together. He'd kept reaching for her throughout the night, unable, it seemed, to get enough of her.

Now she was walking into his bar with this flushed glow on her face, not just from the sex, but from her talk with Theresa, and that made him feel damn pleased with himself. It took him a second to realize she wasn't alone.

Really not alone.

Confused, Cooper frowned, watching as Jess, along with Bailey, Iris, Ira, Vaughn, Dahlia, and Emery, filtered into his bar.

"Jess!" Joey shouted, running across the bar to her. He skidded to a stop inches from her and Jessica grinned, putting an arm around his shoulder to draw him against her.

"How you doing, Joe?" she said, fondness written all over her face.

Joey looked up at her, frowning. "Where have you been?"

She gave him a look of apology. "I had some things to take care of. But I'm back now."

His nephew grinned. "Did Uncle Coop tell you he bought a puppy?"

Oh, shit.

Yeah.

He had forgotten to tell her about that.

Jess's eyes flew to him and she looked like she was struggling not to laugh. "He did not."

Cooper smiled at her. "An Old English sheepdog. The litter is only a few weeks old. I pick him up in five weeks."

"An Old English sheepdog? Those are pretty big, aren't they?"

"I wasn't going to get a teacup." In all the times he'd imagined getting a dog it had been a big one like Chester, his mom's St. Bernard. He'd loved that dog growing up.

She shook her head, smiling. "Big it is."

"Uh, can we get on with this?" Tremaine said, looking impatient and bringing Cooper back to his original confusion.

"What's everyone doing here?"

Tremaine gestured to Jessica. "Apparently your good doctor here has a plan to stop Devlin."

She hadn't said a word about a plan to him the night before. Although to be fair they hadn't done much talking the night before.

Jess glanced down at Joey and then over at Cat.

Cat shrugged at the unasked question. "As long as no one is

planning to swear or plot a murder, he's fine. Joey won't say a word about what happens here, will you, kid?"

Joey mimicked zipping his mouth closed.

Cat made a *See?* gesture.

Satisfied, Jess turned to address everyone. "Between myself and Bailey informing you all, everyone is up to speed with Ian Devlin's suspected plans to blockade the renewal of Cooper's liquor license?"

They all nodded, but Cooper tensed. He hadn't wanted this to be anyone else's problem. The whole point was to get Tremaine to deal with it so no one else would worry about how far Devlin was willing to go to get real estate on the boardwalk.

He gave Tremaine a look that said as much, but the bastard just smirked at him and turned back to Jess.

"We don't know who it is on the city board of licenses that Devlin has bribed. And we don't need to. All we need to do is a little bribing ourselves." She shot Cooper a reassuring look before turning back to his neighbors. "I propose that you all sign a petition stating you will close your doors if Cooper's liquor license—or Antonio's, or the hotel's or the inn's—is not renewed. We'll take the petition to the city board of licenses and tell them that we've received word that someone on the board has been bribed. If that turns out to be true, and they don't do something about it, all doors on the boardwalk will be closed."

Tremaine scowled at her. "You really think they will believe that businesses that rely on tourism to survive will close their doors during the season?"

"Yes." She gave him a wicked smile. "Because those businesses' owners are friends with Vaughn Tremaine and he will be willing to supplement their income until the petition is met by the city board."

Cooper almost choked at the horrified look on Tremaine's face.

"You're fucking joking, right?" said Vaughn.

Jess clapped her hands over Joey's ears as Cat snapped, "Hey, kid in the room!"

He held up a hand. "Apologies. But still." He glowered at Jess. "Are you kidding?"

"It's just a bluff, Vaughn. Everyone knows you have more money than Croesus. You could keep a number of families afloat for a good while."

"No one in their right mind would believe that I would do this."

"He's right." Bailey stared at him in disgust. "He's a selfish, coldhearted bastard. I can't believe you seriously thought he'd help Cooper out, Jess."

An iciness Cooper had never seen before crept into Tremaine's eyes as he stared at Bailey. His tone was equally chilly when he said, "You won't taunt me into doing this, Miss Hartwell."

Cooper had had enough. "Look," he said, rounding the bar, "I appreciate Jess organizing this, and you all coming to hear her out, but Tremaine and I are already on it."

Bailey's eyebrows hit her hairline. "*He's* helping you?"

"I can be helpful when I want to be," Tremaine said.

"I've never seen that side of you."

"I only help the people I like."

It was a direct hit. The first one Cooper had ever seen him volley at Bailey. It seemed he'd had enough of her insults.

Bailey tried to hide her flinch, but it was there.

Tremaine saw it and Cooper watched the muscle in his jaw flex as he jerked his eyes away from her.

Huh.

Maybe Jess was right about those two.

Not that Cooper had time to think about that disaster waiting to happen. "As I said, I appreciate you all coming here, but we'll take care of it."

Jess scowled at him. "Do you have a plan?"

"Not yet."

"Well, I do."

Dahlia spoke up. "I'm signing the petition. Devlin can't get away with trying to bully us. If we stand together he has way less chance of taking from one of us."

"We're signing, too," Iris said.

"We are?" Ira frowned at her, saw her expression, and then turned to the rest of the room. "We are."

"And me," Emery said, surprising everyone in the room. She blushed when they all looked at her. "I have . . . um . . . If Mr. Tremaine . . ." She blushed even harder as Tremaine focused on her. "If Mr. Tremaine is uncomfortable with being used as part of the financial bluff . . . I . . . um . . ."

Jesus. Cooper sighed. It was uncomfortable watching Emery struggle, and he was relieved when Jess let go of Joey to walk over to her friend to place a supportive hand on her shoulder.

It seemed to bolster Emery. "I inherited my grandmother's company. It's worth quite a bit and as a company it is . . . well . . . its profits are public." She looked at Jessica, her fondness for his woman evident. "You're welcome to say that I will be a benefactor to those who would lose income by shutting down."

He could see Jess was as surprised by this information as the rest of them. With Emery not growing up in Hartwell, no one had really known her story. Wealthy grandmother was a new one to all of them.

"That's so great of you, Emery," Dahlia said, giving her shoulder a squeeze.

Emery flushed but gave Dahlia a smile.

"I'm signing, too." Bailey gave Tremaine a look that would have made Cooper want to crawl behind his bar if she'd shot it his way. "It looks like we don't need you after all."

Tremaine flicked his glance from Bailey to Emery. "It was smarter keeping your wealth to yourself, Miss Saunders." He ignored her blush and turned back to Cooper. "We'll use me as the bluff. And no one outside of this room learns about Miss Saunders's inheritance." His gaze fixed on Cat.

She huffed. "Why are you looking at me?"

"Your son."

"Joey won't say anything."

"I won't say anything," Joey said, piping up.

"I don't get it." Bailey looked at him suspiciously, her eyes moving between him and Emery. "Why?"

He gave her a suffering look. "I come from a world of wealth, Miss Hartwell. When a single woman has a lot of wealth it brings out the worst kind of scum to fleece her. When a woman is as beautiful as Miss Saunders, the more scum come scurrying out to get to her and her money."

Emery blushed redder than Cooper had ever seen.

"Why would you care?" Bailey snapped.

"Why do you care if I care?"

"I don't."

"Oh, it certainly looks that way."

"Enough!" Jessica huffed. "Fine. Vaughn is right." She gripped Emery's hand. "It was sweet that you trust us, Em, but no one else should know your business."

"I feel a little stupid," Cooper thought he heard her mutter.

"Don't," Jessica said. "You *can* trust us."

"I'd assume Devlin already knows about it," Iris said, eyeing Emery in concern. "That's why he hasn't bothered her. He knows Emery's got the financial backing to defend herself against him."

Cooper thought he saw a flash of concern on Emery's face. "You think he's looked into me?"

"Yes," Jessica said grimly. "Speaking from experience, I'd say he's looked into everyone in this room."

"Bastard," Bailey huffed and then winced apologetically at Cat.

"Is that settled, then?" Iris said, clapping her hands together. "We sign this damn petition, Vaughn plays the bluff, no one says a word about Emery's grandma's money."

"That sounds about right." Dahlia grinned at her concise summation.

"You don't have to do this." Cooper thought it bore repeating.

Iris shook her head at him. "You're not talking us out of this. We're doing this for you, son. But we're also doing it for all of us. Ian Devlin is a town bully. You have to stand up to bullies or they'll just keep coming back to steal your lunch money."

And because Cooper supposed she was right, he gave in.

Jess took out the petition she'd written up and everyone signed it. After she'd promised to keep them updated, they all left to go back to their businesses, Bailey storming out first, Emery stuttering and blushing as Tremaine held the door open for her, and Dahlia laughing at whatever Iris and Ira were saying to her.

When they were gone Jessica walked over to him as Cat cuddled Joey into her side, whispering at him, probably about keeping quiet about what he'd heard.

"Are you mad?" Jess said, sliding her arms around his waist.

He smoothed his hands up her bare arms and shook his head. "No. It's the only plan we have. Hopefully it works."

"I think it will. This town depends on the boardwalk for tourism. There's no way they will risk you all shutting your doors. The media would have a field day and that would open up a whole can of worms about bribery in the city office."

"It's smart." He nodded, leaning down to press a soft kiss to her mouth. "Thank you."

She grinned at him, bouncing a little in his arms in a giddy way that made him chuckle.

"Jessica," Cat said.

The doc turned in his arms to face his sister and he felt her tense underneath his touch. "Cat."

His sister didn't waste any time smiling at her. "Thanks for looking out for my brother. I'm glad you're staying."

Jess immediately relaxed against him. "Thanks. Me, too. Although"—she shot him a grin over her shoulder—"I need more wardrobe space. Your second bedroom maybe?"

"Wait." Cat stared at them, astonished. "You moved in together?"

Cooper hugged Jess close, giving his sister a look that said, *Back off.* "We didn't see any point in waiting."

"Of course you didn't." Cat shook her head in disbelief. "It's never been slow with you two so I don't know why I'm surprised."

"Are you mad?" Jess said.

"Who cares if she's mad?" Cooper huffed.

Jess frowned at him. "*I* care."

At that Cat gave her a big smile. "Did I mention lately that I like you?"

"Me, too!" Joey cried. "Are you going to be my aunt?"

Now it was Jess's turn to blush a little. "Not right this second."

Cooper wrapped his arms around her shoulders and drew her back against his chest. "Someday, Joe. And you'll be my best man."

Joey smiled. "Really?"

"Of course. Who else?"

His nephew cocked his head to the side. "Will I have to wear one of those stupid penguin suits?"

Cooper flicked a look at Cat. She shrugged. "What? They are stupid penguin suits."

"Probably," Cooper told Joey.

"Oh. Okay. I suppose that would be okay."

There was mirth in Cat's eyes as she studied Jess, who had gone absolutely still in his arms. "Maybe you should stop freaking your girl out with the wedding talk."

He winked at his sister and then pressed a kiss to Jess's neck. "Okay. No more wedding talk. At least for a while."

Jess relaxed at his teasing tone and shook her head. "It's a good thing I'm a little crazy because you all"—she gestured around the bar—"are more than a little crazy."

"Ach." Cat grabbed Joey's hand, striding toward the door. "What's life without a little crazy?"

"Boring," all three of them said.

Cooper grunted in amusement as his sister and his woman burst out laughing, his nephew looking up at his mom, happy whenever she was happy because he was a good kid who loved his mom.

And that was when it hit him.

The piece of the puzzle that had been missing . . . he'd found it.

Because right then, standing in his bar with them, he finally felt like he had everything he'd ever need.

EPILOGUE

Jessica

To say the chair of the city board of licenses appeared extremely uncomfortable with what Cooper and I had to say was an understatement.

"I can assure you that no one on my board would take a bribe," Christine Rothwell said sternly.

"I'm sure you know that what we're suggesting is not outside the realm of possibility," I said.

She looked down at her desk. "And who are you proposing is bribing someone on my board?"

I found her avoidance of my gaze more than a little disconcerting. I hoped like hell that whoever had taken the bribe wasn't the freaking chair of the board.

"You know we can't say who," Cooper said. "That opens us up to slander."

"So let me get this straight." Christine sat back in her chair. "Everyone who has signed this petition"—she gestured to it on her desk—"will close their doors if Mr. Lawson's liquor license isn't renewed?"

"Exactly."

"This is blackmail. You could be arrested for this."

"Maybe so," I said. "But along with a huge hit to the town's economy, there will be a media frenzy. That media, as well as the police, will look into our concerns and I'm not exactly convinced you want them looking into your board."

"We have nothing to hide." She lifted her chin in defiance.

"Are you sure about that? Because we're sure someone on your board has taken a bribe and we're sure we know who paid them off. And we're willing to risk everything on this. Are you?"

Christine considered us, her eyes hard with anger. "Give me a moment while I retrieve your file, Mr. Lawson."

They waited patiently as she typed away at her computer. She studied her screen, her eyebrows pinching together. "You reapplied a few weeks ago . . . and there is a notice on the application." She shot us a wary look. "It has been denied."

Cooper tensed beside me. "Any reason on there for it?"

"It states here that the police have been called to the bar on a number of occasions in the past year for antisocial behavior."

"That's bullshit," Cooper said, sounding calm even though I knew he wasn't.

I glowered at Christine Rothwell. "I'm sure all you have to do is make a few calls to the police for them to deny any such claims."

"And all Mr. Lawson has to do is appeal to the state to have his license renewed."

"That's months in court," Cooper said, sounding less patient. "Perhaps a year. I can't lose out on a year's income, Ms. Rothwell."

"It's the legal way to do this," she bit out. "Not barging into my office to blackmail me."

"We're not blackmailing you," I said. "We're giving you a heads-up. Have you heard of Vaughn Tremaine, Paradise Sands Hotel? He's signed the petition."

"Of course." She nodded, seemingly greatly unhappy to see his name there.

"He's willing to supplement Cooper's income and the income of all the businesses that will be closing their doors. He'll do that while Cooper has to go through the courts to get this mess sorted out. But as I said, all that's going to happen is the police will discover that whoever signed off on this"—I pointed to her computer—"took a bribe to do it. And then your whole office is under investigation."

She studied us and then she nodded. "I happen to be friends with

Sheriff King. I'm going to call him. If you could wait outside in reception while I do so."

Cooper and I did as she asked, waiting impatiently outside her office, sharing frustrated looks. Twenty minutes later Rothwell called us back into her office, looking harried and a little pale.

"Sit."

Once we were seated she gave us a pinched look. "Sheriff King has confirmed there have been no such complaints or call-outs to the bar. He says you're an upstanding businessman, Mr. Cooper."

"I always liked Jeff King." Cooper smiled at me and I gave him a relieved grin in return.

"Yes, well. I can assure you that this petition is unnecessary. Your license will be approved." She waved at her computer.

"And whoever took the bribe?" I said.

She narrowed her eyes on me. "For all I know this is a clerical error. In any case it's now an internal matter."

Meaning she'd fire the asshole but neither that person nor Devlin would be pulled up to the law because she didn't want the police investigating her office.

Cooper seemed to sense my indignation because he gripped my hand tighter. "That's all we wanted, Ms. Rothwell." He stood up and held out his hand to her. "Thank you for your time."

She gave him a clipped nod and we walked out of there with me bristling the whole time.

"They're going to get away with it," I said as Cooper led me out of the building to his truck.

"That's not our fight, Doc." He held the passenger door open for me. "Our fight is with Devlin. And believe me, that's enough to handle for the moment."

On the drive back to his bar, I let his words sink in.

Unfortunately he was right. If Ian Devlin was willing to go to the lengths he had to steal Cooper's place from him, then we needed to concentrate on our fight with him before worrying about anything else.

My cell rang, interrupting our usual comfortable silence. I frowned, not recognizing the number. "Hello. Jessica Huntington speaking."

"Ah, Dr. Huntington," a vaguely familiar male voice said, "it's Dr. Paul Duggan here."

My heart immediately started to race a little faster. "Dr. Duggan. It's nice to hear from you."

Cooper glanced at me and I grinned at him excitedly. He winked at me before turning back to watch the road.

"I'm sorry it's been a few days, but I had to check your references out."

"Right." I waited, nervous.

"Your last employer isn't too happy with you," he said softly, and my heart plummeted into the pit of my stomach.

"I gathered." I felt Cooper's gaze on me at my sad tone.

"However, they did concede you were a good doctor . . . until you up and left with no notice."

"Dr. Duggan, I can explain—"

"You don't need to. This is a small town, Dr. Huntington, and word is you and Cooper are pretty permanent."

"We are," I assured him.

"I'm just going to go on faith that that will keep you here. And truth is, no one as qualified as you has applied for the position."

My spirits immediately picked back up. "Are you offering me the job?"

"I am. Are you accepting?"

"Yes!" I cried out and he laughed at my exuberance. I grinned as Cooper reached over to squeeze my knee, smiling at me, happy for me.

"Then I'll see you at the clinic on Sunday at ten a.m. so we can go over the ropes. You'll officially start Monday morning."

"I'll be there." I was relieved. So freaking relieved I couldn't even explain it. "Thank you."

"You're welcome."

We hung up and I bounced in my chair. "I got a job."

"I heard," Cooper said, amused.

"I'm going to be a doctor again."

He swung a tender look at me. "You never stopped being one, Jessica."

Relaxing back into my seat, I stared out at the town passing us by and I smiled. "Today is a good day."

"Yeah," Cooper agreed.

A banner hung from the ceiling in Antonio's with the words *Bon Voyage, George!* printed on it.

The place was packed with people mingling over the buffet, drinking, and just enjoying their last night with George Beckwith before he left for Nova Scotia.

"I can't believe I threw this party for you, George Beckwith, only to find out you sold your damn store to a chef! A chef! Like we need more competition," Iris grumbled at him.

Her loud annoyance had jerked my gaze from Archie and Anita. They were sitting over in a corner with some people I didn't recognize. Anita looked skinny and tired, but she was out and about and I took that as a sign of strength. A good sign.

As for Archie . . . he was drinking soda.

I leaned in to Cooper. "I'm going to go rescue George."

He nodded, reluctantly letting me go, before turning back to Bailey and Tom.

I hurried over, slipping my arm around George's shoulders. "How you doing?"

"Oh, thank God," he said. "Rescue."

"George!" Iris huffed.

"Sorry, Iris, this pretty lady needs a drink." He guided me quickly away from Iris and over to the buffet. "That woman has always terrified me," he confessed.

I laughed. "She is a force of nature."

He grunted at that, picking up a pig in a blanket.

I studied him, feeling a little melancholy all of a sudden. Not only had I grown fond of him in such a short time, but he and Sarah were the reason I was there.

Maybe Bailey and the rest of the town were right about this place and fate.

It felt like fate had brought me there in the guise of Sarah's letters.

And I'd fallen in love on the boardwalk.

It was nice to think that maybe the legend was real after all.

"I'm sorry you're leaving."

George gave me a kind smile. "Did I thank you yet for bringing Sarah's letters to me? Because thank you, Jessica. You'll never know how much it matters."

I looked over at Cooper and he seemed to sense my gaze, his turning toward me, so soft, so blue, so warm, so loving. "I think I do," I said.

"Maybe it wasn't all for nothing after all," George muttered.

His words pulled my gaze from Cooper to him, only to find George was looking between Cooper and me. "What?"

He smiled. "Maybe it wasn't all for nothing after all. Sarah and I."

Still confused, I shook my head.

That made him smile bigger. "The bigger picture, Jessica. The bigger picture. Sometimes a story is only an important part of a bigger story."

Finally, I understood, and it brought tears to my eyes.

He saw and nodded to the wine. "Drink?"

"I can't," I said regretfully. "Dr. Duggan is showing me the ropes tomorrow for work."

"Oh!" a voice said behind me, and I turned to see Sadie Thomas pushing past a guy to get to me. "I heard you were going to be the new doctor."

I blinked in surprise at her, considering that twice now I'd caught her flirting with my man. "Yes."

"Doc," Sadie said, "I've got a bit of a problem. I was wondering if you'd take a look at it when you have a moment."

"Problem?" I frowned.

"Well, you see . . ." She slipped off her sandal. "Do you see my big toe? Does that look swollen to you? Because it hurts like a bitch. I think I broke it, Doc. What do you think?"

Suddenly I remembered what Bailey had said.

"I think you should put your sandal back on and make an appointment to see me in my office."

She frowned at me. "Is this because of Cooper? Because I've backed off."

I fought hard to hide my smile. "No, Sadie. It's because I'm at a party, not at work."

"Oh. Okay. Just thought I'd ask." She shrugged and sauntered off, not limping, I might add.

George chuckled beside me. "Get used to that, Dr. Huntington."

"Yes. Bailey warned me."

"Think you can cope with it? Small-town life?"

I gazed around at everyone who had turned up to say good-bye to George, and then my eyes fell on Cooper, who was surrounded by his sister, Joey, and my friends. The only people missing were Vaughn and Emery, but I hoped that would change over the coming months.

Antonio's was noisy, rambunctious, full of energy.

It was nothing like the soothing sound of the surf crashing against the shore.

And yet as I stood there, my eyes locked with Cooper Lawson's, surrounded by the people of Hartwell, that feeling I'd gotten the first time I stood on the balcony at Bailey's inn washed over me.

Peace.

At last.

"Yeah," I said, "I can definitely cope with it."

ACKNOWLEDGMENTS

As is usual for any given day, one morning I was in the car with my mum while she told me the plot to the book she was reading. From this conversation sprang one about the dying art of letter writing, and it was in this moment that Jessica's story hit me like a cartoonish bolt of lightning. Quite quickly the idea of setting her story in a boardwalk town on the East Coast followed, as I have a love for boardwalks, and relished the concept of creating a series about the characters in a boardwalk community.

So thank you, Mum, for our daily conversations about everything and nothing. And not just because the kernel of one grew into an entire book series.

Just because.

I also want to thank Georgia Cates, Amy Bartol, Rachel Higginson, and Shelly Crane. All your insights and thoughts at our writer's retreat in Nebraska were inspiring and motivational for this series. Thank you for that, and thank you for being there every day for me. I couldn't ask for better friends. You get it! And I love you for that, and for the incredible quantity of humor and sarcasm we provide as a group. I laugh so hard with you, Horsemen!

There are never enough thank-yous for my agent, Lauren Abramo. Lauren, I couldn't ask for a better champion. I know I'm exceptionally lucky to have you as mine.

Moreover, thank you to my editor, Kerry Donovan, for believing in me and for supporting me in this new venture into Hart's Boardwalk.

You make me a better writer, and I'm incredibly grateful I get to work with you.

Also thank you to all the team at Berkley, including Erin Galloway, my publicist; and the art team for creating stunning cover art.

Finally, as always, a massive thank-you to you, my readers. Thank you, thank you, thank you. A million thank-yous.

Keep reading for a sneak peek at Samantha Young's newest book in the Hart's Boardwalk series,

Every Little Thing

Available in March 2017

Bailey

It was almost impossible for me to drift immediately to sleep when I finally got myself into a bed. You'd think after the long hours I worked, my exhaustion would pull me right under. Unfortunately, I had so many tasks and thoughts and worries whirring around in my brain on any given day that it took a while for my brain to shut down.

After another long day at the inn I'd crashed in the room I kept open at the back of the house. For the longest time I'd done my very best to drag myself home for Tom, but now I didn't have to worry about that, and when I was especially tired, it was nice that I could sleep at the inn. The small room had come in handy, because like all the guest rooms it had its own bathroom, and when Jess was struggling last year I had let her stay there while she worked as my manager.

I reached over for my phone and groaned at the time. I'd thought I was being a good girl going to bed early at midnight. It was one o'clock now and I was still not asleep.

Come to me, goddess of sleep!

I huffed and kicked off the covers, flipping over onto my other side.

Finally, just as I was drifting close to that heavenly oblivion of slumber I heard a creak down the hall from my room. Near my office.

I sat up quietly and listened, wondering if one of my guests was wandering around. The click of my office door opening made my heart rate speed.

None of my guests should be wandering into my office.

And shit. I needed to start locking it.

Out of nowhere, I was hit by the horrible feeling that the person who had opened my office door wasn't one of my guests.

The stairs in the inn were creaky. There was no way I wouldn't have heard someone coming down those.

The blood whooshed in my ears as my heart pounded against my chest. Grabbing my phone, I got out of bed as quietly as possible and tiptoed over to my door.

I winced at the slight snick of the handle turning and froze, waiting. When I was sure I hadn't been heard, I slowly opened it, peering out into my dark hallway. There was a faint light coming from my office. A moving light.

A flashlight.

I felt sick at the violation of someone breaking into the inn.

But also extremely pissed off.

Tiptoeing down the hall, avoiding the all too familiar creaky spots in the floorboards, I got to the office and cautiously peeked my head around the door.

Uncertainty and, yes, not a little bit of fear moved through me at the sight of the tall masked man rifling through my files. My computer screen was on but it was password protected. He was probably looking for something to help him work out the password but he'd find nothing. I had memorized an anagram to remember my complicated password.

The man, dressed all in black, turned his head to the side, and even in the woolen ski mask he wore over his face I recognized him.

Stu Devlin.

I was sure of it.

It made sense. He was probably searching for something that might be useful as leverage in obtaining the inn from me.

Moron!

There was no way that Ian Devlin put him up to this in his effort to amass more boardwalk real estate. Stu's father might be an asshole but he was a much sneakier asshole than his idiot son.

I dialed 911 on my phone as I stepped into the room.

He jerked at my arrival, his head snapping in my direction.

Dark, flat eyes stared at me and I knew without a doubt it was Stu.

"Nine-one-one. What is your emergency?"

"I have an intruder in my establishme— Oof!" His body hit mine before I even had time to react to him suddenly launching himself at me.

My breath slammed out of me as I crashed to the floor, pain juddering through my head as it smacked against the floorboards. At the heavy, warm weight settling over me, my eyes flew open in panic.

Stu's cruel eyes glared down at me as he reached for the phone in my hand. I gripped it tighter, struggling to keep hold of it as his strong fingers clawed at mine. Finally he grabbed my wrist and hammered it against the floor. Pain shot down my arm and I reflexively let go of the phone.

He immediately threw it against the wall, grunting in satisfaction at the sound of it breaking.

Fury roared through me at the shock of him physically attacking me. With my good hand I reached for his mask, my nails scratching him as I tried to drag it off his face so I could finally have evidence to get one of these bastards charged for criminal activity.

"I know it's you!" I screeched as his fingers bit into my hands.

We struggled as adrenaline aided me in my pissed-off quest to unmask the bastard. I wasn't thinking. I was just too angry.

He hissed as I clawed at his arm, drawing blood, and he released me to pull his elbow back, his fist coming toward me as I stared up at him in horror.

But his fist never met my face.

Suddenly he was no longer straddling me because another body had launched itself at him, throwing him off me.

I scrambled to my feet. "Holy fuck." I breathed, stunned.

The other body belonged to the man who was currently wrestling Stu. And that man was Vaughn. A very furious Vaughn.

Stu grunted as Vaughn punched him, but then Vaughn grunted when Stu buried his fist in Vaughn's gut. It was a hard enough hit to wind him, catching him off guard, and off balance. He was quick to his feet though, lunging at Stu, grappling with him. I watched as they fought, Stu deftly avoiding becoming unmasked.

When he landed a punch on Vaughn's face, I'd had enough.

Impulsively I jumped on Stu's back.

And quickly found myself thrown off and at Vaughn.

I felt his strong arms bind around my waist as he pulled me away from an inevitable collision with my desk, and cursed like a sailor at the sight of my attacker sprinting out of the office and out of our grasp.

"Are you okay?" Vaughn said, breathlessly, his hands roaming my body for injury.

I jerked away, unnerved by how much I wanted his comfort right then. "I'm fine."

"You're not fine, you're trembling." He frowned at me.

I narrowed my eyes on his jaw, looking for injury. There was a faint redness that I knew was going to look bad later if we didn't get some ice on it. "*I* didn't get hit in the face."

"Because *I* was there to stop him. What the hell were you thinking?" His eyes darted behind me and he stiffened.

I glanced over my shoulder and my gut churned.

My guests were crowded outside my office, sleepy, disgruntled, and concerned.

"Everything all right?" one of my return visitors, Mr. Ingles, asked.

"A small mishap," I said cheerily, walking toward them as if I wasn't currently wearing a silk camisole and shorts that showed off *way* too much of my body. Or that I was walking through a scattered mess of files and objects that had crashed to the floor during all the violent tussling. "But it's quite all right."

"I'm calling the sheriff," Vaughn said behind me, and even

though I knew it was the right thing to do I squeezed my eyes closed and groaned.

"The sheriff? What happened?"

"Oh, dear. Are we safe?"

I listened to my guests voicing their fears, and wished just once that I could let them think what they wanted, let them leave if they wanted! I was shaken, shocked, hurt, and, frankly, pissed way the fuck off.

The last thing I wanted to do was play the ever-congenial innkeeper.

But I had to.

I opened my eyes and strode in among them. "Please, you are all perfectly safe. Nothing like this has ever happened before, but I can assure you that the intruder will not be returning and the inn will be completely secure. If you'd all like to return to your rooms while I deal with the sheriff—quietly, I promise. Of course I will deduct tonight's room fee from your bill and all day dining tomorrow is free for all guests. On top of that I will issue you all a fifty percent discount if you choose to return to the inn in the future."

As I hoped it would, all my discounts and my freebies worked their magic and my guests trundled back up to their rooms murmuring to one another about the nuisance but also about Mona's delicious muffins and crème brûlée.

Poor Jay. The sous chef was going to have a tough first day in charge.

Wrapping my arms around myself I stared at the entrance to the inn. Both doors were wide open.

"Here." Vaughn appeared at my side.

I glanced at him, surprised to see he was offering me his leather jacket.

Accepting it, I slipped it on, and got a giant, delicious whiff of his cologne as I did so. An inappropriate tingle shot through my breasts and I wrapped the too large jacket shut so he couldn't see my suddenly pebbled nipples. "Thank you," I whispered, staring at him.

Vaughn stared back, concern in his beautiful eyes.

He'd never looked at me like that before.

I felt compelled to say, "I'm okay."

The concern melted under anger. "You're not okay," he snapped. "Was it a Devlin?"

I nodded. "I'm positive it was Stu Devlin."

He cursed under his breath, the muscle in his jaw working. And then that anger was suddenly directed at me. "Why the hell didn't you call the police instead of confronting him?"

My lips parted in surprise at his attack. "For your information I was calling the police *as* I was confronting him. I didn't think he'd throw me to the ground! I thought it was Stu being an ass. I didn't think he'd hurt me." I shivered at the thought.

"Well now he's a dead man," Vaughn said icily.

I felt a rush of sudden desire between my legs at the strangely protective vibe I was getting from him. Unsettled by the feeling, I shifted uncomfortably. "How did . . . Why were *you* here?"

He glanced over at my open double doors. "I sometimes stroll down the boardwalk at night. When I was passing I saw your doors were open. He must have picked the lock." Vaughn's eyes narrowed dangerously. "I knew something was wrong so I came inside to check, and I heard the struggle coming from your office."

Thank God.

Never in my life did I think I'd be grateful for Vaughn Tremaine's presence but I was. In fact I was beyond grateful. I didn't know if it was adrenaline or shock or what . . . but I was a turned-on kind of grateful.

"Well . . . thanks," I whispered, unable to look at him.

If I looked at him he'd know I was imagining stripping that gorgeous dark red sweater right off of him. I glanced at him out of the corner of my eyes. He'd rolled up the sleeves of the sweater, revealing tan, corded forearms.

I had this thing about strong forearms and nice hands on a guy.

Vaughn had both.

I bit my lip at the sight and tried to pull myself together.

What the hell!

It's the adrenaline, I assured myself.

The sound of my garden gate swinging open sent relief through me. A much-needed distraction in the form of Sheriff King entered my inn.

Jeff King had been voted into office the same year my mother's good friend Jaclyn Rose was voted into office as mayor. Jeff was rugged, competent, extremely fair, an all-around good guy and sheriff. He was also widowed. His wife had passed away from cancer eight years ago and the women of Hartwell had been sniffing around him ever since. Without much luck.

Dahlia had had a fling with him a number of years ago, and I think Jeff had genuinely liked her. Unfortunately, she was the wrong woman to start over with. I'd been frustrated, a little annoyed even, when Dahlia broke things off with him—until I remembered my friend was too good at punishing herself. And also that she gave her heart away to someone else a long time ago, even if she refused to admit it.

The sight of Jeff made me feel instantly calmer.

It wasn't that I didn't feel safe. I felt safe with Vaughn standing beside me. But I didn't feel calm. There was nothing calming about being this attracted to a man I wasn't even sure I liked very much.

"Jeff," I said. "I mean Sheriff." I always forgot to call him that when he was duty.

At six feet five, the tall, broad-shouldered police officer seemed to fill the entire space. And I was okay with that. I liked his powerful presence right then more than I could say.

"Hey, Bailey." Deputy Wendy Rawlins stepped into the inn, glancing around, taking everything in. Wendy had been part of our police force for twenty years, and was another good friend of my mom's.

I smiled, glad she was there, too. "Sorry to call you guys out so late."

"Don't be sorry." She frowned. "You've got nothing to be sorry for."

"Crime scene?" Jeff asked.

"Her office," Vaughn replied. "I was taking a walk, saw her doors open, thought I'd check it out. And I caught Stu Devlin attacking her in her office."

Wendy scowled, swallowing what I knew were probably a few choice words, while Jeff looked visibly taken aback. "Stu Devlin. Positive ID?"

"No." I shook my head, furious. "He was wearing a mask."

"Then how do you know it was Stu?"

"Oh come on, Sheriff, I've known him my whole life."

He sighed. "Show me to the office and explain everything from the start."

I did just that, and was weirdly comforted by the fact that Vaughn stayed by my side throughout the whole thing.

Thirty minutes later, Jeff and Wendy had our statements and were standing in the garden of the inn.

"I'll have one of the deputies drop by tomorrow morning to get statements from your guests at breakfast," Jeff said.

"Thank God I already offered them free food," I muttered, put out that my guests would have to be even more inconvenienced.

Vaughn's hand settled on my arm and I looked down at it, shocked by the touch, as I listened to him say to Jeff, "And Stu?"

"All I can do is bring him in for questioning but without a positive ID from anyone I don't have a lot to go on."

"That's bullshit."

"Tremaine," Jeff warned. "It's not that I don't believe you. I'll do what I can. I promise. Bailey, is there anything else I should know that might help me? Bailey?"

"Huh." I jerked my head up from staring at Vaughn's hand. "Oh.

No. Not that I can think of right now. If I do, I'll drop by the station."

"Get some sleep." Jeff nodded and turned to leave.

I waved good-bye to him and Wendy and then turned to Vaughn. I was more awake than ever, and I wasn't ashamed to admit that I didn't really want to be alone right now. "You should get back."

He scrutinized me for a moment, and as if he could read my mind he said, "I spotted a bottle of wine in your office that managed to escape destruction. Want to open it? It might calm your nerves."

I was more than a little surprised by the offer, and also touched. Apparently I was seeing the other side to Vaughn Tremaine that Jess swore was there. Maybe she was right. "Do you want to drink it on the beach? The water always soothes me."

He nodded, amiable.

Actually *amiable.*

"Sure."

I hid my shock as best as I could. "I . . . uh . . . let me change first."

Vaughn's eyes drifted over my skimpy attire and he suddenly looked pissed off all over again. "You do that," he muttered, striding off in the direction of my office.

"Well this is going to be interesting," I murmured. I held the collar of his jacket to my nose and took a whiff. My stomach fluttered of its own volition at the smell of his cologne. *Oh holy hell.* "Very interesting."